Also by Gary Slaughter

Cottonwood Spring
Cottonwood Winter: A Christmas Story
Cottonwood Fall
Cottonwood Summer

COTTONWOOD SUMMER '45

To Tabitha Engelhardt,

COTTONWOOD SUMMER '45

Enjoy!

A Novel

by

GARY SLAUGHTER

Library of Congress Control Number: 2011943603
ISBN -13 978-0-9744206-5-3

Manufactured in the United States of America
Cover and interior design and layout by Danita Meeks
Editing and proofreading by Sharon Yake
Printing and binding by Falcon Press

Published by Fletcher House
P.O. Box 50979
Nashville, TN 37205-0979

For additional copies of *Cottonwood Summer '45,* contact Ingram Books, Inc. or www.fletcherhouse.com.

For Billy Curtis, a.k.a. Danny Tucker --
(December 8, 1938 - June 11, 2011)

My oldest and dearest friend, and
the only man I have ever known
to be loved by every person he met.

And for Joanne --

With my everlasting gratitude
for her untiring effort and enthusiastic support
during all five Cottonwood *seasons.*

CONTENTS

COTTONWOOD SUMMER '45

1 DANNY'S MISSING

I STUMBLED SLEEPILY INTO THE KITCHEN WHERE Mom and Dad were already enjoying a leisurely breakfast. I was confused. On Saturdays, Danny Tucker, my best friend, and I were always up early. Usually we enjoyed a quick, but huge, breakfast before setting off on our early-morning adventures.

"Where's Danny?" I asked, slumping into my chair.

"Good question, Jase," Dad replied. "On weekends, he's always here well before Mom and I are up-and-about. Perhaps he's sick."

"That boy sick?" Mom laughed. "He hasn't even had a sniffle since we've known him. Jase, were you and Danny planning to meet here as usual?"

"Yes. We were going to see if Homer's Bait Shop wanted us to catch night crawlers for them. We need to earn some money this summer."

"I bet I know," Dad asserted. "Danny's working undercover on a new case. He'll be here after he vanquishes another villain and accepts another White House invitation to receive a third medal from President Truman."

I knew Dad was joking, but there was some truth in what he suggested. Danny and I had been honored by President Roosevelt at the White House. That was when we both received our second United States Medal of Courage. The President told everyone in America that we were "brave and patriotic American heroes." Of course, that was before his tragic death on April 12, 1945.

Danny and I always tried our best to protect and defend our neighborhood, our hometown, and our country from its enemies. And, as it turned out, we were pretty good at it. Nonetheless, we knew there was still more work to do.

It's true that Germany had surrendered, and we'd celebrated VE Day just a few weeks before. And, thanks to our courageous fighting men in the Pacific Theater, the Japanese had suffered major setbacks since Pearl Harbor.

However, all but a handful of Japanese defenders on Iwo Jima had fought to the death. This fierce enemy was committed to the fanatical *Bushido Code* that decreed death to be more honorable than surrender. It was a sobering reality throughout America. And our hometown, Riverton, Michigan, was no exception. Needless to say, Danny and I were still on full alert for the bad guys.

My friend's absence deeply worried me. He was always dependable, particularly when it came to eating. His voracious appetite required frequent refueling. It wasn't like him to miss a meal at our house where Mom's oatmeal cookies were always on hand.

Rap! Rap!

The loud knock at the front door startled us. I leaped to my feet to answer it, but I knew it wasn't Danny. He never knocked.

"Maybe it's some news explaining Danny's absence," I speculated hopefully.

Unfortunately I was right.

Chippewa County Sheriff Roy Connors spoke without mincing words. "Good morning, Addisons. Brace yourselves for bad news. Apparently Danny Tucker has been abducted by Otto Klump and a new German POW -- named Shiller -- who works under Otto at the canning factory."

"Oh, Lord," Mom gasped. "Not again!"

MOM WAS RIGHT. LESS than a year earlier in the fall of 1944, Danny had been kidnapped by two ruthless German POWs who had escaped, for a second time, from Camp Riverton. Fortunately I was responsible for rescuing Danny and capturing the POWs, also for a second time.

The people of our town experienced the war differently than most Americans. We were surrounded by the enemy. We saw them every day as they passed by in roaring army trucks on their way to work in our factories and on our farms. Wearing their *PW* uniforms, they were guarded by military police with tommy guns at the ready.

Danny and I had met Otto Klump at our neighborhood canning factory where he supervised a crew of fellow POWs that converted locally grown produce into canned goods for American soldiers and citizens. Since Otto was our friend, the news of his possible involvement in Danny's abduction was disconcerting to say the least.

Shortly after the Tucker family moved into our blue-collar, ethnically-diverse neighborhood, Danny and I had become best friends. His father owned and operated an auto-repair business housed in a huge garage located behind their modest house on New Albany Avenue.

Danny's older sister, nicknamed Queenie for her imperious manner, was the only teenage girl I knew. She made a point of making sure I didn't know her well. Danny's younger brother Chub was best buddies with Sherm Tolna who lived just down the block from our house on Forrest Street. Like Danny and me, the two seven-year-olds were inseparable.

The summer before, Danny and I had established a secret counterespionage organization, called the Forrest Street Guards. FSG's first mission was to keep an eye on Hans Zeyer whom we suspected of being a neighborhood Nazi spy. To provide more feet-on-the-ground, to our regret, we'd recruited Chub and Sherm as FSG junior members.

The two initiates had been formally sworn in under the spreading boughs of our neighborhood's sacred cottonwood tree. As we presided over this hallowed ceremony, Danny and I knew they were too young to fathom the importance of FSG's critical mission. Not even the magical power of the venerable cottonwood could prevent Chub and Sherm from becoming a bane to our existence as a freedom-fighting organization.

Mom and Dad also worked to support the war effort. My father, John Addison, was a skilled tool-and-die maker. He worked full time at the Burke Factory where the ultra-top-secret Norden bombsight was manufactured. This ingenious device enabled American bombardiers to pinpoint Nazi targets from altitudes of 35,000 feet over Germany.

Like many Americans on the home front during the war, Dad had a second job. He ran a part-time, sewing machine-repair business located in a tiny shed next to our Victory Garden.

During the war, every home on Forrest Street had a Victory Garden. And we were not alone. By 1945, an estimated 20 million Victory Gardens produced 40 percent of America's vegetables.

Because my mother, Marie Compton Addison, was a skilled seamstress, she was employed at Camp Riverton, teaching sewing and tailoring to German POWs. Naturally the sewing machines for Mom's training room were provided and maintained by Dad. In the evenings, she and Hans Zeyer, our neighbor, often shared an army car on their way to and from the camp. Hans taught the German POWs about the benefits of American-style democracy. When we learned this from Colonel Butler, the commanding officer of Camp Riverton, we grudgingly scratched Hans from our *Most Wanted German Spy* list.

Danny's huge appetite would have been a burden to most American families during the war. Wartime rationing and shortages of almost every commodity radically altered the menus of people living on the American home front. But we Addisons were fortunate. My mother's parents, Grandpa and Grandma Compton, were farmers. They were more than eager to share their bounty of fruits, vegetables, and meats with us. That's why we saw so much of Danny at mealtimes during the war.

Since he entered our lives, Danny had charmed us all. He was more than my best friend. He had become a part of our family. He was like my brother and my parents' second son. That's why the sheriff's visit was so upsetting to us Addisons on that Saturday morning in June 1945.

AS THE FOUR OF us sat down in our front room, my head was spinning. For a moment, we just stared at each other. Then Mom broke the silence.

"Sheriff, do Danny's parents know what's happened?"

"No, they don't. I drove to their house to tell them, but Sam and Christine weren't home."

"Where could they be?"

"They're at Riverton Memorial Hospital with Sam's father. Apparently he's had a stroke and his prognosis is still uncertain. Queenie was at the house with Chub. She told me about her grandfather."

"What bad timing! Two potentially life-threatening events in their family," Mom lamented. "The poor Tuckers!"

"That's why I didn't say anything to Queenie about Danny. I didn't want to upset her. As you may know, Queenie tends to be -- a bit hysterical at times. After learning about Sam's father, I decided to wait before telling any of the Tuckers about Danny. Hopefully we'll have some good news about the boy soon."

Looking at me, the sheriff said, "Jase, I know that Otto is mighty fond of Danny -- and you too. So even if he's on the lamb with Shiller, I doubt he'd let any harm come to Danny."

"Yes, I think of Otto as a good friend to both Danny and me, Sheriff Connors."

"We'd all like to think that Otto's not involved. But he's the senior POW. And he and Shiller are missing along with Danny and an army truck. Given these facts, we have to consider the worst case scenario -- until we learn more about this case."

"Where's Sergeant Prella, Sheriff?"

The sergeant was the senior military police (MP) officer assigned to guard the German POWs working at the canning factory.

"He's at the hospital too, John," the sheriff told Dad. "After they stitch up his head, they'll keep him there under observation for a couple of hours before releasing him."

The sheriff paused before saying, "I need more details from Sergeant Prella and from Colonel Butler before I feel confident speculating further on this case."

We respected the sheriff's wishes by not pressing him for more details. But I for one was extremely curious about the need to *stitch up* Sergeant Prella's head. I was certain it had something to do with Danny's disappearance.

"Sounds like we all should meet at the hospital," I suggested.

Sheriff Connors' face brightened. "That's a great idea, Jase. Let me radio Colonel Butler and arrange just that."

After returning from his car radio, the sheriff announced, "It's all set. We'll meet at two o'clock at Riverton Memorial -- in the conference room off the lobby. That'll give Sergeant Prella time to recover and join us."

ON OUR WAY TO the hospital, Dad turned on the car radio. While not many 1936 Chevrolet sedans had radios, ours did.

The announcer confirmed America's worst fear, "Dateline, Tokyo. The Japanese Premier Suzuki has announced that Japan will fight to the very end rather than accept unconditional surrender."

Dad turned off the radio. "Boy! That's not good news."

"You got that right, Dad."

As we pulled into the hospital parking lot, Mom turned her attention to the Tuckers. "I hope Sam's father's all right."

When we entered the hospital lobby, we spotted Danny's parents standing with Sheriff Connors. Apparently the sheriff was breaking the news to them about Danny. Because they were concentrating so hard on the sheriff's words, they didn't notice us.

We hesitated for a minute or two. Then Mom announced, "Phooey. I'm going to Christine."

Taking Mom's lead, we surrounded the Tuckers and expressed our wishes for the swift recovery of Grandpa Tucker and, of course, for the safe return of Danny as well.

"Thank you for your kind words. My father's out-of-the-woods. We've been here most of the night. So we were just heading for home when the sheriff hailed us."

After hearing Mr. Tucker's news, we all expressed relief. But I noticed that no one commented on Danny's situation. Perhaps no one dared to do so.

Behind us we heard the familiar voice of Colonel Butler, "Afternoon, folks. I believe you all know Sergeant Prella."

We smiled and shook hands with the two men.

We Addisons held Colonel Butler in high esteem since he'd demonstrated great confidence in Mom by hiring her to teach at Camp Riverton.

After we were seated in the conference room, the first thing Colonel Butler confirmed was, "Folks, we don't know much about Shiller -- he's new to us. But we do know a lot about Otto -- all of which is good. So no one under my command is condemning Otto before all the facts are known."

Something compelled me to utter, "Amen." Everyone nodded affirmatively.

"Sergeant Prella, let's hear from you first. You were there when the crime took place."

"Well, I was until everything went black, Colonel. But I'll tell you all I remember. Since Camp Riverton opened in 1943, the German POWs have worked at the Chippewa Canning Corporation under the supervision of Otto Klump. As a Luftwaffe commissioned officer, according to the Geneva Convention, we couldn't force Otto to work. But he chose to do so. And I can assure you, he's done a bang-up job. Frankly I admire the man."

Then he turned his attention to the crime itself.

"To beat the heat, the POWs start work at five o'clock in the morning. This morning, after Otto had given his men their job assignments, he and I decided to run over to New Albany to pick up a load of pallets at Johnson Wood Products. Otto suggested we take Shiller along. Said he wanted to keep an eye on the new man.

"Otto told me that Shiller was very upset when he heard that the German POWs won't be repatriated until after the fall crops are harvested and processed -- probably sometime in early '46. He's got a wife and family back in Berlin. When he learned the Russians were first to occupy that city, he became obsessed with getting home.

"So the three of us drove to New Albany, loaded the pallets, and headed back to the canning factory. While I was driving along New Albany Avenue, I saw Danny Tucker strolling down the sidewalk -- out by the stockyards. So I stopped and offered him a ride. Danny claimed he was on his way to your house, Jase. Said he'd be happy to ride as far as Forrest Street.

"I got out to help Danny onto the truck. Otto and Shiller stayed in the cab -- or so I thought. I rearranged the pallets to clear a spot for Danny, and then I boosted the boy up to the bed of the truck. Suddenly I felt a sharp pain in the back of my head. That's when the lights went out.

"When I woke up, I was lying next to the curb. The truck -- Danny, Otto, and Shiller -- were gone. I had a heck of a headache, a nasty cut, and huge lump on the back of my head. From the wound, the doctor figured I was pistol-whipped -- probably by a German Luger."

A German Luger!

The seriousness of Danny's situation was abruptly brought home to us.

"I hitched a ride back to the canning factory and called Colonel Butler. That's about it."

Colonel Butler continued, "After talking to Sergeant Prella, I immediately called the sheriff. Because the assault and escape had occurred outside the city limits, I knew he had jurisdiction."

"That's right, Colonel. After talking to you, I hightailed it over to the crime scene. The only evidence I found was Danny's Tigers ball cap," the sheriff said, twirling the hat around his right index finger. "And a large smear of blood on the curb, apparently belonging to Sergeant Prella."

He gently handed the Tigers cap to Mrs. Tucker.

"By this time, we had every patrol car in my department combing the area around the stockyards and stepping up patrols on all routes leading away from the crime scene.

"We also alerted the Riverton police department. Riverton PD patrol cars are now searching for the truck in and around town. Fortunately that truck won't be easy to hide, making me hopeful that we'll find them soon.

"I'm afraid that's about all we have to report for now. Assuming we find the truck sometime between now and sundown, why don't we meet back here at seven o'clock. We should have more to go on by then."

As an afterthought, the sheriff, looking at the Tuckers, added, "If we haven't found that truck by sundown, I plan to bring in the Michigan State Police. And eventually the FBI may have to get involved."

THE TUCKERS HURRIED OUT of the hospital, explaining that they were eager to share the good news about Grandpa Tucker with Queenie and Chub. Before they departed, they offered to pick us up and drive us back to the evening meeting.

As Mrs. Tucker walked away, her left hand held Mr. Tucker's calloused fist, and on her right index finger she twirled Danny's Tigers cap. I took that as a good sign.

When we arrived home, I suddenly realized that I was very depressed. My best friend was in danger, abducted by at least one dangerous and desperate escapee. And my other friend Otto's role in this terrible nightmare was still a mystery to me.

Was Otto a danger to Danny as well?

Mom sensed I needed a diversion. "Jase, you haven't eaten anything but a couple of cookies all day. You need a good meal to perk you up. How about having some of that bean soup and corn bread that we brought home from the farm last night?"

Since I was a very young boy, I'd spent the majority of my summer days and nights at Grandma and Grandpa Compton's farm. Being an only child, with both Dad and Mom working in war-related jobs, I was used to being alone. At the farm, I also spent much time by myself. Even after I learned to drive a team of workhorses, I usually worked alone.

Like all Michigan farmers back in those days, Grandpa spent nearly all of the long summer days driving his teams of horses back and forth across the fields. Using his horses, he employed one of the dozen farm implements, enabling him to plant, nurture, and harvest a wide variety of crops. For the most part, working the fields was a one-man job. With two teams of horses, I became one of those men, at the early age of eight.

My grandmother, a recently-licensed driver, found any excuse to hop into her 1934 Hudson Terraplane Coupe and race about Chippewa County on various errands, some necessary but most contrived. Her errands freed her from her solitary housework to visit with friends, neighbors, and family members. Grandma had a high need for social interaction.

Whether I was alone or spending time with my grandparents, my days at the farm provided a rare opportunity to hone my creative imagination and expand my knowledge of how things worked. I learned by observing and understanding the nature of each intriguing facet of that stimulating place.

I was captivated by the various elements used in farming. Myriad barns and outbuildings, each built to meet a specific need required by the complex process of raising and harvesting a wide range of animals and plants. Like their neighbors, my grandparents' farm produced crops not only for cash but for family consumption.

At the farm, the nearby woods, fencerows, and creeks created a rich habitat for dozens of varieties of wild animals, fish, and birds. I never tired of walking the fields, lanes, creek beds, and wooded paths to observe and learn the ways of these fascinating creatures. All these alluring attractions provided a feast for my young and fertile mind.

Though less cerebral, I also feasted on Grandma Compton's down-home farm cooking. To me, it far exceeded the taste and comforting pleasure available from either the Addison or the Tucker kitchens or for that matter from any of the great collection of restaurants that dotted the downtown streets of Riverton.

Strangely, until Mom suggested Grandma's bean soup, I hadn't felt the least bit hungry. But, once the prospect of farm food entered my mind, my mouth immediately started to water. I quickly realized just how famished I was.

"Thanks, Mom. I really am awfully hungry."

Dad adored Grandma's bean soup. I've never forgotten how he *tailored* that dish to enhance its flavor.

First, he finely diced a raw onion, producing at least a cup of tongue-burning tidbits that he carefully mixed into the steaming soup. Then he broke Grandma's delicious, freshly-baked corn bread into small cubes and lightly dropped them into his bowl. Finally he painted the surface of the steaming mixture with shake-after-shake of black pepper.

His first large spoonful always elicited a half-groan and half-meow. This dish was indeed his very favorite.

After finishing every last bite of Grandma's latest bestowal, Dad and I pushed our chairs away from the kitchen table and relaxed with our hands clasped behind our necks.

"Boy! That was good," we both agreed.

For a brief time at least, the plight of Danny, and Otto perhaps, seemed worlds away.

"Why don't we stretch out in the front room?" Dad suggested. "You wouldn't mind. Would you, Marie?"

"No, you two sleepyheads go take a nap. I'll clean up the kitchen first. Then I have to prepare for my tailoring class at Camp Riverton tonight. I want to master that new buttonhole-maker you provided us before I try to teach the POWs how to use it."

Before Mom had finished her last sentence, Dad and I were curled up in the front room. He chose the sofa. And I nestled down in his large overstuffed chair. Dad's heavy breathing told me he wouldn't be awake long. I allowed myself to join him in slumber.

"HEY, YOU TWO SLUG-A-BEDS! Wake up -- now! The Tuckers just honked. Time to go to the hospital," Mom pleaded. "I'll wait here for the limousine to take me out to the camp."

I awoke with great difficulty, not knowing where I was or what time it was. Still dazed, I followed Dad out the front door and into the Tucker's station wagon.

Mrs. Tucker took one look at me. "Have a good nap, Jase?"

"*Erupmet jolp*," I responded politely, still rubbing my eyes.

"From the sound of it, I'd say you did," Mrs. Tucker chuckled. "Lucky you! We couldn't relax at all. Once Queenie learned her grandfather was going to be fine, she turned her attention to Danny. She interrogated us incessantly for two straight hours about Danny's predicament. She posed question after question that she must have known we couldn't answer. Honestly! That girl can sometimes be a real *pill*."

I had two reactions to Mrs. Tucker's comment.

First, I'd never thought of Queenie as being a particularly caring sister. Her ardent concern for Danny was somehow endearing to me. But I had to be careful thinking those thoughts with respect to Queenie. After all, this was the young woman that I'd nearly *done-in* by means of my homemade bow and arrow. I won't go into the details.

Suffice it to say, afterwards, I was extremely happy that I possessed only mediocre archery skills. Had I been a better shot --. Well, you get the idea. My father curtailed my progress in that particular sport by converting my carefully-constructed bow and arrow into kindling wood for the potbellied stove in his shed.

In addition, I'd never heard anyone, except Grandma Compton, refer to someone as *a real pill*. And Grandma used that term very infrequently, reserving it for the true scoundrels of the world. One of whom was the former manager of our neighborhood Graham Market who refused to donate even a penny to rebuild the home of our friends and neighbors, the Matlocks, after it had been destroyed by fire. When E.F. Graham, owner of the grocery chain, heard about this uncharitable public relations faux pas, he quickly cashiered that *pill* of a manager.

When I thought of the tragic Matlock house fire, I remembered how Otto and his crew of POWs from the canning factory had bravely rescued Mrs. Matlock and her newborn baby from the blazing house. How we neighbors cheered Otto and his crew that day. We pounded those poor POWs on their backs until they begged for mercy. Because these memories evoked mixed emotions about Otto, I quickly decided to think about something else.

There was an amusing side to that whole Matlock episode. I chuckled to myself when I thought about how Danny had cleverly manipulated Mr. Graham into donating almost all the food for the fund-raising finale. Yes, the powerful grocery-chain owner was putty in Danny's hands. His ability to bend adults to his will was an uncanny facet of his genius.

When we arrived at the hospital, Mr. Tucker proclaimed, "Right on time! Let's go see what Colonel Butler has to report. I'll bet he has good news for us."

We entered the conference room but no one was there. While we looked at each other for an explanation, the answer was delivered by the hospital receptionist. "Sorry you had to wait, folks. I didn't see you come in. Colonel Butler just called to say that he and the sheriff are running late for your seven o'clock meeting. He apologizes for any inconvenience."

"This can't be good news," I muttered aloud.

Everyone nodded in agreement.

Ignoring our mood, the receptionist offered, "Perhaps you'd like to go down to the cafeteria. They have some fine bean soup if anyone is hungry."

Dad and I looked at each other through squinted eyes. We could barely maintain our composure. We assured her we would be fine. Then she left to resume her normal duties, which apparently consisted of delivering bad news.

THE DELAY WAS AGONIZING. I was tired of waiting to hear of Danny's whereabouts. My only thought was that *no news* is not always *good news*. In fact, during my year-long best friendship with Danny, *no news* generally meant that something had gone wrong. After all, this was wartime and things have a tendency to go wrong when life and death are at stake.

Danny had been in so many dire straits and nasty scrapes since we'd met that I was beginning to believe he was a magnet for trouble. Not that he wasn't adept when it came to ducking punches thrown his way, but just how many lives is one cat allowed beyond the proverbial nine? Even a cat with Danny's intelligence, clairvoyance, and plain good luck must run out of chances at some point.

Recognizing that pessimism had begun to dominate my thinking, I decided to take a walk. On entering the lobby, I saw Colonel Butler's car pull into the driveway. Sheriff Connors followed him into the parking lot.

I rushed back to the conference room and announced their impending arrival.

"Thank, God!" Mrs. Tucker exclaimed. Danny's mother seldom used the Lord's name *in vain*. In this case, she'd have reasoned that she merely used it *in earnest*.

When the colonel and the sheriff entered the room, we were greatly relieved to see them. Before either man had spoken a word, the receptionist entered the conference room once again. "Sorry to interrupt, folks. Sheriff, you have a call from your dispatcher -- out at the front desk."

He rose immediately and hurried from the room. Within a couple of minutes, he was back. His face was ashen.

"What's wrong, Sheriff?" Colonel Butler asked.

"They found the truck all right. It was abandoned at the Riverton Airport."

"The airport!" we all cried simultaneously.

"Why the airport?" Dad asked.

"Because Luftwaffe Oberleutnant Klump is an aviator," I reminded everyone.

"That's right, Jase," the sheriff confirmed. "Otto is now piloting a four-passenger, single-engine airplane -- a bright red Staggerwing Beech -- stolen from the hangar right next to the abandoned truck. And he took off without filing a flight plan. According to the duty air controller, before he lost visual contact, the airplane was flying due west. But we've no idea where he's heading."

"I know exactly where he's headed!" I shouted. "Milwaukee, Wisconsin! That's where Otto spent his childhood -- before returning to Germany to join the Luftwaffe. He's got a lot of friends and family there."

"Well, I'll be darned. He must have masterminded this caper after all. Now I'll have to involve the Michigan State Police and the FBI."

"Sheriff, if they're headed for Milwaukee, perhaps the army should handle this case. Without too much trouble, I can see that they receive a splendid welcome when they land there," Colonel Butler promised solemnly.

"How's that, Colonel?" Dad asked.

"The Milwaukee airport is Mitchell Field -- named after a Milwaukee native -- Brigadier General Billy Mitchell. I'm sure you've all heard of him. He's regarded as the *Father of the U.S. Army Air Force.*"

While the adults all nodded their heads, I made a mental note to remember Billy Mitchell.

"Earlier this year, Mitchell Field was leased to the War Department for use as a POW base camp. Over 3,000 POWs are interned there. This doesn't include over 250 officers and military police who are responsible for guarding the POWs."

"I'm surprised you know so much about this. Why is that?" Mr. Tucker inquired.

"I'm friends with the commanding officer of that POW camp. His name's Colonel Jenkins. I owe him a favor. I could repay that favor by giving him the gift of two escaping POWs, a stolen airplane, and an innocent boy."

"That sounds great, Colonel. All except the *innocent* part," Mrs. Tucker quipped. She always had a positive attitude in the most trying situations.

"One last thing -- there's a squadron of P-51 Mustangs -- you know the new pursuit airplane -- stationed at Mitchell Field. They might come in handy if Otto tries to make a run for it."

After hearing Colonel Butler's news, Mrs. Tucker reasserted her positive attitude. "Well, there's one good thing that could come of all this," she observed. "After spending all this time with two Germans, Danny should return home speaking fluent German."

"Ya Bolt," I agreed, echoing my best friend's favorite German phrase.

COLONEL BUTLER SUGGESTED THAT we adjourn for the time being.

"You go home and rest up while I return to Camp Riverton to make arrangements for a proper *welcome* for Danny's abductors when they land in Milwaukee."

As an afterthought, the colonel asked, "Sheriff, could you come along in case we have to coordinate with the local authorities over in Wisconsin. You'd know more about that than I would."

The sheriff agreed to join him.

"Based on my estimated flying time to Milwaukee, this operation should be wrapped up in an hour or two. Why don't we all meet back here at the hospital -- say at nine o'clock?"

Instead of driving home and then back again, we decided to wait at the hospital. Colonel Butler and the sheriff showed up early this time. They had news all right but it was *not* good.

"Well, here's the crux of it. We don't know where they are. They didn't enter Milwaukee airspace. We have to assume they headed off to some other destination. They had enough fuel for about four hours of flying -- and that would be at a moderate speed. Chances are they've either refueled by now and are still flying. Or they're on the ground -- who knows where?" The colonel paused. "Anything to add, Sheriff?"

"Well, there is one other scenario that I'm sure is on everyone's mind. The airplane could have had problems causing them to go down."

Mrs. Tucker gasped. We all looked with concern in her direction.

The sheriff continued. "We anticipated that and have called on the Coast Guard and the P-51s at Mitchell Field to conduct a land and sea -- or in this case -- *lake* search of every square inch of territory in a wide swath extending from Riverton to Milwaukee. We set that up as soon as we were certain they hadn't landed -- about an hour ago.

"This may not pass the *so-what* test, but Colonel Butler and his friend Colonel Jenkins in Milwaukee did a heck of a job setting up the welcoming party for Otto and Shiller. They were very upset not to bring this bizarre case to a close an hour ago."

At this point, Colonel Butler was looking at his shoes.

While I spoke for myself, everyone joined me in thanking the colonel for all he'd done. We also thanked the sheriff.

They both agreed to continue to monitor the search from Camp Riverton and come to our homes the minute they learned anything of importance. We all watched them as they hurried toward their cars.

"Danny's rescue couldn't be in the hands of two more competent men," Dad observed. "We're lucky to have them on the job."

"Well, they sure know the *innocent victim* well enough," I agreed.

"Jase, over this past year, just how many times have they rescued Danny and you from the clutches of nasty villains?"

I wasn't sure I accepted the premise of Dad's question so I politely disagreed. "Well, I'm not unappreciative of what they've done to help us on numerous occasions, but I wouldn't say they've ever had to *rescue* us. Admittedly they've always been there when it was time to take custody of the dozen or more bad guys we've had in our possession this past year."

I smiled to myself and thought, *Boy! Wouldn't Danny be proud of how I'd defended our honor.*

"Jase, you're too much. You sound just like Danny," teased Mrs. Tucker as she pinched my cheek, a little too hard I thought.

While we waited in the lobby, no one uttered a word. Strangely, as we drove home with the Tuckers, silence reigned as well. We got out of the Tucker's car, exchanged a few mutually encouraging words, and then watched as they drove out of sight.

Once again, my mood soured and I began to think the worst. I pondered what my life would be like without Danny. For some crazy reason, one of Danny's favorite malapropisms popped into my head, *All's swell that ends swell.*

"Dad! Everything's gonna be fine. *All's swell!* Just like Danny says."

AFTER REACHING RIVERTON AIRPORT, Otto had parked the truck behind the hangar located at the far west end of the field. This insured that the truck was well out of sight from the main road and the airport terminal.

The sleek, shiny-red Staggerwing Beech airplane parked inside the hangar was one that Otto knew would take them where they wanted to go. He also knew that he could fly it competently.

During the day, especially on Saturdays, the airport was bustling with employees, pilots, and passengers. No one in his right mind would attempt a heist and takeoff with all this activity around them. It was best that the POWs not be seen, even from a distance. Any Rivertonian back in those days could spot the prominent *PW* emblazoned on the uniforms worn by all POWs.

Danny was the only one of the trio who wouldn't stand out. Well, now that I think about it, perhaps I'm mistaken. For the first three years that I knew him, Danny wore the same uniform every day. A tee shirt of alternating maroon and dirty yellow stripes was tucked carelessly into crumpled tan cotton shorts. Several passes of an adult-length, brown-leather belt embossed with bucking broncos and branding irons circled his waist.

But the most dramatic element of his fashion statement was the floppy pair of canvas infantry leggings, surplus from the Great War, I guessed. If fully laced, they would have extended upward, well past his knees. Two scuffed, brown work shoes, in need of new soles and laces, poked out from under his doughboy specials.

Describe that get-up to anyone, young or old, in our part of town and they'd shout out the name *Danny Tucker.* It was his trademark.

So the trio waited. And waited some more. By dusk, the number of people began to lessen. Cautiously they crept from the truck into the hangar. Otto and Shiller agreed on seating assignments. Of course, Otto would take the pilot's seat in front on the left. Danny would sit in the copilot's seat on Otto's right. Shiller wanted both backseats so he could keep tabs on Otto and Danny.

Despite his tenuous situation, Danny decided he might as well enjoy the moment. Setting aside his concerns, he told Otto that he was extremely honored to assume the role of copilot and would do his level best to make Otto proud. As Grandma Compton would have put it, "Danny was pleased as punch!"

After he had gone through his checklist, Otto started the powerful twin engines. When everyone had buckled his seat belt, Otto taxied the sleek red airplane to the head of the runway. He revved up the engines, released the brake, and pushed the throttle forward. Within seconds, Otto was powering the stolen Staggerwing down the runway and into its takeoff. After they lifted off, everyone including Danny felt a sense of elation. They'd done it!!!

However, from the elevated control center, the duty air controller watched the scene through the large plate-glass window. Because this airplane that had just taken off was owned by his brother-in-law, he was very familiar with the Staggerwing. He also knew immediately that something was wrong.

He picked up the radio microphone to scold his friend.

"Beech 4761, this is Riverton Control. *Mr. Perfect Pilot*, it's not like you to forget to file your flight plan before taking off. Why don't you come about and land your pride and joy? Then we'll make you legal before you head out of here. Over."

The unexpected blast from the radio reverberated around the cockpit, causing all three passengers to flinch. Otto nervously peeked over his shoulder to see how Shiller was taking this abrupt order from the ground. Shiller was clearly on the verge of panic. Just as Otto was about to advise patience and calm, the *innocent boy* shocked both POWs.

Copilot Danny, assuming power granted to him by Otto, decided something had to be done. He snatched the radio microphone and transmitted the following message, "Riverton Control. This is Daniel Tucker, Copilot of Beech 4761. I'm leading a top secret mission for Edgar J. Hoover, Director of the FBI in Washington, DC.

"I made the decision to commandeer this airplane and take full responsibility for my action. I'm not authorized to reveal the identity of my passengers or our destination. If this troubles you, I suggest you discuss it directly with J. Edward Hoover. But remember -- this is a wartime emergency. Unless you want to look silly, I'd advise just keeping it to yourself. Over and out!"

Danny folded his arms and leaned back in his seat. Then he glanced at Otto whose eyes were as big as saucers. Danny responded with his sly grin that most people would have perceived as a smirk.

Shiller jabbed the back of Otto's neck with the Luger and barked, "Was ist los?"

He demanded to know what was going on.

Otto calmly explained all that had just transpired. Shiller pondered Otto's words for a minute. Finally he burped a grunt of approval at Danny who gave Shiller a sly grin/smirk of his own.

Feeling a sense of relief, Otto brought the aircraft around and settled on a heading of 275 degrees -- nearly due west. In about three-and-a-half hours, they would be landing in Milwaukee. Then Danny and he could give Shiller the slip and explain the situation to the authorities there. Surely Otto would be exonerated from what some people back in Riverton were accusing him.

As soon as Otto settled on the heading of 275 degrees, Danny snatched the chart folder from the large leather briefcase at his feet and studied it feverishly. After a few seconds, he slammed the folder closed and turned to Otto.

"Oberleutnant Klump, come right to your new heading of 085 degrees. Over."

A combination of years of military conditioning and Danny's commanding demeanor resulted in Otto's complete compliance with his copilot's order.

Otto jammed the yoke fully over to starboard. The powerful aircraft tipped radically to the right. Once he'd settled on his new course, Otto reported, "Steady on new course, 085 degrees. Sir!"

"Very well," the copilot replied, adding a pinch of Navy lingo for good measure. "Steady as she goes, helmsman."

They were now heading nearly due east.

Once again, Shiller demanded to know what was going on. "Oberleutnant, was ist los?" he screamed.

When Otto replied in German, Danny couldn't understand most of the words. But there was one phrase that pleased him very much. It was when Otto explained, "Wir gehen nach Milwaukee."

Danny thought to himself, *That's right, Shiller, old boy. We're going to Milwaukee, Wisconsin. Just keep believing that. Keep believing that and we'll all be fine.*

Soon Danny was bothered by a gnawing thought. *Maybe Otto knows we're not going to Milwaukee, but has he figured out just where we're going?* Danny put this concern out of his mind. He was sure their destination would soon be revealed to all those aboard.

Once again, he was right as rain.

WHEN DAD AND I returned from the hospital, he picked up his *Riverton Daily Press*, which he always read from cover to cover. This was particularly true during the war years. I always believed his need to track progress in the war had something to do with the fact that so many of his close friends had signed up right after Pearl Harbor and had been sent overseas.

However, Dad could not join them. Like many skilled laborers in our neighborhood, Dad was deferred from military service because his occupation was deemed critical to the war effort. He had no choice in the matter.

"Jase, did you hear that SS Reichsfuhrer Heinrich Himmler committed suicide? Somehow I must have missed that. By now, it looks like most of the top Nazis took the coward's way out. I'm not surprised.

"They're still fighting hot and heavy on Okinawa. That's been a real tough nut to crack for our troops there. Just like Iwo Jima.

"And the Japanese are still fighting on in Mindanao -- in the Philippines. I wonder if they'll ever surrender. Or will it be another fight to the death?"

Even though it had been more than a month since Dad had read the news accounts on the subject, I still couldn't forget about Adolph Hitler committing suicide. He had caused the world so much pain. Yet he removed himself from it without one word of apology or regret. *Incarnate evil* was how Dad described Hitler.

Dad seldom solicited my response but I was okay with that. I still learned a lot. Besides, following his example, I read the newspaper almost every day myself.

His news briefing over, he headed for the shed.

As the war wore on, because of the extreme shortage of ready-made clothing, more and more people were forced either to make their own or to repair worn items. This meant Dad spent more and more time on his sewing-machine business. So for hours each evening, he wasn't really at home. He was out back in his shed where his repair shop was located. With Mom working several evenings each week at the POW camp, I was often alone in the house for several hours each day.

Once Danny and I became best friends, we devised myriad ways to entertain ourselves during the times I had normally spent by myself at home. This would have been one of those times. But I found myself alone again, trying to decide what to do. The day had been long and trying. Of course, Danny's whereabouts and welfare were still very much on my mind.

I decided to turn on the radio and tune in to one of my three favorite mystery theaters, which included *Suspense*, *Sherlock Holmes*, and *Inner Sanctum*. Dad called these three, "Scary but smart shows." These were among many high-quality radio programs broadcast back in those days. But I was frustrated. It was too late to listen to these evening shows. I turned off the radio and snatched up Dad's *Riverton Daily Press*.

I was startled by the sound of footsteps on the front porch. I put down the newspaper and tiptoed to the front-room window. Warily I pushed back the curtain and peeked out. The glow of the street light, obstructed by the thick foliage of our box elder tree, cast a dark shadow over our front porch. Still I was able to recognize the person standing there. It was Queenie.

But why doesn't she knock?

When my eyes adjusted to the darkness, I learned why she was hesitant to reveal herself. She was sobbing. I couldn't remember ever seeing her cry. Of course, I'd only known her for about a year and, after all, she was three years older than I. She was a teenager while Danny and I were still only 11.

I wasn't sure what to do. *Should I go to the door and invite her in? Or should I wait until she knocks?* It was nerve-wracking. I decided to wait her out. And soon I heard a gentle tapping on the front door.

"Jase, it's Selma. May I come in?"

Selma? I must have made a mistake. But I'd been sure it was Queenie.

"Come on, Jase. I saw you at the window. It's Queenie. Let me in."

Queenie's name is Selma? Who knew?

When I opened the door, she pushed her way inside. I wondered if she were angry with me. My mind went back to that terrible bow-and-arrow incident. *Was she here to get even?*

But I quickly realized she was simply exhausted. She looked terrible. Her eyes were red. Her nose was running. And her hair, that she always meticulously styled, was in tangles.

"Gee, Queenie. Please sit down."

She fell onto the sofa and closed her eyes.

"Please tell me. What's wrong?" I implored cautiously. Queenie and I hadn't had much in the way of a personal, one-on-one relationship. Unless you count the times she had slugged me in the arm for annoying her. That was about all the *contact* we ever shared.

"Well, Jase, what do you think? I'm worried sick about Danny. And I don't understand how Otto could be involved with this. What are we going to do?"

For the first time since we'd met, I felt included in her life. We shared a mutual love for Danny and a mutual concern for his safety. We also shared that frustrating state of not-knowing, which for those people who really care is crazy-making.

"Do you want to go for a walk? Maybe down to Pete's? We could buy some pop and sit on the bus-stop bench."

It was about the best I could come up with. While I expected Queenie to reject my idea out-of-hand, to my surprise, she seemed pleased.

"Sounds great. It's a pleasant evening. The air is so fresh and cool. I like walking. And I'm kinda thirsty too. Thanks, Jase."

She stood and held out her hand. We walked hand in hand, out the door and down the sidewalk toward Pete's Grocery-Liquor-Hardware Store.

Looking back on that evening, I imagine Queenie would have been about five feet tall. But I'm certain I was at least twice that tall, myself.

AFTER AN UNEVENTFUL TWO hours of flying and no further radio traffic, Shiller seemed to relax a bit. But Otto remained tense as he watched the sun setting behind them. He hoped Shiller's geography was as poor as his judgment.

Being a member of the *Master Race*, Shiller should have known that Wisconsin was due west of Riverton, Michigan, on the other side of Lake Michigan. Since departing from Riverton, the Staggerwing had been flying due east over miles and miles of, not lake, but verdant Michigan farmland.

The ever clairvoyant Danny, somehow sensing Otto's concern, began singing the University of Wisconsin fight song.

On Wisconsin! On Wisconsin! Plunge right through that line.

Danny had a magnificent voice so the other two men in the cockpit joined right in.

Ahn Visconseen! Ahn Visconseen! Ploonge right trooo dah lines.

They had the first stanza down cold. But there was a small problem. That was the only stanza Danny knew. Not wanting to spoil the fun, Danny simply repeated himself

On Wisconsin! On Wisconsin! Plunge right through that line.

Ahn Visconseen! Ahn Visconseen! Ploonge right trooo dah lines.

After six iterations, the old school spirit began to wane. After the eighth iteration, it sputtered and mercifully died altogether.

But Danny was certain that he'd made his point. Again he thought to himself, *That's right Shiller old boy. We're going to Milwaukee, Wisconsin. Just keep believing that. Keep believing that and we'll all be fine.*

Danny snuggled down into his cozy blanket of smugness and closed his eyes.

Squawk!

The second blast from the radio shattered the silence. Everyone in the cockpit was on high alert.

"Calling unidentified aircraft! Calling unidentified aircraft! This is Selfridge Air Control. You have just entered military airspace. You are ordered to change course to 180 degrees. Maintain your current elevation and airspeed. Please comply immediately. Over."

Without hesitation, Otto carried out the order by coming right to course 180 degrees. They were now flying straight south.

"Selfridge? Selfridge? Was ist das, Oberleutnant?" shouted Shiller.

Otto answered calmly, "Selfridge ist der Name des Milwaukee Flughafen."

Name of the Milwaukee Airport?

Otto was so convincing that for a moment Danny almost believed him.

"Calling unidentified aircraft. This is Selfridge Air Control. Change of course acknowledged. Please identify yourself immediately. Over"

Once again, the copilot snatched the radio microphone from its bracket and transmitted the following message: "Selfridge Air Control. This is Beech 4761, flying out of Riverton, Michigan. Over."

"Beech 4761. What's your destination? Over."

"Selfridge Air Control. Our destination is Selfridge Airport in *Milwaukee*. From there we intend to fly to Berlin. Over."

Shiller smiled when he heard Danny mention *Berlin*.

"Beech 4761. Say again. Over."

"Selfridge Air Control. Stand by to copy. Over."

"Go ahead. Over."

"Selfridge Air Control in *Milwaukee*. Copy the following. Sugar Oboe Sugar. Over."

"Beech 4761. Copied that. Can you clarify? Over."

"Selfridge Air Control. Clarification follows. Stand by to copy. How Oboe Sugar Tare Able George Easy. Did you copy? Over."

"Aha! Understood. Roger. Out."

Danny wasn't sure if Otto had caught on to his ploy, but he was sure that Shiller was in the dark.

Without consulting Otto, he turned to Shiller and explained, "You may not have understood all of my conversation so I want to fill you in on the details. I made arrangements for us to land at Selfridge Field in Milwaukee and transfer to a larger airplane for our flight to Berlin. The air controller will get back to us as soon as they're ready for us to land. I hope you're pleased to be on your way home."

After Otto's translation, Shiller was overjoyed. He unbuckled his seat belt and reached over the back of Danny's seat and gave him a big hug. Danny smiled back at him and shook his hand. Otto was amazed at how Danny had played Shiller. He was still musing to himself about the mystery of Danny's brain when he saw them.

The flight of four P-51 *Mustangs* streaked out of the setting sun toward them at breakneck speed. Within a minute, the four sleek, fully-armed warplanes gracefully settled into position on all sides of the Staggerwing. One each on the airplane's starboard and port wingtips. One dead ahead of them and the fourth on their tail.

"Our escort has arrived," Danny announced matter-of-factly.

Otto translated Danny's words, "Unsere Begleitpersonen sind hier."

"Beech 4761. This is Mustang Flight Leader. Are you the gentlemen who are heading for Berlin? Over."

"Mustang Flight Leader. This is Daniel Tucker, Copilot of Beech 4761. Are preparations for our landing and connections to Berlin all set? Over."

"Beech 4761. Master Tucker, we have conferred with your friends back in Riverton. They are eager to insure that proper preparations are made as well. We will have a little party on the runway for you and your companions before you depart for Berlin. Do you copy? Over."

"Mustang Flight Leader. I copy loud and clear. Roger Dodger. Over and Out."

THE MUSTANG FLIGHT MAINTAINED a tight formation around the Staggerwing as the flight leader fed Otto course, altitude, and airspeed corrections, positioning the Staggerwing on a proper approach for landing at Selfridge Field. Danny continued his role as radio talker.

"Wow! Otto, look at that beautiful sunset," Danny exclaimed. "I've never flown before. Are sunsets always this beautiful -- from up here?"

"Everyting ist, Dahny, mein friend. Everyting is bootifful. Understoods?"

Danny understood all right. Otto was aware of what kind of party was being prepared.

When the sun sank beneath the horizon, darkness fell over them. In the distance, all was black except for a single brightly lighted strip that Danny assumed was their destination. In a few minutes, the Mustangs and the Staggerwing Beech began to descend rapidly. Danny could see clearly now that the runway they were approaching was completely illuminated but either side of the runway was bathed in total darkness.

The Mustangs followed the Staggerwing downward until the airplane's landing gear touched the surface of the runway. Then like magic the Mustangs roared off into the darkness, never to be seen again by those in the Staggerwing cockpit.

When Otto brought the airplane to a halt, Danny looked out to see at least twenty U.S. Army jeeps, with their blinding headlights shining brightly now, forming an ever-tightening circle around the airplane. As they came closer, Danny could see that each was equipped with a .50 caliber machine gun mounted in the back of the jeep. In each jeep, there were two soldiers, not counting the machine gunner and driver, who were pointing tommy guns at the cockpit. Because Shiller was leaning back in his seat, he didn't have a clear view of the *party* that was forming all around them.

Suddenly the Staggerwing shuddered from the *explosion* of sound emitted from a megaphone on the lead jeep. This eruption made the previous radio *blasts* seem like whispers by comparison:

PLEASE STEP OUT OF THE AIRPLANE
WITH YOUR HANDS IN THE AIR. NOW!

Before the order was completed, a dozen soldiers charged the cockpit. Otto and Danny instinctively opened their doors. Two soldiers reached inside and yanked the pilot and his copilot from their seats. With the two *innocents* out of the way, the other soldiers moved to each side door and trained their tommy guns on Shiller. The terrified POW threw his Luger onto Otto's empty seat and raised his hands.

The party was over.

"JASE! JOHN! WHERE ARE you? Danny's safe! Danny's safe!" Dad and I had closed the shed and were heading up the walk to the back porch when we heard Mom's voice.

"That's terrific!" I screamed back. "Where is he?"

We converged with Mom and Colonel Butler in the kitchen.

"Where is he?" I repeated.

Colonel Butler replied, "Otto and he are on their way back from Selfridge Field. The Army Air Corps is flying them into the Flint airport. We have a driver on the way to pick them up."

"Selfridge Field? Why there? What happened to Milwaukee?" I asked, more confused than ever.

"They flew from Riverton straight to Selfridge -- that's a U.S. Army Air Corps base near Mount Clemens. It's located north of Detroit on Lake St. Clair."

"Oh, yeah. I remember now. But whose idea was it to fly there instead of Milwaukee? I bet it was Otto. Right? Or maybe Shiller has some family there. Or ..."

I was still confused.

"It was Danny's idea, Jase," Colonel Butler told us.

"Danny! Well, what do you know!" exclaimed Dad.

"Wait a minute. Otto's coming home too. Does that mean ...?" I sputtered.

"Shiller abducted both Danny and Otto. He needed Otto to fly the airplane. Danny cleared Otto of all wrongdoing as soon as the three were taken into custody earlier this evening. From what I gather, during the flight, Otto and Danny colluded to outwit Shiller. Fortunately, because Shiller is a relatively recently-captured POW, he speaks very little English. That helped Danny and Otto pull the wool over his eyes. When Otto landed, MPs surrounded the aircraft, rescuing Otto and Danny and disarming and capturing Shiller."

"That's great news, Colonel. I knew Otto could never do anything to hurt Danny," I vowed, not revealing a tiny doubt that I had harbored about Otto's innocence. After all, he was raised in Milwaukee.

"Do the Tuckers know that Danny's safe?" Dad wondered.

"Yes," explained Mom. "Colonel Butler and I went there to give them the news before coming here. Naturally they were greatly relieved. And, Jase, Queenie wanted me to thank you again. But she didn't say for what."

I re-experienced the warm glow of my time spent with Queenie earlier that evening. It meant a lot to me. I suddenly realized that the warm glow I was feeling could very well be coming from my red cheeks. I felt a need to explain. "She and I took a walk to talk about Danny. She was pretty upset."

Mom gave me a hug. "That was a very nice thing to do, Jase."

"I have another question about Otto. How did he know how to get to Selfridge Field from here?" Dad asked, still puzzled.

"Apparently *he* didn't know but Danny did. When the Selfridge Field Commanding Officer inquired how Danny knew, Danny told the C.O. that he'd learned it in Boy Scouts."

"Boy Scouts? What does that mean, Colonel?"

I answered Dad's question. "Map reading. Danny knows how to read maps. I bet there were maps in the airplane. Right?"

"You're right, Jase. There was a full set of charts in that Staggerwing Beech they stole. Danny read the correct chart and told Otto what direction to fly. All during the flight, the two of them made Shiller think they were still flying to Milwaukee."

"What about IFF, Colonel?"

Having a top secret clearance because of his work with the Norden bombsight, Dad knew more about air defense tactics than he had ever revealed to us.

"IFF? What's that?" I asked Dad.

"The colonel answered my question. It stands for *Identification Friend or Foe*, a piece of equipment that lets you know whether an incoming airplane is friendly or not."

"Was the Staggerwing Beech identified as a friendly?" Dad asked.

"The C.O. told me it was *not* determined to be a friendly airplane. That's because it was civilian as opposed to military. All Allied military airplanes are equipped with IFF gear. In these cases, they generally contact the unidentified airplane by radio and route them away from restricted airspace -- say around a military airbase. They also often scramble a flight of fighter airplanes to intercept the intruder and make a visual identification."

"Did they do either of those things in the case of the Staggerwing Beech?" Dad inquired.

"They did both."

Dad had a confused look on his face. "Could the fighter planes have shot the Staggerwing Beech down?" Dad asked with trepidation.

"Yes. If the unidentified airplane doesn't cooperate or if it's a real enemy, this being wartime, they're authorized to shoot it down."

"But instead, they let it land. And I still don't understand how the soldiers knew to surround the airplane when it landed," Dad confessed.

"John, you're no more confused than I was when I talked to the C.O. But he told me -- as I'll tell you -- Danny will clear it all up for us when he gets here."

Knowing Danny, I couldn't resist replying, "Don't count on it."

A CAR DOOR SLAMMED, followed by footsteps running up the front walk. Without bothering to knock, Danny banged open the front door and dashed to the kitchen where we were waiting for him. He made his grand entrance by declaring, "Hi, everybody. Sorry I'm late for breakfast."

You're only 15 hours late, I told myself.

"I'm starved. Mrs. A -- are there any of your oatmeal cookies left?"

Mrs. Tucker entered the kitchen just in time to scold her son, "Danny! Why that was very rude. You cannot be discourteous to Mrs. A -- I mean Mrs. Addison."

"You're right, Mom. Sorry Mrs. A -- Addison. I really don't care for any of your delicious oatmeal cookies. Perhaps some other time. Thank you."

"Oh, brother!" virtually leaped out of my mouth.

"I'd surely like one of those cookies, Marie," Dad declared, with a wink.

Mom brought the whole cookie jar down from the cupboard and set it in the center of the kitchen table. Everyone, including Danny's mother and father, took one.

"Okay, Danny. Tell us how you did it," I ordered.

"Did what?" Danny asked as he chomped down on his third or maybe fourth cookie.

"Don't keep us in suspense. Why didn't the Selfridge airplanes shoot you down? And how did the soldiers know to surround the airplane when it landed?" I demanded, cutting to the chase.

"I sent an SOS over the radio."

"An SOS? Now just how did you do that, Danny?" I was becoming impatient.

"Jase, remember when Mr. Shurtleif, our neighborhood air-raid warden, gave us that big envelope full of army things last summer? You remember -- it had the airplane spotter cards and that other stuff."

"Oh, yeah. I remember."

"Well, in the bottom of the envelope, I found a copy of the Phonetic Alphabet that's used by the army to fool the enemy."

"So you used the Phonetic Alphabet to fool Shiller and to alert the base. Is that it?" Colonel Butler asked.

"Sure did! I used the Staggerwing's radio to send an SOS to Selfridge Air Control. I radioed 'Sugar-Oboe-Sugar.' That's an S-O-S."

"Did he understand right away?"

"No. He asked me to clarify my SOS message."

"What did you do?"

"I sent him How-Oboe-Sugar-Tare-Able-George-Easy. Earlier I'd told him my name and that we were from Riverton. He got the message and called Colonel Butler. Right, Colonel?"

"That's exactly right, Danny," the colonel confirmed, still looking a bit puzzled.

"Oh, I got it," I shouted. "You spelled out H-O-S-T-A-G-E!!!"

"Right you are, Jase, my boy. Now please pass the cookie jar, Mrs. A."

AS BOYS GROWING UP in Michigan during World War II, Danny and I were acutely aware of the importance of Selfridge Field to the war effort.

Selfridge Field was built in 1917 on 640 acres of land in Harrison Township, Michigan, near Mount Clemens. The land was leased from Henry B. Joy, the founder of the Packard Motor Company. The field was named after Lt. Thomas Selfridge who died in 1908 while flying as a passenger in an airplane piloted by Orville Wright. Wright survived the crash, but he suffered serious injuries and was hospitalized for several weeks. Lt. Selfridge was the nation's first soldier to die in an airplane crash.

During World War I, Selfridge Field, the country's newest air training facility, became home to the First Pursuit Group, one of the oldest combat groups in the Air Force. By definition, "Pursuit" or "P" series airplanes are high-speed, long-range fighter airplanes designed and equipped to pursue and attack enemy aircraft.

During World War II, two pursuit airplanes were highly successful in this mission against Japanese Zero fighter airplanes in the Pacific Theater, namely the single engine P-51 *Mustang* and the twin-engine P-38 *Lightning*.

Author's Note:
Lew Lockhart, a good friend of mine, lives in nearby Franklin, Tennessee. During the war, from bases in New Guinea, Lew and his fellow Army Air Corps pilots flew the vaunted P-38s. On many occasions, they successfully tangled with Zeros while carrying out attacks on Japanese positions in the Southwest Pacific. During 1943 and 1944, Lew flew an incredible 171 missions against the enemy. Two of his colleagues were the top Aces of the war: Richard Bong (40 kills) and Thomas McGuire (38 kills).

On a personal note, Lew, at the age of 58, took up long-distance running. Since that time, he has won over a hundred trophies. In fact, he completed three, full marathons after the age of 60. In addition, Lew is a voracious reader, especially of histories. Naturally he's also a loyal Cottonwood *fan. I consider myself privileged to know this exceptional man.*

Perhaps the most famous member of the First Pursuit Group was Captain Edward "Eddie" Rickenbacker, who was an American fighter Ace in World War I and a Congressional Medal of Honor recipient. He was also a race-car driver, an automotive designer, and a pioneer in air transportation. Of course, he enjoyed a longtime career as the head of Eastern Air Lines.

In 1924, a young Army Air Corps cadet named Charles Lindbergh was stationed at Selfridge Field. In 1927, after completing the world's first trans-Atlantic flight, Lindbergh returned to Selfridge. His airplane, the *Spirit of St. Louis*, was escorted by a squadron of 22 pursuit airplanes from Selfridge.

General William "Billy" Mitchell was also stationed at Selfridge Field during World War I. One of the most famous and controversial figures in the history of American airpower, Mitchell was court-martialed for his insubordination and insulting behavior toward his military superiors.

Following his death, however, he was recognized for his contribution to his country. President Franklin D. Roosevelt gave him a posthumous commission as Major General. And Mitchell is the only individual after whom a type of American military aircraft is named, the B-25 *Mitchell* bomber.

Selfridge Field was known as the *Home of Generals* because more than a hundred members of the First Pursuit Group rose through the ranks to become Air Force generals. These included Curtis LeMay, Jimmy Doolittle, Emmett "Rosie" O'Donnell, and of course Billy Mitchell.

During World War II, three squadrons of the 332nd Fighter Group, popularly known as the *Tuskegee Airmen*, also trained at Selfridge Field. The *Tuskegee Airmen* were determined young men who enlisted to become America's first black military airmen, at a time when many people thought that black men lacked the intelligence, skill, courage, and patriotism needed to succeed as American military pilots. But the *Tuskegee Airmen's* stellar record of service during World War II proved their detractors wrong.

After the war, the newly formed U.S. Air Force initiated plans to integrate its units as early as 1947. In 1948, President Truman enacted Executive Order Number 9981, which directed equality of treatment and opportunity in all of the United States Armed Forces. This order, in time, led to the end of racial segregation in the military forces. It was also the first step toward racial integration in America.

AFTER WE HAD SAID our goodbyes and the Tuckers and Colonel Butler departed, we Addisons sat down in the front room. Naturally we were exhausted, but none of us really felt like going to bed. Dad suggested we tune in to Gabriel Heatter's late night newscast on our console radio. Heatter was known for his morale-boosting broadcasts during the arduous days of the war. He was our favorite radio commentator.

I turned on the switch and yellow-white light beamed from the dial. After a few seconds of scratchy *squeaks*, we heard Heatter's catchphrase that always began his program.

"Good evening, everyone. There's good news tonight.

"Dateline: Mount Clemens, Michigan. Early this evening, a flight of four *Tuskegee Airmen*, flying P-51 pursuit airplanes, was scrambled to intercept an unidentified aircraft, which had entered Selfridge Field's restricted airspace. The intruder was a Staggerwing Beech single-engine civilian airplane carrying two escaped German POWs and an innocent eleven-year-old boy. The flight of P-51s escorted the intruder to Selfridge Field where it landed. The two POWs, one of whom was armed with a German Luger, were recaptured and the innocent boy was returned to his anxious family who resides in Riverton, Michigan."

2 JUST REWARDS

AFTER SATURDAY NIGHT'S EXCITEMENT AND THE resulting late bedtime, I allowed myself to sleep in the next morning. The sound of Mom preparing breakfast awoke me. Even though the sun was up, I was still sleepy. So I didn't get out of bed until the mouth-watering aroma of Grandpa's farm bacon, eggs, and toast floated into my tiny bedroom and tickled my nose.

I slipped into my tee shirt, shorts, and black basketball shoes and headed for the bathroom to brush my teeth. Unlike other boys I knew, I enjoyed brushing my teeth. I derived satisfaction from the ritual of shaking an ample measure of Squibb's Tooth Powder from its brown and yellow tin onto my left palm, wetting my toothbrush from the tap, and mixing my own *toothpaste* before thoroughly scouring my teeth with this tasty blend. I felt rather sad each time I rinsed this early morning treat out of my mouth.

By the time I reached the kitchen, Mom and Dad had finished eating. As usual, Dad was reading the Sunday morning edition of the *Riverton Daily Press*. And Mom was focused on the latest *Saturday Evening Post*.

After exchanging good mornings, I asked, "Has Danny been here?"

"Nope. No sign of him yet."

"I hope he hasn't been abducted again," I quipped, trying to make a joke. When no one laughed, I corrected myself. "Naw! That couldn't be it. He probably slept in just like me."

While Mom was serving my breakfast, I heard footsteps on the back porch. Suddenly the kitchen door burst open and there was Danny, dressed in his Sunday uniform. That is to say, instead of his olive-drab army cap, he was wearing his recently-rescued Tigers baseball cap. The rest of his garb remained the same.

"Hey! It's the star of the Gabriel Heatter newscast," Dad announced. "Did you and your family hear the show, Danny?"

Danny smiled. "Yep, we all heard it -- and so did everybody at the Good Mission Church."

I wondered how Danny knew that, but I was wise enough not to ask.

Because our parents allowed themselves the luxury of sleeping in on Sunday mornings, Danny and I always left home early to carry out our self-assigned duty of visiting as many churches as possible. Because of Danny's perpetual state of hunger, the selection of churches depended solely on the quantity of the food offerings provided for the church's flock.

For several reasons, the Mission was our first stop. Every morning at six o'clock, a full breakfast was served to its residents, consisting of neighborhood and transient bums. Danny always contended that a hearty breakfast was essential to good health in growing boys like us. While I didn't have Danny's appetite, I did enjoy the sumptuous offerings at the Mission as we called it.

The Mission was only a block away, located at the corner of Forrest Street and New Albany Avenue. As luck would have it, this location was directly across the street from Pete's Grocery-Liquor-Hardware Store. This was convenient for many Mission *guests* who thought it wise to *check in* after indulging in Pete's offerings of fortified red wine or *affordable* whiskey. Those guests, unable to check in formally, spent the night snoozing together on the Mission's commodious front porch.

In addition, the sunrise religious service was mandatory for all guests in residence, including those on the porch. Danny and I thoroughly enjoyed the rousing sermon delivered by Reverend Squires. How better to start our day than by being severely warned of the consequences of not changing our sinful ways. Yes, it was invigorating all right. But the *pièce de résistance* of the service was

Mrs. Squires' piano renditions of our favorite hymns, delivered to a pulsating boogie-woogie beat.

"Danny, why don't you sit down while I fix you some breakfast? How do bacon and scrambled eggs sound?"

"No, thanks, Mrs. A. I just finished a big breakfast at the Mission."

"Hey! Why didn't you come and get me before you went?" I asked indignantly.

"I did. But everybody in the house was sound asleep so I just went alone."

We were accustomed to Danny entering our house without knocking, but I wasn't sure how I felt about his coming in and wandering around while we were sleeping. I was about to express my concerns when Danny beat me to the punch. "I wouldn't normally come in when everybody's asleep, but I didn't want to carry the big can I brought for you down to the Mission."

"You brought us a big can of something? Where is it?" I demanded, not sure that this wasn't another of Danny's fibs.

"It's under your bed."

I was almost speechless, but I managed to say, "Why did you leave it there?"

"Didn't want anybody to steal it."

"Who's going to steal it?"

Danny gave me a funny look and changed subjects. "Chub's gotten very possessive about *his* cans so it's harder for me to bring them over lately."

Danny's younger brother Chub had been the center of a family controversy revolving around the subject of tin cans. As a form of financial assistance, Grandpa Tucker had given Danny's family several hundred cases of canned goods from the remaining stock of his grocery store that closed when he retired. At the time, Danny's father was just starting an automotive-repair business so Grandpa Tucker's generosity was greatly appreciated.

The family stored the cans in their basement on shelves built by Danny's father. Because the cans of various sizes contained a broad spectrum of foods, it wasn't unusual for the Tucker family to open two or three cans for each meal. Recycling the cans became a family ritual. This event involved washing the can, opening the can's bottom and pushing it inside the can, removing its wrapper, and finally squashing the can flat before dropping it into a burlap sack.

Bohunk Joe, a friendly neighborhood bum, would come by each week with his pushcart to pick up the bulging burlap sack. From there, he pushed the sack, with others he'd collected, to Southside Junk Yard where he was paid a few pennies for the metal. This modest payment allowed him to make a selection from Pete's finest for his supper that evening.

During his family's recycling ritual, Chub's job was to remove the paper wrapper from each can. One day, Chub decided he could get a head start on his job by unwrapping all the cans in the basement before they made their way upstairs for meals. Before he was discovered, Chub had managed to unwrap nearly ninety percent of the cans.

After administering a proper punishment for Chub, the family entered what they called the *Mystery Can* phase. Before each meal, they would select two or three wrapper-less cans and open them to determine each meal's menu. So when Danny brought a can of food to our house as a gift, we had no idea whether it contained catsup, soup, or peaches.

"Since Chub unwrapped all our cans, we've focused on the smaller cans, like #1s," Danny explained. "They're the 11-ounce cans. And #2s, the 20-ounce cans. That way, if it's something we don't want to eat with the meal -- or just don't like -- there's a smaller amount to deal with. We're going through the small cans pretty fast. We'll soon be down to just the larger cans. Like #3s with 32 ounces, #4s with 58 ounces, and #5s with 110 ounces -- that's almost a gallon.

"We opened a #5 for lunch the other day and it was *creamed onions*. Last week, one of them was *mustard*. That's a lot of mustard for one family to eat before it goes bad."

"But I don't understand. Why's Chub more possessive?"

"I really don't know. He spends hours in the basement, playing with the cans. He reorganizes them about every two days. He's even started giving them names. I walked down to the basement the other day, and Chub was talking to a #4 that he was calling *Howard*. It's pretty pathetic."

Mom knew it was time to change the subject. "Do you boys realize what day this is?"

"Sunday," Danny told her smugly.

"This is the day JB leaves for Nashville for the summer."

JOHNSON BRADFORD AND HIS mother Rose had come to Riverton from Nashville, Tennessee, to live with our friends and next-door neighbors, Patrick and Mary Reilly. Rose and Mary were sisters.

Rose's late husband had been a Navy doctor assigned to the *USS Arizona* (BB-39), which was sunk during the Japanese sneak attack on Pearl Harbor on December 7, 1941. Dr. Bradford was among the 1,177 *Arizona* crewmen who lost their lives on that fateful day. After her husband's death, Rose suffered from severe depression and was no longer able to work as a nurse.

Johnson Bradford was a wunderkind in any sport he tried. Before his mother's *indisposition*, as Mrs. Reilly called it, he had been enrolled in Stony River Academy, a prestigious, private boarding school in Nashville. There, Johnson received some of the nation's best basketball coaching. But when the family money ran out, Johnson had to drop out of school. He and his mother moved to Riverton where he enrolled in Hamilton School, joining Danny and me in the sixth grade.

At first, we couldn't decide whether we liked or despised Johnson Bradford. For one thing, he persisted in wearing his preppy clothing to our extremely *unpreppy* school. For another, his combed-down long, oily hair was an anathema to us. But his most egregious character flaw was his habit of calling every adult either *sir* or *ma'am*. And his tendency to say *please* and *thank you* to everyone. In short, Johnson Bradford was far too *genteel* for us.

However, when we saw the sports trophies that he'd won, we changed our appraisal of him. And after seeing what he could do with a basketball in the school gym one day, we took him on as our *cause*. Within days, he was wearing unpreppy clothing, sporting a real American haircut, and uttering *sirs* and *ma'ams* less frequently.

All that remained was to change that *name*. Who else in the State of Michigan had two last names? No one! That's who. So Johnson Bradford became *JB*, our good friend.

When JB told us about his summer plans, we were very happy
for him. His old coach at Stony River Academy had invited JB
to coach at the school's summer basketball camp. Although JB
wouldn't be paid, he could sleep in the boys' dormitory and eat his
meals in the school dining hall at no cost.

Best of all, JB told us that the coach had agreed that Danny
and I could spend nearly two weeks with JB. We also would sleep
in the dorm and eat in the dining hall at no cost to us as well.

JB suggested we plan to arrive on Friday so our stay could span
two weekends, allowing him to show us the sights in and around
Nashville. All we had to do was pay for our round-trip train fares.

"Mom, how much is a round-trip ticket to Nashville?"

"Well, I really don't know. The train ride takes about 18 hours.
JB's leaving at ten o'clock this morning and will arrive in Nashville
around four o'clock tomorrow morning. He gains an hour because
Nashville is on Central time. You could ask him about the price
when he comes over this morning."

"Or we could walk down to the train station and ask the ticket
master," suggested Danny.

Danny always preferred doing things the long, hard way.

"Jase, let's go count our money. All right?"

As we made our way to my bedroom, I heard my mother ask,
"Like me to refill your coffee, John?"

"Thanks. I'm going to finish the paper before we go to the
farm today so I can fill your dad in on the latest news."

Just two days before, Danny and I had counted what was left
of our bait supply earnings from the summer before. We only had
$17.13. I was positive that Danny remembered this, but I went
along just to humor him.

Danny and I had been fortunate to find a good job the
summer before. Homer Lyle hired us to be the sole suppliers of
fresh-caught bait for his bait shop. We spent the summer catching
night crawlers, chubs, minnows, and crickets.

We replaced Homer Jansen who had enlisted in the Marine
Corps. However, Homer's military stint was cut short in the
Philippines by a Japanese sniper's bullet. Mercifully his wounds were
not serious enough to end his bait-supply career. Last fall, Danny and
I had gracefully resigned so Homer could reassume his old position.

We stored our bait supply earnings in the locked bank that I kept on my dresser. When I reached under my mattress to retrieve the key to my bank, I felt a large lump beneath the innersprings. I quickly withdrew my hand and looked under the bed.

"You *did* put a large can under my bed while I was sleeping."

"You doubted me?"

"No! You *never* fib."

We both chuckled at that one.

I retrieved both the bank key and the #10 can. I opened the bank and dumped its contents on the bed. Besides two arrowheads and five Indian Head Pennies wrapped in ancient wax paper, out tumbled what was left of our bait money.

"You count it this time," I insisted.

Danny took his time unfolding each bill carefully and sorting the loose change by denomination. When he finished, he announced, "It's all here. $17.13. Just like last time."

"You doubted me?" I replied sarcastically.

Ignoring my attempt at humor, he stated emphatically, "The round trip fares are almost $40 each. We need to get a job -- in a hurry."

"What do you mean by *almost?*"

"The tickets cost $39.03, but we need some tip money. So that's almost $40 each."

How Danny suddenly knew the cost of our train fares was beyond me. But my past experience with the mysterious mind of Danny Tucker told me that $40 would prove to be accurate.

WHEN OUR NEIGHBORS ARRIVED, we settled in our front room. Everyone seemed on edge. Perhaps JB's imminent departure was finally becoming a reality.

Mom broke the ice. "Your summer in Nashville sounds exciting, JB. Are you looking forward to it?"

"Yes, ma'am," JB replied. "To be honest, it's a dream come true. But a part of me dreads the thought of being away from you all -- my friends and family."

"Well, if you're having fun, the summer will be over in a flash. Then you'll be home again," Mom assured him.

JB's mother turned to Danny and me. "I hope you'll be able to visit Johnson this summer. You'll love Nashville."

"JB, you were kind to make arrangements for the boys to stay at the school. I know they're already making plans to find jobs to pay for the trip," Mom informed him.

That was Danny's cue. "How much is the round-trip fare, JB?"

"The train fare is just over $39, but you need some extra money for tips. So I'd say you'll need about $40."

Danny turned to me and winked. Then he explained to JB, "We only have to earn $62.87 more to make the trip."

"Don't forget to bring a little extra for sightseeing expenses -- bus fares, tickets, snacks, and so on."

"Snacks? With Danny along, that means we'll have to earn about *$362.87.*"

Danny nodded his agreement.

"Oh, Danny. We were in Lansing yesterday shopping for luggage and new basketball shoes for JB. But we heard Gabriel Heatter last night," Mrs. Reilly pointed out. "I'm certainly glad you're home safe and sound. What an ordeal you must have had."

"It was actually fun. I'd like to do it again," Danny admitted.

I believed him.

"Well, I'm just glad you're home safe and sound," Mrs. Reilly repeated.

"Where's Mr. Reilly," I inquired.

"He wanted to wash the car before taking Johnson to the train station."

"Oh, that reminds me," Mrs. Reilly told us, "We know of a possible short-term job. Mr. Reilly's cousin is Edward Gray who owns Gray's Funeral Home -- right next to the library. He asked Mr. Reilly if Johnson could assemble a team of three or four boys to do a job for him. He thought the boys could make a good amount of money in just a couple of weeks. And you could start as early as tomorrow -- if you're available."

"Oh, that sounds very promising, boys," Dad speculated.

"Since Evelyn, his only child, works at the funeral home, she's not able to do the job," Mrs. Reilly added.

"I saw her picture in the *Riverton Daily Press*. She was the Valedictorian in the recent graduating class from Riverton High. She's a very pretty girl," Mom replied.

Mrs. Reilly nodded her head, smiling proudly.

"We're definitely interested, Mrs. Reilly," I affirmed without conferring with Danny.

"If you'd like to know more about the job, we could stop by after the train station and tell Mr. Gray that you'll be down -- say later today -- to discuss it with him. I suggest today because the funeral home is always open on Sunday afternoons and evenings. He'll definitely be there."

"That sounds great, Mrs. Reilly. Please tell him that we'll come down right after we get back from the farm -- probably in the late afternoon. Is that okay, Mom? Dad?"

Danny didn't say a word.

JB's mother looked at her watch and announced, "Well, we should be leaving, folks."

As we reached the Reilly driveway, we saw that Mr. Reilly had just finished drying his car with his chamois. "Didn't want to go to the train station with a dusty car on a day as important as this," he explained.

We shook JB's hand and he gave us both a hug.

"Don't forget to write us with your address," I reminded him. "We'll send you updates on what's happening in Riverton."

As Mr. Reilly pulled out of his driveway, he honked his horn. We all waved goodbye.

I felt a swell of emotion, rising in my chest. I suddenly realized that I was going to miss JB very much. On the other hand, I was extremely happy that he was given the opportunity to do something he loved. Without a doubt, this weekend had been an emotional roller-coaster ride.

On the way back to the house, Dad said, "Say, that job opportunity sounds promising. Doesn't it?"

"Yes, it does, Dad. Gee! Maybe we can start tomorrow."

For the first time, Danny weighed in. "Just one minute, here. This Gray man runs a funeral house. Right?"

"Home," I reminded him, to no avail.

"Yes," Dad agreed.

"Then he has funerals at his house. Right?"

"Yes."

"Who's always at those funerals, Mr. A?"

"Family and friends of the deceased, I suppose. Why?"

"And who is the *deceased?*"

"What? It could be anybody. I -- I don't understand your question, Danny," Dad finally admitted.

Dad wasn't the only one. "Anybody else got the answer yet?" Danny pressed on.

"Nope! No! Not at all," I sputtered, impatiently.

"Well, I'll tell you who they are. They're dead people! That's who they are. And I'm not going to work with dead people. No, sir. I have my limits!"

"Danny I'm sure --," Dad tried to say.

"I'm sure too. No corpses."

"Well, I'm sure you won't be working with corpses. But you can make sure of the nature of the job before you say you're interested," Dad reasoned.

But Danny wasn't finished. "If we can't find a way of earning some real money -- fast, we'll just have to go talk to the hobos under the Ann Arbor Bridge."

"What on earth for?"

"We'll ask them to show us how to hop a freight train down to Nashville!"

"Are you serious, Danny?"

"Well, Jase. Just how bad do you want to see JB?"

Before I could answer, Danny whipped his red farm handkerchief out of his shorts pocket and quickly tied it around his neck.

"All 'Board," he hollered.

Dad looked at Mom and shook his head.

THE MINUTE WE WALKED in the door, Dad returned to reading his newspaper. "Wait a minute! I think I know how you boys can make $100. Look at this," he declared, holding out the newspaper.

In the *Local* section there was a picture of a young man in a U.S. Army private's uniform. Below the picture, the following article appeared:

DESERTER
FBI OFFERS $100 REWARD
FOR CAPTURE AND CONVICTION
OF FORMER RIVERTONIAN

Former Riverton resident, Donald Douglas, the subject of a nationwide manhunt, is wanted for desertion from the U.S. Army. Douglas is the son of former Riverton banker, Harold Douglas, who was president of the now bankrupt Riverton First National Bank.

As chairman of the Chippewa County Draft Board during the months following Pearl Harbor, the senior Douglas was accused of unduly influencing the draft board to grant his son Donald a military deferment based on a nervous condition from which the son allegedly suffered.

The majority of Riverton citizens perceived the son's only ailment was extreme cowardice. This blatant exercise of undue influence during a period of national emergency resulted in the complete exodus of Riverton First customers causing the bank to close its doors and file for bankruptcy.

Harold Douglas and his son moved to Detroit where the senior Douglas secured a low-level position with the Thrift Savings Bank of Detroit. Mrs. Douglas remained in Riverton to care for her aging mother, Mrs. Thelma Dixon, longtime Riverton resident. Unconfirmed sources informed this newspaper that Mrs. Douglas has filed for divorce.

In September 1944, the son was drafted into the U.S. Army. He was ordered to Basic Training at Fort Custer near Kalamazoo, Michigan. After two weeks of training, he absented himself from the confines of the base without permission. He has been Absent Without Leave (AWOL) for more than six months so he is now officially considered a deserter.

Sources informed this newspaper that the FBI suspects that the fugitive intends to return to Riverton to contact his mother and an unidentified young woman that he had dated when they were fellow students at Riverton High School.

Neither of the senior Douglases cared to comment on the plight of their son.

The FBI has offered a $100 reward for information leading to the arrest and conviction of Donald Douglas. Anyone with such information should contact the FBI's Detroit Field Office whose telephone number is Gratiot 2-5000.

"Danny, this is good timing for us. How would you like $100 to finance our trip to Nashville?"

"Jase, you might as well book those tickets. I'm certain I know how we can nab Douglas Donald."

We might first try getting his name right, I thought to myself. But I didn't correct my friend. I simply started daydreaming about the two weekends of Nashville sightseeing that we would enjoy after we collected the reward money.

"Hey, Mr. A., I'm starved. Isn't it about time we headed to Grandma Compton's house for Sunday dinner?"

From my perspective, Danny had two loves in his life, his love of food and his love of Grandma Compton for loyally meeting his need for constant nourishment.

Just as we were preparing to leave, there was a knock on the front door. Dad answered it and greeted Chuck Nichols. Chuck was a *Riverton Daily Press* reporter and newscaster for WRDP, the radio station owned by the newspaper.

"Come in, Chuck. I can't imagine why you're here."

Both men laughed.

"Danny, there's someone here to see you."

Chuck Nichols was our friend, and the only journalist we trusted to write objectively about our heroic exploits. As a result, we'd given Chuck the exclusive rights to our stories on a number of occasions.

When we first met Chuck in the summer of 1944, he wrote the story about how we managed to capture two POWs who had escaped from Camp Owosso with the assistance of two young women who lived right in our neighborhood. In the fall of 1944, Chuck hosted a radio discussion with Governor Thomas E. Dewey, Danny, and me. We had helped the governor during his 1944 Presidential election campaign. Of course, we also lent support to FDR during that campaign as well. We tried to be as evenhanded as we could in that regard.

In short, Chuck was as close to being our personal press agent as he could and still be objective and earn his salary from the *Riverton Daily Press* and WRDP.

"Hi, Danny. I heard Gabriel Heatter's show last night. Congratulations! It was a good piece all right, except I didn't buy that *innocent boy* angle. Knowing you, I'll bet you played the shell-and-pea game with Shiller -- and then Otto and you lowered the boom. Am I right?"

Danny answered Chuck with a sly grin and a wink.

"Nevertheless, looks like you brought down another villain -- with help from Otto, I realize. And, I suppose, you did get a bit of assistance from the Army Air Corps. But -- I'd be interested in telling our readers -- and listeners -- just how you pulled it off."

Danny nodded his agreement.

"I was hoping you could meet with Otto and me out at the POW camp -- today some time. That would allow me to write a story for tomorrow's newspaper and for my news program tomorrow evening. I've cleared this with Colonel Butler who'll make arrangements for us to meet with Otto anytime that's convenient for you. Are you okay with this idea?"

"I think we can squeeze it in. Let's see -- we're just leaving for Grandma Compton's farm for Sunday dinner. Yum! Then we have to go to the Gray's Funeral House -- I mean funeral *home* -- to see about a job. We're taking the train to Nashville to see JB who's a basketball coach there this summer. Maybe we could do it after the funeral home. I'd like Jase and the Addisons to be there too."

"I think that can be arranged," Chuck replied. "Would it be all right if we meet at the camp?"

"That should work," Dad assured him.

"Sounds good. What time shall I tell the Colonel we'll be there, John?"

"Tell him we'll be there at eight or nine o'clock," Danny said, answering for Dad.

Chuck went away whistling, confident that he'd have a whale of a story in time for his noon deadline the next day.

Of course, that all depended on Danny, which is sometimes risky.

AS DAD TURNED ONTO New Albany Avenue, he suggested, "Danny, we better stop to let your folks know you're going to Grandma Compton's with us."

"I already told them -- this morning before I came over."

This was typical of Danny. Of course, he was always welcome, but why he never waited to be invited bothered me some.

All four of Grandpa and Grandma Compton's children were married and had families of their own. And they all lived within 50 miles of the farm. There was an unwritten rule that the entire Compton clan was expected to come *out home* every Sunday afternoon for dinner.

The war had ruined the family's perfect attendance record. The oldest son, my Uncle Tom, had enlisted and was serving as a tank-repair instructor at the Armor School at Fort Benning, Georgia. But his wife, my Aunt Esther, would be there with her three children, my cousins Carol, Bobby, and Jane.

My mother's sister, Aunt Maude, was also excused. Her husband, my Uncle Van, had been awarded the Congressional Medal of Honor after fighting in Belgium during the Battle of the Bulge. The two of them had spent the last six months touring the country to introduce America to our latest national hero and to convince people to *Buy War Bonds*. Their baby son, my cousin Little Johnnie, was at home in Washington, DC, being taken care of by a special nanny, furnished by the War Department. Yes, there were a number of pleasant perquisites for Medal of Honor recipients.

Among Mom's siblings, Aunt Maude was my favorite. The summer before, when Uncle Van was sent overseas, Aunt Maude came to live with us. She and I shared my tiny bedroom in our small bungalow on Forrest Street. When Little Johnnie was born, he became the third occupant of my postage-stamp size room.

When we pulled into the circular driveway, we could see Grandpa and Mom's other brother, my Uncle Raymond, standing at the edge of the farmyard looking eastward onto the newly mowed hayfield. Each man's shotgun was broken open and hanging over the crook of his left arm.

"Are they going hunting, Jase?" Danny asked.

"Too early for hunting season," I answered. "But you'd never know it by the way Mick is madly barking and leaping into the air."

Mick was Grandpa's loyal fox terrier and one of my most ardent fans. Mick could always induce me to take him hunting. During the summer, Mick and I *hunted* often. My *shotgun* was usually a dried stalk of field corn or a branch that had been broken off the old elm tree by a gust of wind. Mick didn't care. He could flush pheasants quite capably whether or not anyone shot at them with a noisy shotgun.

As much as he enjoyed it, Mick wouldn't hunt with just anyone. In fact, Grandpa and I were the only two people in the world Mick agreed to hunt for.

"They're trapshooting, Danny," Dad explained.

"What's a trap? Oh, yeah! I think I remember. It's a small duck. Right?" Danny guessed.

"No. Actually it's a pigeon," Dad told Danny, leading him along.

"Are you allowed to shoot them this time of year?"

"You can shoot them all year round," I added, joining the tease.

"Are they good eating?"

"Nope."

"Why not?"

"Because they're made of clay. You use them to practice your shooting," Dad noted, putting Danny out of his misery.

When we got out of the car, Mom headed for the kitchen, balancing two enormous bowls. One was filled with egg-yolk colored potato salad and the other contained a three-bean salad, which were her contributions for today's feast. We walked toward the shooters. Grandpa and Uncle Raymond turned to greet us. Grandpa welcomed Danny with, "If it isn't the hero of Selfridge Field. Did they make you a captain while you were there? Or will you have to wait until you get to Washington?"

Grandpa slapped Danny on the back. Remarkably Danny actually blushed.

"How's that new 16-gauge shooting, Raymond?" Dad inquired.

"I'm really pleased with it. The gun fits me perfectly. And it's so well-balanced -- and light."

"Let's show them, Raymond," Grandpa suggested. "Are you ready to try for two?"

"With this huge audience, that's a lot of pressure, Dad. But go ahead. Let's give 'er a try."

Grandpa picked up two clay pigeons and loaded them into the spring-powered launcher on the ground in front of him.

"I'm adjusting their flight path to make it interesting for you, Raymond."

"*Interesting?* Just what I need."

"You can do it. Are you ready?"

"Ready, Dad."

Grandpa launched the pair of clay pigeons. The *birds* glided gracefully out over the field. Their flight paths differed in direction and in altitude, but their speed was the same, that of a pair of fleeing cock pheasants.

In rapid succession, Uncle Raymond quickly took aim and fired one barrel. **Bam!** Then he adjusted his aim and fired the second barrel. **Bam!** We cheered when both birds exploded, creating a puff of brown dust that slowly drifted to the ground. Mick the fox terrier leaped high into the air and barked his congratulations.

"Raymond! Nice shooting! Real nice shooting!" Grandpa acknowledged proudly.

When we applauded Uncle Raymond's fine marksmanship, a wide smile spread across his face.

"Could Jase and I practice shooting clay pigeons with our new shotguns next weekend? We gotta get ready for hunting season," Danny implored.

"Raymond. All right if we let the boys get in some shots next weekend?"

"Sure. The more the merrier. Haven't convinced Tommy and Teddy to take an interest yet. Perhaps Jase and Danny will light a fire under my boys. I'll be sure to have my launcher and plenty of clay pigeons. Be sure to bring plenty of light bird shot -- say 7½ to 8½ shot size. I'm using 7½ for my 16-gauge."

As Uncle Raymond, opened a new box of shells, Grandpa asked, "What have you boys been up to lately?"

"Grandpa, I won't spoil it for you. But you'll learn all about it. There'll be a big article about Danny and Otto in Monday's *Riverton Daily Press*. You can read it on Tuesday," I promised.

When you lived in town, paperboys delivered the *Riverton Daily Press* to your porch within an hour of two of its printing each day. But the newspaper was mailed to subscribers who lived more than a mile from the Riverton city limits. When the Rural Free Delivery (RFD) mailman delivered Grandpa's newspaper, the news was already a day old.

"Let's go in and join the womenfolk," Grandpa suggested. "I'm sure they'll all want to shake your hand, Danny."

"That's okay. I can eat with one hand."

At Grandma's Sunday dinners, each of her four *kids*, as Grandma still called them, brought enough food to feed everyone present. This didn't count the massive quantities of meat, poultry, and game that Grandma routinely prepared for the family. Nor did it count Grandma's supply of baked goods, including homemade breads, muffins, biscuits, dinner rolls, and an assortment of pies, cakes, and cookies. She was in the habit of baking something every morning, even when summer temperatures were unusually high.

Like all the Sunday dinners he attended, today would be like going to heaven for Danny. He'd not only wallow in the food, like one of Grandpa's porcine pets, but he'd also wallow in the attention of his four adoring women admirers. The more he ate the more the Compton women *Ooooed* and *Ahhhhed* over him.

After the weekly feast, the men removed the lace tablecloth from the dining room table and dealt the cards. It was an adults-only game. *Adult* was defined as any male, regardless of age, who could fathom the game of *Set Back*. I'd been accepted as a bona fide player when I was ten. As of yet, Danny hadn't taken enough interest in the game to be qualified. He spent his time in the kitchen, breaking records in terms of the number of helpings he could stow away.

The women remained in the kitchen to clean up and wash dishes. Huge parcels of leftover food were packaged for whoever displayed even a mild interest in portions of leftover meat, potatoes, breads, or desserts.

This process wasn't a quick or quiet one. It was peppered with loud assertions like, "Ma, this is far too much for us. Divide it in half and give it to Betsy and Esther."

"No, Ma. I brought that. I can't take it home with me. We'll just have to drop it off at the county home."

"If I take all this food, what'll you and Dad eat this coming week?"

Knowing we had to leave early to go to the funeral home to meet with Mr. Gray, Dad sat out the last few hands of *Set Back*, waiting for Mom to announce that she was ready to leave. To shorten the divvying-up ritual, Mom agreed to take far more food than she normally did. She calculated that the food wouldn't go to waste with the daily visits from Danny.

By the time we left the farm, it was almost four o'clock. So Dad suggested a new plan. "Instead of stopping at our house, let's drive directly to the funeral home."

Danny reminded us of his *limits*. "Don't forget. Any corpses and the deal's off."

WE PARKED ALONGSIDE THE building and walked toward the front entrance of Gray's Funeral Home. When we entered the building, we were greeted by an attractive young woman, seated at the front desk. She stood and extended her hand to Mom. "Hello! Welcome to Gray's Funeral Home," she said, flashing a dazzling white smile that set off her lightly reddened lips. "How may I help you?"

I noticed she wore light eye shadow that accentuated her sparkling azure-blue eyes. She had fine classical features and a trim figure. She could have easily won a beauty contest over any of a dozen top Hollywood stars that Mom and I saw regularly in first-run movies at the upscale Chippewa Theater.

Danny took charge. "We're here to meet with Mr. Gray about a job -- as long as there are no corpses involved. Okay? This is Mr. and Mrs. Addison. That boy there is Jase Addison. He's my best friend. I'm Danny Tucker."

"Oh, yes. Mr. Reilly dropped by earlier so we've been expecting you. I must say that I've been most eager to meet you two boys.

Over this past year, I've followed reports of your heroism and brave deeds in the *Riverton Daily Press* and on WRDP. I even heard Gabriel Heatter's radio show last night. What an honor to meet you both. I'm a devoted fan."

Danny's eyes glazed over. If he had opened his mouth, his tongue would have hit the floor. His silly grin reminded me of someone from the movies. *Ye Gads!* Danny had become Peter Lorre.

"You're very kind to say those nice things about the boys. We're very proud of them. Could you please tell us how to find Mr. Gray?" Dad requested politely, trying to move things along. "It's been a while since we've seen each other. We were high-school classmates."

"Yes, father -- that is Mr. Gray -- mentioned that to me. Well, by now you've probably guessed -- I'm Evelyn Gray."

"I saw your picture in the paper, Evelyn. Congratulations on being Valedictorian. What a great honor for you," Mom told her.

Evelyn's rose-colored blush complemented her tasteful makeup. She thanked Mom profusely. Then she told us, "We have a good number of visitors this evening. Let's take the easy route. Follow me please."

She led us back out the front door and down the sloping driveway that took us behind the funeral home. When we rounded the corner, we saw the open doors of a spacious three-stall garage. The first two stalls housed a pair of somber black hearses that transported recently-departed Rivertonians to their final resting places.

The vehicle from the third stall had been pulled out onto the wide cement driveway in front of the garage. Standing in stark contrast to the hearses was an enormous, fire-engine red Cadillac ambulance. The gold lettering on its side read *Chippewa Ambulance Service.*

Mr. Gray stood behind the shiny ambulance. He wore spotlessly-clean white coveralls and was holding a flowing rubber hose that extended from a sizeable reel mounted on the wall at the far side of the parking area. He'd just finished rinsing the vehicle.

"Father, this is Mr. and Mrs. Addison. Their son Jase and his friend Danny Tucker. Folks, this is my father Edward Gray."

Mr. Gray placed the sponge and chamois on the ambulance hood, wiped his hands on his coveralls, and walked toward us. He shook Dad's hand enthusiastically and smiled warmly. "My old friend, John Addison. How long has it been, John?"

"Years, Ed. Too many years, I'd say."

"Sorry, Mrs. Addison -- boys. John and I were once very close friends. I guess we just grew apart. I'm very happy to meet you all. Welcome!" He shook our hands too. "Why don't we go inside? There's a small meeting room on this level where we can make ourselves comfortable while the boys and I discuss a potential business arrangement."

"Father, I really should get back to the front desk," Evelyn said politely. "I was pleased to meet all of you. I hope to see you again soon. Goodbye."

After she had gone, Mom told her father, "Mr. Gray, she's a charming young woman. I saw her Valedictorian picture in the newspaper. You must be very proud of her."

"Yes, indeed, Mrs. Addison. After she graduated from school, Evelyn decided to join me here in my business. That pleases me greatly. My late wife, who worked here with me, would have been proud as well. Evelyn was our only child."

Mr. Gray started for the basement entrance door. But Dad stopped him. "Before we go inside, I must say that this vehicle is beautiful. It looks brand new. Cadillac hasn't made any civilian cars or trucks since early 1942. Where did you get this, Ed?"

By February 1942, all American automakers had shut down their production lines to comply with a nationwide production freeze on civilian vehicles. Those 1941 and 1942 models in inventory were rationed out for selected military and civilian uses. Automakers quickly converted to the manufacture of jeeps, armored cars, tanks, airplanes, and other military equipment, including grenades, bombs, and engine-powered landing craft. Civilian automobile production did not resume until late 1945.

"I was lucky to find it. There was a small-town fire department down near Pontiac that was abolished after being consolidated into the county department. Back in 1940, some wealthy resident left a bequest, stipulating that the money be used to buy a brand new, red Cadillac ambulance. Soon after the consolidation, for some reason, the county auctioned it off. I won the auction. Sort of like the color. It will set us apart from the hospital. Their only ambulance is white."

The basement conference room was furnished with crisp chrome and black leather chairs, encircling a large highly-polished light gray, marble-topped table. The fluorescent light fixtures mounted on the ceiling immersed the room in sterile blue-white light.

When we were all comfortably seated, Mr. Gray folded his hands and spoke in a prideful tone.

"Over the years, I'm pleased to say that -- thanks to the support of the people of Riverton -- the business my wife and I started some 25 years ago has done very well. We've served hundreds of families in our community when they were enduring their most difficult hours.

"In the same situation, most men would consider themselves a success. But I hit a couple of rough spots along the way. My wife passed away eight years ago. And I went through another difficult time with someone else who's very close to me. These experiences have caused me to rethink my priorities. I've decided it's time for me to give back to our community."

I couldn't help wondering who the second rough spot involved.

"Let me acquaint you with some facts. The population of Riverton is 10,000 and if you draw a circle with a 15-mile radius, encompassing New Albany and the other small towns in the area, you can add another 3,000.

"Before I purchased the Cadillac, there was only one ambulance in this community to serve its 13,000 citizens. This is totally insufficient. When my pleas to the hospital board to add at least two more ambulances fell on deaf ears, I decided to remedy the situation myself.

"I want to provide *emergency services* for accidents or fires. And *transportation services* for patients too ill to drive or take the train to places like Ford Hospital in Detroit or Sparrow Hospital in Lansing.

"The Cadillac is the first of at least five ambulances that we'll need. I'm forming a not-for-profit organization to own and operate this service. I will personally donate all the ambulances as well as the money to hire top-notch emergency medical personnel and drivers. By charging reasonable fees, I think eventually the service can be financially viable. If not, I'll donate some more. That's it. Any questions?"

We were all stunned by this news. Finally Dad spoke to his old friend. "You're doing a very generous thing for our community, Ed. Thank you."

"Yes, indeed," Mom concurred.

Danny added with a twinkle in his eye, "I think it's a good idea to hire Jase and me and some of our friends to drive these ambulances. We don't charge much for our services. Do we, Jase?"

Mr. Gray suddenly did turn gray. "Oh, my dear boy, I'm sorry to have caused you to think --."

When Mr. Gray's voice petered out, Danny pulled back his barb. "Just pulling your leg, Mr. G. We think your idea's great. Don't we, Jase? How can we help?"

"Thanks, Danny. Here's what I have in mind. I want you boys to promote this idea throughout the community. We need to contact every person in town and in the outlying towns and villages. And I mean personal contact by clean-cut boys like Jase and you -- and others you think can do a good job. Here, look at these brochures."

He handed us each a handsome booklet sporting a patriotic, but tasteful, red, white, and blue color scheme. The brochure outlined the benefit of each service and its cost.

"These brochures are so impressive -- and very informative," Mom noted.

"I'll say!" Dad agreed. "They cover everything."

"I don't want to advertise in the paper or on the radio. I want the personal touch. I want you to walk through town and hand one of these to every person you meet. Look them in the eye and tell them honestly how this service will benefit them and their families. Go into the neighborhoods all around town. Knock on doors. Give them to people on buses, in restaurants, and at the stockyards. Be there for shift changes at our factories. Wherever you can find people, I want you to be there, smiling and telling each one of them the good news."

Finally Mr. Gray asked, "Can you do it, boys?"

"You bet!" I replied enthusiastically.

Danny was less susceptible to Mr. Gray's pep talk. He needed more facts before making a decision.

"How many brochures do you have for us to distribute, Mr. Gray?"

"I've had 5,000 printed for starters. When they're gone, we'll stop to assess how successful our approach has been. I hope you can distribute the first 5,000 in less than a month."

Danny pressed on. "What do you plan to pay your distributors?"

"For the quality job, I think a penny for each brochure distributed would be fair."

"What if the boys distributing the brochures were each wearing two Medals of Courage on their shirts? That would make a difference, I'll bet. What do you say, Mr. Gray?"

"Well, Danny, you're quite a negotiator. Let me think now. Does two cents a brochure sound about right to you?"

Danny smiled and held out his hand to Mr. Gray who shook it with apparent relief. Then Mr. Gray reached into his suit-coat pocket, pulled out his handkerchief, and wiped his brow.

We agreed to start first thing in the morning. While we were being escorted to the door, I calculated the total in my mind.

"Wow! That's $100!" I whispered to Danny.

Danny nodded and pointed out, "Think of it, Jase. By this time next month, we'll have collected two $100 rewards."

For some reason, I believed him.

AFTER OUR FUNERAL HOME stop, we turned west on Main Street and headed out of town. About a mile past the city limits, we saw the halo of light that hovered above Camp Riverton. Our POW camp, like hundreds of camps across America, had been established in early 1943 on the site of an old CCC camp.

The Civilian Conservation Corps (CCC) was a part of President Roosevelt's *New Deal*. During the Great Depression, this program provided jobs related to the conservation and development of natural resources on land owned by federal, state, and local governments. To be eligible to work, applicants had to be men who were unemployed, unmarried, and between the ages of 18 and 25. Some 2.5 million American men worked in CCC jobs over the course of the program's existence between 1933 and 1942.

Camp Riverton's POW population ranged from about 600 in the winter to well over a thousand in the summer months. POWs were used to plant, cultivate, harvest, and process various crops grown on farms in the area around Riverton.

At each corner of the double, barbed-wire square enclosure, stood a tall watchtower crewed by two MP guards, one manning the .50-caliber machine gun and the other the gigantic searchlight, whose ominous beam slowly swept back and forth over the camp like a giant white shark.

We turned into the long driveway that led to the main gate where an MP guard halted us and shined his flashlight into every square inch of the interior of our modest 1936 Chevrolet sedan. After completing his thorough inspection that included a careful reading of Dad's driver's license, the guard's intrusive demeanor suddenly disappeared.

He gave us a big smile, leaned into the front window, and said, "Danny and Jase. Congratulations on all you've done for our country. I'm proud to know you." Then he turned to Mom. "Good evening, Mrs. Addison. It's nice to see you again."

"Good evening to you too, Chester," Mom replied. "Thanks for your kind words to the boys."

Then he stepped back, saluted, and snapped, "Straight ahead to the HQ building. I think you know the way. Colonel Butler, Otto Klump, and Mr. Nichols are waiting for you there."

After we left the gate area, Dad asked, "You know that guard well, Marie?"

"Sure. He's nearly always on watch when I arrive here with Hans Zeyer and the other instructors."

"The way he treated us when we first arrived made me think that he was -- new or something. Kinda officious, I thought."

"Oh, Chester puts everybody through that routine. Even Colonel Butler. Because it's his job, no one objects."

"Oops. I guess I better change my attitude," Dad allowed.

"Don't worry Mr. A. I'm with you," Danny assured Dad. "I thought he was very opsious too."

The bright light around us insured that Danny had seen me roll my eyes and shake my head.

"Jase," Danny asked. "Are you having a migraine headache? Maybe we can get some *assburn* when we get inside."

Mom's guffaw punctuated Danny's suggestion.

When we reached the HQ building, we parked and went inside. The guard at the front desk led us to Colonel Butler's office. After a round of greetings, we sat down at the highly-polished hardwood conference table off to one side of his spacious office.

We hadn't seen Otto since a few days before the abduction. Mom smiled and professed, "Otto, some people assumed that you'd master-minded the abduction, but I want to assure you that no one in either the Tucker or Addison family had any doubt that you'd act in Danny's best interest."

Otto's face turned red. He looked down at his hands and affirmed, "These two boyz ist very important to Otto. I vould protect zem like dey ist mein own childrenz."

"We know that Otto. Thank you," Mom assured him.

Then she turned to Chuck Nichols, who was making notes on his reporter's pad. "Chuck, thank you for offering to set the record straight. I know you'll do a fair job."

"I was just recording Otto's words. I think they'll make a fine opening for my story."

Otto nodded affirmatively.

"Well, Danny. Before you arrived, Otto and Colonel Butler filled me in on most of the details of the abduction. But I'm a bit unclear about a couple of things that I need to ask you about. All right with you?"

"Shoot!" Danny barked with a dramatic sweep of his hand.

Danny and I had heard Humphrey DeForest Bogart use that line in about two dozen movies over the course of the previous year.

Chuck plowed ahead. "The air controller at the Riverton Airport gave me a transcription of what you transmitted to him just as Otto had lifted the Staggerwing off the ground. Let me read it so everyone knows what you said."

Chuck Nichols read the following:

Riverton Control. This is Daniel Tucker, Copilot of Beech 4761. I'm leading a top secret mission for Edgar J. Hoover, Director of the FBI in Washington, DC. I made the decision to commandeer this airplane and take full responsibility for my action. I'm not authorized to reveal the identity of my passengers nor our destination. If this troubles you, I suggest you discuss it directly with J. Edward Hoover. But remember -- this is a wartime emergency. So unless you want to look silly, I'd advise just keeping it to yourself. Over and out!

Those of us in the room, who knew nothing about this radio message issued by Danny, were stunned.

"Danny, because you've had dealings with Director Hoover before, I want to be sure that there was no truth to your statement that you were on a *top secret mission* on behalf of Mr. Hoover. Is that correct?"

Danny seemed puzzled by Chuck's question. Then he stated flatly, "I was only using this as a tactic to fool the enemy."

Initially Chuck seemed satisfied by this response. But then he seemed puzzled. "Danny, by *the enemy* -- are you referring to Shiller -- your abductor?"

"Righteo, Charles, me boy."

I gave Danny a dirty look and he just winked at me. He was really into himself and it made me uncomfortable.

"But I thought Shiller understood very little English."

"Of course, I spoke English. All the better to fool him with. If I'd spoken German, there was a chance that I wouldn't have fooled him. Right?"

I had to bite my tongue. I didn't want to reveal that Danny's command of German was limited to one phrase. *Ya Bolt.*

Moving on, Chuck attempted to clarify some facts. "You told your folks, the Addisons, and Colonel Butler you were able to put Otto on a course to Selfridge Field because there were charts in the Staggerwing's cockpit and that you'd studied map reading in Boy Scouts. Is that correct?"

"Yes, indeedy."

"Being able to read a map is a far cry from setting a perfect heading for Otto to fly directly from Riverton Airport to Selfridge Field. Otto stated he flew over a hundred miles without having to change course once. How did you come up with what appears to have been the exact course?"

"Boy Scouts again. We learned how to read a compass."

Since Chuck looked a bit puzzled again, Danny elaborated. "One, reading maps. Two, reading compasses. I just put the two together and told Otto what course to steer. It's as easy as one plus two. Piece of cake."

"Okay. Okay. Danny. Let's just leave well enough alone here. I believe you told folks that you found a *Phonetic Alphabet* sheet in some materials that Mr. Shurtleif gave Jase and you last summer. And that you used that alphabet to spell out *SOS* and the word *HOSTAGE* in your radio messages to Selfridge air control. You didn't have that sheet with you, did you?"

"Nope. I memorized it last year though."

"Just for the record, could you recite that alphabet to me now?"

Without taking a breath, Danny recited the entire military *Phonetic Alphabet* with lightning speed.

"Able, Baker, Charlie, Dog, Easy, Fox, George, How, Item, Jig, King, Love, Mike, Nan, Oboe, Peter, Queen, Roger, Sugar, Tare, Uncle, Victor, William, X-Ray, Yoke, Zebra."

"Wow! That was impressive. How do we know they were all correct?" Chuck asked, foolishly as it turned out.

Danny reached into his back pocket and removed a folded sheet of paper, which he handed to Chuck.

"Check me. Ready?" Without waiting for Chuck's answer, Danny began, "Able, Baker, Charlie, Dog, Easy, Fox, George, How, Item --."

Mercifully Danny stopped when he saw me put my hands over my ears.

"Any other questions, Chuck?" Danny inquired, amiably for a change.

"Just one more, Danny. It appears that you're pretty handy with a radio microphone. Where'd you pick that up?"

"I learned to speak on a microphone when Jase and I appeared on your radio show with Governor Dewey last fall during his Presidential campaign."

"That's right! I remember now. The Governor is certainly a big fan of yours."

"That's the day Governor Dewey recruited me to carry out secret missions for J. Hoover Edgar," Danny declared smugly.

That was the show-stopper.

WE DROPPED DANNY OFF in his driveway and headed for home. When we entered the kitchen, Mom suggested, "This has been a long day. How about a simple supper of scrambled eggs and home fries?"

While Mom prepared the food, Dad returned to his Sunday paper. I sat down on our sofa and fought off sleep while listening to Dad comment on stories that he thought were important.

"According to reports, Japanese troops have completely withdrawn from China. Wow! This says that Chinese casualty numbers are staggering. Since the 1937 invasion by Japan, the Republic of China has suffered an estimated 3.5 million *military* casualties and over 10 million *civilian* casualties. That's horrifying. Don't you think so, Jase?"

That was the last of Dad's news summaries that I heard before I descended into a deep, soul-nourishing sleep. Grandpa and I were loading hay in the field just south of the cow barn when Mom gently shook my shoulder. "Jase, you fell asleep. Do you want some supper -- or would you rather just go to bed?"

The aroma of Mom's special scrambled eggs and home fries decided for me. "No, I'm awake, Mom."

We'd just settled at the kitchen table when we heard voices from the backyard. They were boys' voices. One was Danny's.

Wham!

The back door suddenly banged open. There stood Danny, Chub, and Sherm. Sherm was the son of Sergeant Tolna who was Dad's best friend and a member of the Riverton Police Department. The Tolnas lived just down the block from us on Forrest Street.

"Sorry to interrupt your supper, but this won't take long," Danny assured us as he tightly gripped the two younger boys by their shirt collars and shoved them into the kitchen. "These young FSG members want a piece of the action. I say we cut them in for a small chunk. It may save us some time. Then we can start looking for another job a little sooner. I told them we were being paid *a penny* per brochure," Danny prevaricated, with a wink. "What do you say, Jase?"

I wasn't up to agreeing to swindle two otherwise honorable FSG brothers, but I was also hungry and sleepy so my resistance was low. Despite the fact that Mom and Dad were both shaking their heads, with mixed emotions, I nodded my agreement.

As Danny unceremoniously hauled the two younger boys back out the kitchen door, he admonished them, "Be here at eight o'clock sharp. If you're one second late, you're both fired."

After slamming the door, he turned to Mom. "Boy, those eggs and home fries smell dee-licious! I just love the way you cook, Mrs. A."

Without saying a word, Mom stood up and went to the refrigerator for more eggs.

THE NEXT MORNING BEFORE sunup, I awoke to the noise of rattling dishes and the slamming of our refrigerator door. I pulled on my shorts, my best tee shirt, and my basketball shoes and headed for the kitchen.

When I arrived, Danny was sitting at the kitchen table eating the large bowl of cold, greasy-looking home fries that Mom had placed in the refrigerator the night before. A thick coating of catsup covered the potatoes.

"Save any for me?" I asked as I sat down at the table.

"Nope, you'll have to make more for yourself," he mumbled between gulps. "Just kidding. Grab a fork. We got to eat fast and get down to the funeral home. Chub and Sherm will be here shortly."

"But Danny, it isn't even six o'clock yet. No one will be there."

"Sure they will. They run a 24-hour ambulance service, don't they?"

"Oh, I hadn't thought of that."

"Put some toast in -- four pieces. One for each of us," Danny ordered.

"Aye, aye, captain," I replied sarcastically as I opened the bread box.

"I've put together a sales pitch for everyone," Danny announced, handing me a piece of wadded up paper. "See what you think of it."

I unfolded it and, despite the wrinkles, I could decipher the following words:

Good morning sir or madam,

Because the Riverton Memorial Hospital is too cheap to purchase additional ambulances to help poor Riverton citizens who have emergencies, Mr. Edward Gray, owner of Gray's Funeral Home, is going to purchase five ambulances with his own money to make sure Riverton citizens are safe again.

You can use Mr. Gray's ambulances for fires and accidents or if you just want to lie down when you travel to Detroit or Lansing.

Here is a brochure that tells all about the new service.

Remember, don't be blue. Go Gray!

Have a nice day.

I was stunned by what I'd just read. I quickly handed it back to Danny without saying a word.

"Glad you liked it. We'll make the young frogs memorize it -- and tell them they can't work until they get it down pat. Okay with you?" Danny asked nonchalantly.

"Well, I -- ah -- have a few suggested changes. In fact -- I'll be right back," I sputtered.

I went to my bedroom to find something to write on. When I reentered the kitchen, I saw Danny slathering the four pieces of toast with thick coatings of peanut butter and jelly.

Using Danny's first draft as a guide, I wrote a version of my own. When I finished, I handed it to Danny. "Yours needed a few tiny edits."

This is how my version read:

Good morning, sir (or ma'am)!

To supplement the ambulance service provided by Riverton Memorial Hospital, we are proud to announce the opening of a new and reasonably-priced, 24-hour ambulance service to be operated from Gray's Funeral Home located conveniently in downtown Riverton.

Soon our fleet of five, state-of-the-art ambulances will provide not only emergency services in case of accident or fire, but also routine transportation for ailing patients being treated at hospitals, including Ford Hospital in Detroit and Sparrow Hospital in Lansing.

This brochure describes our services and tells how to contact us in case of an emergency or the need for professional medical transportation services.

Thank you for your time.
Have a nice day.

Danny read it quickly and sputtered, "Mine was better, but this is pretty good too. Let's go with yours."

Again, reflexively, my eyes rolled backward.

Bang!

Chub and Sherm stumbled through the kitchen door without knocking.

As I stared at the pair in disbelief, I heard Mom say, "My goodness! What's this? A meeting of the FSG? May I fix some breakfast for you, boys?"

"No, Mrs. A. We're about to leave for work. We want to get there early on the first morning -- to make a good impression. And thanks for the home fries. I liked them cold too, Mrs. A."

Mom was stricken with a mild look of bewilderment. Who could blame her?

"Okay, let's get going. Mom and Dad need room to have their breakfast," I ordered, pushing everyone out the back door.

"Wait!" Danny ordered, holding his hand up like a policemen stopping traffic. "Aren't you forgetting something?"

"What?"

"Our Medals of Courage!"

"Oh, shoot. Be right back," I promised, heading for my old baby bank where all our treasures were stored.

After Mom pinned our medals squarely in the middle of our tee shirts, she patted us both on the heads. We left under a barrage of good luck wishes from Mom and Dad. I couldn't help thinking that it was *their* good luck to get rid of all of us. Now they could enjoy a peaceful breakfast for a change.

Danny insisted on marching to work with the senior FSG members in the front rank and the juniors in the back. When we'd fallen in properly, Trooper Tucker assumed the role of drill sergeant.

"Hip -- two -- three -- four. Hip -- two -- three -- four.

"Go to yer left -- yer right -- yer left -- yer right -- left -- right."

For the most part, we did fine with the *Hip* verses, but we were definitely out-of-synch when he sang out his *Go Tos*.

I concluded that Danny would have repeated these two verses about 12,000 times before we reached the funeral home so I suggested we rehearse our sales pitch.

"Okay, Jase. Get your sales pitch out and start reading it -- real loud. Stay in step, everybody!"

I tried my best to match my words with our cadence, but it was next to impossible.

We marched up Forrest Street to New Albany Avenue where we did a clumsy *column right*. Then we marched another mile or so down to Addison Street where we did another *column right*. I must say that our second turning maneuver was more successful than our first. That is to say, Chub managed not to trip Sherm this time.

When we reached Riverton's main corners, the intersection of Addison and Main, all four of our sales team demonstrated a remarkable command of my sales pitch. During the final mile as we marched west along Main Street to the funeral home, we really nailed it. We were ready!

We arrived at the funeral home before seven o'clock. We walked down the driveway to the entrance to the garage. The huge doors were closed and all vehicles were nestled inside.

Danny boldly went to the entrance door and banged on it loudly with his clenched fist. We heard a voice from inside. The door was opened by a man who looked as if he'd just stepped out of an operating room. He was dressed in a white cotton gown tied at the waist, a white mask, and a surgeon's cap. I noticed his gown was slightly stained. When I deduced what this man had been doing, my stomach did a flip.

When he removed his mask, I recognized him as one of the men we'd seen dressed in a black suit, standing outside a viewing room the day before. "Come on in, boys. You must have gotten up before breakfast this morning." This was also Grandpa Compton's favorite early-morning one-liner.

Danny couldn't resist asking, "Is your name Compton by any chance?"

Initially the poor man was taken aback. But he recovered nicely. "No, it isn't," was all he mumbled. He quickly reassumed his friendly demeanor. "Mr. Gray should be along shortly. He always comes in early. Why don't you wait inside?"

When we reached the door to the meeting room, Sherm and Chub stopped in their tracks.

They conferred briefly and then announced. "We don't want to go in there!"

"Why not?" Danny hissed impatiently.

"There might be dead people in there," Chub whimpered.

What? Dead people at a funeral home. How silly! That's what I thought, but this is what I said, "Do you two want to make ten dollars apiece or not? Going once. Going twice."

They glanced at each other, then turned, and scampered into the meeting room.

Once we were seated at the table, the man bid us adieu and left us to ourselves.

"What should we do while we're waiting?" I asked.

"For one thing, I'm not going to try to find out what that guy's working on," Danny vowed.

"What do you mean?" implored Sherm.

"Yah, what do you mean?" parroted Chub.

"Forget it. You guys are too young. Let's rehearse our sales pitch. You first, Sherm."

After 950 solo attempts each, the younger FSG members finally got it down pat. At that moment, Mr. Gray poked his head into the meeting room and greeted us.

"Good morning, Danny. Jase. Who are these young fellows?"

After we introduced our assistants, demonstrating far more courage than usual, Sherm asked, "Mr. Gray, would you like to hear our sales pitch? I could reseat it for you?"

Not to be out done, Chub insisted, "I want to reseat it too."

"Well, darn right I'd very much like to hear that. Who wants to *recite* first?" he inquired, tactfully ignoring the *reseating* faux pas.

Danny and I looked at each other in awe after each of the frogs had *reseated* his sales pitch perfectly. Chub even concluded with a deep bow from the waist, emulating a practice patented by his older brother Danny.

Mr. Gray was extremely pleased with my version of the pitch. "Yes. Its attributes are many. It's succinct and to the point. It's compelling -- very persuasive. It's classy but very businesslike. Yep. I really like it!"

By this point, I could see that Danny was a little edgy. I assumed it was because, mercifully, he hadn't been able to share his original draft with Mr. Gray.

"Well, time's a wasting, fellows. I'll bet you're eager to get out there and meet people. Right?"

"Right you are, Mr. G. When can we get our hands on those red, white, and blue beauties?" Danny asked with great aplomb.

"The brochures are stored in the closet over there."

He opened the door to reveal a stack of 50 cartons, four feet wide and at least six feet high.

"Oh, I borrowed these from the *Riverton Daily Press*. He reached into the closet and brought out a half-dozen, sturdy canvas bags with shoulder straps. I recognized them as the bags our neighborhood paper boy used when he delivered our paper. The name of the newspaper was printed boldly on each side of the bag.

The name, *Riverton Daily Press*, reminded me to be sure to buy an early edition to read Chuck Nichol's article about Danny and Otto's adventure. I reminded Danny, "Let's not forget to pick up a newspaper."

"What for?"

"To read the help-wanted ads, silly," I replied sarcastically.

"Okay," Danny answered as if I were serious.

"Danny, I didn't mean --."

"I know, Jase. I know," he said, patting me on the hand.

SHERM AND CHUB WERE promised a penny for each brochure they personally presented to a Riverton citizen. This offer was based on two conditions. First, they had to report for work neatly dressed, including well-scrubbed tennis shoes. Second, they had to present the sales pitch flawlessly with every brochure they presented.

I suggested that we had not emphasized the penny-per-piece rate. I thought it would be more motivating to tell them they would each get ten dollars for distributing all 1,000 brochures that would be allocated to each of them. Danny agreed. We counted on their not yet having long division in school.

Naturally we also failed to mention that for each thousand brochures they distributed, the partnership of Danny and Jase would also be paid ten dollars. No sense in confusing their little minds with unnecessary details.

By working a full day in the crowded downtown area, we calculated that the two shrimps should be able to distribute a combined total of 500 brochures a day. This meant that we would be rid of them in no more than four days.

Jase and I decided to take the less densely populated neighborhoods surrounding the downtown area and the business places located along the streets and roads that led out of the city in all directions. We figured that it'd take us six to eight days to distribute our allotment of 3,000 brochures.

Because the brochures were printed on coated paper stock and thus quite heavy, we knew that Chub and Sherm couldn't carry as many as we could. So we put 250 brochures in Chub's newspaper bag and the same number in Sherm's.

Danny and I each put a thousand brochures into our bags. The weight of our full bags was just short of being too heavy for comfort. Nonetheless, we took more than we were likely to distribute in one day, just to feel macho.

We started the two boys on North Addison Street at the north edge of the downtown area. Sherm took the west side of the street and Chub took the east. We instructed them to visit every business they came to and to give their sales pitch and a brochure to every person they met, even to people walking on the downtown sidewalks. They were to travel south on Addison Street until they ran out of brochures. At that point, they were to walk back to the funeral home and wait for us to return.

After watching them making their way south, we decided to cover the more affluent neighborhoods on the north side of town. Doing these neighborhoods instead of the downtown area meant more walking per brochure delivered, but it was time spent walking in the shade of the tree-lined streets and not on the sunbaked concrete of the downtown sidewalks.

Danny and I began to look forward to calling on homes and visiting neighborhood grocery stores. The people we spoke to were very interested in what we had to say. No one refused a brochure.

We also enjoyed traveling by bus to New Albany, the Chippewa County seat, which was located four miles to the south and east of Riverton. When we arrived there, we set up shop on a location that was equidistant from the county court house and the county sheriff's office. Right across the street from where we stood was New Albany's business district. So dozens of curious shoppers crossed the street to find out why we were attracting such a crowd.

I reminded Danny of our success at selling cans of household oil to benefit our scout troop during the past summer. We'd really made a killing at Riverton's numerous war production factories. At four in the afternoon, we positioned ourselves between the long lines of workers punching in to work the second shift and the long lines of workers punching out after working the first shift. Most of those leaving the factory were headed for one of the many nearby bars and taverns to relax a while with their friends before going home for supper.

We decided to repeat that strategy. Luckily we'd hit a gold mine of willing brochure recipients. So we decided to concentrate on factories and bars until our supply was diminished.

Believe it or not, it only took us four days to go through our 3,000 brochures. And Sherm and Chub took exactly four days because of Parkinson's Law, which states that work expands to fill the time available to complete that work. By the end of only four days, we were making our way back to the funeral home to settle up with Mr. Gray. He had told us we could find him in his office located near Miss Gray's front desk on the main floor.

As the four of us passed the driveway leading down to the garage doors and basement, Sherm suddenly let out a yelp.

"Oh, no!" he cried. "I still have one brochure left in my bag. What am I going to do? Will I still get my ten dollars?"

When he started to pout, Chub joined him. Soon the two were standing in front of the funeral home wailing.

"Knock it off! Knock it off!" I ordered. The crying ceased as quickly as it had begun. "Tell you what, Sherm. Take this brochure down and put it under the windshield wiper of the new ambulance. Run -- and hurry back up here -- so we can go inside and get our money from Mr. Gray."

In a split second, Sherm had snatched the brochure from his paper bag and was running down the driveway toward the garage area. For some reason, Chub dropped his bag and ran like a madman after Sherm. Danny looked at me and shook his head.

"They're both crazy," I concluded.

Danny nodded his agreement.

We watched as both boys rounded the corner of the building at the bottom of the drive and disappeared from sight. Two seconds later, the pair reappeared at the bottom of the driveway, running wildly back up toward us. Sherm was still waving his brochure. Both of them were yelling at the top of their lungs, but neither of us could make out what they were saying.

As they neared, I finally understood their words, "Corpus! Corpus! Corpus!"

Corpus?

By the time they reached the top of the driveway, both of the red-faced shrimps were out of breath and perspiring profusely.

Finally Sherm managed to spit out, "Corpus! Corpus -- in the anbalance."

"There's a corpus in the anbalance," Chub yelled, supporting his fellow shrimp.

"Let's check it out, Jase," Danny ordered.

We ran to the bottom of the driveway and stopped. Before proceeding, we peeked around the corner of the building. There was the ambulance, all right, but nothing seemed to be out of order. Cautiously we crept up to the vehicle and peered through the back window. Sure enough, we saw the form of a man lying on the stretcher. A chill of cold fear tiptoed up my spine.

Before I could assimilate what I'd seen, Danny tugged on my sleeve and motioned me to follow him around to the side of the vehicle closest to where the man was lying. When we were in position, we slowly raised up to take another peek.

There he was. But he was no *corpus*. He was a young man lying on the stretcher. He was also sleeping soundly and snoring softly. What he was doing there, I could not imagine.

Danny signaled me to follow him to the back of the ambulance. He then whispered, "Do you recognize his face?"

I thought he looked familiar, but I couldn't be sure so we crept back toward the *body* to take a closer look. Suddenly it struck me. I'd seen that face just hours ago on the front page of the *Riverton Daily Press.* The underlying headline struck me between the eyes.

FBI OFFERS $100 REWARD

Danny and I tiptoed to a spot behind the ambulance to determine what to do next. We stopped under the reel of hose Mr. Gray used to wash his new red plaything. Suddenly I had an idea. I quietly unwound a long length of hose from the reel and walked to the side of the vehicle.

Danny quickly realized what I intended to do.

I carefully pushed the tip of the hose through the left door handle and pulled a length of hose off the reel toward me. I walked around to the right door handle and repeated the process. Then I threaded the hose through the back door handle. Finally using my scout training, I tied a square knot of hose tightly against the back door of the ambulance. Our $100 *corpus* was securely trapped inside the ambulance.

Then Danny whispered in my ear, "Let's open the hood -- very quietly."

I wasn't sure why that was necessary but I trusted Danny's judgment.

We tiptoed back to the front of the ambulance where I slowly released the hood latch and opened the hood. I held it high enough for Danny to do his work on the engine. Deftly he removed the distributor cap, pulled back, and motioned for me to close the hood. I quietly did as he indicated.

When our quarry was snuggly imprisoned inside, Danny ordered, "Let's go call the police."

We ran up the driveway, collected Sherm and Chub, and ran into the building. We saw that Miss Gray wasn't at her front desk so we burst into Mr. Gray's office. He was startled by our abrupt entry, but he soon regained his composure.

"Are you boys finished distributing our brochures?" he asked. Chub nodded his head and stuck out his open palm. Sherm followed suit. But Danny did not. Instead, he assertively instructed Mr. Gray to call the police.

Without questioning Danny, Mr. Gray made the telephone call. Then he turned to us. "The police are on their way, boys. I sure wish I knew what was going on."

"Thank you, sir. When the police arrive, please direct them to your ambulance. We'll be down there waiting for them," Danny instructed politely. "After they're gone, we can settle up. Oh, you'll want to put this someplace where it won't be harmed."

Danny handed the distributor cap to Mr. Gray.

Then he turned to us and gave us our instructions, "Sherm and Chub, you stay here and wait for the police with Mr. Gray. Jase, we'll go down and guard our reward money."

We started to leave Mr. Gray's office when Danny stopped. "Oh, I forgot something. No one has presented you with a brochure, Mr. Gray."

Danny pried Sherm's last brochure from the shrimp's grimy paw and handed it to Mr. Gray. Turning to the boys, he instructed, "Each of you give Mr. Gray the sales pitch you memorized."

As we left for the ambulance, Sherm and Chub were arguing about who should go first. Danny turned to me and boasted, "Two $100 paychecks in one day. What have you got to say about that, Jase, old boy?"

"Only one thing, Danny. Only one thing."

I leaped into the air and shouted, **"Nashville here we come!!!"**

AFTER WE WERE ALL seated at the conference table, Mr. Gray began to introduce us to Sergeant Tolna, but he stopped when the sergeant raised his hand. "I'm very familiar with all of these young men, Mr. Gray. Jase, Danny, and Chub are friends and neighbors and --."

"And I'm his son!" shouted Sherm. He quieted down when Danny *gently* kicked his shins under the table.

"Do you know the identity of the man you arrested, Sergeant?" Mr. Gray inquired. "I didn't get a look at him before your officers took him away."

"Yes, we have a positive identification. In fact, one of the arresting officers was a high-school classmate of the man. He is definitely Donald Douglas who --.""

"Oh, no!" cried Mr. Gray.

"Are you all right, sir?" Sergeant Tolna asked as Mr. Gray removed his glasses and rubbed his eyes vigorously with the heels of his hands.

"Excuse me, Sergeant. I'm fine. Please go on with what you were saying."

"Because of the positive identification, we called the FBI field office in Detroit to tell them that Douglas was in our custody. By now, two carloads of FBI agents are on their way to Riverton. They'll take him back to Detroit and turn him over to the Military Police at Fort Wayne. He'll be formally charged with desertion at that time. The FBI says it's an open-and-shut case. This being wartime, he'll most likely serve a life sentence in Leavenworth."

"That's good news, Sergeant. Just what he deserves," Mr. Gray replied, with a wide grin. "Yes, sir. I --.""

Apparently Sergeant Tolna, like the rest of us in the room, was attempting to understand why this news appeared to make Mr. Gray so happy. But not one of us asked.

Sergeant Tolna changed the subject. "Jase, I understand you were responsible for tying the ambulance doors closed with the hose. Douglas could have never opened any of the doors with the car tied up like you had it. That was quick thinking. Well done!"

Being singled out made me feel slightly uncomfortable so I attempted to share the credit. "Thank you, Sergeant Tolna. But I couldn't have tied that knot without Danny's help."

"Yeah, we helped too. We found the crook in the anbalance," chirped Chub.

"Yeah, we helped too. We found him in the anbalance. Right, Chub?" echoed Sherm.

Danny disagreed. "You told us you found a *corpus*. Jase and I found the deserter. Now kindly zip those lips."

Mercifully Sergeant Tolna intervened with a question for all of us, "Does anyone know how he got into the ambulance in the first place?"

"He just opened the door," explained Danny as if everyone should know that answer.

"No, I always lock the ambulance -- and I usually park it in the garage. But for some reason, I guess I forgot to do that last night."

"Something's not right here," Sergeant Tolna mused. "But I can't put my finger on it."

"Let me ask you, Danny -- since Douglas was tied up tight, why did you remove the distributor cap?"

"To keep him from driving away of course," Danny answered, rather harshly I thought.

"How could he possibly do that?" the sergeant demanded to know.

"By using the keys that were hanging in the ignition," Danny said slyly, looking at Mr. Gray.

"Oh, brother. So that's where I left them," Mr. Gray sputtered, scolding himself.

Danny nodded his head.

"Well, that clears up a lot of things. But I do have one question for you, Mr. Gray. Of all the places in Riverton to take a nap, why did we find Donald Douglas on your doorstep, so to speak?"

"I suspect he came here hoping to rekindle a romantic relationship he once had with my daughter Evelyn. But I can assure you Evelyn would have had nothing to do with that no good rascal. Suffice it to say, he has brought a lot of pain to this family. In my opinion, life in prison is too soft a sentence compared to what he deserves."

Danny and I looked at each other knowingly. I was sure he was thinking of Mr. Gray's words on the day we first met him.

In the same situation, most men would consider themselves a success. But I hit a couple of rough spots along the way. My wife passed away eight years ago. And I went through another difficult time with someone else who's very close to me. These experiences have caused me to rethink my priorities. I've decided it's time for me to give back to our community.

3 JOB HUNTING

ON MOST MORNINGS DURING THE SUMMER OF 1945, I was awakened by the sound of Danny entering our kitchen. But the Friday morning following our capture of Donald Douglas was very different. What woke me that morning was the lack of sound.

After awakening, I lay in my bed wondering why I hadn't heard Danny arrive. He was very late. After all, the sun had been shining brightly for nearly an hour.

My hunger pangs finally compelled me to get out of bed and head for the kitchen.

"Danny! You're here. I didn't hear you come in. How long have you been here? Have you had anything to eat? Did you get a postcard from JB yesterday? Mine has a picture of the Ryman Auditorium. JB says maybe we can see the Grand Ole Opry if we have enough money. Tickets are 25 cents apiece."

Danny didn't seem to hear me. There was no evidence of his having eaten anything since his arrival. That was most unusual. Instead, he just sat there staring at the wall.

"Danny, what's wrong?"

Slowly he turned to me and announced, "We can't go to Nashville."

His words shocked me. "Why on earth not?"

"We don't have enough money."

I hadn't expected that explanation for his morose behavior. In my mind, I quickly inventoried our trip money. After paying the FSG shrimps ten dollars each, we had netted $80 from Mr. Gray. We still had $17.13 of leftover bait money. It probably wouldn't cover our incidental expenses in Nashville. But the $100 reward money for capturing Donald Douglas was bound to arrive shortly.

What was Danny thinking?

He seemed to read my mind. "I saw Sergeant Tolna this morning. He was on his way to the police station early -- to handle Donald Douglas' paperwork. He told me we wouldn't be getting our reward money until -- perhaps -- next year."

"Next year! That's preposterous!"

Shoving last Sunday's newspaper across the table, he nearly shouted, "Here! Read this."

I grabbed the paper and read the notice aloud, starting with the headline.

DESERTER
FBI OFFERS $100 REWARD
FOR CAPTURE AND CONVICTION
OF FORMER RIVERTONIAN

"Stop, Jase! Read that headline again -- carefully this time."

I slowly read it again. "-- $100 Reward for Capture and Conviction --. And *conviction?* That means a trial -- and that could take months!"

"Exactly! That's why we can't go to Nashville!"

"Don't be hasty, Danny. We can get a job somewhere and earn the money we need."

"Earn $100 before JB comes home? What are we going to do? Rob banks?"

"Don't be silly, Danny. There has to be a way."

"Sure! We'll just find us a rich uncle, Jase."

"Danny! That's it! Who's one of the richest men in Riverton?" Danny smiled from ear to ear.

"My old friend, E.F. Graham, that's who. Jase, you're a genius. Let's each get a couple of nickels out of your bank and go see the old boy."

"I have a better idea. It's not even seven o'clock yet. So why don't we have a good breakfast and, after that, take the bus to Mr. Graham's office?"

"Good idea, Jase. Please pass the peanut butter and pickles."

MR. E.F. GRAHAM was the wealthy owner of Graham Markets, a chain of 35 neighborhood grocery stores, located throughout Riverton and New Albany. As mentioned earlier, Danny's shrewd manipulation of Mr. Graham had given their relationship a rather shaky start.

But since the fall of 1944, when two dangerous, escaped German POWs had stolen Mr. Graham's limousine and kidnapped Danny in the process, these two former adversaries had become good friends. Because of Danny's friendship with me, I was accepted as a member of their mutual admiration society. Of course, it hadn't hurt that, with some help from Mick the fox terrier, I was responsible for discovering the POWs' hideout, rescuing Danny, and recovering Mr. Graham's Cadillac limousine, whose trunk was filled with valuable shotguns, wallets, and hunting gear.

Mr. Graham's generosity toward the two of us was never in question, but we'd never taken advantage of our friendship with him. By asking for a job, we were entering new territory. After all, this was an exceptional situation. Thus, we reasoned, exceptional measures were required.

While we waited for the eight o'clock Chippewa Trails downtown bus, we sat on the bus-stop bench with our old friend, Buddy Roe Bibs. Bibs was an on-again, off-again resident-trustee of the Good Mission Church. On this particular morning, Reverend Squires would not have been pleased with Bibs' condition. Instead of performing his trustee duties, Bids was sleeping off a bit of a bender.

We tried not to disturb him while we waited, but it was a bit difficult because he kept falling over onto Danny. When we saw our bus approaching, we carefully propped Bibs up against the box-elder tree that supported the bench and tiptoed onto the bus.

We slammed our two nickels into the coin box and took our usual seats right across from Mr. Smalley, our favorite bus driver. Danny enjoyed *helping* Mr. Smalley by offering suggestions on coping with traffic challenges in the road ahead. Of course, if it's true that help is defined by the recipient, I'd have to say that Mr. Smalley would have preferred a rabid Tasmanian devil, rather than Danny, seated right across from him.

WHEN THE BUS STOPPED at the main downtown station, we said goodbye to a much-relieved Mr. Smalley and headed for Mr. Graham's offices located on the second floor of the Graham Building. The downtown Graham Market occupied the building's first floor.

We climbed the stairs and entered the offices. The first person we observed was an attractive young woman with curly blond hair. She wore a carefully-ironed white blouse with long sleeves. I noticed she wore no makeup or jewelry of any kind.

Beyond the reception desk, about a dozen men were seated at small metal desks. Each man wore green eye shades and sported garters on the arms of heavily-starched white dress shirts. Each desk was equipped with a huge Marchant Calculating Machine that noisily recorded figures that were being punched into its wide keyboard by the eye-shaded men.

Beyond those desks, we observed a row of well-appointed executive offices that overlooked Addison Street. We concluded that Mr. Graham's office must be the large corner one with the highly-polished, dark-wood door embossed with gold lettering that we couldn't quite read from the reception desk.

"How may I help you, boys?" the receptionist asked. Then she cocked her head. "I think I know who you are. Is it Jase Addison and Danny Tucker?"

"Yes, ma'am. That's us. We would like to speak with Mr. Graham if that's possible," I requested politely.

"Well, he's awfully busy, but I'm sure I can persuade him to spend a minute with two such illustrious visitors. Please take a seat while I ask him if he can see you now."

We sat in the visitors' chairs and watched the receptionist pick up a telephone and push a button. We heard a faint *buzz* emanating from behind Mr. Graham's door.

During their brief conversation, the receptionist nodded her head four or five times. Finally she said, "Yes, sir," and hung up the telephone. She stood and walked out from behind her desk. I was amazed to see how tall and thin she was.

"Mr. Graham will see you now. Please follow me."

While we trailed behind her, Danny jabbed my ribs with his elbow. "I told you this was a brilliant idea," he whispered.

"Glad I thought of it," I whispered back.

Danny shot me a dirty look followed by a smile.

Mr. Graham didn't wait for us to enter. He flew out to meet us. He shook our hands, put his arms around our shoulders, and led us inside his luxurious office.

"Please take a chair, boys. Make yourselves comfortable," he said affably as we all sat down at a small table in the corner of his office.

"To what to do I owe the pleasure of this visit, may I ask?"

Danny deferred to me by nodding his head, signaling that I should answer the question.

"Well, Mr. Graham. To get right to the point, Danny and I are here to ask you for a job. We need to earn some money -- real soon -- so we can take a train to Nashville, Tennessee, where we plan to spend ten days with Johnson Bradford."

At the mention of JB's name, Mr. Graham's eyes lit up.

"JB. Isn't that what you boys call him?"

We nodded our heads.

"What a talented basketball player that young fellow is! I saw a number of his games when he played for the Riverton YMCA team. Of course, you boys know about that. You were on that team as well. What's JB doing in Nashville for goodness sakes?"

I told him about the basketball camp at Stony River Academy. And about our being able to stay at the school during our visit.

"Why that's just super, boys. Nashville's a great place to visit. And to be able to spend some time with your friend, JB. That's just super!"

"We thought we had enough money for the trip, Mr. Graham, but we only have about half of what we need."

I told him about making $80 working for Mr. Gray and about our role in capturing Donald Douglas. And about the delay in collecting the $100 reward. "We were counting on that reward money, but now we have to find a job instead."

"Boys, I saw Mr. Gray at the Rotary Club breakfast meeting this morning. He told all of us how you captured that scoundrel Douglas. He was tooting your horns like mad. I'm very proud of you.

"To be totally honest, Mr. Gray told me about the reward money delay. And he was so pleased with your work that he recommended that I consider hiring you. So before you arrived, I talked with some of my staff about that possibility. We identified an opportunity that might just interest you. If you hadn't shown up this morning, I was planning to drop by this afternoon to tell you about it."

"We knew you wanted to talk to us, Mr. Graham. That's why we're here," Danny declared, fibbing again.

"Well, boys, in terms of a job opportunity with Graham markets, I have some good news and some bad news. Which do you want to hear first?"

"The bad news, please," I insisted.

"Listen, fellas. You've always been straight with me -- well almost always," he vowed, winking at Danny. "So are you ready for the bad news?"

"Ready," I said.

"Shoot," Danny replied, with a slight Humphrey Bogartian accent.

Mr. Graham chuckled at Danny's response, but after that he turned serious.

"First, we do have two job openings but they're only temporary. We need two extra stock boys for three weeks, starting this coming Monday.

"As stock boys you'll be opening cases of food, affixing proper prices to cans and boxes, and restocking shelves. It's not easy work. There's heavy lifting involved. But you boys are strong so I'm confident you can manage the job just fine.

"When you run out of restocking work, the store manager will assign you to other work. That might involve sweeping floors, washing windows, emptying trash, or cleaning bathrooms. So dress accordingly. And please, boys, no shorts. Long trousers are required for all male employees.

"The hours are not ideal for young fellas like you. Each day, you'll work from 4:00 a.m. until noon. That's eight hours a day, six days a week. Monday through Saturday.

"For the most part, you'll be filling in for people on vacation. So we'll know ahead of time where you're needed. But you could also fill in -- at the last minute -- for someone who might call in sick. So you fellas would be floaters, assigned to various locations. Counting our stores in Riverton and New Albany, we own and operate 35 Graham Markets. Over the course of your three weeks with us, I predict that you'll probably do some work in almost every one of our stores.

"I know you boys like to do everything together. But there may be times when you'll be assigned to different stores. Our smaller stores simply don't have enough restocking work to make good use of two stock boys.

"Before we get to the good news, why don't I pause to answer any questions you might have so far?"

"Would it be okay if we wear our Boy Scout uniform pants, Mr. Graham?"

"Why I guess it would --. Sure, Danny. Why do you ask?"

"They're the only long summer pants we own that fit us right now," Danny confessed. "We plan to use some of our earnings to buy some other long pants for our trip to Nashville."

How did Danny come up with this idea? But he was absolutely right. So I nodded my agreement.

"I see. Good thing for Graham Markets that you two are Boy Scouts, by golly," Mr. Graham snickered, slapping his thigh. "Any other concerns?"

"I have one, Mr. Graham. The city buses don't run at 4:00 a.m. So unless we can walk to our jobs, we would have to ask our folks to drive us to work. Is that right?"

"Well, now. That's part of the good news. During your time with us, you'll report directly to Harry Samson who's our vice president for store operations. All of the store managers work for him. And he and the managers start work at 4:00 a.m. Harry comes to this office and oversees our operations from here. If any store needs a temporary stock boy or two, Harry can run you over to that store. And if you need to move between stores the store managers involved will take care of that for you. Wherever you are at noon, we'll have someone drive you home -- or to the nearest bus stop."

"So our folks should bring us here to this office by four every morning. Is that right?"

"Goodness sakes, I left out the best news. Harry lives in New Albany. He'll be happy to stop by and pick you up every morning. Your folks needn't be involved. No, sir."

I was greatly relieved to hear this piece of good news. Suddenly this job opportunity seemed very feasible.

"What does this job pay, Mr. Graham?" Danny bluntly inquired.

"You're gonna like this good news, boys! Because it'd be difficult to fill this position with anyone as reliable as you two boys, we would pay you 50 cents an hour. That's 10 cents more than the minimum wage. And 10 cents more than our permanent stock boys are paid."

Author's Note:
At the end of the war, the minimum wage for an average job was 40 cents an hour. A gallon of milk cost 62 cents. A loaf of bread cost nine cents. A new car was $1,000 or a luxury car like Cadillac was $2,500. Of course, there were no new cars for sale at that time.

I reflexively began calculating figures in my head. But Mr. Graham completed my task.

"That's 48 hours a week times 50 cents an hour. So that's $24 a week for three weeks for a grand total of $72 each. So the two of you'll take home a combined total of $144. That's more than your $100 reward money. How does that sound?"

Danny stood up and grabbed Mr. Graham's hand. You got yourself two Class A stock boys, Mr. G. Thank you very much!"

Then Danny turned to me and asked, "All right with you, Jase?"

"All right indeed!" I exclaimed as I shook Mr. Graham's hand.

"That's terrific, fellas! Follow me. I'll introduce you to Mr. Samson."

OUR MEETING WITH MR. Graham had gone so well that Danny felt like celebrating our good fortune. Instead of spending our nickels on the bus, we decided to splurge. And walk home instead.

"Where should we go, Danny?"

"Let's go to the Woolworth lunch counter. Maybe Aunt Maude is there," Danny joked.

While Uncle Van was in Europe fighting the Nazis, Aunt Maude had worked behind the lunch counter at Woolworths. She was such a popular waitress that her tips amounted to more than twice the income from her wages. Danny and I made a point of stopping there often to see her and to sample the latest concoctions offered by the creative crew in the kitchen.

When we sat down on the stool, Aunt Maude's close friend, Molly O'Brien, waved at us and pointed her index finger upward, letting us know she'd be with us as soon as she finished taking the order from the customer sitting a couple of stools away. We perused the *Cold Drinks* section of the menu.

"Look! They still serve cherry cokes. Hmmm! That sounds good to me. How about you, Jase?"

"Here's a new one. A lime phosphate. Wonder what that tastes like."

"Let's ask Molly."

"Look, Danny. They still have fresh lemonade too. And chocolate cokes. I can't decide."

"Hi, boys. Heard anything from Aunt Maude lately?"

Before I could answer Molly's question, she began telling us about *her* latest letter from Aunt Maude.

"Last time she wrote, she was in Idaho with your Uncle Van. Or was it Montana? On a war bond drive. She said they were on stage with Bob Hope who introduced Uncle Van as the country's latest Congressional Medal of Honor recipient. After the show, they drove back to their hotel with Mr. Hope. What an exciting life they have!"

Danny looked bored so he returned to his inspection of the menu.

"Have you decided, boys?"

Danny ordered a lime phosphate. I stuck with my old favorite, cherry coke.

"Anything else, boys?"

We both shook our heads.

"That'll be ten cents. You can pay when you're finished with your drinks. I'll be right back with your order," she told us as she dashed off to the soda dispenser and the flavored syrup section of the food preparation area.

A minute later she returned with our frost-covered drinking glasses brimming with ice and the sweet nectar of exotic flavorings. She laid our paper straws next to our glasses and scurried off to wait on a newly-arrived customer.

Danny tore off the bottom of his straw wrapper and dipped the tip of the un-torn end into his lime phosphate. Then he pointed the wrapper-covered straw upward and blew hard into the unwrapped end of the straw. The wrapper shot to the ceiling where it stuck like an arrow among the dozens of other wrappers that hung there like a flock of upside-down white bats.

Molly shot Danny a disapproving look.

"Nice shot!" I had to admit.

"Thanks. You gonna shoot yours?"

"Naw! Makes Molly mad. She says straws drop down on people's food and they complain. I've never seen it happen, but I promised Aunt Maude I'd never do it again."

"I didn't promise not to do it. Can I shoot your wrapper to the ceiling? Please!"

Reluctantly I agreed -- with one proviso. Danny had to promise to shoot my wrapper when Molly wasn't looking our way.

After tearing off the end of my wrapper, Danny dunked it into my cherry coke. He explained that it was my wrapper so it should be stuck on the ceiling using my drink as stickum.

As soon as Molly turned her back, Danny launched his missile.

But Molly was no fool. When she heard the *whooshing* sound of Danny's launch, she turned and immediately assumed that I was the villain.

"Jase Addison! Shame on you! You promised never to do that again. You know it's not sanitary. How would you like a dirty old wrapper to drop off the ceiling into your cherry coke? I expected more of you. Wait until I see your Aunt Maude."

I thought she was making far too much of the incident. Besides I wasn't the one who launched the wrapper. But I was feeling stubborn enough not to let her know that fact.

Danny looked at Molly. Then he turned to me and let me have it.

"I agree with Molly, Jase. Shame on you."

I zapped him with one of my most deadly if-looks-could-kill stares. I was being double-teamed and I didn't like it one bit.

After Danny had his fun, he did something that I'd seldom seen him do before. He beckoned to Molly who stormed toward us. When she arrived, I could sense that she was still furious with me.

"Miss Molly. I have to set the record straight. Jase didn't shoot that second straw. I did. And I'm very sorry. I didn't realize how important it is to you and your customers. I promise I'll never do it again. Will you *please* forgive me?"

I swear that during this exchange Danny batted his eye lashes at Molly. But in any case, she melted like butter on a griddle. She nearly swooned in the white-hot heat of Danny's charm. Molly couldn't help herself. She patted Danny on the head and softly told him, "That's all right, Danny. You didn't know any better. You're forgiven."

Then she turned to me. I expected an apology. Boy! Was I mistaken. "But, Jase, you do know better. You ought to be ashamed of yourself for not warning poor Danny. You know how I feel about shooting wrappers at the ceiling. But no! You let him take the blame when you could have easily prevented this whole incident."

Danny looked at me and immediately laid down his nickel. I followed suit.

"Let's get out of here before she changes her mind again," he suggested.

So much for our celebratory drink at Woolworths.

ON OUR WAY HOME from our successful job-hunting trip, we decided as we often did to take a short detour. We found ourselves at the Grand Trunk Railway Station, located close to the intersection of Addison Street and New Albany Avenue. We decided to stay and watch the arrival of an incoming train.

Why this seemed like a good idea escapes me at the moment. Nonetheless, we found ourselves standing there on the platform with two or three dozen people who, unlike us, were expecting the arrival of friends or family. Their loved ones were soon to be delivered by the monstrous Grand Trunk steam engine, *chugging* and *hissing* its way up the tracks toward us.

"Jase, what are *you* doing here?"

Needless to say, I was startled by this question. A question, I might add, that sounded moderately accusatory. The robust good feelings generated by our recent job offers were immediately replaced by a potent array of defensive emotions. This all occurred even before I could identify my assailant.

However, I soon had my answer. I turned around and there stood Aunt Esther, whose eyes were fixed on me as if I were a poisonous snake. Not being at all sure of my reason for being there on the platform, I didn't answer her question. My hesitancy seemed to upset her. Her dismay was palpable.

This was a confusing situation for me. For years, Aunt Esther had hugged and squeezed me more than she had any of my first cousins, including her own three children. Naturally these years of affection conditioned me to feel very special in the eyes of the lady who was now viewing me as if I were that aforementioned reptile.

My common sense told me that whatever had caused Aunt Esther's ire, it would be prudent for me to remember that she was a large and very strong lady. No one, especially a boy of eleven years, would relish being *bopped* by Aunt Esther. Recalling the size of the bicep, now hidden under the frilly sleeve of her calico housedress, I backed out of range of her lethal right hook.

Suddenly Danny came to my rescue. He insinuated himself between me and my accuser and gave her a friendly wave, animated by five wiggle-fingers. His gesture seemed to charm her. "Hi, there. It's me, Aunt Esther. Danny. From Sunday dinners at the farm. I'm the one who loves your macaroni and cheese. And your mashed potatoes and gravy. And your cranberry sauce too. Remember me?"

Aunt Esther immediately did what she does best.

She snatched Danny up off the platform and, using her powerful arms, crushed him to her considerable bosom. She rocked him back-and-forth and up-and-down. His head disappeared and his lifeless arms and legs flopped from side-to-side. He looked like a turkey hanging by its neck in the butcher shop.

Having been subjected to that viselike grip many times before, I hoped my best friend had managed to take a deep breath before being swept off his feet. From personal experience, I knew he had no possibility of breathing, considering where his face was now buried.

Mercifully she dropped him to the platform and kissed him on the head. Without a word, he turned toward me. A goofy smile creased his beet-red face. "She remembers me," he wheezed.

Lucky you! I thought.

Then Aunt Esther turned her attention to me. "Jase, are you alone?" she inquired, almost desperately.

"I'm just here with Danny. Nobody else."

"Thank God! Please don't tell *anybody* you saw me here. It's a surprise. Uncle Tom is coming in on this train. He's home from the army -- on furlough. We want to surprise everybody at the farm on Sunday. Please promise me you'll keep this a secret."

"I promise, Aunt Esther."

"Oh, thank you, Jase. Thank you, my dear."

She moved toward me. I knew what was coming. I took a deep breath. Closed my eyes and crossed my fingers. As my body left the platform, I relaxed and allowed her familiar perfumed softness to envelop me.

Faintly I heard Danny's voice. "I'm next, Aunt Esther!"

BECAUSE WE HAD INADVERTENTLY become privy to the conspiracy that was afoot, Aunt Esther suggested we stay and greet Uncle Tom when he arrived.

"Danny, I have a job for you to perform when Uncle Tom steps off that train," she told us as she reached into the giant purse hanging on her arm."

"A job?" Danny asked curiously.

She handed Danny a brand new camera. "Yes, you can be the official photographer. Uncle Tom sent this Brownie Hawkeye camera that he bought in the camp PX. It's fully loaded with 620 film. And here's an extra roll. There are a total of 24 shots in those two rolls. Your job is to take as many pictures as you can of Uncle Tom's homecoming. Okay?"

"Great! But what about Jase?"

I was just thinking the same thing.

"I want Jase in the pictures too. After all, he's family."

"Gotcha," Danny replied.

"Okay, let's get a couple of you two with the big engine in the background."

Snap!

You can imagine Uncle Tom's surprise when he stepped off the train and saw Danny and me standing on the platform with Aunt Esther.

Snap! Snap!

All of Grandma and Grandpa Compton's children were handsome. They were endowed with fine features, including dark wavy hair, black eyes, and stunning figures in the women and superb physiques in the men. Uncle Tom was no exception. And when he was in uniform, my mother told us he looked *smashing*. For that reason, I paid particular attention to his uniform that day when he arrived. I observed he was sporting new staff sergeant stripes. I wondered if Aunt Esther noticed them. With his knapsack slung over his shoulder, he made his way through the crowd and gave Aunt Esther a long hug.

Snap! Snap! Snap!

"Welcome home, sweetheart," she whispered, after kissing him warmly.

Finally he turned his attention to us boys. "Hello, Jase," he said, while shaking my hand.

Snap! Snap!

Danny walked up and stuck out his hand too.

"You must be Danny. Great to meet you, son. Fine looking camera you've got there!"

Danny just smiled.

Snap! Snap!

He turned to Aunt Esther and joked, "I didn't know the town elders were sending Riverton's two most famous heroes to meet my train. How about that? Boys, Aunt Esther sent me all of your newspaper clippings. You have a remarkable record of service to your country. I'm proud of you both."

We walked down the platform. But neither Danny nor I could feel what was beneath our feet. After hearing Uncle Tom's words, we were both walking on air.

"What happened to our plan to keep my arrival a secret, Esther?"

Snap! Snap!

Danny rewound the first roll of film and masterfully inserted the second roll.

Click. Grrrrind. Click.

"Quite by accident, the boys were here at the station -- when I came over from MEM to meet your train. As Jase will tell you -- when I saw him here -- I was quite upset. Not at him personally -- of course -- but at not being able to keep your arrival a total secret as we planned."

Without being asked, Danny offered, "The best-laid plans of mice and men do often go awry."

"Burma Shave!" I added for a bit of comic relief. Uncle Tom was the only person who snickered at my attempted humor. The others didn't seem to be amused.

"Maybe I should get on home before another family member walks up and shakes my hand. Have you told the kids I'm coming?"

Snap! Snap!

"No, I thought you could surprise them. They should be at the house when you get there."

"Where's the car, Esther?"

"It's over there in the MEM parking lot. Just a short walk."

Snap! Snap!

"What time do you have to be back on the job, Esther?"

"There was no set time. I just punched out. Now I'll punch back in and work until the shift ends at 4:00 p.m. I've got so much overtime that I'm not concerned."

We arrived at Uncle Tom's large black 1936 Ford four-door sedan.

Snap! Snap!

"How's the old car running, Esther?"

"You'll see. She purrs like a kitten. I think my driving makes her very happy."

"You're sure you have a ride home now? I could stay until the shift ends."

"No, go home and spend some time with the kids. I'll be home around five o'clock."

Addressing Danny and me, Uncle Tom explained, "I'd take you home, but I'm afraid your folks might see me and spoil the surprise."

We assured him that we actually preferred walking, which was true.

Snap! Snap!

He waved goodbye and yelled, "Don't forget, you fellas -- mums the word."

Snap! Snap!

Danny yelled back, "Bring your shotgun to Grandma's, Uncle Tom. We're gonna shoot clay pheasants."

For some reason, Uncle Tom didn't reply. He just kept on driving.

Snap! Snap!

Click!

Having shot two rolls of film, Danny resigned from his photographer job and handed the Brownie Hawkeye back to Aunt Esther.

"Got some pretty good shots, Aunt Esther," he assured her.

She kissed the top of his head and we said our goodbyes. We watched Aunt Esther until she disappeared through the MEM entrance door. Then we set off walking toward New Albany Avenue.

On the way home, Danny inquired, "Jase, what does MEM stand for?"

"Michigan Electric Motors. They manufacture specialized small electric motors used in military equipment like army airplanes, tanks, torpedoes, and bomb sights."

"Wow! I had no idea."

"I know that because so many of my family members have worked there at one time or another," I informed him. "How MEM grew before and after the war began is an interesting story.

"Starting a number of years before Pearl Harbor, the War Department began upgrading America's military equipment. MEM was awarded a number of government contracts to build these special motors, and they hired lots of Riverton people to work there.

"Both Uncle Van and my father worked there before the war. In fact, Uncle Van and Aunt Maude took Mom to the hospital. When I was finally born, Uncle Van went down to MEM where Dad was working the night shift. He wanted to tell Dad that he was the father of a little boy. Because Dad worked all over the shop, Uncle Van walked around the outside of the building, yelling into the open windows, asking if Dad were there. He finally found him and told him about me.

"After Pearl Harbor with all their male workers signing up for military service, MEM was desperate to hire more workers. So they put on a big push to hire women. That's when Mom, Aunt Maude, and Aunt Esther went to work there. Even Grandma Compton worked at MEM for a while."

"When Dad joined the navy," Danny told me, "Mom went to work in Grandpa Tucker's grocery store. She worked there even after Dad was discharged from the navy. Because he was wounded at Pearl Harbor and spent a couple of years in hospitals, she needed to work to support our family. She worked there until Dad started his auto-repair business at our house last summer. Now she does Dad's books. That's when Grandpa Tucker decided to retire and close the store."

"Dad works at the Burke Factory. They do a lot of top secret work out there. But he doesn't talk about it at all."

"Do you think you'll work in a factory when you grow up, Jase?"

"Not if I can help it. I want to go to the University of Michigan and get a good education so I can do something different."

"Sounds good to me, Jase. Why don't we go together?"

"It's a deal," I vowed.

Danny nodded and we shook hands on it.

Could it ever happen that way? I wondered.

4 WE CAN DO IT!

THE WAR OPENED A NEW CHAPTER IN THE LIVES OF
American men and women emerging from The Great Depression
of the 1930's. After the men were shipped off to war-torn Europe
or the Pacific, millions of women were desperately needed in
factories, offices, and military bases to work in jobs traditionally
held by men. By the end of the war, 18 million women accounted
for one-third of the country's workforce. Over 350,000 women
were serving on active duty in the various branches of the
military, and 127 American women had secured official military
accreditation as war correspondents.

BEFORE THE WAR, WORKING wasn't new to minority and
lower-class women. They had always worked. And during the
Depression, the country was opposed to the idea of middle-class
women working because they would have taken jobs from men.

However, when the United States entered the war, it was
critically important to increase the production of war materials
dramatically and immediately. At first, the idea of women working
in factories wasn't taken seriously by factory management. But
attitudes changed when large and lucrative defense contracts were
being signed at the same time that droves of male factory workers
were enlisting in the military. During the war, a full half of all

American men between the ages of 18 and 40 were in uniform. Employers were simply left with no alternative. While desperate for workers during the war, companies agreed that hiring women would be acceptable, but only for the duration of the war.

Since the women's response to joining the workforce was slow, the government launched a propaganda campaign to *sell* them on the importance of their contribution to the war effort. Thus, the fictional character of *Rosie the Riveter* was created. Rosie was the ideal worker -- patriotic, hard-working, loyal, and extremely attractive. Needless to say, many real-life Rosies did not fit that *attractive* image.

In 1942, the song *Rosie the Riveter* became very popular, particularly the version recorded by the *Four Vagabonds*. This version caught on and rose on the *Hit Parade*.

The May 29, 1943 cover of *The Saturday Evening Post* carried the Rosie image as created by the popular cover artist, Norman Rockwell. A few months later, this image appeared on a government poster with the motto, *We Can Do It!*

Women just graduating from high school were recruited. But it became apparent that still more workers were needed so married women were recruited as well. At first, women with children under the age of 14 were requested to stay home. Then as the demand for workers became even more acute, only women with children under six were encouraged to stay home.

Patriotic as well as economic incentives were factors in women's decisions to join the workforce. Plus they began to enjoy the benefits of learning new skills and proving themselves in traditional *men's* jobs. And the extra money certainly came in handy, especially if the *man of the house* was serving in the military.

When the United States entered the war, 12 million women were already working. By the end of the war, that number had grown to 18 million. While three million women worked in defense plants, the majority worked in the service sector, freeing men to take better paying jobs or to join the military. The clerical sector's demand for women exceeded supply. Women preferred clerical jobs because the hours were shorter, wages were better with good job security, and the work was less strenuous.

Working women were encouraged to buy war bonds. Because wartime rationing and shortages meant there was little to buy, women invested heavily in bonds. After the war, bonds were used to buy houses and luxuries not available during the war.

Many working women suffered from the fatiguing effects of the *double shift*. That is, working both a full-time job at the office or factory and another full-time job taking care of the family and the home. More than half of the working women in America were also full-time homemakers.

After the war when men returned to the workforce, companies forced women to accept lower-paying female jobs or simply laid them off. While the image of women had changed during the war, it was temporary and superficial. Most women returned to their former roles as mothers and homemakers when the war ended.

In 2000, a new national park was created in the wartime boomtown of Richmond, California. *Rosie the Riveter World War II Home Front National Park* was established as a tribute to the sacrifices of the generation of wartime female workers. A memorial walkway, flanked by metal structures, evokes the hull of a ship. The park's landmarks include a housing development built for shipyard workers and Shipyard No. 3, which was the only permanent shipyard at the facility.

During the war, by utilizing round-the-clock shifts, the Kaiser Richmond Shipyard built 747 ships. The *USS Red Oak Victory*, an ammunition ship that was built there, is being restored by a group of World War II veterans. This ship was named for an Iowa town that lost the highest percentage of its sons on the battlefield.

FOLLOWING THE BOMBING OF Pearl Harbor, the number of required military personnel escalated rapidly. Soon it became apparent that more women would be needed to fill military jobs normally reserved for men. This would release greater numbers of military men for combat duty.

When the call for women recruits was issued, wives, mothers, sisters, daughters, and fiancées responded enthusiastically. On the first day of recruiting, May 27, 1942, lines of women eager to volunteer were overwhelming. The Washington, DC, recruiting office ran out of application forms twice during the first day. In New York City, 1,400 women stood in line for more than eight hours to sign up.

Most women volunteered out of a sense of patriotism. However, other women signed up for the opportunity of advancement, to learn new skills, to travel, or for adventure and excitement.

First Lady Eleanor Roosevelt lent her support to the effort to recruit women for the military. She visited college campuses with military directors Mildred McAfee of the WAVES (Navy), Oveta Culp Hobby of the WACs (Army), Ruth C. Streeter of the Women Marines (USMC), and Dorothy C. Stratton of the SPARS (Coast Guard).

The following is a brief description of the major women's military units, their size, and their function during World War II:

Women's Army Corps (WAC) (Army - 140,000 women)

WACs performed some 235 different jobs formerly reserved for men. These jobs ranged from repairing trucks to making aerial surveys. The women awoke to *reveille* every morning and endured the same regimen as men in the army. However, they did not handle weapons or participate in tactical training.

Women Accepted for Voluntary Emergency Service (WAVES) (Navy - 100,000 women)

The WAVES performed shore-duty tasks for the navy, including clerical support, driving military vehicles, operating control towers, repairing and maintaining everything from plumbing to parachutes. While WAVES were never assigned to combat duty, they served as gunnery instructors for sailors. In late 1944, they were given permission to travel to safe areas like Hawaii, Alaska, and the Caribbean.

Dr. Grace Hopper was the most renowned member of the WAVES. In 1943, to help the war effort, she left her position as an associate professor of mathematics at Vassar and joined the WAVES. As a navy lieutenant, she was assigned to work at

Harvard University on the computation of ballistic trajectories. She accomplished work by using the Mark I, the first electronic digital computing device and a forerunner of the modern computer.

On one occasion, she discovered the reason the Mark I wasn't operating properly. A moth had somehow found its way into one of the machine's relays. This gave birth to the term *bug*, which describes a computer programming error. After the war, she remained in the Naval Reserves. At Remington Rand, she created the first English-language computer programming language called COBOL.

After retiring from the reserves in 1966, she was recalled in 1967 and promoted to captain in 1973. In 1985, by a special act of Congress, she was promoted to the rank of Rear Admiral.

At her second retirement in 1986 at the age of 80, having served for 43 years in the navy, she received the Distinguished Service Medal, the Defense Department's highest honor. Shortly after her death in 1992, the *USS Hopper* (DDG-70), a guided missile destroyer, was named after Grace Hopper. The *Hopper* is the only United States naval vessel to be named after a woman.

Author's Note:
I've devoted many words to Grace Hopper as a tribute to her many accomplishments and to our friendship. During the 1970s and 1980s, at a number of national computer conferences, we shared the stage as keynote speakers. Not only was she a brilliant computer scientist, but she was an entertaining and popular speaker.

I remember vividly how audiences looked forward to her trademark stage prop that she used to demonstrate the speed by which electrons travel through computers. Before each of her talks, she'd give a 16-inch length of plastic-coated copper wire to people seated near the podium.

Later during her talk, she'd ask those with the wire, "What do you have in your hand?"

At first, no one knew the answer. But, over the course of time, because she used this prop over and over again, whenever she asked the question, audiences would shout, "A nanosecond!"

Grace would smile and say, "That's correct."

Then she'd explain, "Astronomers measure great distances in the universe by light-years. That is, the distance light travels in a vacuum

*in one Julian year. Because electrons travel at approximately the speed
of light, I wanted you to see how far an electron travels in one-billionth
of a second. That is, one nanosecond."*

Grace Hopper or Amazing Grace, *as her fans called her, used her
nanoseconds to the delight of audiences for decades. I was proud to be
her friend.*

Women's Air Corps Service Pilots (WASP) and Women's Auxiliary Ferrying Squadron (WAFS) (Army Air Corps - 2,000 women)

These two groups of female pilots ferried airplanes for the
Army Air Transport Command from manufacturing plants to
Army air bases, transported supplies, and taught men how to fly.

Newly recruited WASPs and WAFSs entered an intense
training program where they spent 16-hour days drilling, mastering
Morse code and map-reading, and flying single- and twin-engine
airplanes. While they proved faster with instruments and smoother
at the controls than men, women were restricted to ferrying
airplanes. These units of female pilots flew more than 60 million
miles in less than three years.

Perhaps the most renowned WAF pilot was Cornelia Fort, a
Nashville native from a wealthy family, who chose the unusual
occupation of airplane pilot and instructor. Before the war, she
moved to Hawaii. When the Japanese bombed Pearl Harbor, she
was in the air giving a flying lesson. Though Japanese pilots tried
to shoot her down, she escaped.

When the government solicited women to volunteer to pilot
military airplanes, she joined the WAFS. In 1943, she was involved
in a fatal accident when another American pilot collided with her
airplane. Cornelia Fort was the first American woman to die in the
military service during World War II.

Women's Reserve of the U.S. Marine Corps (USMCWR) (Marines - 23,000 women)

Women Marines were assigned to over 200 different jobs
including radio operator, photographer, parachute rigger, driver,

aerial gunnery instructor, control tower operator, motion picture operator, auto mechanic, telegraph operator, and cryptographer.

The USMCWR also maintained cameras used for air reconnaissance, directed air traffic, repaired aircraft engines, drove service vehicles, and performed various ground jobs at Marine air stations.

United States Coast Guard Women's Reserve (SPARS) (Coast Guard - 13,000 women)

The name SPARS was a contraction of the Coast Guard motto, *semper paratus*. The English translation from Latin is *Always Ready*. During peacetime, the Coast Guard is a component of the Department of Treasury, but during war, the Coast Guard becomes a part of the Department of the Navy. Like the WAVES and WAC, SPARS women performed a wide variety of duties to free male members of the Coast Guard from stateside duty for assignments overseas.

Army Nurse Corps (ANC) (Army - 60,000 women) and Navy Nurse Corps (NNC) (Navy - 14,000 women)

The need for nurses in the military increased dramatically as the war progressed. These nurses worked in state-side hospitals, in field hospitals, on hospital ships, and in rehabilitation centers around the world.

In Europe and in the Pacific, they risked their lives daily, serving on or near the front lines. The most difficult aspect of their work was to help soldiers adjust to the psychological damage of the combat experience.

In all, more than 200 Army nurses lost their lives during the war. 1,600 Army nurses and 565 WACs received combat decorations, including the Distinguished Service Medal, Silver Star, Bronze Star, Air Medal, Legions of Merit, Commendation Medal, and Purple Heart.

THE WAR ALSO OFFERED new opportunities for women as war correspondents and photographers. Like most women recruited to perform *male jobs*, when the war ended, these women were expected to step aside for returning veterans, their former male colleagues. By 1968, there were fewer female foreign correspondents than before the war.

Prominent women war correspondents and photographers include the following:

Clare Boothe Luce is best remembered as a congresswoman, ambassador, playwright, and spouse of Henry R. Luce of *Time-Life-Fortune.* She covered World War II battlefronts and faced house arrest in Trinidad by British Customs. Her draft article for *Life* about poor military preparedness in Libya proved too accurate for Allied comfort. However, this reporting did lead Winston Churchill to revamp the Middle Eastern military policy. Her first non-fiction book *Europe in the Spring* was written to convince fellow Americans of the danger of isolationism.

May Craig not only served as a Washington correspondent for the Guy Gannett newspaper chain, but she provided eyewitness accounts of V-bomb raids in London, the Normandy campaign, and the liberation of Paris. To report the news firsthand, she broke strict rules that had kept women out of airplanes and off ships.

For the record, Guy Gannett newspapers were not in any way associated with today's Gannett communication chain.

Dorothea Lange documented the change on the home front among ethnic groups and workers uprooted by the war. After the relocation of Japanese-Americans into internment camps in the West, she was hired to photograph Japanese neighborhoods, processing centers, and camp facilities for the War Relocation Authority. In 1972, the Whitney Museum in New York incorporated 27 of her photographs into an exhibit about the Japanese internment. Her photographs were described as "Documents of such a high order that they convey the feelings of the victims as well as the facts of the crime."

Therese Bonney's images of homeless children and adults on the back roads of Europe touched millions of viewers in the United States and abroad. She pledged, "I go forth alone, try to get the truth, and bring it back and try to make others face it and do something about it." She was twice decorated for military bravery.

Toni Frissell, best known today for her high-fashion photography, moved from the *soft news* of fashion to the *hard news* of the front page by volunteering her services to the American Red Cross, Women's Army Corps, and the Eighth Army Air Corps. She produced thousands of images of nurses, front-line soldiers, WACs, and orphaned children. Her images of the fighter pilots of the elite 332nd Fighter Group, the *Tuskegee Airmen*, were intended to develop a positive attitude about the fitness of blacks to handle demanding military jobs.

WOMEN ENTHUSIASTICALLY VOLUNTEERED TO fill jobs normally reserved for men in peacetime. To free men to enlist, they worked in offices and in defense factories producing materials of war. In the military, they relieved men who could be deployed to combat areas. In the nursing field, they dispensed aid and comfort to the wounded, And in the news media, they reported battlefield conditions.

These women were living proof of their motto:
We Can Do It!

5 THE HEIST

AS WE STROLLED ALONG NEW ALBANY AVENUE, Danny asked, "Jase, are you hungry?"

So much had happened during the morning that I hadn't thought much about eating. That is, until Danny mentioned it. "You bet I am!"

"Let's go to my house and open a couple of cans. Maybe we'll get lucky."

"Good idea."

We didn't notice the Riverton police car pulling up beside us until we heard a familiar voice. "So there you are. I've been looking for you boys."

"You're looking for us, Sergeant Tolna?"

"I sure am. I owe you fellas a lunch. How about the Chop Suey Diner?"

Danny immediately opened the car door and hopped into the front passenger seat. "Hurry, Jase," he urged, waving me into the backseat.

When Danny was hungry, it was unwise to cause any delay in his next meal. So I quickly jumped into the car.

"We're all set, Sergeant Tolna. Let's get a move on!" Danny ordered.

"Sergeant Tolna, what's the occasion? Why did you invite us to lunch?"

"I don't want to tell you. You'll have to guess."

"Car 15, Dispatch. Lieutenant Tolna, the MEM payroll has just been stolen. And get this! The thief was dressed in a Riverton police officer's uniform. Chief Remke will be on his way shortly. He's rounding up the CSC as we speak.

"Oh, another thing -- Officer Pryorski, who was scheduled to make the payroll run today, appears to be missing. I can't raise his patrol car by radio. Over."

"Dispatch,15. This sounds bad. I'm six blocks away. I'll be there in a jiffy. Thanks for the heads-up, Clint. Out."

Lieutenant Tolna snapped on his siren and tromped down on the gas pedal. "Hold onto your hats, boys. Looks like our lunch will be delayed."

We raced into the MEM parking lot, the same lot where Danny and I had waved goodbye to Uncle Tom. We skidded to a stop at the factory's front entrance.

"I'd like you boys to come with me. I'll need your sharp minds and intuition on this one. I still can't believe someone, dressed as one of us, robbed the payroll."

The armed, uniformed security guard at the front door waved us through his checkpoint and gave us directions to the payroll office, located at the end of the first floor hallway, just outside the wide doors leading into the factory itself.

The payroll office consisted of two sections.

The front section was further divided into a pair of wide walkways. Arrows painted on the floor defined the *IN* walkway, which led employees past two pay windows. Arrows on the *OUT* walkway led them from the payroll office into the main hallway.

The back section of the room was located inside a sturdy wrought-iron cage. The pay windows were openings in the cage with flaps that could be padlocked after the payroll was disbursed. A heavy steel door allowed access to personnel who worked inside the cage. That door stood open, its chain and padlock hanging uselessly from the door handle.

All Riverton factories and other businesses paid their employees on Fridays. Merchants stayed open until nine o'clock that night to take advantage of the surge in spending power of the newly-paid Rivertonians.

Back in those days, nearly all businesses paid their employees in cash.

Inside the cage against the back wall, stood a huge, floor-to-ceiling safe. Its two massive steel doors were wide-open. Except for a tall stack of payroll ledgers on the bottom shelf, the safe appeared to be empty.

White cotton money bags were strewn over the floor of the caged area. Each had the words *Riverton Second National Bank* stenciled on its side and appeared to be empty as well.

A thin, bald-headed man, wearing a starched white dress shirt and bow tie, sat upright in the middle of the bag-covered floor. A matronly lady dressed in a white nurse's uniform was bending over the man. She'd just finished taping a gauze pad to the shining dome of his head.

Two armed, uniformed security guards stood at one side, watching the proceedings.

When we entered the payroll office, the two MEM guards greeted us enthusiastically. They seemed *relieved* to be *relieved* by a *real* police officer. The younger one introduced himself, "Hello, Lieutenant. I'm Mark Houseman, head of MEM security. This is Security Guard Ted Braden."

"Jeff Tolna," the lieutenant replied, shaking the two men's hands. "Our chief is on his way with our CSC -- the Crime Scene Crew."

Turning to us, Lieutenant Tolna said, "You may have heard of these young men. Gentlemen, meet Jase Addison and Danny Tucker. They'll be assisting me on this case."

Lieutenant Tolna allowed a brief period for the two men to praise our past deeds. Then he got down to business.

"I'd like you to brief me on what happened here. Perhaps it'd be best if we stepped out of the cage. We want to keep the crime scene as undisturbed as possible."

The head of security began his briefing.

"Each Friday, we need $7,000 to meet our payroll for the three shifts of MEM employees. As you know, the Riverton police department transports that amount of cash from the Riverton Second National Bank to our safe -- there inside the cage.

"Your officer parks his patrol car and enters the bank. Armed bank security guards escort the officer to the safe where the money is counted and placed in a special container that is padlocked to a handcart of sorts. The officer signs a receipt for the cash before leaving the bank.

"Then a bank security guard escorts the police officer to his car and helps him load the cart and locked container into his trunk.

"After that, the police officer drives here and parks at our front entrance. The MEM guard there calls one of my men who comes to the police car, helps your officer lift the container and cart out of the trunk, and escorts the police officer and the cart to our payroll office. Once the police officer and cart are safely locked in the cage with Mr. Hanna, our paymaster, my man returns to his post."

"Let me interrupt you there, Mark. Isn't this police officer nearly always Officer Pryorski?"

"I'd say he makes the delivery about 40 times a year. Some other police officer delivers the payroll about one week a month. In fact, if I recall right, you made the delivery a couple of years back. Right?"

"You've got a good memory, Mark," Lieutenant Tolna observed cheerfully. Then he got back to business. "Are you notified when it's *not* going to be Officer Pryorski?"

"No, sir. We're not. My men tend to know your officers so we've never had a problem accepting substitutes from time to time. If a person wearing a Riverton police uniform and driving a Riverton police car delivers us $7,000, until now, we haven't been overly concerned.

"But, based on what happened here today, I'd say it's time to revisit our procedure -- with your help, of course."

"We'll be happy to work with you on that. But right now it looks like this horse is out of the barn. Now just for the record, it was *not* Officer Pryorski who delivered the money today. Right?"

"That's correct. Neither the guard at the entrance nor the guard here recognized the perp. Mr. Hanna -- the man over there who was hit on the head -- didn't recognize him either.

"Before you arrived my men huddled and came up with a pretty good description. I had my secretary type it up for you," Houseman explained, handing the folded piece of paper to the lieutenant.

"Very good. Very good indeed. That's definitely not Pryorski's description. And it doesn't fit any of the other officers in the department either.

"Please take me to a phone so I can have our dispatch notify our patrol cars to be on the lookout for this rascal.

"We'll also notify Sheriff Connors so he can alert his patrols all over the county. If this guy is smart, he'll dump that police uniform and police car posthaste. But maybe we can get him before he does so."

"That's not going to happen," Danny whispered in my ear.

"Why not?"

"This fellow is far too smart to be caught doing something dumb."

Danny had a good point. Darn it!

WHEN CHIEF REMKE ARRIVED with the CSC, we moved to a conference room down the hall from the payroll office, allowing the crew to inspect the crime scene for forensic evidence and fingerprints.

Lieutenant Tolna briefed the chief on what we'd learned up to that point in time. He showed the chief the description of the suspect and informed him that he'd notified dispatch to send the description to all Riverton patrol cars and to the sheriff's force as well.

"I also sent one of my investigators over to the bank with this description to see if they concur. Want to make sure we're only dealing with one perp. He'll ask the bank officials to secure the area that the suspect visited. After CSC is finished here, I'll send them over to the bank to gather evidence as well."

"Good thinking, Jeff. What's next?"

"Mark, do you think Mr. Hanna is up to joining us?"

"Yes, sir. He's eager to talk, Lieutenant. I'll bring him in."

Mr. Hanna was still a bit shaken by the experience, but his anger fueled his attitude. "I feel like a fool. I've never let a stranger into that cage before. If I don't know a police officer, I make a point of calling Mark here to verify that he's on the level. But I was in a hurry. So I took a shortcut. I deserved a conk on the head."

"Could you tell us exactly what happened, Mr. Hanna?"

"Of course. Ted Braden -- one of Mark's men -- escorted the man into the payroll office. They were chatting with each other in a friendly manner -- about the Detroit Tigers' prospects this year. Ted called the man Officer Finlay -- so I assumed Ted knew him.

"In any case, I opened the cage door and let the stranger inside. Once I'd locked him and his money cart inside the cage, Ted said goodbye and left the payroll office.

"Normally it takes ten or fifteen minutes to count the money, sign the receipt, and so on. Once I have the money locked inside the safe, I unlock the cage and the police officer leaves -- unescorted -- on his own.

"I had opened the safe and was clearing room for the payroll. Naturally I had my back to him. That's when I felt a severe pain in my head. I assume he was carrying a blackjack or perhaps he hit me with his revolver.

"That's all I remember until I woke up when my assistant came in and found me."

"Did the man say anything to you after Braden left the payroll office, sir?"

"When I had told him I wasn't quite ready to count the money, he told me not to rush. Said he had all the time in the world. Seemed like a real friendly fellow to be honest with you. I guess his words gave me a false sense of security."

"So he got away with the entire $7,000. Is that right, Mr. Hanna?"

"I can only assume what was in the cart. I never saw it -- let alone count it. You could check with the bank to make sure they filled our order completely. That is to see how much the stranger signed for. But chances are you'll find that he took $7,000 in new cash."

"New cash? How do you mean?"

"In addition to the weekly payroll money, we always have a supply of cash on hand. Some of our suppliers insist on being paid in cash. To them, C.O.D. means *Cash on Delivery*. And their invoices often run in the hundreds of dollars."

"Any idea how much money was in the safe before the suspect arrived?"

"I have to look at my ledger, but I'd estimate there was at least $3,000 in the safe. I can give you that exact amount before you leave. In fact, our auditors were here this week, and we haven't used any cash since they departed. The exact number will be in their report as well."

Wow! I thought, *$10,000. Not a bad haul for a friendly stranger.*

"Do you have anything else to share with us, Mr. Hanna?"

"Just a couple of observations. This stranger did his homework. He knew just when we would have the entire payroll in that cage and the safe door opened so our permanent supply of cash was at risk."

"I hate to say it, but it almost sounds like an inside job."

"You must be reading my mind. There are many aspects of this robbery that lead to that conclusion," Lieutenant Tolna observed. "What's your other observation, sir?"

"All those empty bags on the floor tell me a couple of things. First, the stranger was smart enough not to attempt to fill his cart with bags full of money. They would be too bulky. He wouldn't be able to fit a bagged $10,000 or so into his cart.

"Second, he was in no rush. He was smart, deliberate, and cool. This whole robbery was done with -- well -- military precision."

"Any other questions for Mr. Hanna?" Lieutenant Tolna asked perfunctorily. "If not, I think we should go see how the CSC boys are doing."

Everyone headed for the conference room door. Everyone except Danny I should say.

"Mr. Hanna, I have a question for you. Does MEM have a cafeteria?"

"Why, yes, young man. We have a fine cafeteria."

"Are boys and police lieutenants allowed to eat there?"

"Ah -- of course -- they are. Stop back at the payroll office. I'll see if I can find you some free meal passes."

"That won't be necessary, Mr. Hanna. Will it Lieutenant Tolna?"

Chief Remke declared, "Jeff, when we get back to the station, I'd like to take another look at the age requirements for new police recruits. I think we could use a man like Danny on the force."

"Sorry, Chief, but Jase and I already promised J. Edward Haver that we're going to be FBI agents. But thanks for asking."

The chief just shook his head and snickered.

ON OUR WAY TO the MEM cafeteria, we stopped to check on the Crime Scene Crew. "Got anything for me?" Lieutenant Tolna asked the crew leader.

"We lifted four different fingerprints from inside the cage. But we've found no physical evidence that definitively points to the thief. I'd say this fellow was extremely careful -- almost like he knew what we'd be looking for, Lieutenant."

"How much longer do you need to be here?"

"The assistant cashier is rounding up all the payroll staff, including Mr. Hanna. We have to take their prints too and match them with the ones we lifted. Just so you know -- there are four people with access to the cage area. So we may be looking at no prints from the perp. As I mentioned, he's a careful fellow. In any case, it should be about another half-hour, I'd guess."

"They'll be expecting you over at the bank as soon as you finish up here."

"Yes, sir."

"The boys and I are going to grab a bite of lunch in the cafeteria here. Can I bring you and your crew a sandwich or something?"

"No, thanks, Lieutenant. In this job, we never know where we'll be at meal times. Because it could be out in the middle of nowhere, we always bring a sack lunch from home. They're in the van. We'll eat on our way to the bank."

"Understood. Let me know if you hear anything from dispatch about the perpetrator or about Officer Pryorski. We'll be in the cafeteria. Then we'll head for the bank."

"Yes, sir."

Having to feed hundreds of workers across three shifts, the MEM cafeteria's menu offered a wide range of selections. The long cafeteria line ran in front of an equally long steam table where those selections were displayed in great quantities.

That day's hot offerings included roast chicken, meat loaf and gravy, hamburgers and hot dogs, and chop suey. Of course, there were various side dishes including mashed potatoes, all kinds of steaming vegetables, and soups, along with breads, biscuits, and rolls. And there was an extensive selection of desserts.

This wide array of choices made Danny's first cafeteria dining experience a difficult one. He couldn't decide what he wanted.

Then he couldn't decide how much of the selection to place on his tray.

Because Danny insisted on going through the line first, his decision-making difficulty caused great angst among the impatient diners in line behind him, including Master Jase Addison and Lieutenant Jeff Tolna.

Finally I lost patience. "Danny, make up your mind and let's get on with our lunch. You're taking so much time that my food is getting cold. Besides we've got to get to the bank. Geez!"

Apparently Danny was wearing his *angst deflector* because he ignored my *suggestion* to pick up the pace.

"I've got an idea. Watch my tray, Jase," Lieutenant Tolna said. "I'll be right back."

The lieutenant walked back to the table where we'd picked up our trays, silverware, and napkins. He removed a clean tray from the stack and brought it to where we were stalled in the line.

"Here, Danny. Maybe this will help."

Danny smiled and snatched the tray from the lieutenant's hands. Then, after lining up his pair of trays on the tray slide, Danny literally ran along the steam table grabbing dish after dish, piling them higgledy-piggledy onto his trays.

When we reached the cashier, her eyes popped wide-open. "Are you planning to eat all that food, young man?"

"No. I'm planning to feed some of it to my dog. You *do* have paper bags for leftovers. Don't you?"

The cashier's mouth fell open. She was speechless. When she regained her composure, she murmured, "I'll see if I can find something for you to use to carry home your leftovers."

"Please don't bother, ma'am. I have my own leftover container," he explained as he patted his stomach.

While Danny carried his second tray to a nearby table, Lieutenant Tolna informed the cashier that we three were together. So she added up the total for our four trays.

"The total is $2.15," she announced.

"$2.15!" I gasped. "That's too much."

"It's fine, Jase. I've got it," Lieutenant Tolna assured him, reaching for his wallet.

"Hold it right there, Lieutenant Tolna. Your money's no good here. I'll take care of it. You and Jase head for the table while I settle up."

Not wanting to create any more fuss in the cafeteria line, we blindly followed Danny's orders and dazedly walked to the table. A minute later Danny returned. Without a word of explanation, he sat down to begin his mammoth feast.

Something told me not to ask the question, but I couldn't help myself. "Danny, you didn't have any money. How did you pay for our lunches?"

"I didn't."

"Who did?"

"Mr. Hanna!"

"You mean free passes? When did you have time to get them?"

Danny winked and shot me a sly grin.

Oh, Danny!

BECAUSE OF OUR EXTENDED lunch hour, we arrived at the bank later than Lieutenant Tolna had hoped. He apologized to the CSC leader who had arrived with the crew well before Danny had finished his main courses. Not to mention the time needed to consume four gigantic desserts.

"Sorry we're late. We were delayed at MEM. Anything to report?"

"I'll start with MEM. As predicted, all four prints we lifted were those of the four people authorized to be in the cage. So we haven't a thing to go on from our investigation at MEM. Well -- except the description of the perpetrator.

"So that leaves the bank. There's a *caged area* here as well -- the area beyond that ceiling-high locked gate. The bank vault's inside the cage. The gate key is kept at that guard desk. Not just anybody can go in there. That's the good news.

"The bad news -- the access list looks like the cast of *Gone with the Wind*. All the bank officers and directors. The tellers and assistants. A total of 33 people. Don't know when the marble in there's been polished last. We've got fingerprints on top of fingerprints inside the cage. We'll be working here for days. If our luck's the same as it was at MEM, I'm not sure we'll have anything when we finish."

"Did people here look at the description of the perp?"

"Oh, I forgot -- your investigator showed the description to all the employees who saw the man when he picked up the money. Everybody agreed the description matches that man."

"Good! At least, we're only dealing with one perp."

"Yep, but this perp knows the ropes. He's a smart cookie all right."

At the mention of cookie, Danny remembered a morsel of dessert that he had stored in his shorts' pocket in case of an emergency. We all turned toward Danny when we heard the *crunching*.

"Chaaalaate kwoooeee," Danny explained with his mouth full. "Fawn looosch," he further articulated.

Lieutenant Tolna and I looked at each other and laughed. Danny just frowned but continued crunching.

We wished the CSC leader luck and left the bank. Just as we got to the car, the leader yelled from the bank door, "Lieutenant, dispatch just called me. They found the car and Officer Pryorski. They want to talk to you."

Lieutenant Tolna gave him a thumbs-up and picked up the radio microphone.

"Dispatch, Car 15. Over."

"15, Dispatch. A sheriff's deputy found Pryorski's patrol car -- in the woods near the intersection of Riverton Road and Barrington Road. Pryorski was locked in the trunk. Deputy broke the lock and let him out. Didn't have a uniform on -- only his underwear. No sign of the perp or the car keys. Deputy's waiting for you there. Sheriff Connors will be there shortly. Over."

"Dispatch,15. Has Chief Remke heard this? Over."

"15, Dispatch. That's affirmative. Chief wants you to double-time it out to Pryorski's car. He'll round up CSC and join you there. Over."

"Dispatch,15. Clint, call the deputy back. If they haven't found the key, dispatch a tow truck. Tell them not to hook up -- just stand by. Also tell the deputy to tape off the area surrounding the car -- out to 25 feet. Then keep everybody out of there. CSC can comb that area first. If it gets dark before they get to the car, we'll tow it to our garage so CSC can see what they're doing. Clint, you follow all that? Over."

"15, Dispatch. Roger, Lieutenant. Wrote it all down. Over."

"Dispatch,15. I'm on my way. Oh, Danny and Jase are still with me. Have a car go by and tell their parents what's going on. Over."

"15, Dispatch. Wilco. Out."

Again, Lieutenant Tolna started the engine, snapped on the siren, and tromped down on his gas pedal. We sat back in our seats and enjoyed the ride.

"Jase, do you realize that Pryorski's patrol car was found close to your grandparents' farm?"

"That's right. Danny, that's the place where you sprained your ankle -- this past spring -- when the gypsies picked you up."

Closing his eyes, Danny sighed, "Wasn't Gisella just beautiful?"

I visualized the stunning gypsy woman and her family. We weren't the only ones who fell for these gypsies. Grandma and Grandpa Compton practically adopted them.

As we flew out Riverton Road, for some reason, I recalled the last time we'd heard the car radio, just before we sped off to MEM. That's when we learned about Lieutenant Tolna's promotion. And when he told us he owed us a lunch.

Despite the tenseness of the situation, I asked, "Did your promotion have something to do with us, Lieutenant Tolna?"

Danny opened his eyes and listened intently.

"Absolutely! Every time you fellas solve a crime and I arrest the criminal, I get the credit for it. For example, the Douglas case resulted in my receiving an impressive Letter of Commendation from the FBI. When Chief Remke read his copy, he decided my performance during this past year merited my being promoted."

"Congratulations again, Lieutenant Tolna. That's just wonderful!" I told him.

"Yeah, me too! Congratulations, Lieutenant," Danny added.

"Thanks, fellas. But there's only one thing wrong with it. That FBI letter should have been addressed to you -- not me. So that's why I offered to buy you lunch. As I told you, it's the least I can do. And I still owe you."

"Let's go back to the MEM cafeteria," Danny suggested.

"Ugh!" I replied. "Why on earth would we want to go through that again?"

"Because I still have six free lunch passes in my pocket."

I'm a fast learner so I didn't ask the obvious question.

WHEN WE ARRIVED AT the crime scene, Sheriff Connors had a special request for Lieutenant Tolna. "Jeff, I know you'll want to question both these fellows. But I'd appreciate your questioning Deputy Larson first, before you question Officer Pryorski. He's been here for over an hour now. I'd like to release him to resume his patrol."

"You bet, Roy."

After shaking the deputy's hand, Lieutenant Tolna asked, "Tell me how you discovered the car, Deputy."

"I was driving east on Riverton Road when I noticed tire tracks leaving the road and disappearing into the woods -- right about here. From the road, the tracks showed up real good in the wet grass."

"What made you stop?"

"This is my regular patrol area so I know it rather well. When I passed this point earlier in my shift, I was pretty sure there were no tracks here. So I stopped to investigate. I followed the tracks past that brush and into the woods. And there it was -- a Riverton patrol car."

"How did you know Officer Pryorski was in the trunk?"

"When I opened the car door, he heard me and gave out a muffled shout and banged on the trunk lid. I looked for the keys to unlock the trunk, but I couldn't find them anywhere. So I went to my car and got my tire wretch and the base from my tire jack. Using the wretch as a punch and the base as a hammer, I punched that lock through the truck lid. When I opened the lid, there was Officer Pryorski -- gagged and tied up like a Christmas present. I removed his gag and untied him. All he had on was his underwear so got my poncho and galoshes from my car for him to wear."

"Assuming our perp drove the patrol car here, do you think he escaped on foot? Shall I call in some tracking dogs?"

"I had time to think about that. I believe he had a car parked -- up there a piece -- at the end of the lane running along the creek and into the woods. The brush is so high in there that he could have hidden behind it. Besides if somebody -- even myself -- would have seen a car parked in there, it wouldn't raise any suspicion."

"Why's that?"

"This time a year, people park in that lane to pick asparagus. That meadow is just covered with wild asparagus right now."

Danny and I looked at each other. Just a year ago the two of us picked a large basket of asparagus with Grandma Compton in that very meadow.

"Sparagrist," Danny whispered, using his naïve pronunciation of the delicate vegetable. We both smiled.

The deputy continued, "Heck, I pulled in there the other day myself. Picked some sweet wild asparagus to have with my lunch."

He stopped and gave the sheriff a sheepish look. Apparently he was uneasy making that admission.

"I did the same thing when I was a deputy just like you!"

The sheriff turned back to the Lieutenant. "If the perp did park at the end of the lane, he could walk through the woods from here to get his car without being noticed from the road."

"That's what I concluded," Deputy Larson told us.

"If you're right, this fellow had this heist planned out to the finest detail. This guy's really beginning to impress me."

"Deputy, I think that's all I need for now. Thank you for your assistance. If you remember anything more, radio the sheriff. If we need anything more from you, we'll be in touch. By the way, you did a very professional job of handling this situation. Well done!"

Deputy Larson smiled and shook hands with all of us. Then he literally galloped back to his car.

Danny had a parting observation. "If it rains tonight, he'll be one wet deputy."

SINCE OUR ARRIVAL AT the site of the hidden patrol car, something had bothered me. But I couldn't put my finger on it. While I watched Deputy Larson's patrol car disappear in the distance, it suddenly struck me.

"How'd he get into Riverton?" I blurted out.

"What's that, Jase?" Lieutenant Tolna asked.

"That's right, Jase. How *did* he get into town," echoed Danny. "After he parked the car way out here, he had to get into town somehow. Did he hitchhike or what?"

Lieutenant Tolna looked at Sheriff Connors. "Darned good question, Roy. Why didn't we think of that?"

Then the lieutenant turned to the raingear-covered Officer Pryorski and inquired, "Can you shed any light on this, Paul?"

"Well, that's not the only unanswered question I have. How did he know that I'd be pulling into Trumble Park just minutes before I was scheduled to pick up the money from the bank?"

"Wait a minute! Let's start at the beginning," Lieutenant Tolna advised. "I assume you started your shift at eight o'clock as usual."

"That's right, sir. On Fridays, I usually drive my normal patrol -- in the southeast part of town -- for a couple of hours before going to the bank to pick up the MEM payroll money.

"At about nine o'clock, Dispatch radioed to tell me that a car belonging to a man hiking in Trumble Park had been broken into. He reported the thieves had stolen a camera and a trench coat."

"Did Dispatch give you the man's name?"

"Clint claimed his name was Finlay. Said he'd called from the pay phone there by the swimming pool."

"That's the name the perp used at MEM."

"Well that squares, Lieutenant. Anyway, I high-tailed it over to Trumble Park, thinking I might catch somebody -- wearing a trench coat and carrying a camera -- leaving the park. When I turned into the park, a man flagged me down. I guess it must have been Finlay. But he wasn't wearing a trench coat. And he had no camera that I could see."

"Did you think it was the man whose car was robbed?"

"I did at first. But I've since realized that this fellow was at least half-a-mile from that pay phone. So he couldn't have gotten up to the park entrance that fast -- at least not on foot. But, to my regret, I stopped my car and asked him how I could help.

"He pulled a gun on me and ordered me to step out of the car. He removed my revolver from my holster and threw it into my backseat. He had the drop on me so I did what I was told.

"We both got back into the car -- he kept me covered the entire time. Then he ordered me to drive to the upper parking lot. When I stopped the car, he ordered me to remove my uniform -- shoes, socks -- everything. Then he forced me to walk into the woods where he bound and gagged me. Then he tied me to a tree."

"Good grief! That couldn't have been a very pleasant experience for you."

"Definitely a low point in my law enforcement career, Lieutenant. To add insult to injury, the mosquitos up there are unmerciful. I'm going to take a bath in calamine lotion as soon as I get home tonight."

"We'll try to get you there shortly, Paul. What else can you tell me?"

"Not a whole lot. He came back a couple of hours later -- wearing my uniform. Untied me from the tree and marched me back to the car. He removed the money case and cart from the trunk. The way he hefted it, I assumed it was full of money. He put it in the backseat. Then he pushed me into the trunk and slammed the lid shut. He started the car and drove for -- I don't know -- about a half-hour, I guess."

"I could feel the car slowing down. Then I was jostled around -- presumably as he drove off the road and into the woods here. I heard the door slam and that was about it -- until Deputy Larson opened the car door and I made as much noise as I could."

"You've been through quite an ordeal, Paul."

"Yes, sir. I guess you could say that. But there's some good news. I got a real good look at the son of a -- the perp. I'll never forget what he looks like. Never in my life. No, sir."

Lieutenant Tolna removed a folded piece of paper from his pocket and handed to Officer Pryorski.

"Take a good look at this, Paul. Is this Finlay -- or whatever his name is?"

The officer read the description carefully. Then he advised, "This is right on the money all right. Except for a couple of things."

"What do you mean, Paul?"

"First of all, this description says that the man is 6' 2" tall. I don't think he was that tall. When he returned to untie me from that tree, he was wearing my uniform. And it fit him perfectly."

"What you're saying is that you're not that tall. That right?"

"Exactly! I'm only 5' 10" -- or 11" at best."

"I see your point. This merits some more investigation."

"And another thing -- there's nothing here about his accent."

"An accent? What kind of an accent?"

"The man who took my car had a deep *Southern* accent. Reminded me of a guy I once worked with -- born and raised in Tupelo, Mississippi."

"That's strange. Nobody's mentioned that."

"If he did make that phone call -- which I doubt -- maybe Dispatch can corroborate this. In any case, this guy was definitely a Southerner."

Danny turned to me and drawled, "Theem suth-on-ahs ah awll ahlike."

So are smart-aleck Rivertonians, I thought, but didn't say.

AT LIEUTENANT TOLNA'S REQUEST, Danny and I continued to work the case all Friday evening and the next day. Late on Saturday afternoon, Chief Remke called us all together to review our progress. All those playing key roles in the investigation were assembled at City Hall in the large conference room normally used for Riverton City Council meetings.

"Sheriff, since you and Lieutenant Tolna have been running this joint investigation, I suggest the two of you share the podium here today. If anyone else has additional information, share it after the sheriff and the lieutenant finish. One more thing -- what's discussed in this room today is confidential. Please keep it that way."

Lieutenant Tolna spoke first. "Because the case had its start here in Riverton and then spilled over into Sheriff Connors' jurisdiction, I'll go first. This crime was committed only 30 hours ago. It's not unusual to have *some* unanswered questions at this point in an investigation.

"But this case is a corker. Candidly we have very few *answered* questions -- even after applying the resources of almost every Riverton police officer, half the Sheriff's department, and our entire Crime Scene Crew.

"You'd think we'd be better off than we are. After all, we have ten people who saw the man who committed the crime. We have a written description of this fellow, but we can't even agree on his height or whether he speaks with a Southern accent.

"Furthermore, Officer Pryorski was the last person to see the man. And that was as he was being pushed -- bound and gagged -- into the trunk of his own patrol car. We have no fingerprints, no physical evidence, and, worst of all, this fellow has now seemingly vanished from the face of the earth. I'm no quitter -- but frankly -- I'm not sure what more we can do at this point in time."

"Chief, I'm in complete accord with Jeff," agreed the sheriff. "I hate to say it, but we've just come up empty on this one."

"Thank you for your candor, gentlemen," the chief replied. "That's what I expected you to conclude. And in your shoes, I might think the same thing. However, I'd like you to know that since I arrived here at the office this morning, I've received telephone calls from five members of the MEM board of directors -- and the president of MEM. I've also talked to four newspaper reporters -- three of them work for the largest newspapers in the state.

"Each of them posed the same question. When are we planning to request help from the Michigan State Police -- or the FBI -- or both? I believe I already know the answer, but I'll ask anyway. Would it do any good to ask for their assistance?"

"Chief, if I'd thought they could help us, I would have recommended it yesterday. I've never been too proud to ask for their help. But I honestly don't think they'd have any better luck. But, of course, that's your call, Chief."

"Hate to sound like a broken record here, but once again I completely agree with Jeff," added Sheriff Connors. "Wish I didn't."

The chief looked at everyone in the room and then observed, "I'm afraid you've overlooked a potent crime-solving resource, gentlemen. Anyone know what I'm talking about?"

No one said a word.

"I'd like to tap into that resource right now. Danny and Jase, what do you think about this case?"

Danny spoke first. "We're making a number of false assumptions."

I immediately concurred with Danny.

"Tell me, boys," Chief Remke implored, "What are those assumptions?"

"That's what we have to find out. So we need to start all over," Danny stated emphatically. "Right, Jase?"

"Once again, I completely agree with Danny."

Grinning from ear to ear, Chief Remke declared, "I couldn't have said it better myself. Get a move on, gentlemen."

6 LOSS OF A FRIEND

WHEN DANNY AND I ARRIVED HOME ON SATURDAY evening, we were simply exhausted. Before parting, we agreed that we needed a day of rest. Besides the MEM case had come to a standstill. In this situation, the best remedy is often benign neglect.

On Sunday morning, when we picked up Danny, he was cheerful and energetic. He proudly carried his new single-barrel, 20-gauge shotgun to our car where Dad placed it in the trunk with our two shotguns. Dad had purchased an extra supply of shells packed with size 8 shot as Uncle Raymond had suggested. Since the three of us had 20-gauge shotguns, we all could use the same shells.

The one thing I liked about skeet shooting is that you really got a chance to shoot. On a number of hunting days during the previous hunting seasons, Dad and I had loaded shells into our shotguns in the morning, hunted all day, and unloaded those very same shells when we returned to Grandma's house. When you hunted pheasants, rabbits, or especially squirrels, you never knew how many shooting opportunities would present themselves.

When we pulled into the driveway at the farm, Uncle Raymond and Grandpa were arranging the launcher and clay pigeon boxes on the strip of grass between Grandpa's vegetable garden and the east hayfield. As usual, Mick was barking and leaping into the air. The mere sight of shotguns generated his patented, acrobatic fits of enthusiasm.

Mom wished us luck and took the dishes she'd prepared to Grandma's kitchen. We men carried our shotguns and shells to the skeet-shooting site. We were agreeing on the sequence of shooters when Aunt Esther, my three cousins, and the *surprise guest* pulled into the driveway. Aunt Esther honked the horn furiously to signal her arrival.

"Well, I'll be. Look! It's Tom," Grandpa announced with delight. "Tom! Tom! What are you doing home?"

All of the women poured out of the kitchen onto the driveway. We men laid our shotguns on the grass and hurried over to join them. Uncle Tom was inundated with a mad flurry of back-slaps, hugs, and handshakes.

Because we peppered him with so many questions, he didn't bother to respond until the siege subsided.

"I was lucky enough to get a ten-day furlough. Came up by train. Arrived this past Friday morning. We thought we'd surprise everybody. Almost didn't work though. These two rascals were at the station when my train pulled in. They always seem to be in the right place at the right time," Uncle Tom joked as he scoured our heads vigorously with his knuckles.

"Boys, did you keep your promise not to tell?" Aunt Esther asked.

When we nodded yes, she rewarded each of us with a deep dive into her soft and massive bosom. When she'd finished crushing us with affection, she announced to Danny, "I made one of your favorite dishes. It's in the trunk. Why don't you take it to the kitchen? Put it in the heating oven -- you know -- in the top of the stove."

As Danny lifted the towel-wrapped baking dish from the car trunk, he pronounced, "Hmmm! It's macaroni and cheese, I bet."

And I bet Danny would consume a hefty sample before we began our skeet shooting.

While the men followed Grandpa back to the skeet-shooting site, the women followed Danny to the kitchen. He was in heaven, a place filled with food and adoring women.

"Oh, Jase. Stop a minute, please. I have a favor to ask."

Aunt Esther reached into her massive purse and withdrew a dollar bill and two rolls of film. "I'm taking a week off work -- so

I won't be coming into Riverton until Uncle Tom leaves. Besides after the robbery at MEM, nobody's doing anything there but talking about that. I'd like to have these pictures developed and printed before Uncle Tom leaves for Fort Benning next Sunday night. Could you please take these to Rick's tomorrow -- or the next day?"

"Sure, Aunt Esther. We're going downtown tomorrow. Danny and I are starting our new jobs at Graham Markets."

"That sounds wonderful, Jase. What'll you be doing?"

I told her all about our duties as floating stock boys. I also told her about our planned Nashville trip.

"That will be a great experience for Danny and you. I've always wanted to visit Nashville."

Finally Aunt Esther handed me the dollar bill. "Please have them make two sets of prints. One for Uncle Tom -- and the other for me. Tell them we'd like the standard print size. The dollar will more than cover the cost, but you keep the change and add it to your travel fund. Okay?"

"Okay! Okay, Aunt Esther. Thanks," I said, carefully stuffing the rolls of film and dollar bill down into my shorts' pocket.

She gave me another bear hug. Lucky me! I was one hug ahead of Danny. And the day was still young.

THAT SUNDAY THERE WERE six potential shooters, four men and two boys. With only one clay-pigeon launcher there would be a long wait between shooters.

Recognizing this, Grandpa volunteered to operate the launcher. In a modest way, he reminded us that he didn't need any practice to bring down a pheasant. And he was absolutely right. Owing to an unfortunate foundry accident, years before, Grandpa was as he put it, "Blind in one eye and can't see out of the other." Nonetheless, using his antiquated, wired-together, single-barrel 12-gauge shotgun with a missing trigger guard, he never missed a bird. During any season, Grandpa's total of bagged pheasants was greater than the combined total of the birds bagged by his two sons and two sons-in-law.

Uncle Tom also declined to participate. He explained, "The army requires all of us to go to the firing range once a week.

Frankly I've just about had my fill of shooting. It's certainly not something I'd choose to do when I'm on a furlough."

So that left Uncle Raymond, Dad, and me. Whether Danny could tear himself away from the food and females was anybody's guess. So we started without him. We agreed that each person would shoot four times per turn. This would give us ample opportunity to adjust our aim and hopefully pop the pigeon by at least the fourth shot.

I took the first turn. Because I was still breaking in my new shotgun, my accuracy wasn't up to the level it had been when I was using my old 4-10 gauge shotgun. In short, out of my first four pigeons, I just *scared* the first three. And I managed to put about two BB's into the fourth. Of course, my biggest fan didn't care. Mick always leaped, barked, and whimpered his encouragement no matter how well I did.

When Danny heard my first shot, he broke away from his harem and ran hurriedly toward us.

"Don't forget me. Wait up everybody."

Danny took the second turn. Believe it or not, Danny squarely nailed three out of his first four birds. It was downright disgusting.

"How many did you get, Jase?" he probed greedily.

"I can't tell you. It's a military secret."

"That bad, huh?" Danny knew me pretty well.

After Uncle Raymond and Dad both matched Danny's performance, I gave serious consideration to joining the *ladies league* in the kitchen.

Before my second attempt, Grandpa made a suggestion. "You're not used to shooting a gun this heavy, Jase. Hold it tighter against your shoulder -- to keep it steady -- and don't relax until after you've shot. That's it. You'll get more kick that way, but you'll be more accurate."

I followed Grandpa's advice and tied Danny's record.

"Yoo-hoo! Dinner's on the table. Come and get it, men," Aunt Esther hollered from the screened-in porch.

I followed the others' example of unloading my shotgun, breaking it, and laying it on the grass. Mick didn't like the idea that we were stopping. He tugged on my shoestrings and gave me one of his fake growls.

"We'll be back after dinner, boy," I told him as I scratched him under his chin. "You hungry?" He was hungry all right. Hungry for some more *hunting*. While the rest of us left for the kitchen, Mick dutifully stood guard over our shotguns, eagerly awaiting our return.

Now that's what I call dedication!

ON NORMAL SUNDAYS, WHEN all family members were present, the adults sat at the large dining-room table located in the front room. We children were relegated to the kitchen table and the extra card table that together provided seating for my five cousins, Danny, and me.

However, on this Sunday, because Danny and I had spent our time with the adults, we were invited to sit with them. I thought it strange that all five of my cousins seemingly had no interest in shooting.

Frankly I'd almost forgotten they were at the farm. After they heard Aunt Esther's dinner call, however, it was hard not to notice them. They poured out of the horse barn like rats leaving a sinking ship. I liked my cousins all right, but not more than shooting clay pigeons or hunting for real birds, like pheasants.

During a lull in the conversation, Mom broached a subject that placed Danny and me in a quandary. "We haven't seen much of Danny and Jase lately," she proudly announced. "They've been very busy, assisting the Riverton Police Department and the Chippewa County Sheriff's office on the MEM robbery case."

"Great! Give us the straight story," Aunt Esther demanded. "On Friday afternoon, the rumor mill kicked into high gear and it hasn't stopped. People called me at home all day yesterday. I even got a call this morning before we left home."

"I'm sorry, Aunt Esther. But --." I tried to tell her about the rules laid down by Chief Remke.

"Was it really an inside job? Was Mr. Hanna taken away in handcuffs? Is there a woman involved? Speak up, Jase. Give us the goods!"

"But Aunt --."

Danny raised his hand like a policeman directing traffic. In this case, Danny was telling me to stop. So I jammed on the brakes.

"Aunt Esther, there's something important that you should know."

"Oh, good! Is it -- ?"

Danny gave her the old stop sign too. Only he wasn't sitting across the table from her as he was in my case. That is to say, his stop sign was resting on the tip of her nose. It seemed to have gotten her attention. With her eyes crossed, she stared at his hand. Apparently it had some sort of hypnotic effect. She was in a trance.

"As I was saying," Danny continued, without removing his hand. "We're unable to discuss any of the details of this case. We gave Chief Remke our word. We can't tell you about the involvement of the Michigan State Police or the FBI. Or about the man who was dressed only in his underwear. Or about the attempts to bribe Jase and me with free lunches from the MEM cafeteria. Or the need to take the fingerprints of 37 suspects. We can't even tell about the key role that asparagus played in this case."

"Asparagus?" Mom repeated.

He paused and looked at me. "Have I missed anything, Lieutenant Addison?"

"No, you've just about covered everything, Chief Tucker. Well, perhaps there is one item you missed."

"What's that, Lieutenant?"

"You can't tell anyone about the wet deputy either."

"Good catch, Lieutenant!"

"Aunt Esther, there'll be not one word spoken about the wet deputy. Agreed?"

Having set the record straight, the chief locked his lips with his invisible key and threw it over his left shoulder.

Fini!

FOR THE FIRST TIME in Compton recorded history, we men decided to forego the usual after-dinner game of *Set Back*, choosing instead to return to our pursuit of that elusive fowl, the clay pigeon. When Mick saw us emerge from the house, well before our normal time, he immediately jumped into the air and performed a picture-perfect pirouette.

After the four shooters had each completed five turns, our accuracy was remarkably improved. Creating dust bunnies from three out of four clay pigeons became the rule, not the exception. We all felt proud of our shooting.

Dad called a time-out to inventory our remaining shotgun shells. While he sorted through the empty shell boxes on the ground, we all searched our pants and shirt pockets. Mick helped by sniffing the empty shells, which we had raked into a neat pile away from the launcher to keep them from being underfoot.

When the inventory was completed, Dad announced the result, "After all that shooting, I'm sad to say -- we only have eight shells left. I vote to give Danny and Jase the last pair of turns. Hearing no objection, who wants to go first?"

In a rare gesture of civility, Danny announced, "I'll be last. You go first, Jase."

"Ready, Grandpa."

Bam! Puff!
Bam! Puff!
Bam! Puff!
Bam! Puff!

I ended my day with a perfect four-for-four turn. Mick was ecstatic. Dad, Grandpa, and Uncle Raymond delighted. And Danny was determined. Determined to equal my feat.

Apparently Danny thought he needed help to increase his chances of matching my score. So he boldly requested, "Uncle Raymond, may I use your double-barrel shotgun for my last turn."

"Why - ah - sure, Danny. Why not?"

Danny hadn't used the double-barrel before so he wasn't familiar with its double-trigger. Uncle Raymond tried his best to show Danny how to use it, before loading the shotgun and handing it to Danny.

"Now, Danny. Grandpa, will only launch one pigeon so don't pull both triggers. If you do, you'll waste a shot. Do you understand?"

Danny nodded his head, impatiently.

I guessed that Danny regretted his decision to use a shotgun that he'd never fired before. But Danny could be very stubborn at times. And this was one of those times.

Proudly he raised the shotgun to his shoulder.

"Ready, Grandpa."

Bam! Bam! Puff!

"Nice shooting, Danny. Really nice. But I'm afraid you pulled both triggers. Do you want to go back to your single barrel?" Uncle Raymond asked gently.

"No, I'd like to try and get it right. Okay?"

"I understand. Here let me load it for you."

Uncle Raymond broke the gun and slipped a shotgun shell into each barrel. He closed the breech and handed it back to Danny.

"Are you all right, son?"

Danny nodded his head. He waited a second or two. With a look of determination, he glanced at me and then at Grandpa. Then he turned to study the probable path of the next pigeon. He was ready.

"Ready, Grandpa."

Bam! Puff!

"Nuts!" Danny yelled. "I did it again."

"No, Danny. That was perfect. One shot. One pigeon," Uncle Raymond assured him.

"I don't understand. I fired two shots again."

Danny brought the shotgun down from his shoulder.

"I know I shot two --."

Bam! Yelp!

Danny's second shot caught Mick at the top of his pirouette. The lifeless dog flipped in midair and fell heavily to the ground.

Grandpa and Dad ran to help poor Mick. But it was too late.

"Oh, my God, John. Oh, my God," Grandpa sobbed. His shoulders shook with grief.

"Come inside with me, Bill. We'll take care of everything. Let's go in through the back door," Dad advised, gently leading Grandpa by the elbow.

I turned my attention to Danny. From all appearances, he was in a state of shock. Uncle Raymond was trying to pry the empty shotgun from Danny's clenched fists as he consoled the boy.

Danny stared straight ahead with a ghostly, blank look in his eyes. Finally he unclenched his fists and the shotgun fell to the grass. Uncle Raymond made no attempt to pick it up. He focused only on Danny.

"Danny, this was an accident. You didn't mean it. It was just a terrible accident. But Mick had a long, wonderful life. And when this happened, he was doing what he loved to do."

"Come on, Danny. Let's go sit down on the running board."

Danny obediently sat down next to Uncle Raymond.

When I came closer, Danny looked up at me. Tears welled up in his eyes. His face twisted and he cried, "I killed Mick. Jase, I killed Grandpa's dog. What am I going to do, Jase?"

Looking down on Danny, I wanted to cry, but I couldn't. I felt intense anger, all directed at Danny. Inside I was screaming, *Mick was my dog too. You killed my dog.*

How can I ever forgive you, Danny?

A FEW SECONDS AFTER Grandpa and Dad entered the kitchen, the Compton women flew into action. Grandma and Aunt Betsy shouldered the burden of comforting Grandpa. Aunt Esther and Mom ran outside to take charge of consoling Danny.

When Dad emerged from the back shed, he was carrying Mick's bed and blanket from behind the kitchen stove. Uncle Tom was walking behind Dad with Grandpa's shovel over his shoulder. Dad walked to where Mick had fallen. He gently lifted Mick and placed him in his bed.

Then he turned to me and told me, "Your Grandpa wants you to bury Mick in the orchard -- under the first snow apple tree. He said you'd know the spot."

I certainly did know the spot. It's where Mick and I always rested after our long sessions of *cornstalk* hunting. I'd lean back against the smooth bark of the apple tree and close my eyes. I often fell asleep there with Mick curled up beside me, his chin resting on my leg. After my naps, I'd awaken to find Mick standing watch over me. He was a good dog and my loyal friend for years. Yes, I knew just the spot.

Dad and my two uncles watched silently as I carefully shoveled the black soil to shape Mick's grave. I dug a deep grave so nothing would disturb his remains and buried Mick lying in his bed, covered with his blanket. He was resting exactly as I'd always seen him on cold winter mornings, curled up behind the kitchen stove.

When I finished my work, Dad laid his hand on my shoulder and spoke softly, "Later, Grandpa and you can agree on a marker for Mick's grave."

"Yes, Dad. That's a good idea."

When we were about to return to the house, I saw Grandpa enter the orchard and walk toward us. When he reached us, I could see that he'd been crying. But he looked down on Mick's grave and told me, "Good job, Jase. Thank you."

He put his arm around my shoulders and the two of us stood there in silent meditation. Out of respect, the three men left us alone and walked back to the house.

After a while, Grandpa squeezed my shoulders and advised, "He was a good dog, Jase. And we'll both miss him -- very much. But he's gone and we have to move on."

"Yes, I know, Grandpa," I said bravely, trying not to cry.

"Now that Mick's resting, you have another job to do. Danny is hurting badly. You're his best friend. He needs you at his side."

"But he killed Mick, Grandpa!" I blurted out, releasing some of my anger.

"I know, Jase. I know. But even I share some of the blame. I know better than to put a loaded gun into the hands of a boy before he knows exactly how to fire it."

"Danny is stubborn, Grandpa. And he can't admit that he doesn't know things."

"You're right, Jase. Danny's pride was a factor. But so was that complicated double-trigger. And we adults failed to exercise good judgment. All these factors combined to cause this terrible accident. But now you have to go to him. He knows how much Mick meant to you. So tell him you forgive him. He needs to hear that from you, Jase."

"Have you talked to him, Grandpa?"

"He's lying on the backseat of your car, Jase. He told your mother that he'd never be able to face me again. After you tell him how I feel, he'll change his mind. Then I'll have a talk with him. Not today. Maybe next Sunday. Time always makes things better."

"We're starting our new jobs at Graham Markets tomorrow."

"That'll be good therapy. Give my best to my old friend, E.F. Graham. He'll be saddened to hear about Mick. Remember how Mick ran circles around those fancy hunting dogs that E.F. brought out here last fall. What a hunter that old Mick was!"

"He was the best, Grandpa. If you could keep up with him, that is."

Grandpa chuckled. I couldn't help but join him.

"That's the attitude. Let's not forget the good times we had with old Mick. Now go to Danny and help him snap out of it."

"I'll do my best, Grandpa."

But I would soon learn that my best wouldn't be good enough.

DURING OUR JOB INTERVIEW with Mr. Graham, he told us that our hours were, and I quote, "Not ideal for young fellas like you." When my alarm clock and my parents' alarm clock loudly rang out at exactly 3:00 a.m., the truth of his statement was forcefully driven home.

This unusually early morning reveille was a necessary evil. By my estimate, I'd need 45 minutes to wash up, dress, eat a good breakfast, and walk to the bus-stop bench with Danny. Mr. Samson agreed to pick us up there at precisely 3:45 a.m. Normally our family wake-up call arrived some two hours later, at 5:00 a.m.

To keep me company, my parents offered to get up when I did. Because this would only last for three weeks, they thought they could tolerate the revised morning routine for this relatively short period. But on this first morning, I'm sure they regretted their decision. In fact, all three of us had had a rough night.

The cause of our sleeping difficulty was Danny's stubborn refusal to be consoled. Instead of following Grandpa's suggestion of accepting our forgiveness for his part in the accident and then move on, Danny had chosen to wallow in his guilt and grief.

Frankly by the time we got home from the farm, I was ready to pop him one. In my opinion, he was playing it for all it was worth. And if there's one thing I can't stand, it's attention-seeking behavior.

When the Tuckers learned what had happened, they were extremely upset. After offering their condolences to Grandpa and me, they turned their attentions to Danny. They smothered him with words of compassion and empathy. But Danny adamantly refused to accept their gifts of comfort.

Because we'd seen this show before, we removed our sails from Danny's wind and headed for home where we were in for a fitful, short night's sleep.

As I thought back on Danny's behavior, I could feel the resentment rising in my chest. So I decided to put him out of my mind. That didn't work.

When he entered the kitchen, Danny hollered in a cheerful voice, "Anybody home?"

"Why are you so happy? I thought you were feeling sorry for yourself," I said sharply.

By this time, Mom and Dad were in the kitchen too. "I gotta hear this," Dad admitted to Mom.

"Jase -- Mr. and Mrs. A -- I was very wrong yesterday so I came here to apologize. It was rude and selfish of me to refuse your kind words of forgiveness and comfort. I hope you'll take me back as your friend.

"I know how much Mick meant to everyone -- but especially to Grandpa and you, Jase. I'm so sorry the gun went off. But as everybody told me -- and I refused to accept -- it *was* an accident. However, I shouldn't have been shooting a gun that I didn't understand. So I'm partially to blame. But there's nothing any of us can do about that now. Mick is gone. I only hope we can remember his wonderful qualities -- and try our best to put this behind us."

I glanced at Mom and Dad. Like me, they were wearing expressions of amazement. Dad was the first to speak. "Danny, I agree with every word you just said. And of course, we forgive you. You never have to worry about our friendship and affection for you. Without you in our lives, the world would be very dull. Welcome back, Danny."

With that, we formed a four-person hug-huddle in the middle of the kitchen.

A while later as we waited at the bus stop for Mr. Samson, I asked Danny why he had changed his attitude and accepted our caring concern.

His one-word answer was *Queenie.*

Then he explained. After we left the Tucker house the night before, Queenie made it abundantly clear to her family, as well as many residents in our part of town, that she *refused* to have a brother who was permanently stuck on the *pity pot.* To punctuate her position, she stormed out of the house, slamming the door so hard that the dishes rattled and clanked in the kitchen cabinet.

"I didn't want Queenie to be mad at me. And I didn't want you -- or your parents -- or any of the Compton family -- to be mad at me either. So I decided I needed to change my attitude. It doesn't mean I'm not awfully sorry about shooting Mick. I'd do anything to change it. But now, instead of being part of the problem, I need to be part of the solution."

"Part of the solution? What does that mean, Danny?"

"I think we ought to find Grandpa a new hunting dog. Pronto!"

Why hadn't I thought of that?

AS WE WAITED FOR Mr. Samson, I suddenly realized how much had happened since we'd met the man. Two events dominated my thoughts. The MEM payroll robbery and Mick's death. I was about to share this revelation with Danny when Mr. Samson's car pulled up. Right on time.

"Been waiting long, boys?" he inquired, with a friendly smile.

"Only a minute or two, Mr. Samson. We were watching the early morning sky. The sun will be up soon," I replied.

Danny added, "We're excited about coming to work for Graham Markets. Do you have any idea where we might be working today?"

"I don't know. But that's part of the fun of being a floating stock boy. I'm an authority on the subject. That was my first job with Graham Markets when I started about 20 years ago."

"Do you like the grocery business, Mr. Samson?" I asked.

"To be honest, Jase, I've never worked in any other business. I started as a stock boy during the summer and after school when I was a freshman in high school. Came here full-time after I graduated. Been here ever since. Frankly I love the grocery business. But that has a lot to do with Mr. Graham. I guess you'd say he's like a father to me."

When I first saw Mr. Samson on the day of our interview, I wondered if he were Mr. Graham's son. They were about the same size and build. Their haircuts were identical. And they wore the same conservative dark business suit, white shirt, and gray necktie. Their highly-polished black, wing-tipped shoes were also identical.

"You see I had no family. I was raised in the Dorcas Home in Riverton."

Because the Tuckers had lived in New Albany before moving into our neighborhood the year before, Danny was unfamiliar with many things known by life-long Rivertonians. "What is that, sir?" Danny asked.

"Some people would call it an orphanage. I was an orphan, Danny. So I just called it home."

A Dorcas Society is a local group of people, usually based in a church, with its original mission of providing clothing to the poor. In 1891, six ladies founded the Riverton Dorcas Society. They made clothes for Riverton's poor children and served them supper. Over the years, their day-care center evolved into a home accommodating 28 children who lived under the watchful eye of a matron.

Every week a chart was posted telling the children their chores for the coming week. A Riverton High School teacher, assisted by the boys, planted a garden to supply fresh fruit and vegetables. Local organizations supplied canned food and clothing. Monetary contributions from the Riverton Community Chest helped offset costs.

By the time we parked in the Graham Markets downtown parking lot, I'd concluded that Mr. Samson wasn't only a sharp businessman, but a fine individual as well. I could tell Danny felt the same way. We walked up the stairs to the main offices to see where we would be working on our first day.

"I don't think Mr. Graham mentioned it, but there may be occasions when none of our stores require stock-boy assistance. At those times, we may use you at our main warehouse where there are a number of jobs for fellows like you. I remember that I worked one entire summer there when I was in high school."

"We're very flexible, Mr. Samson," I assured him.

When we walked into the main offices, Mr. Samson approached the receptionist desk, where I saw the same tall woman with curly blond hair. She smiled warmly at us. "Congratulations. This is your first day at Graham Markets. Hope you'll be here for many more. We could use some bright young fellows like you."

It was a whole-hearted welcome. We thanked her profusely.

Then she got down to business. "Both boys are needed at New Albany #3. When you drive them over, you can stop by the new construction site. Mr. Graham is there, reviewing plans with the contractor. He wanted me to tell you he needs your opinion on a number of items. Says -- after that he's going to visit Mr. Morgan and the *new arrivals.*"

"Thanks, Sally."

We walked briskly back to the parking lot.

"Looks like you'll get a chance to say hello to Mr. Graham at the construction site. Save him the trouble of seeking you out. He likes to welcome new employees on their first day with the company. Then I'll drop you off at New Albany #3. That's the store located on New Albany Avenue near Courthouse Park."

"We shopped at that store -- last spring -- during the Camp-O-Ree in the park. Real nice manager there. Pretty too."

"You've got a good memory. And you've accurately described Miss Bridges. We only have three women managers in our stores. She was promoted temporarily when the war broke out. The store manager signed up for military service in the Army Air Corps. After the war, he's been promised his old job back. So she'll go back to being his assistant manager."

"We like working for beautiful women, Mr. Samson," Danny assured him.

From what I observed this morning, the only attractive woman that Danny ever worked for was Queenie. On second thought, he'd do most anything for Aunt Maude. And for Mom of course. And for Mrs. Tucker as well. Danny was definitely putty in the hands of any attractive woman.

When we pulled up to the construction site, I saw Mr. Graham's black Cadillac limousine.

"What kind of store are you building here, Mr. Samson? Seems like a lot of construction activity. Must be a big one."

"Well, boys. This is not a single store. This is a collection of stores. It's called a *shopping center*. This will be Chippewa County's first. When the war ends -- hopefully soon -- we expect to build a number of these centers in this part of the state. Of course, each will have a Graham Market."

"There's Mr. Graham. He's coming out of that construction trailer. Let's go and say hello."

As we walked across the grassy field toward the trailer, Mr. Graham spotted us and gave us a big friendly wave. We waved back. "Howdy, boys! I noticed you made it to work on time. That's always a good practice to follow, especially on the first day of a new job."

We thanked him again for our jobs and told him that we were looking forward to working with Miss Bridges today.

"She's dandy! You're going to like working with her."

We told him that we'd already done business with her and were very impressed. That seemed to please Mr. Graham very much.

"Mr. Samson, my meeting with the construction folks brought up a number of points that I think you should be in on. Why don't you run the boys over to #3 and drop back here? Probably take a half-hour of your time."

"Yes, sir. Sally mentioned that to me. Ready, boys?"

We said goodbye to Mr. Graham, and as we were leaving, he asked, "On Friday, you mentioned you were going to do some skeet shooting at the farm this past weekend. How'd you shoot? And how's my old friend, Bill Compton, doing? Did he shoot that old wired-together 12-gauge?"

Danny's face suddenly reddened. I thought he might burst into tears again. So I answered Mr. Graham's last question first. "Grandpa Compton wanted me to say hello to you. He was very pleased about Danny and me working for Graham Markets."

"That's good. That's real good. So how did you boys shoot, Jase?"

There was no avoiding it. "There was a terrible accident, Mr. Graham."

"Oh, Good Lord. Was anyone hurt?"

His question made me feel extremely uncomfortable. I didn't want to lie to Mr. Graham, but I was also concerned about Danny. He had just resumed his normal frame-of-mind. I feared he might backslide.

"Jase doesn't want to tell you, Mr. Graham. But I will. I accidentally shot and killed Mick. Grandpa Compton is real sad. So is Jase. And so am I. I couldn't sleep last night. Mick was such a good dog. And he really liked hunting for you that time."

I was concerned that Danny would be unable to break this news without crying. But I wasn't expecting the tears that welled up in Mr. Graham's eyes and flowed in profusion down his cheeks. Of course, both Danny and I joined him. And Mr. Samson reached for his handkerchief as well.

Without saying a word, Mr. Graham stepped toward us and wrapped his long arms around us. We just stood there for several minutes until we all had regained our composure.

Mr. Graham was the first to speak. "What a terrible, terrible loss you've experienced. I know your Grandpa Compton and you loved that old Mick. Heck, you were the only two people on earth that Mick would hunt for. And what a hunter he was. Ran circles around my dogs -- Ham and Bullet -- last year. Remember that, boys?"

"Yes, sir. Danny and I were just talking about that yesterday."

Mr. Graham knelt down and spoke to Danny, "I can't imagine how you must feel. I'd gladly change places with you if I could. You were brave to be so forthright when you told me. You must feel just awful."

"I did -- last night especially. I was so -- upset. I haven't even talked to Grandpa Compton yet. And I shot his dog -- I shot Mick."

Mr. Graham took Danny into his arms and held him for a few minutes until Danny's sobs subsided.

Danny pulled away from Mr. Graham and declared, "But Jase and I decided something this morning. We're going to find a new hunting dog for Grandpa Compton. Pronto!"

Upon hearing that news, Mr. Graham stood up and slapped us both on the back. "That's a terrific idea, boys. And I've got just the dog for him too. Or maybe I should say just the puppy -- or puppies -- for him. Isn't that right, Mr. Samson?"

"You're right six different ways, Mr. Graham. That is, six healthy, newly-weaned English setter puppies. Every last one pedigreed and registered -- sired from a line of champion show dogs. And with a father like Bullet and a mother like Lady Gray, they'll all be super hunting dogs. Yes, sir."

"Tell you what, boys. You let Mr. Samson take you to your jobs, but I'll pick you up at noon with Joe Morgan's truck. You remember him -- my dog trainer. He was there hunting with us last fall at the Compton farm."

We remembered him all right. He's the one who was treated to a shower delivered by a mother skunk. That event rather spoiled his day.

"We'll load up all half-dozen puppies. Then we'll drive over to Grandpa Compton's and let him pick out one. By jiminy, that'll cheer him up. You can count on that, boys."

Danny looked at me and winked.

"It's great to be a part of the solution. Right, Jase?"

WITHIN MINUTES OF LAUNCHING our grocery career, Danny and I agreed that Miss Bridges was the ideal store manager for us beginners. She was friendly and welcoming. She was patient and caring. Most importantly, she *taught* us rather than *told* us what to do. On top of it all, she was cheerful about it.

Miss Bridges inspired us to believe that lifting heavy cases of canned vegetables off the dusty top shelf, removing each can from its case, and affixing the price tag was a noble stepping-stone on the path to building America's economic strength and winning the war.

After processing our 10,000th case of cans, or so it seemed, I began to doubt my readiness for retail excellence. I knew Danny shared my feelings when he sat down on the floor and let out a huge, "Whew!"

Miss Bridges possessed an uncanny sense of timing. She came to our rescue with an offer we couldn't refuse. "Wow! I'm amazed by how much you boys have accomplished. You need to take a break. How about a cold bottle of pop?"

Didn't I say she was the ideal store manager for us beginners?

When we finished our break, Miss Bridges gave us another job. We went to the receiving platform and carried fresh produce into the store. Then she showed us how to prepare each variety of vegetable before placing it in the display cooler.

Danny and I caught on quickly. Carrying out Miss Bridges' instructions was tantamount to creating a work of art. And we had a wide variety of media from which to choose.

My first creation was a stunning *Mushroom Monet*. Danny topped me with his *Potato Picasso*. I countered with a clever *Radish Renoir*. But Danny took the trophy with his magnificent mixed-media piece, *Turnip-Lettuce Toulouse-Lautrec*.

When Miss Bridges opened the store at 7:00 a.m., newly-arriving customers were in awe of our artistic accomplishments. However, Miss Bridges didn't comment on our work. Perhaps our creations had rendered her speechless.

With such a variety of tasks, completed under the caring tutelage of Miss Bridges, our first day of work passed quickly. Before we knew it, Mr. Graham entered the store and greeted our mentor.

"How did my young friends perform today, Miss Bridges?"

"Superbly, Mr. Graham. They were quick studies and hard workers. They completed my entire list of tasks in record time. And, on top of that, they charmed customers with their creative vegetable displays."

I might be wrong, but I swear I saw Miss Bridges wink at Mr. Graham when she got to the vegetable topic. After all these years, I have yet to understand what would have caused that wink. Perhaps it was a speck of dust raised by the frantic pace of our work in the storeroom.

"That's fine, Miss Bridges. Glad to hear it. Well done, Jase. Well done, Danny."

Danny responded with his trademark bow from the waist. I swear both Miss Bridges and Mr. Graham snorted.

"Let's get you out of here before Miss Bridges changes her mind about your work."

We followed Mr. Graham out to a pickup truck parked in front of the store. The truck door panel read *Morgan Kennels*. A heavy canvas tarpaulin, tied at the corners, fit snugly over the bed of the truck. Mr. Graham untied one corner.

"Come take a peek, boys."

We stepped up onto the bumper and looked in. There on the straw-covered bed of the truck were six enchanting English setter puppies. Each puppy was marked differently with an assortment of black and white patches. Unlike their parents, the puppies' hair was short, silky-soft, and wavy. When the puppies saw Danny and me, they galloped toward us, stood on their hind legs, and licked our fingers furiously.

"How old are they, Mr. Graham?"

"Let's see. Well, Jase, they were weaned in their fourth week and that was three weeks ago. So they're about seven weeks old -- still on puppy mush."

"Puppy mush?"

"After they're weaned, we feed them puppy mush until their systems can tolerate adult dog food. They're just about ready to eat adult, dry dog food now."

Mr. Graham tied the canvas down and we hopped into the truck.

"Did either of you see a puppy you especially liked?"

"No, they're all cute," Danny said for both of us.

When we pulled into the driveway at the farm, Grandpa opened the screened-porch door and walked our way.

"Howdy, Bill. Terribly sorry to hear about Mick. That was one special dog. Yes, sir. We'll surely miss him come hunting season. Boys thought we should come out and cheer you up."

Danny opened the door and stepped out. Then he turned and ran toward Grandpa. The two of them hugged each other. Grandpa whispered something in Danny's ear. Danny nodded his head. Then they walked hand-in-hand toward the truck.

"Thanks for coming by, E.F. Why are you driving the kennel's truck? Something happen to your Cadillac?"

"The boys and I needed it to bring your birthday present."

"Birthday present? My birthday's on Ground Hog Day."

Mr. Graham got out of the truck and untied the tarpaulin.

"I guess we're a little early. Right, boys?"

"Or a little late," Danny added.

"Come here and take a look, Bill."

Grandpa peered over the side of the truck and grinned from ear to ear. Then he stuck his hand down among the bustling fur balls. Half the puppies licked his hand while the other half nipped and pulled his shirt sleeve.

"See one you like, Bill?"

"You can't be serious. Unless I miss my guess these are English setters that were bred to be show dogs. They're valuable property. I couldn't accept --."

"Grandpa, please do," Danny pleaded.

That seemed to move Grandpa. He nodded at Danny and looked back at Mr. Graham.

"Are you sure, E.F.?"

"You bet! I promised the boys. I can't go back on my word. Can I?"

Grandpa grinned again. Then he reached down and picked up one of the puppies. She was different than all the others. She had a black patch over each eye.

"This one is awful frisky. I'll choose her."

"Frisky! Grandpa, that'd be a good name."

"Frisky! You're right, Jase. Frisky it is."

Now it was Danny's turn to grin from ear to ear.

Later Mr. Graham dropped us off at the bus-stop bench. While he drove away, Danny and I watched until his truck was out of sight. Before Danny left for home, I asked, "What did Grandpa whisper in your ear?"

He said, "I forgive you, Danny. Have you forgiven yourself?"

"That's why you nodded, huh?"

"You bet!"

WORKING IN THE GROCERY business was very enlightening to Danny and me. As insiders, we learned the details of grocery store operations. But we also learned about the government-imposed process by which groceries had to be purchased during the war. This program was called *rationing*. Based on irate comments expressed by customers and declarations of utter frustration by grocery clerks, we quickly concluded that rationing, at the retail level, was universally despised.

Many unpopular government rules and regulations have been manifestations of noble principles, just causes, or strategic necessity. Rationing was one of these.

In the months leading up to Pearl Harbor, the Roosevelt administration implemented plans to refocus the American economy on preparing for and winning an all-out, multi-front war.

Transforming the undermanned and ill-equipped American armed forces to a state of readiness, capable of taking on the battle seasoned and well-equipped armies of Germany, Italy, and Japan, was an overwhelming challenge. This required full mobilization and a dramatic redirection of the consumption of foods and other goods from the civilian population to the military. To provide the necessary resources, stabilize prices, and curtail inflation during this massive military buildup, price controls and rationing were mandatory.

In the summer of 1941, the Office of Price Administration (OPA) was established to administer this program. In less than a year, some 8,000 local ration boards were in place.

Rationing altered the way of life of every American citizen. Common foods and durable goods disappeared from store shelves. In their place, a complicated, confusing, and burdensome system of rationing was imposed on everyone.

The OPA's plan was simple in theory. Rationing was a *dual currency* system in which rationed goods carried two prices, dollars and ration points, both fixed by the OPA. To purchase goods, consumers needed both the cash and the necessary ration points, denominated by red and blue tokens and stamps. The government undertook the massive task of issuing ration books to all Americans.

In early 1942, clothing rationing was restricted to silk, wool, rayon, and nylon. Silk, used to manufacture women's stockings, was needed to make parachutes. To achieve the look of hosiery, women turned to staining their legs and drawing a seam line down the back of their legs. Wool was needed for military uniforms, and different materials were substituted for civilian clothing. Because metal used in zippers was needed to make guns and bullets, small snaps, buttons, or ties replaced zippers. Design elements of clothing, including the length, cut, and material of styles, were greatly affected by these restrictions. Photos of women from the war years invariably show them wearing extremely short skirts and dresses.

In May 1942, car owners were limited to five gallons of gasoline a week. By the end of 1942, half of the automobiles had either a B sticker (supplementary allowance for war workers) or a C sticker (vital occupation such as a doctor). Truckers had a T sticker for unlimited amounts.

In May 1942, sugar was the first food item to be rationed. In November 1942, coffee was added to the list with one pound of coffee allotted for a five-week period. Meat, fruits, and vegetables were added, as were automobile tires. Shortly all areas of daily life were affected, including walking because even shoes were rationed in February 1943.

Rationing of canned vegetables and fruits, meats, cheeses, fats, oils, and canned fish followed. Canned fruit could require as many as a 100 points so most Americans restricted their menus to include this luxury only once during any four-week period. And canning your own fruit was difficult because sugar was on the ration list.

Citizens could earn more points while helping the war effort. The OPA instituted a system of rewarding extra ration points in exchange for certain household by-products. Kitchen fats and oils were used in the manufacture of explosives so these items were collected and taken to supermarkets and butcher shops where people were paid by the pound in cash and ration points.

In America, the unpopular rationing system ended shortly after victory over Japan in August 1945. In September, the rationing of gasoline and fuel oil, as well as enforcing a maximum speed limit of 35 mph, ended. In October, shoe rationing stopped. However, sugar rationing in some parts of the country continued until 1947. European countries were not as fortunate as the United States. Because most European economies had been destroyed during the war, rationing persisted for many years. In Great Britain, for example, some form of government rationing continued until 1955.

The question is, "On balance, did the OPA do a good job?" Objectively the correct answer is *yes* and *no*.

During the war, through our sacrifices (whether voluntary or coerced by the OPA), we Americans managed to outfit the most formidable military force in the history of the world. Equipped with up-to-date weaponry and adequate provisions, our fighting men did a commendable job.

On the other hand, there was one area where the OPA utterly failed. While unemployment virtually disappeared during the war, despite the OPA's efforts, food and fuel prices soared. Food prices rose 44 percent during the war years. It wasn't until after reestablishment of peacetime institutions that tools were put in place to control inflation effectively.

There were other unintended consequences of rationing. Hoarding of scarce foodstuffs and materials. Creating black markets to bypass the constraints of rationing. Smuggling of scarce goods across borders. Selling from army stockpiles by dishonest servicemen.

In summary, OPA should be given an A for effort and, at best, a C+ for results.

7 LONG PANTS

OUR THREE-WEEK STINT AS GRAHAM MARKETS' floating stock boys had finally come to an end. The first week had proved to be the most difficult for us. Rising at 3:00 a.m. and working eight hours a day for six straight days was extremely demanding, to say the least. Generally we arrived home at about 1:00 p.m. and were ready for bed within an hour or two. We simply weren't accustomed to the rigors of working real jobs.

Miraculously by the middle of the second week, we began to get used to the strenuous routine. Actually we started to enjoy ourselves. After our stamina improved, we looked forward to working for the various store managers and meeting the customers from diverse neighborhoods throughout Riverton and New Albany.

Our job was supposed to last exactly three weeks, but we neglected to take the Fourth of July into account. July 4, 1945, fell on Wednesday during the third week of our stint as floaters. Unlike previous Independence Days, Danny and I simply rested and, despite pressure from our families, did not participate in any of the usual festivities.

Because Graham Markets were closed on that holiday, Danny and I agreed to return for our final day of work on the following Monday that fell on July 9th. Fortunately on that last day, we returned to New Albany #3, where we'd spent our first workday under the friendly management of Miss Bridges.

Unbeknownst to Danny and me, with the help of Messrs. Graham and Samson, she'd planned a small lunchtime going-away party for us. In addition to hot dogs, potato chips, and strawberry pop, the menu featured a special cake from Tootie's Bakery, inscribed with the following words, *To Danny and Jase, Enjoy Nashville!* To finish our feast, we eagerly devoured a mouth-watering wedge of chocolate cake covered with a thick, powdered-sugar frosting.

After lunch, Mr. Graham presented our earnings along with a flurry of effusive compliments on how well we'd done our jobs. While his overly kind words were somewhat embarrassing to me, Danny had no difficulty accepting the full measure of Mr. Graham's kudos.

"Danny, here's your envelope. And Jase -- yours too. I agreed to pay you boys $72 each. But each of you'll find $80 in your envelopes. You deserve this bonus because of the glowing reports I received from more than two dozen store managers for whom you worked during the past three weeks. And many of our valued customers were impressed by your courtesy and helpfulness."

While Mr. Graham shook our hands, he added, "We want you to return to work for us again -- during school vacations and summers as well. Well done! And have a wonderful trip."

Danny looked at me and let out a *whoop!*

"Jase, now we can buy some long pants."

AFTER COMPLETING OUR LAST day of work, we finally allowed ourselves the luxury of a lazy afternoon. We sprawled out on the steps of our back porch and stared at the robins digging for worms in our Victory Garden.

We exchanged our Nashville postcards from JB and reread them for the umpteenth time. Mine showed a picture of Union Station where JB told us he'd meet our train. Danny's card had a picture of the Belle Meade Theater where JB's basketball camp group had gone to see *Anchors Aweigh*. We'd seen a preview of this new musical comedy at the Chippewa. Imagine Gene Kelly dancing with an animated *Jerry Mouse*! Lucky guy! We knew this film wouldn't come to Riverton before that fall.

By three o'clock, each of us had counted the money in our pay envelopes at least 14 times. It was more money than either of us had ever earned. Just the feel of the eight ten-dollar bills nestled in our envelopes was downright thrilling. We sat there on the steps, aglow with pride of our accomplishment.

"Let's see. How much money do we have now?" Danny inquired for the fourth time since we'd arrived home.

Without the hint of impatience, I answered Danny's question one more time. "We've got $16.93 leftover bait money. $80 from Mr. Gray. $160 from Mr. Graham. That's a total of $256.93 not counting the $100 reward money."

"Oh, yeah. That's right. Now I remember. We'll certainly be able to afford our round-trip tickets and spending money -- and even some long pants too. Right, Jase?"

"But don't you miss wearing shorts?" I asked in earnest.

"Naw! I'm used to wearing my scout pants. I like long pants. They make me feel more grown-up. How about you? Besides we can afford long pants now."

Danny was right about one thing. If we were going to wear long pants, we needed more than just the two pair of scout pants that we wore at Graham Markets. We were lucky to get two-day's use from a pair before our mothers had to wash them. You would be amazed to see the grimy dirt and dust that collected on unopened cartons of tin cans in the storage rooms of grocery stores. During the first week or so, until we learned how to avoid getting them so dirty, we changed our pants nearly every day,

Danny was right about another thing. Since we'd started working in long pants, I'd gotten used to them. In fact, I hadn't bothered to put on my shorts. Not even on Sundays or on the Fourth of July when we didn't work. Perhaps I associated long pants with our responsible jobs at Grahams. In any case, I felt more comfortable with Danny's position. I too felt more grown-up in long pants.

"Danny, if it's warm tomorrow, let's wear our shorts one more time. Then our mothers can wash both pairs of our scout pants. Okay?"

"Good idea. Whattaya wanta do for the rest of the day?"

"Later, we can listen to our favorite programs on the radio."

"Okay."

Needless to say there's not a whole lot to do when you're an unemployed, floating stock boy.

DURING WORLD WAR II, children's programming was broadcast in the late afternoons. Programs included thrilling serials with cliff-hanger endings guaranteed to keep young listeners tuning in day-after-day.

American children, fascinated with airplanes, fought the war in front of the radio. *Don Winslow of the Navy* took them into the thick of battle through stories of a naval aviator who bombed ships and attacked Nazis. *Hop Harrigan* was an eighteen-year-old free-lance aviator, who became a *big brother* to younger children. He flew bombing missions, engaged in dogfights with enemy airplanes, managed to escape from Nazi concentration camps, and dodged German bullets to rescue his friends.

On *Hop Harrigan,* children were urged to join the Junior Salvage Army and collect scrap materials that could be used to build military supplies. On *Terry and the Pirates,* children were invited to become good-luck mascots for the U.S. Army Air Corps by having their *names and messages go to war* in a B-25 bomber.

Superman, Dick Tracy, and *The Green Hornet* protected the American home front from saboteurs and spies. *Captain Midnight* and *Terry and the Pirates* went abroad to fight the enemy. All young radio listeners were urged to fight the enemy by buying War Stamps, by planting Victory gardens, by writing letters to servicemen, and by collecting scrap, used cooking fat, tin, rubber, and newspapers.

Radio stations also encouraged children to sell War Bonds and Stamps. Station WGR in Buffalo created a Commando Corps of young people who received armbands for identification and who could, by increasing their sales, move up the ranks from *Private* to *General.*

SUDDENLY WE WERE JARRED out of our reverie by the arrival of our crime-fighting partner, Lieutenant Tolna.

"There you are. I knocked on the front door but no one answered. So I thought you might be out here. Are you still working for Graham Markets?"

"Today was our last day. In the last month, we've earned $356.93 -- including the $100 reward. So we're going to buy some long pants and go to Nashville," Danny bragged nonchalantly.

"Well, that's impressive. I hear a lot of people wear long pants in Nashville. So you'll fit right in," Lieutenant Tolna told Danny.

"We heard that too," Danny responded, not catching the joke.

"I wanted to give you an update on the MEM robbery. The update is simple. We have no new leads or any significant additional information. I'm sorry to say that the case is right where it was three weeks ago. Nowhere! Naturally with all the effort we've put into solving this one, it's mighty discouraging. You fellas had any thoughts since we last talked?"

Frankly I'd nearly forgotten about the case. Since we started working at Graham Markets, Danny and I hadn't even talked about it, let alone had any fresh insights. But I didn't want to admit that to Lieutenant Tolna.

"We haven't come up with anything either. But with our job ending, maybe we can spend more time on the case," I suggested, glancing at Danny for approval.

Upon hearing my words, Lieutenant Tolna shrugged his shoulders and admitted, "That doesn't surprise me. You've been awful busy, and this is a real tough case to figure out. Well, let me know if you have any breakthroughs. I'll keep you informed from our end."

After Lieutenant Tolna left, Danny articulated my feelings exactly. "We've really let Lieutenant Tolna down. Let's try to break this case before we leave for Nashville. You with me, Jase?"

"I couldn't agree more. Let's go back over the details one more time."

We spent the rest of the afternoon reviewing the facts of the case. But at the end of that process, we were no closer to having an answer than when we began.

"Jase, let's go down to Pete's for a bottle of pop. Maybe that will help."

An hour later we returned to the back porch. At Pete's, we had each enjoyed two bottles of strawberry pop, perused the recently-arrived comic books, and had an interesting conversation with Pete himself. But we were still stuck.

"Danny, do you think this case is solvable?"

"Right now it sure doesn't look like it. Have you ever heard of a perfect crime?"

"Not until now, Danny," I admitted. "Not 'til now."

OUR WORK AT GRAHAM Markets had not only been hard labor and long hours, but it had greatly disrupted our normal routine. One of the aspects of daily life that suffered was my keeping abreast of progress of the war in the Pacific.

Each morning at breakfast, Dad briefed me on the latest war news, but my sleep-deprived brain wasn't very receptive and sometimes forgot the details. But I do remember a few significant pieces of good news during this period.

On June 18th, a few days after we started working, Japanese resistance ended in Mindanao in the Philippines. And on July 5th, the liberation of the Philippines was announced. General MacArthur had indeed returned, and the islands were now in American and Filipino hands.

During World War II, President Roosevelt coined the name *United Nations,* referring to the 26 nations who committed their countries to continue fighting together against the Axis Powers of Germany, Italy, and Japan. Representatives of 51 countries met in San Francisco to draw up the United Nations Charter that was signed on June 20th.

There was also good news from Okinawa. On June 22nd, the Japanese resistance had ended. At great cost, the Allies finally occupied this strategically important Japanese island. Okinawa, a Japanese Prefecture, was located in the Ryukyu Islands a mere 350 miles southwest of the Japanese home islands. The four Japanese airstrips on Okinawa were required to support the assumed-to-be inevitable invasion of Japan itself.

Launched on April Fool's Day in 1945, the invasion of Okinawa, code-named *Operation Iceberg*, was the largest amphibious landing of the Pacific war. Some 300 American warships, 1,200 landing craft, and 187,000 American and British soldiers and sailors took part in the operation.

Okinawa was defended by 117,000 battle-seasoned Japanese soldiers. During the battle, Japanese kamikaze pilots made nearly 1,500 suicide attacks by crashing their explosive-laden airplanes into American ships. In all, 79 of our ships were sunk, killing 5,000 American sailors. The Japanese lost 16 ships including the world's largest warship, the battleship *Yamato*.

Like the battle for Iwo Jima, the Japanese defenders fought to the death. Over 100,000 Japanese soldiers were killed and only 7,000 were captured. American casualties were high as well with 12,513 killed and 38,916 wounded. Of the 435,000 Okinawan citizens, nearly 150,000 were also killed. During the three-month battle, 90% of the buildings on the island were destroyed.

Both sides suffered extraordinarily heavy losses during this bloody battle.

NOT HAVING TO ARISE at 3:00 a.m. lifted a heavy burden from my shoulders. Ironically, however, the expectation of a normal night's sleep was so exciting that the very thought of it kept me awake. I have no idea when I finally dozed off.

The next morning Danny noisily tromped into my bedroom and roughly shook my shoulder. Thinking I was dreaming, I simply rolled over and treated myself to another breath of ether.

Danny shook me again, harder this time, and ordered, "Come on! Get up! It's almost eight o'clock. I've had three breakfasts already -- and I've run out of things to say to your mother. **Get up!!!**"

While that did the trick, I couldn't seem to open my eyes. They were glued shut with crusty *sleepy bugs* as Dad called them. When I finally managed to pry my lids apart, there stood Danny in the blinding morning sun that streamed through my bedroom window. It was indeed at least eight o'clock. In my fogginess, I failed to realize that he was wearing his old familiar uniform, the centerpiece of which was his crumpled tan cotton shorts.

"You wore your shorts! I thought long pants made you feel grown-up," I observed somewhat disapprovingly.

He countered by reminding me, not so kindly, of our agreement to wear shorts on this, our first morning of unemployment.

The cobwebs finally cleared. "Oh! Yeah. That's right! Then I'll wear shorts too."

I had no difficulty locating them. They were hanging on the peg inside my closet door, right where I'd hung them nearly four weeks earlier. As I slipped them on, I felt some strange objects in the left pocket. I reached in and pulled them out. I was shocked by what I saw. "Oh, no! Aunt Esther's film! And her dollar bill," I cried. "I completely forgot about this!"

"She's going to squash you, Jase!"

"But we saw her at the farm -- on two Sundays -- since she gave me this film. Why didn't she say something? I just can't believe this."

"Nothing to worry about. She probably forgot. But we can't cry over spilt water. Let's --."

"Milk," I interrupted.

"Milk? Good idea. Let's get a glass of milk -- after that we can catch the bus down to Rick's Grill."

"No, I meant -- it's spilt *milk*."

"Jase, you're not making sense. I don't think you're awake yet. Let's go," Danny directed as he headed for the kitchen.

Before following him, I extracted four nickels from my bank for our bus fares to and from Rick's. When I reached the kitchen, Mom turned to me, "Don't be too hard on yourself, Jase. We all forget things. Danny has the perfect solution. Catch the next bus to Rick's, and you'll have the pictures well before we go to the farm this coming Sunday. Okay?"

With his arms folded, Danny haughtily expressed his approval by nodding his head as Mom spoke.

Sometimes he can really be a jerk, I thought to myself. But I quickly dismissed my negative thoughts. After all, he had come up with a sound plan, on the spot, before I was barely able to speak.

Located next door to the Chippewa Trails bus station, Rick's was a combination restaurant, drugstore, and travel shop. In fact, there was a double-glass door between it and the passenger waiting room. People waiting for buses could enter Rick's to browse for books and magazines, postcards, playing cards, or stationery in the *Travel Needs* area of the store. Local riders found it a convenient place to have prescriptions filled or film developed and prints made. And Rick's *Fountain Grill* offered some of the best food in Riverton. Serving sizes there were colossal and prices were downright cheap.

When we entered the store, Danny held out his hand. I dutifully handed him Aunt Esther's rolls of film and the dollar bill. After patting me on the shoulder, he made a beeline for the *Photo Center*.

Behind the counter, an extremely attractive young woman smiled and asked, "How may I help you, Mister Tucker?"

Her pulchritude and recognition of Riverton's renowned hero combined to deliver a sneak punch to Danny's stomach. He stammered, seemingly incapable of completing a sentence. While he sputtered and spat, I walked up beside him and lifted the film and dollar from his hand.

"We need to have this film developed and two sets of standard-size prints of the 24 pictures on these rolls. And please put each set of prints in a separate package. When may we pick up the prints? Do we pay now?"

"I understand your needs completely, Mr. Addison. The prints will be ready -- first thing -- on Friday morning. You can pay us at that time. The cost is 79 cents. Any other questions?"

"Just one. How do you know our names?"

"Oh, I've been acquainted with you for more than a year now. You see, my regular job is photo technician at the *Riverton Daily Press*. I just work here part-time, when someone is out sick or on vacation. I developed all the photos of Danny and you that appeared in the paper. Oh, yes. I know all about you two boys and all your heroic deeds."

When she gave me a wink and a smile followed by a soft pat on my hand, I lapsed into a *catatonic* state of my own.

8 TIPPING POINT

SINCE WE WERE EAGER TO HAVE AUNT ESTHER'S
photos in hand as soon as possible, Danny and I arrived at the
Photo Center well before 7:00 a.m. on Friday morning. Rick
had just opened the store and he welcomed us as we entered.
Apparently we were his first customers of the day.

"I don't usually handle photo department business. But let's see
if I can help you fellas." Rick pawed through a stack of completed
orders laying on the counter. "I'm looking for two identical
packages of prints under your name. And they were to be ready
this morning. Right, Jase?"

"That's right, Mr. Rick."

"These orders were finished last evening for pick up this
morning. They haven't been filed alphabetically in the drawer yet.
I'll have to sort through the whole stack. It'll only take a second."

I nodded my head and watched as he rummaged through
the film packages. When he reached the bottom of the stack, he
stopped and shook his head.

My spirits plunged to the soles of my shoes.

"Oh, wait. I bet I know where they are," he continued, opening
the wide drawer under the counter. "Let's see *A* for Addison. Yep!
Here they are. She must have done these on Wednesday evening.
Let's see. Yep! That'll be 79 cents exactly, Jase."

I reached into my pocket for Aunt Esther's dollar bill.

"But before you pay, why don't you sit down at one of the booths and go through them? Make sure they're just what you were expecting."

"Thanks, Mr. Rick. Sounds like a good idea. These are photos that Danny took of my Uncle Tom's homecoming at the train station. He came home on furlough from Fort Benning -- about a month ago. I -- ah -- misplaced the rolls of film. Just found them the other day. So we do want to be certain they're in good shape before giving them to Aunt Esther."

We took a seat together at the nearest booth. Each of us opened a package. I was pleased to see that the photos were crisp and clear. And they were numbered and packed in the order they were taken, starting with the first roll and ending with the second.

"Danny, you took some fine shots that day. You're a natural. Had you ever used a camera before?"

"Nope. Just lucky I guess."

"I can see you're doing a careful job, boys. Thought you could use a little energy boost," Rick said as he set two steaming mugs of hot chocolate on the table. "On the house. Take your time and make sure you're completely satisfied with the photos."

We thanked our host profusely, took a deep sip of the rich beverage, wiped the chocolate moustaches from our top lips, and continued to examine each shot. Not that it was planned, but as we went through the 24 photos, we found ourselves looking at the same photo at the same time and sharing our observations.

When we turned over photo #24, I gasped. My heart began to race.

Danny stood up and yelled, "Holy Crow! Do you see what I see, Jase?"

"I certainly do! Mr. Rick, do you have a magnifying glass?"

"Sure. Let me dig it out from behind the counter. Here it is."

Danny and I took turns using the magnifying glass to examine photo #24. When we finished, I nodded my head at Danny who broke into a broad grin. "Let's get over to police headquarters -- right now, Jase!"

"After you, Dr. Watson!"

"Righteo, Mr. Holmes!"

We gulped down the last of our hot chocolate, carefully repacked the photos, and headed for the cash register. We returned the magnifying glass, paid the 79 cents, thanked Mr. Rick over and over for the hot chocolate, scurried out the door, and ran all the way to the police station.

When we arrived, we breathlessly informed the desk sergeant that we must see Lieutenant Tolna. We insisted it was very important.

"Boys, he's in the field investigating a hit-and-run auto accident at the moment. He shouldn't be long. Dispatch can reach him immediately if this is really urgent."

Danny took charge. "Thank you, Sergeant. Would you please have Dispatch radio the lieutenant the following message? *Jase Addison and Danny Tucker are waiting for you at police headquarters with the evidence needed to solve the MEM robbery case.* And Sergeant, you might want to radio the same message to Sheriff Connors and Chief Remke."

The sergeant's eyebrows nearly leaped off his forehead. Without a word, he turned and hurried to the radio room. We heard Clint, the radio operator, let out a whoop!

Danny shook his head and announced, "Mr. Addison, I have a feeling this is going to be a very good day."

"You're right as rain again, Mr. Tucker."

THE DESK SERGEANT SUGGESTED we wait in the Riverton City Council conference room where we'd met before. So we made our way down the hall and took our *regular* seats at the highly-polished, cherry-wood conference table. We sat silently, both of us deep in thought.

After a few minutes, Danny revealed what was on his mind. "Jase, I got to thinking. Maybe this picture isn't enough evidence to solve this case. I think it is, but maybe we jumped the gun."

Danny's words caused me to wince, because I was thinking exactly the same thing. Suddenly my optimism was crushed by the ponderous weight of self-doubt. I looked at Danny and nodded my agreement.

"It's too late to worry about it now, Jase. When the others arrive, let's just show them what we have and let them decide."

Within minutes, we heard a chorus of excited voices in the hallway. The conference door banged open and in walked Lieutenant Tolna, Chief Remke, and Sheriff Connors. They were all smiles as they shook our hands and patted our shoulders.

"All right, boys. Don't keep us waiting. Tell us what you've got," Lieutenant Tolna instructed.

I answered him by shoving both copies of photo #24 across the table. After examining it carefully, they turned to us with expressions of excitement mixed with confusion.

Then they peppered us with a flurry of questions. After an approving nod from Danny, I answered for both of us.

"Exactly where was this picture taken?"

"In the MEM parking lot. The patrol car shown is in the driveway leading to the MEM main entrance."

"When was it taken?"

"About 11:00 a.m. on Friday, June 6th. A few minutes before the MEM payroll robbery."

"Who took this picture? How did you boys come into possession of it?"

"Aunt Esther asked Danny to take pictures of Uncle Tom's homecoming -- from Fort Benning -- at the train station. Then she requested that we have these prints made. We just picked them up this morning at Rick's. This picture was the last one in the batch."

"You mentioned the train station, but why was Danny taking pictures at MEM?"

"Because Aunt Esther works at MEM, her car was parked in the lot there. Just after this shot, Uncle Tom drove her car home. As Danny and I were walking home, Lieutenant Tolna picked us up. We were on our way to lunch at the Chop Suey Diner when he was dispatched to investigate the MEM robbery."

Chief Remke's final questions were the clinchers. "Jase, what made you boys think this picture would solve the MEM robbery case?"

"Well, the driver of Officer Pryorski's patrol car is wearing a Riverton police uniform. He also fits the MEM security guards' description of the robber."

"How did you know this is Pryorski's patrol car?"

"The number on the back fender is 125 -- the same as the number on the car the deputy found on Riverton Road."

"Right. Anything else, Jase?"

"In the backseat, you can see Officer Pryorski peering out the window -- still wearing his uniform. When this picture was taken, he was supposedly tied to a tree in Trumble Park, wearing nothing but his underwear. If Officer Pryorski was still wearing his uniform, the driver wasn't wearing Officer Pryorski's uniform as he told us."

"So what do you conclude from this evidence, Jase?"

"Officer Pryorski obviously lied to us. So I believe these two men planned and committed the MEM robbery together. The MEM paymaster told us he suspected this was an inside job. Officer Pryorski was very familiar with the MEM payroll procedure. Apparently he's our *insider*."

The chief thumped the conference table. "Dang! If I don't agree with you. Well done, fellas! Well done! I was beginning to think we'd never get a break on this case."

Turning to Lieutenant Tolna and Sheriff Connors, he asked, "Do you gentlemen have any other observations or conclusions?"

Both men agreed that our discovery of the photograph had indeed broken the case wide-open. But each cautioned that much more investigation and evidence-gathering was needed to insure a conviction. Everyone concurred that before confronting Officer Pryorski, his partner-in-crime had to be identified, and a connection between him and Pryorski had to be established. If Pryorski was unaware of our suspicions, he might become overly-confident and slip up, leading us to his partner.

Danny and I were greatly relieved that our discovery had garnered so much unabashed enthusiasm.

"Gentlemen, we need to involve the city attorney in this case," Chief Remke advised. "But he's tied up in court this morning. Why don't we meet back here this afternoon at two o'clock? Meantime, boys, we need enlargements of that photograph. If you could leave the negative with us, we'll return it this afternoon."

As we were departing, Chief Remke reminded us, "Needless to say, everything we have discussed here is Top Secret. Please keep it just among the five of us. We can't tip off Pryorski."

We all agreed and bid our farewells. Lieutenant Tolna offered us a ride home. We accepted, saving a nickel apiece in the process.

When he pulled up at our house, he joked, "I don't know how you boys do it. But if you don't knock it off, I'll go broke buying you lunches."

"Not a problem, Lieutenant Tolna. I'll just pay another visit to Mr. Hanna. I'm sure he'll want to give me some more free passes for the MEM cafeteria."

BY REPUTATION, CHARLES PETERSON was a thoroughly competent, no-nonsense lawyer. As Riverton's city attorney, not only did he insure that all laws and regulations passed by the city council met the highest legal standards, but he also acted as Riverton's prosecuting attorney in criminal cases. In court, he earned a well deserved reputation as a formidable opponent to any and all defense attorneys who opposed him there. He seldom lost a case, owing in large part to his meticulous process for collecting, organizing, and presenting evidence and for his careful vetting and preparation of witnesses for the prosecution.

Because Danny and I never had any dealings with Mr. Peterson, we were completely unprepared by his take-charge manner. The moment the meeting began, he quickly assumed the role of titular chairman and quickly demonstrated the strength of his leadership style. Remarkably Chief Remke, Lieutenant Tolna, and even Sheriff Connors immediately relinquished control of the proceedings to this man.

Not long after our *chairman* called the meeting to order, I began to feel uneasy about the *balance of power* in the room. Danny's silence was a dead giveaway. I prepared myself for the inevitable clash of the titans, and I didn't have long to wait.

Ignoring Danny and me, Mr. Peterson addressed his first comments to the three men in the room. "Gentlemen, I'm uncomfortable with the presence of these boys in this meeting. Despite their reputations as amateur sleuths, they're not law-enforcement officers. I fear a defense attorney might question the appropriateness of their presence. And I want to avoid having to explain or defend this to a judge and jury, if and when this case goes to trial."

Before any of the three men could react to Mr. Peterson's words, Danny launched his counterattack.

"Chief Remke, do you have the enlargements of photograph #24?"

"Yes, Danny. Here they are."

"I think we made a mistake in allowing you to do that. Technically that photograph belongs to Aunt Esther. So we better collect those enlargements and be on our way."

"But Danny -- I," the chief sputtered.

Turning to Sheriff Connors, Danny continued, "Sheriff, because the escape vehicle was recovered outside city limits, perhaps this case rightly falls under your jurisdiction. Do you think the Chippewa County attorney would be interested in seeing this photograph? I'm sure Jase and I could convince Aunt Esther to turn it over to him."

Then Danny ordered, "Let's go, Jase."

"Whoa! Whoa! Wait a minute, Mr. Tucker. First of all, I'm sure that we could subpoena the photograph and obtain the evidence that way," Mr. Peterson asserted. "So why don't you --?"

Ignoring Mr. Peterson, Danny turned to me. "Jase, are you absolutely sure of the time and date that photo was taken? If I were called as a witness in court, I'd have to say I honestly don't recall. Perhaps my memory would improve if the Chippewa County attorney asked me."

Mr. Peterson was visibly upset.

"Let's go, Jase," Danny barked again.

Chief Remke handed me the envelope of enlargements, and I rose from my chair. Danny and I marched solemnly toward the door.

Then Lieutenant Tolna intervened. "Jase! Danny! Boys, please come back here and sit down."

Turning to Mr. Peterson, the lieutenant asserted, "This is my case and I say the boys stay."

"I agree," boomed Chief Remke.

"I also agree," chimed in Sheriff Connors. "Let's get on with this meeting. I have work to do back at my office."

Mr. Peterson's face turned beet red. He paused for several seconds and finally took a deep breath. "Now I know why you two fellas are so successful at solving cases. I take my hat off to you. And I humbly apologize for treating you so shabbily. I was wrong and I hope you'll forgive me. I'm now convinced that we need you on this team if we're going to convict these two rascals."

He stood up and walked toward us with his hand extended. We shook it and took our seats.

Danny smiled. "Any chance of getting a snack or some pop before we continue?"

THE ENTIRE TEAM READILY agreed to adjourn for a much needed time-out. We made our way to the police lounge where vending machines offered cold pop, candy bars, and peanuts.

Since access to the lounge was normally restricted to members of the Riverton Police Department, Danny and I had never been there. The carpeted room was furnished with comfortable dark-brown, leather arm chairs and coffee tables stacked with copies of the *Riverton Daily Press* and magazines including the *Police Gazette*. In one corner stood a well-worn card table covered with poker chips, decks of playing cards, and boxes of wooden kitchen matches. On a counter against the wall near the door, set a steaming coffee pot and several cartons of various doughnuts, apparently a staple in a police officer's diet.

"Here, boys. This is on me," Mr. Peterson declared as he handed each of us several nickels from his pocket.

We thanked him and made our selections.

Upon returning to the conference room, our first order of business was to finish our snacks and to reestablish rapport. This latter objective was accomplished by discussing a topic on the minds of everyone in the room. Would the Detroit Tigers take the American League pennant and finally make it to the World Series this season?

Later I would learn that on October 10, 1945, at Wrigley Field, the Detroit Tigers won Game 7 of the World Series by defeating the Chicago Cubs by a score of 9 to 3. In the *Detroit News*, H. G. Salsinger reported that "Detroit beat the Cubs with TNT, meaning Trucks, Newhouser, and Trout, and they beat them twice with 'N.'"

After service in the Navy, Virgil Trucks returned to the Tigers on the last day of the regular season and was the winning pitcher of Game 2 of a doubleheader. Hal Newhouser won Games 5 and 7 in the World Series, including the last game. In Game 4, Dizzy Trout beat the Cubs by a score of 4 to 1 on a five-hitter. He went 1 and 1 in the Series with an ERA of 0.66.

This was the Tigers' second World Series championship since their entrance into the American League in 1901. Two Tigers, Hank Greenburg and Tommy Bridges, were the only players remaining from the winning 1935 team. Left fielder Greenberg had missed four seasons while he served in the military, but he rejoined the Tigers after his discharge on July 1, 1945. In his first game, he hit a home run. In the 9th inning on the last day of the regular season, Greenberg clinched the American League pennant by hitting a grand-slam home run.

In the 1945 season, Detroit pitcher Hal Newhouser, also known as *Prince Hal*, won 25 games and was named the American League's Most Valuable Player for the second consecutive season. Newhouser and Greenberg were the only two players from the 1945 team elected to the Baseball Hall of Fame.

When Mr. Peterson called us to order, it was clear that his tone and tenor had changed dramatically. He suggested that each team member offer a plan for moving forward with the investigation.

As a gesture of reconciliation, he suggested Danny share his thoughts first.

"Thank you, Mr. Peterson. I've thought a lot about this question. Our first priority must be to identify, locate, and arrest *Finlay* -- or whatever his name is. There are two ways to go about this. First, we could shadow Officer Pryorski, hoping he'll lead us to Finlay. Or we could confront Office Pryorski and *induce* him to reveal Finlay's identity and whereabouts.

"However, we have to be realistic. It's been nearly a month since the robbery so there's a good chance that Finlay is already on the lamb. If so, it may be difficult to locate him regardless of which plan we follow."

"That's sound thinking, Danny," Mr. Peterson observed. "Who wants to add to Danny's thoughts?"

Chief Remke replied, "If Officer Paul Pryorski were not a good officer, I wouldn't trust him. So I would definitely favor the first plan. However, having hired Pryorski and observed his performance for the past four years, I'm certain that he's no bad apple.

"His references from his teachers, scout master, priest, and even Sheriff Connors were impeccable. And his performance reviews from Lieutenant Tolna have been the best in the department. Evidently some strong external factor must have intervened to cause him to behave in a manner that runs totally contrary to his character. So I too vote for the second plan. Let's get him in here and find out why he did this."

"Lieutenant Tolna, you've worked with this man on a daily basis for the last four years. What's your opinion?" inquired Mr. Peterson.

"The chief is right. Officer Pryorski in my opinion is -- or perhaps *was* -- the best police officer in the department. I was about to recommend him for promotion to corporal. I planned to make him assistant shift commander for the midnight shift. The reason for the promotion and new assignment is that he's highly respected and well-liked by all his peers. For example, he regularly stays after hours with the other bachelors on the force, playing poker in the lounge. They have a real fraternity built solely around the trust and friendship they share with Pryorski. I definitely vote for the second plan."

"Jase, what's your take on this matter."

"Based on how well the robbery was planned and executed, we know that Finlay is a pretty smart fellow. So -- regrettably -- I suspect he's long gone by now. However, if I'm wrong and he's still in the area, I would vote for the second plan. Bring Officer Pryorski in as soon as possible and *induce* him to lead us to Finlay. Time is of the essence."

"Sheriff, you wrote an extremely positive letter of recommendation for Pryorski," Mr. Peterson stated. "Why was that?"

"I'm glad you called on me last, because frankly I'm totally biased when it comes to Paul Pryorski. You see I've known Paul since he was a young boy. The Pryorski family farm adjoins my brother's farm, located -- I'm somewhat sorry to say -- on Riverton Road not more than a half-mile east of where Paul's patrol car was found by my deputy."

"So there's little doubt that Pryorski knew about the lane leading to the asparagus patch where we suspect Finlay's car was parked. Is that right, Sheriff?"

"I'm afraid so, Mr. Peterson."

"Thanks for that clarification. Please continue."

"Paul's father very much wanted his son to take over their farm, but Paul always wanted to be an officer of the law. When his parents died after long illnesses that ate up most of the family savings, Paul asked my brother if he'd be interested in purchasing the farm. Paul confessed that he really needed the money. So, about three years ago, my brother bought the farm at a fair price. Paid Paul several thousand dollars in cash -- with the help of a bank mortgage. Paul leased the family home from my brother, and he still lives there."

"Another question, Sheriff. With money in the bank and a bright future in law enforcement, it'd appear that Officer Pryorski is rather well-fixed. Is that right?"

"That's correct, Mr. Peterson. A career in law enforcement was Paul's life-long ambition. He worked hard to learn all he could, starting at an early age. When Paul was in high school in New Albany, he'd come over to our office after school. He took out trash, fetched coffee, ran errands -- anything to make himself useful. He did this almost every day all during high school.

"Believe me he was a pleasure to have around. He was polite, upbeat, and bright. Everyone liked him. I guess you could say that he became our *intern*. Because he'd skipped taking the school bus, I arranged for one of the deputies on patrol to run him home every evening so he wouldn't miss supper.

"Despite the enormous amount of time he spent at our office, he got straight As all through school. Somehow he even managed to earn himself an Eagle Scout badge. To top that off, his priest selected him as lead altar boy at church. I don't know how he found time to accomplish all he did. But that's Paul for you."

"If that's the case, why didn't you hire him, Sheriff?" Mr. Peterson wondered.

"Unfortunately, at the time he graduated, we didn't have a single opening. My deputies were all young men. And as both family men and officers of the law they were exempt from the military draft. To top it off, they're an exceptionally bright and professional group of men. So I don't expect any of them to ever be fired because of sub-par performance.

"Since I knew it'd be years before we had a job for Paul, I called Chief Remke to see if he had any openings. The chief had just lost two good men -- resigned to enlist in the army. I advised Paul to apply and sent the chief a glowing letter of recommendation. The way I figured it, our loss was Riverton PD's gain. At least Paul was in the profession he loved.

"I still stand by that recommendation, Mr. Peterson. Officer Paul Pryorski is an exceptional individual and a fine police officer. Needless to say, I vote for the second plan. Let's have a talk with Paul and get to the bottom of this. Pronto!"

"Thank you, gentlemen. I think we have a consensus. The second plan is the way we'll go. Chief, who should interview Officer Pryorski?"

"Mr. Peterson, there are two people among us who Officer Pryorski could never lie to -- Jeff Tolna and Roy Connors. Officer Pryorski is working the evening shift nowadays. Comes on duty at two o'clock this afternoon. How would that work for you, Roy?"

"That'll allow me time to get back to my office to check on some things. Jeff, why don't the two of us huddle -- around one o'clock -- to work out our game plan?"

"Sounds good, Sheriff. Let's meet here in the conference room. When we finish our planning session, we'll have Officer Pryorski join us."

"I'll keep my schedule clear if you need my legal advice," promised Mr. Peterson.

"I'll contact everyone when it's time to reconvene this team," added Chief Remke. "And don't forget -- everything that we've discussed is strictly top secret."

"Danny and Jase, I have some paperwork to clean up regarding the hit-and-run accident this morning. It won't take long. Then I'll give you a ride home so you can have lunch and come back later if the chief needs us all," Lieutenant Tolna told us.

While we were driving home, it dawned on me. The team, including Mr. Peterson, had accepted everything that Danny and I had recommended.

Maybe we were pretty exceptional too.

WHEN WE ARRIVED HOME, Mom offered to fix us lunch. We gladly accepted and sat in our regular places at the kitchen table.

While she was assembling two big baloney sandwiches with mustard and dill pickles, Mom asked, "Where've you two been all morning?"

I smiled at Mom and began to share all that had happened since we left the house. "Danny and I went to Rick's to pick up Aunt Esther's pictures."

Sensing what I was about to reveal, Danny kicked me sharply on the right shin.

"Ouch! Why'd you do that, Danny?"

Predictably he answered by locking his lips with his invisible key and tossing it over his shoulder. Then he lipped the words, *Top Secret*, and winked at me conspiratorially.

Realizing he was right, I told Mom, "We're involved in the investigation of the MEM robbery, but we can't say anything more about it -- at least not yet, Mom. Hope you understand."

Having lived through a number of our previous cases, Mom understood completely. As she served our sandwiches and large glasses of milk, she inquired, "Do you have to go out again this afternoon?"

"We may be called to meet again -- sometime after two o'clock," Danny replied.

"I'll be going to a Stanley Party this evening so you boys and Dad can have scrambled eggs whenever you come home. How's that sound?"

"Thank you for being so understanding, Mrs. A. This is pretty important business. No telling when we'll be home," Danny told her with a sigh as he examined his fingernails.

I was just about to deliver a kick to Danny's shin when we heard a loud knock at the door. Mom gestured for us to stay at the table and headed for the door.

"Hello, Marie. Are the boys here?"

"Yes, Jeff. Please come in."

Lieutenant Tolna entered the kitchen and quickly assessed the state of our lunch.

"I would appreciate your finishing as quickly as possible, boys. Chief Remke wants to reconvene the team. He'd like us there as soon as possible."

Danny and I gulped down our milk, grabbed what remained of our sandwiches, and headed for the door.

"Bye, Marie."

"Bye, Mrs. A."

"Bye, Mom. Have fun at the Stanley Party."

In 1931, Frank Stanley Beveridge was a successful Fuller Brush salesman who saw potential in door-to-door selling. He and Catherine O'Brien founded a company called Stanley Home Products that sold high-quality household cleaners, brushes, and mops. Based on the Fuller Brush model, salesmen went door-to-door carrying cases of home-cleaning products to sell to housewives.

By 1940, Stanley Home Products changed its model of individual sales to *Stanley Parties* that could maximize sales. At parties, salesmen demonstrated products in living rooms of women, who offered their homes and invited friends to learn about the newest products. This way salesmen could take multiple orders. For her efforts, the hostess was given a *hostess gift* of a toaster, coffee pot, or free Stanley products.

This model opened the door for women, and during the 1940s many women earned extra *pin money* or supported their families from jobs with Stanley. By 1950, company sales hit a record of $70 million.

The Stanley Party Plan became the training ground for many well-known company leaders like Mary Kay Ash of Mary Kay Cosmetics and Brownie Wise of Tupperware. Today Stanley representatives sell by catalog, one-on-one, by telephone, and on the Internet.

AS WE SPED UP Forrest Street toward New Albany, Danny advised, "Better hit the siren, Lieutenant T."

To humor Danny, the lieutenant hit the siren button as we turned onto New Albany.

Screeeeam!

My adrenaline surged, causing my chest to swell with excitement. Danny dropped his sandwich and for the first time since we'd met, he seemed utterly unconcerned about his loss of food.

Within ten minutes, we'd taken our seats in the conference room. The only team member missing was Mr. Peterson.

Danny, pulling what remained of his recovered sandwich from his pocket, was in the process of devouring it, when Chief Remke called the meeting to order.

"Mr. Peterson will be with us in just a minute or two. He's taking care of some important paperwork to enable us to move forward rapidly with this case."

I noticed that Sheriff Connors' demeanor was very subdued. In fact, he appeared to be extremely sad, not a state that I'd ever observed in him. I poked Danny who had apparently noticed the same thing. He gave me a concerned look and shrugged his shoulders.

"Sorry to be late, gentlemen," Mr. Peterson said as he entered. "Let's get right to it. Officer Pryorski has resigned from the Riverton Police Department. He has been taken into custody. And in exchange for his full cooperation in the apprehension of Sergeant Michael Pickard and his partner and for his willingness to testify for the prosecution at the trial, he'll be granted full immunity. This means, he'll not be charged with any crime and will serve no prison time."

"Whoa! This is making my head spin. First of all, who's this Sergeant Pickard?" Lieutenant Tolna asked.

"Nominally Pickard is a highly-decorated, combat-seasoned U.S Army sergeant, currently assigned to the MP security detail at the Grand Blanc Tank Plant, just south of Flint. He earned his current state-side assignment because -- for some time -- he was a POW. Captured by the SS during the fighting at Anzio.

"Those attributes aside, his importance in the MEM case is owing to the fact that he's also a card shark, con man, extortionist, thief, and all-around nasty scoundrel. As such, I'm devoting all my effort to putting him behind bars for the rest of his life."

"Three hours ago we were completely in the dark. How do you know all this now?" Lieutenant Tolna asked.

Danny and I nodded our heads in agreement. This was unbelievable.

"Good question. Sheriff, why don't you fill everyone in?" Mr. Peterson suggested.

The sheriff immediately snapped out of his funk and reassumed his businesslike demeanor. "After leaving here earlier, I drove straight to New Albany where I found Paul Pryorski waiting for me in my office. When I entered, I saw his badge and holstered pistol stacked neatly on my desk. He looked like he'd lost his last friend. His eyes were red from lack of sleep -- and tears -- I suspect."

"What did he say?" I asked.

"First, he asked for my forgiveness -- and then for me to accept his resignation. He told me that I was responsible for -- for his becoming a police officer so it was only fitting for him to end his career with me. I asked him why he was doing this."

The sheriff was choking on his words, but no one reacted with anything but respect and rapt attention. "He regretted bringing dishonor -- to me, to the Riverton Police Department, and to himself. He confessed being an accomplice in the MEM robbery and lying about it -- to me and to his fellow Riverton police officers."

"What was his state of mind, Sheriff?"

"He admitted that he'd thought long and hard about writing a note of confession -- and shooting himself. But in his religion, suicide is a sin. He also considered killing the man -- Pickard -- who had blackmailed him into participating in the robbery. But again his conscience prevented him from killing another man in cold blood. He had no choice but to face the music."

"What did you do next?" Chief Remke asked.

"First, I put a call in to you, but you were in the field with the mayor and wouldn't be back for another hour. So I called Mr. Peterson who advised I bring Paul to his office."

"Let me pick it up there. When the sheriff and Pryorski arrived, I arranged for an interrogation room and a stenographer. With the sheriff's help, we obtained a full and detailed confession from Pryorski. While the stenographer typed the confession, I briefed Judge Jenkins on the case. Taking into account the coercion that Pryorski was subjected to, he concurred with my granting Pryorski full immunity for his cooperation."

"What *coercion* are we talking about? Tell us more about that, Sheriff," Lieutenant Tolna implored.

"Here's the short version. We all know that Paul is a sharp poker player. He seldom loses -- at least when he's playing for kitchen matches. But after he got his farm money, he thought he'd try playing for real money. Confident in his ability, he started looking for a game of high-stakes poker. He learned of an after-hours club on the outskirts of Flint where he could play with the pros. He had no idea that the game was rigged by Pickard and another crook who acted as if he were the club's impartial dealer. Paul became their latest patsy.

"On his way out of the place one night, Paul overheard the two colluding about how they were going to fleece their next sucker. But at this point, Paul had gone through all his farm proceeds and was into Pickard for another $3,000."

"Good grief, Sheriff, how could he have allowed this to happen?"

"Jase, once a man is hooked on gambling -- especially if he's always won -- it's nearly impossible for him to stop gambling until he wins back his losses -- or goes completely broke. It's a compulsion that affects all classes of people in our society."

"In this case, Pryorski's compulsion must have cost him over $10,000," Chief Remke noted.

"That's right. And coincidentally it was just about equal to the amount stolen in the MEM robbery. This was where the coercion came in. Pickard hounded Paul unmercifully, threatening to expose him if he didn't cooperate in the robbery."

"Wait a minute! Where's Pickard now?" Lieutenant Tolna asked.

"He's working his day job at the Tank Plant and his night job at the after-hours club near Flint."

"Why don't we issue an arrest warrant and have the FBI pick him up while he's in uniform at the plant?"

"We want to catch him in action at the poker game. I called my counterpart in Genesee County who has had his eye on Pickard and his associate for a long time. With Pryorski's assistance, we think we can arrest the pair in the next evening or two for illegal gambling and racketeering charges and additionally charge Pickard for extortion and robbery," the sheriff explained. "We can also close the doors on that after-hours club."

"It still amazes me that Pickard isn't on the lamb by now. He's just sitting there, fat and happy, waiting for us to pick him up. How do you explain that? Is he nuts?"

Mr. Peterson rendered his opinion. "Lieutenant, it's called *hubris* from the Greek, meaning an exaggerated pride or self-confidence that leads to the downfall of a hero in a classical tragedy. Because of his hubris, Pickard has deluded himself into believing that the power of his own personality, coupled with Pryorski's shame and guilt, will protect him from any threat from the law. He's dead wrong because, unlike Pickard, Pryorski is fundamentally a good, decent, and honorable man."

Danny summed it up his own way. "Never try to blackmail an Eagle Scout."

Amen

ON SATURDAY, WE WAITED all day to hear of Pickard's arrest and arraignment. By Sunday morning, we still hadn't heard a thing. Danny had just arrived to join us on our regular trip to the farm for Sunday dinner. Danny wouldn't think of missing this weekly ritual.

Danny and I had each received another postcard from JB. The picture on mine was the Parthenon in Centennial Park. Danny's showed Sulphur Dell, a baseball stadium. We both agreed that Nashville must be a huge city compared to Riverton.

As Mom assembled her contributions to the Sunday feast, Dad was soaking up all the war news from the Sunday edition of the *Riverton Daily Press.*

"Wow! General LeMay launched an attack on Japanese cities involving a thousand B-29s. Says he won't be content until every major city in Japan is burned to the ground. My gosh! What more will it take before they surrender?"

As history would show, it would take months of more death and destruction, including the dropping of two atomic bombs, before Japan would finally accept defeat and surrender unconditionally.

"Somebody just pulled up outside," Danny announced. "It's Lieutenant Tolna. Maybe he's got news for us."

We opened the front door and Lieutenant Tolna entered with a smile on his face.

"Does that smile mean what I think it means?"

"Sure does, Jase. Last night, the Genesee County Sheriff and his men, along with FBI agents from the Detroit Field Office, raided the after-hours club and arrested Pickard and his partner. There are more charges against them than I can remember. But needless to say with Officer Pryorski's testimony, Pickard will soon be on his way to a long, long vacation. And his card-shark partner won't be seen for a very long time as well."

"Congratulations, Jeff!" Dad declared exuberantly.

"Don't give me any credit. The tipping point for this case came when Danny and Jase discovered that photograph."

"What photograph?" Mom asked, looking at us.

"You mean you haven't told your folks how you solved this case? Shame on you," Lieutenant Tolna said in jest. "You better fill them in quickly before they read about it in tomorrow's newspaper. Oh, that reminds me. I have it on good authority that Chuck Nichols is on his way here with his photographer Artie."

"We're about to leave for the farm. They may have to wait until tomorrow," Danny advised. "But before we go, Jase and I have questions about some details that don't quite line up."

"Shoot!"

Danny wanted to know, "How tall was Pickard? Was he 6'3" or could he fit into Officer Pryorski's uniform? And why did the photo show them both in uniform? And did Pickard speak with a Southern accent?"

"Whoa! Let me see if I can cover these questions before you go on," Lieutenant Tolna responded, holding up his stop-sign hand.

"Pickard is over six feet tall and does *not* have a Southern accent. Pickard ordered Pryorski to lie about this just to confuse folks. His uniform was from those we keep in the closet off the police lounge at city hall. The department owns all the Riverton Police uniforms so there are always spares in the closet."

"Was there an actual robbery at Trumble Park?" Jase asked.

"No. Pickard made up that story and called in the report. Then got back in Pryorski's patrol car and headed for the Second National Bank to pick up the payroll. And Pryorski was never tied up in the woods either."

"When he was in the backseat, why did Officer Pryorski raise his head just as Danny snapped the picture? And why did he let us see him in uniform?"

"Pryorski stuck his head up to help Pickard find his way through the parking lot to the front door. When Pickard picked up the payroll at the bank, Pryorski was hiding under a dark blanket on the back floor of his patrol car. And he was hiding there when Pickard robbed MEM. Pryorski was wearing his own uniform all that time.

"On their way to ditch the patrol car along Riverton Road, Pryorski removed his uniform. After Pickard locked him in the trunk, Pickard carried Pryorski's uniform and blanket to his car parked in the lane. Later he disposed of both."

"I assume that Officer Pryorski picked up Pickard at his car in the lane on his way to work. Is that right?" Danny surmised.

"Yes. According to police department regulations, officers who live within five miles of city hall can take their patrol cars home with them after their shifts and drive them back for their next shift. Since Pryorski lived more than five miles away, he made arrangements with Sheriff Connors to park his patrol car and his personal car at the sheriff's office.

"So on the morning of the robbery, when Pryorski picked up Pickard at the lane, he was driving his personal car. Pickard had already dressed in a uniform from the storage closet. After they picked up Pryorski's patrol car, they changed drivers. That's when Pryorski hid under the blanket."

"No wonder Mr. Hanna -- the MEM paymaster -- thought the robbery was executed with *military precision*. You have to give Pickard credit. He developed a masterful plan," I observed.

With a bit of Bobby Burns, Danny closed the MEM case as he'd begun it, "The best-laid plans of mice and men do often go awry."

BECAUSE OF OUR UNEXPECTED visit from Lieutenant Tolna, we departed later than usual for our Sunday visit to the farm. When we approached the driveway, it was clear that something unusual was happening. Every member of the Compton family was outside talking with the passengers of two familiar cars that evidently had arrived just a few minutes before us.

"Hey, there's Sheriff Connors! And that's Chuck Nichols and Artie, his photographer. What are they doing here?" Danny wondered aloud.

"Well, obviously Chuck wants to interview you boys. And take a few pictures," Dad reasoned.

"But I wonder why the sheriff is here," I added.

When we pulled into the driveway the entire crowd turned and walked in our direction. After parking, we had difficulty getting out of the car, because *our fans* were pressing their faces to our windows and blocking our doors.

Finally Dad rolled down his window and pleaded, "If everybody will just step back a little, we can get out."

While we were climbing out of the car, I saw Frisky jumping up and down next to Grandpa. The first person to pounce on us was Aunt Esther. Once again, she swept Danny and me into her bosom where she delivered her patented crush-hug. To break her stranglehold, Danny retrieved the packages of pictures from his pocket and waved them in front of her face. Mercifully Aunt Esther dropped us to the ground and began riffling through the prints.

"These are great shots, Danny. You're a wonderful photographer. Based on what Sheriff Connors tells us, you boys discovered that one of these pictures contained evidence that enabled police to solve the MEM robbery case. I wondered why you hadn't given me my prints until now. I bet you were working undercover. Right?"

"Yep!" Danny exclaimed, before I could answer.

Danny looked at me, smiling slyly.

As I stammered, Aunt Esther exclaimed, "I'm so proud of you boys!"

"Good work, fellas. Do you mind if Artie takes a shot of you handing the photos to Aunt Esther?" asked Chuck Nichols.

After the photo session, Chuck wondered if we had some time for a few questions. While he didn't come right out and ask, he knew that he'd have the exclusive rights to our story. He was the only truly, trustworthy reporter that we knew.

Sheriff Connors had a better idea. "Chuck, you may not have heard this yet, but Chief Remke has called a press conference for three o'clock tomorrow afternoon. We're setting up a panel at the high school auditorium -- like we've done before. Panel members will be the Genesee County sheriff, Chief Remke, Lieutenant Tolna, Danny, Jase, and myself. I suggest you postpone your session with the boys until after the press conference. That way you'll have a better context for your questions."

"Thanks for the heads-up, Sheriff. Sounds like a great idea." Chuck turned to us. "Would that be okay with you, boys?"

We enthusiastically nodded our agreement.

Sheriff Connors suggested, "If it's all right with your folks, I'd like to talk some with you boys to prepare them for the press conference. Why don't I come back about 2:30? That should give you enough time to grab a bite to eat and for me to have a short visit with my brother who lives just a mile away."

"That'd be fine, Roy," Dad replied.

Mom agreed.

"Let's eat!" Danny ordered, dashing toward the house.

By the time I reached the kitchen, Danny was ensconced in his favorite seat at the kitchen table. All around him, Grandma Compton, Aunt Esther, Aunt Betsy, and Mom were busy opening the serving dishes and packages of food so the feast could commence. I wouldn't have been surprised to see Danny lick his chops like the proverbial jungle cat. In fact, his appetite had many of the attributes of a wild animal.

At the agreed-to time, I heard the crunch of the sheriff's tires as he pulled into the driveway. To give my young cousins a thrill, he touched his siren.

Brreeep!

The crowd of youngsters raced out the screen door and onto the driveway, begging the sheriff to do it again. He was a pushover when it came to pleasing little boys and girls so he accommodated them one more time.

Brreeep!
Brreeep!

To provide us with a bit of privacy, I suggested we take seats at the picnic table under the maple tree next to the house. No one would bother us there. After we were seated, the sheriff told us he had something to tell us.

We waited, but he didn't say a word. I wondered if he were teasing us. As I would soon learn, he was most likely thinking about how he'd phrase his message.

He finally spoke. "Well, this is not for public consumption, but I thought you fellas deserved to hear it first."

"Hear what?" Danny asked.

"Paul Pryorski's given up any hope of returning to law enforcement. There isn't a police department in the country that would hire him when the news hits the wire services after this afternoon's press conference. So he has decided to pursue another line of work."

"What other line of work, Sheriff?"

"Farming."

"Farming? I thought he hated the idea of being a farmer. Why farming?" I wondered aloud.

"As it turns out, Paul told me that he never *hated* farming. He just *loved* law enforcement. Now that his dream of being a police officer is shattered, he has to do what's practical. Besides he's already got a job offer."

"From whom?"

"My brother wants Paul to work for him. Since he bought the Pryorski farm, he's learned that working two farms is too much for one man. Because he knows and respects Paul immensely, he's asked Paul to help him."

"Wow! That's good news. Will Paul stay in the old Pryorski house?"

"Yep! That's part of the deal."

"What's the other piece of good news?" Danny wanted to know.

"When the after-hours club was raided, they found nearly $50,000 in the safe. Under the supervision of the court -- after restoring the money taken in the MEM robbery -- the remainder will be divided up among those people who were swindled. So Paul stands to recover at least a portion of what he lost."

"That's good -- I think. But shouldn't he pay some price for going wrong. That's a tough one to sort out," I admitted.

"Jase, your words are nearly identical to Paul's when I told him about the money."

"So he doesn't want his share of the money?"

"Not exactly. Instead of keeping it, he told me he'd rather earn it back over time working for my brother."

"For goodness sakes, what *is* he going to do with it?"

"He's donating his share to his church."

"Holy smokes!" Danny cried.

You can say that again.

BY THE TIME OF the press conference, reporters from all over the country had gotten wind of the MEM robbery, the alleged kidnapping of a Riverton police officer, and the arrests following the raid on the Flint after-hours, poker swindle. The critical role that two young, renowned national heroes played in solving the case only served to intensify the reporters' ravenous hunger for a delectable scoop. Naturally the heroes to whom I refer were none other than Danny Tucker and Jase Addison.

After we'd seen Chuck Nichols at the Compton farm the afternoon before, he had sped off to WRDP. Upon his arrival at the radio studio, Chuck interrupted normal programming to issue a series of special reports about the case and the imminent press conference. This special reporting continued all day Sunday and Monday, until just minutes before the press conference.

When we filed across the stage of Riverton High School's auditorium, our impressive procession comprised five law enforcement officials plus Danny and me. The only key person missing was Mr. Peterson whom, I was told later, eschewed press conferences. In his role as Riverton's prosecuting attorney, he preferred tight control of information that might later be used as evidence in court. Not insignificantly he personally had little or no respect for any reporter except Chuck Nichols.

While Chief Remke assumed his position behind the podium, we took our seats in the row of the folding chairs situated behind him. The auditorium was abuzz with chatter among eager reporters who sat in the front, reserved section and among our family, friends, and neighbors who filled most of the remaining seats.

The chief called for order, introduced himself, and opened the conference by reading a short and concise statement, outlining the key facts of the case. In deference to Mr. Peterson, he carefully avoided speaking directly about actual evidence in the case. Then he introduced the remaining five of us and told the reporters that we would be best able to answer their questions.

When Sheriff Connors was introduced, I suddenly remembered that apparently he'd been so excited about the news of his brother's arrangement with Paul Pryorski and about Pryorski's donation to his church that he'd forgotten to *prepare* us for the press conference.

After enduring two tedious hours of repetitious questioning by the reporters, Chief Remke concluded the conference. As on previous occasions, without a word of thanks, the throng of reporters rose as a body and rushed out of the auditorium, leaving us staring down on empty seats.

The boorish reporters elbowed their way up the stairs to the typing classroom where they fought each other for use of the twenty upright *Underwoods*. After a flurry of frantic pecking, with stories in hand, they rushed to the Grand Trunk Railway Station to browbeat Riverton's only telegraph operator into filing their copy ahead of the competition.

The only reporter who failed to join the throng was Chuck Nichols. He greeted us and our parents and asked if he could come by the house for an interview and a few photos. Naturally we agreed. Once again Chuck would have exclusive rights to our story.

The others could learn a few things about reporting from Chuck.

9 BE PREPARED

FOLLOWING OUR INTERVIEW WITH CHUCK NICHOLS
and a cold supper, consisting of leftovers from Sunday dinner at
the farm, we drove to the Ann Arbor Railroad station to check the
train schedules. We were surprised to learn that the connections
JB used to travel to Nashville were no longer available. Our best
connections would prove more complex and our trip much more
time-consuming than his.

Because Danny and I had only traveled by train on one
previous occasion, we really didn't care. Our attitude was the
longer the train ride, the better. No matter what, we were bound
and determined to make the entire trip an adventure.

The fall before, Grandma Compton was our chaperone when
we traveled to Chicago to be on Don McNeil's *Breakfast Club*
radio show. That was when J. Edgar Hoover called the show
from Washington, DC, and presented us with our first Medals of
Courage.

After conferring with Mom and Dad, we decided to leave
Riverton on Thursday, July 19th, and depart Nashville on Sunday,
July 29th. This would give us nearly ten full days with JB. And
it would allow us three days to prepare for our trip. All we really
needed to do was purchase long pants and luggage, which we'd
worked so hard to be able to afford.

The travel time for our southbound trip would be 19 hours and 28 minutes, following the schedule below:

SOUTHBOUND

New York Central #78
Riverton   Leave: 11:33 p.m. (ET)
Jackson   Arrive: 1:30 a.m. (ET)

New York Central #45
Jackson   Leave: 1:40 a.m. (ET)
Chicago   Arrive: 6:15 a.m. (CT)

Pennsylvania RR #308 (*South Wind*)
Chicago   Leave: 8:00 a.m. (CT)
Indianapolis Arrive: 11:30 a.m. (CT)
Indianapolis Leave: 11:33 a.m. (CT)
Louisville   Arrive: 1:45 p.m. (CT)
Louisville   Leave: 2:56 p.m. (CT)
Nashville   Arrive: 5:55 p.m. (CT)

The northbound trip would take us about four hours longer for the return. The travel time for our northbound trip would be 22 hours and 27 minutes, following the schedule below:

NORTHBOUND

Louisville & Nashville RR #98 (*Pan American*)
Nashville   Leave: 12:20 p.m. (CT)
Louisville   Arrive: 4:45 p.m. (CT)
Louisville   Leave: 5:00 p.m. (CT)
Cincinnati   Arrive: 9:15 p.m. (ET)

Baltimore & Ohio RR #58
Cincinnati   Leave: 11:45 p.m. (ET)
Toledo   Arrive: 5:30 a.m. (ET)

Ann Arbor RR #51
Toledo   Leave: 7:55 a.m. (ET)
Riverton   Arrive: 11:47 a.m. (ET)

Just as Danny had predicted, our round-trip tickets would each cost $39.03, including a seat reservation charge of 50 cents for the *South Wind* and the applicable federal excise tax of 15%. Dad wrote a check for our tickets. When we arrived home, we agreed to hide the tickets under my mattress and pay Dad for the tickets out of our travel fund.

Because we were at the railroad station, Dad suggested that we send a telegram to JB, informing him of our arrival date and time. I'd never sent a telegram before, but it only took a few minutes and cost 35 cents.

Dad also requested three copies of our schedule, one for Danny and me and one each for our parents.

While the agent prepared copies of our schedule, he asked, "You boys ever traveled by train before?"

"Only once. We took a train from Riverton to Chicago with my Grandma Compton."

"So you're still novice railroaders. Eh?"

Danny shrugged his shoulders and examined his fingernails. "We haven't traveled a lot, but we do know a lot about trains around here though."

"Oh, you do, huh? Do you know when the first rail service reached Riverton?"

Without hesitating, Danny responded, "In 1856. After several failed attempts, Chippewa County saw the completion of a railroad line known as Detroit, Grand Haven, and Milwaukee. It was a division of the Grand Trunk system."

"Well, I'll be darned. You *do* know your history."

Without replying to the incredulous agent, Danny nodded and continued, "That same year, a train reached Riverton. Stations along that line were Riverton, Durand, Vernon, Corunna, Owosso, and Burton."

"What do you know about the Michigan Central?"

Danny continued. "In 1862, a line of the Michigan Central Railroad between Lansing and Riverton was completed. Bribery was used to get that railroad routed and constructed. By a verbal contract, the right-of-way -- a strip of land 100 feet wide -- was turned over to the railroad without any form of payment to the landowners.

"For this *gift,* all donors, their families, and relatives visiting them, could ride free on any passenger train over any part of the railroad. They could even embark or debark at their homes instead of the station, if they wished. Later this agreement was cancelled and everyone was forced to pay. Stops at individual homes were eliminated."

By this time, we Addisons were astonished. Mom whispered, "Where did Danny get all this information?"

It was time for me to shrug *my* shoulders.

"What about the Chicago and Northwestern?" the agent asked, trying to stump the expert.

"In the 1880's, the Chicago and Northwestern Railroad Company was incorporated into the Grand Trunk Company and renamed the Grand Trunk Western. This system had immense freight traffic and a double track its entire length. This important line brought considerable business to Chippewa County by establishing a junction here in Riverton with three other railroad lines."

Anticipating the agent's next question, Danny continued. "In the late 1800's, the Toledo, Ann Arbor, and Northern Michigan Railway Company, now known as the Ann Arbor, entered Chippewa County. Its shops and roundhouse were located in Riverton, which became an important railroad center. These facilities grew in size and importance doing all kinds of repair work."

Danny finished with his *coup de grâce.* "The period between 1910 and 1915 was the peak of freight and passenger traffic. Six daily passenger trains and the Midnight Flyer passed through Riverton. Some passenger trains had express, mail, and baggage cars, as well as a smoking coach and a few day coaches. Some trains added a Pullman sleeping car and a dining car as well."

When Danny concluded his remarks, all of us were dumbfounded. After shaking his head for a full minute, the ticket agent admitted, "Well, young feller, you really know your stuff. I'm mighty impressed. Mighty impressed indeed. When you return from Nashville, perhaps you'd agree to speak at our Riverton Railroad History Club. Meets at the Riverton Library at 7:00 p.m. on the third Thursday of each month -- except for Thanksgiving of course."

"I know about it. My Grandfather Tucker is a member. He gives me copies of your newsletter to read."

"So that's how he knew!" Mom whispered in my ear again.

On our way back to the car, Mom observed, "I've never heard you talk about railroad history. Does that subject really interest you?"

"Not really. But it pleases Grandpa Tucker. And that's why I read it."

"Well, I'll be," Dad chuckled.

Wisely changing the subject, Mom suggested, "Boys, how about going shopping tomorrow?"

"How many pairs of pants do you think we'll need, Mrs. A?"

"For ten days, I shouldn't think you'll need more than three pairs, Danny. You could take your Boy Scout pants as backup if you want. They won't take up much space in your suitcases."

Before dropping Danny off at his house, we agreed to take the 9:00 a.m. downtown bus.

"Oh, I almost forgot. You boys should wear your long pants and good shoes tomorrow. Then we can show the clerk the right length of pants," Mom advised. "See you in the morning, Danny."

"Right. I'll be there at my regular time," Danny replied, confirming his breakfast reservation.

When we pulled out of the Tucker driveway, Dad suggested, "Maybe we should adopt Danny. Make him an official member of our family."

Spontaneously Mom and I both laughed. Then we fell silent. I don't know about Mom, but I wondered if Dad were serious.

"LET'S START AT MADISON'S," Mom suggested. "They carry both luggage and boys' clothing."

"They sell Boy Scout clothing too," I reminded the two of them.

When we arrived, Mom headed straight for the men's department.

"May I help you, madam?" It was the genial clerk that I remembered from the Christmas before when we'd shopped for ties but settled for hankies for our fathers' gifts. "Oh, hello, boys. Nice to see you again."

"We'd like to see what you have in long pants for these boys," Mom explained.

"Unfortunately we have nothing in long pants -- for boys or for men either. It's the rationing. I'm terribly sorry, madam. And I don't believe any other store in town will be able to help you either."

"Do you have any long pants in the Boy Scout department? You know -- uniform pants like these we have on?"

"I'm really not certain. Let's go down there and ask Mr. Markel."

Mr. Markel delivered more bad news. "We're completely out of Boy Scout uniform trousers. Been back-ordered for months. Can't say when we'll have any. Sorry, ma'am. Boys."

As we left the store, Mom suggested, "Let's try Weinstein's."

Weinstein's department store was Madison's direct competitor. Every Riverton shopper preferred one or the other. I could never see much difference in the two stores. But for Mom to suggest Weinstein's was very unusual. She was an ardent Madison customer.

We heard the same apology at Weinstein's.

"Let's try Montgomery Ward," Mom suggested.

The same apology.

"That's all right. We'll try J.C. Penney's."

The same apology.

"Well, this is discouraging, boys. But while we're here, we might as well look at luggage. From what I saw in the window, they're having quite a sale on Samsonite suitcases."

"What are Samsonite suitcases?" I asked Mom.

"Strong enough to stand on," answered Danny.

"That's right, Danny. How did you know that?"

"I saw an ad in *Collier's* magazine. It showed a pretty woman standing on a suitcase and those words were spelled out under her picture."

"Well, I'll be."

If it really were a *pretty woman*, I wondered how Danny managed to notice the words. But I didn't say anything.

One of Penney's clerks removed two identical, reddish-brown, leather-looking Samsonite suitcases from the front-window display.

"These are on sale for $8. Normally they sell for $10," he explained. "They're genuine Samsonite so they're --."

"Strong enough to stand on?" Danny inquired casually.

"Why, yes. They are that strong. I'm amazed that you knew that, young man."

"I read a lot."

"Do you think these would be large enough to hold clothing for ten days, Mrs. A?"

"Oh, I think so, Danny -- especially if you pack carefully. It's a good value, boys. But it's your money. And your decision."

Danny and I looked at each other and nodded. I reached into my pocket, removed a $20 bill, and handed it to the clerk.

"Please come with me to the sales desk. I'll write up your sale and get your change."

When he'd finished writing our order, he placed it and the $20 bill in a basket that was suspended from a wire that stretched upward to the cashier's desk located above the sales floor at the back of the store. Then the clerk pulled down sharply on a short length of rope. This action launched the basket from a catapult. The basket sped up the wire and disappeared through an opening in the wall at the top of the store. Within a minute, the basket was launched by the cashier and sped toward us. When it landed, the clerk removed our receipt and four crisp dollar bills.

"Seventeen. Eighteen. Nineteen. Twenty," the clerk counted out my change as he placed each bill into my hand. "Thank you, sir. We appreciate your business. Please come again."

"What do you call that contraption?" Mom asked the clerk.

"It's called a *Rapid Wire*. Made by a Detroit company called Rapid Service Store Railway Company. It really saves us time. And we only need one cash register in the store."

"Well, you learn something new every day. Thank you," Mom declared.

As we turned to leave the store, the clerk stopped us. "I beg your pardon. I almost forgot --. This month, all customers who purchase Samsonite luggage are entitled to a special gift. I have them back at the luggage display. I'll go get two of them and be right back."

"Special gifts! What could they be?" Mom pondered.

"Here we are. These beautiful luggage tags are especially designed for sophisticated travelers like you gentlemen."

The clerk handed us each a handsome leather tag complete with straps to attach to the handles of our suitcases.

We thanked him and asked, "How do they work?"

"First, when you lift up this leather flap, you'll see a name card showing through the plastic window. The card shows your name, address, and phone number. For privacy purposes, you keep the flap closed over the card. That way no one can see your name."

"These are very classy -- and practical. But how do you get the card out of the tag to record the information?" Mom asked.

"To remove the card, simply slip the buckle straps out of the card holder like this. Then remove the card, record your information, slip the card back into the holder, and replace the straps. Then use the straps to attach the luggage tag to the handle of your suitcase."

After Danny and I practiced what the clerk had shown us, we attached the tags to our suitcase handles. We were pleased and duly grateful. We thanked the clerk again and shook his hand.

He gave us one last word of advice. "It's very important to fill out your cards and attach your tags before leaving for your first trip. If your baggage-claim check is lost or if your baggage is misplaced by the airline or rail service, this is the only way to insure that your luggage will be returned to you."

We soberly assured him that we would follow his advice.

"Good luck, gentlemen. Bye, ma'am," he said as we left the store.

We carried our suitcases back to the bus station. When our bus arrived, the driver stored our new luggage in the baggage compartment so we wouldn't have to lug it in and out of the bus. At Forrest Street, we retrieved our suitcases and carried them toward our house. When we reached Mrs. Mikas' house, as usual, she was outside sweeping her front walk.

"Hello, Mrs. Mikas," we chimed.

"Goinz on a treep?"

"We're going to see JB in Nashville. We went shopping for long pants but none of the stores had any."

"Loog pintz -- for you boyz?"

"That's right. For Danny and Jase," Mom told her.

"Don't buy zem. I got plenty loog pintz. You kahn have zem. Beloog to Ivan -- and Theo. Kum in. I shooz you," Mrs. Mikas announced, waving us up her walk.

In all the years that we'd lived on Forrest Street, I'd never been on the second floor of Mrs. Mikas' house. That was the location of the bedroom belonging to her two sons. Both had been killed in action, one in North Africa and the other during the Normandy invasion. Gold Stars hanging in Mrs. Mikas' front window memorialized their deaths.

From the appearance of the room, Mrs. Mikas had not removed anything since her two sons left for the army. Two huge closets were jammed with clothing, including sizes worn by her sons when they were our age.

"Triz on. Take alz yah wantz."

"Oh, my goodness, Mrs. Mikas. Are you sure?" Mom implored.

"Ya. Ya," Mrs. Mikas assured her. "Take alz. Pulesse."

Mom and Mrs. Mikas waited downstairs as Danny and I tried on pair after pair of pants. When a pair fit us, we walked downstairs and modeled them for the two admiring women. We each selected five pairs of long pants that fit us well and five more pairs that we would grow into. We neatly folded the 20 pairs of pants into our new suitcases for ease in carrying them home.

We thanked Mrs. Mikas profusely as we made our way out the door to her front porch. She hugged us, pointing to the Gold Stars in her window. She tried to say something to us, but her tears began gushing. She had to settle for hugging us again. We understood and patted her back as she squeezed us.

Just as we were walking up our front walk, Dad pulled into the driveway. "Hey! I see you got some new luggage there. Have any luck finding long pants?" he hollered.

"We got ten pairs each, Mr. A. Not bad luck at all."

"Wow! That must have depleted your travel budget some. Huh?"

"Not a penny, Mr. A. Not a penny," Danny assured my incredulous father.

BEFORE LEAVING FOR THE POW camp, Mom suggested that Danny and I try on the pants so she could measure them. Then she could take them to the camp and have her tailoring students lengthen the trouser legs by dropping the hems an inch or two. Apparently the Mikas boys were shorter than Danny and I.

"I'll just make a list of how much each pair should be lengthened. Fortunately almost all of them are without cuffs -- and looks like there's adequate material to work with. My students won't have much trouble with them. And they'll look so much better when they're hemmed properly."

After Mom measured my first pair, she recorded the required lengthening adjacent to a description of the pants. *Jase's gray gabardine slacks. Lengthen one and a quarter inches.* "Okay, Jase. Go into your bedroom and try on your next pair while I measure Danny's pants."

"You got it, Mom."

After measuring Danny's pants, I heard her say, "Danny's tan, light-wool slacks. Lengthen one and three-quarters inches. Good, Danny. Now bring me another pair."

It took Mom less than 15 minutes to record all the required adjustments.

"If we fold them neatly, I think we can get all 10 pairs of pants into one suitcase. Let me help you with that."

Mom deftly folded the pants and placed them into one of the suitcases.

"There. Now I'll only have to carry one suitcase tonight. When I come home, we can send Danny's pants home with him in one of the suitcases so he can add his socks, shoes, shirts, and so on."

Because Mom was very organized, she started supper before leaving. Dad would be responsible for finishing the meal preparations. Tonight the menu was spaghetti with meat sauce and garlic bread. Having invited Danny to stay for supper, Mom quadrupled the portions of food just to be on the safe side. Since spaghetti was one of Dad's specialties, he gladly assumed the chef's role.

As usual, Mom would eat dinner in the POW mess hall. This enabled her to converse with her students before class. She claimed it helped build rapport and gave the POWs an opportunity to exercise good manners and speak English. Mom always failed to note that she was an attractive woman who undoubtedly appealed to the POWs for that reason as well.

"There's the car," Mom announced, after we all heard a tap on the car horn from the street.

"Let me help you with the suitcase, Marie," Dad offered.

"Thank you, John. It's quite heavy."

We said our goodbyes and headed for the kitchen. Perhaps with our help, Dad could speed up things there. I realized that during our search for pants today, we'd forgotten about lunch. I was amazed that Danny hadn't objected. He seldom went an hour without some form of caloric replenishment.

"Danny, did you realize we forgot to eat lunch today?"

"Oh, I didn't forget. I just thought it was more important to finish shopping before we took the time to eat."

I couldn't believe my ears. Who was this stranger inhabiting the body of my friend?

Perhaps it was a combination of our missing lunch and Dad's special touch in preparing this particular meal, but dinner was delicious. Even Danny remarked about the fine taste of Dad's offerings that evening. This was very unusual because Danny generally placed a much greater value on the *quantity* of food rather than its quality.

Having two and three helpings of spaghetti and garlic bread kept us at the table for more than an hour. By the time the dishes, pots, and pans were washed, it was nearly nine o'clock.

"Danny, why don't you wait until Mrs. A gets back? At that time, we can take your suitcase to your house in our car. Do your parents know where you are?"

Danny nodded his head nonchalantly and added, "They always assume I'm here. So they don't worry."

"You boys want to play some gin rummy?"

"Sure, Mr. A. Let's play for kitchen matches."

By the time we'd played a full game of rummy, we heard a car door slam outside.

"It's Mom," I speculated. "Let's help her carry in the pants."

The three of us headed for the door. We were greeted by an Army MP. Evidently he was Mom's driver whom she had enlisted to carry the heavy suitcase.

"We were just coming outside to help. But bring it right in, Sergeant. Just place it here on the sofa. That's it. Thank you."

Dad shook the man's hand and patted him warmly on the arm.

"All the pants altered, Marie?"

"Mission accomplished. They did the hems in record time. Gee, I'm proud of the skills they've developed since I have been working with them."

"You're just a good teacher, Mrs. A."

"And you're just a good flatterer, Mr. Tucker."

What an understatement!

ON TUESDAY MORNING WITH Mom's help, we inventoried the many items we had to pack before setting off for Nashville.

First we focused on the contents of our suitcases.

- Belt
- Handkerchief
- Hat
- Jacket
- Pajamas
- Robe
- Shirts - Long Sleeve
- Shirts - Tee
- Shoes - Basketball
- Shoes - Dress
- Shorts - Basketball
- Shorts - Underwear
- Shorts - Walking
- Slacks - Boy Scout
- Slacks - Dress
- Socks - Basketball
- Socks - Dress
- Sweater
- Sweatshirt
- Swimsuit

Then we inventoried the contents of our toiletry kit, which would be packed in our suitcase.

- Comb
- Soap
- Toothbrush
- Toothpowder

That was easy! Finally we inventoried the items we would carry in our pockets.

- Cash
- Chewing Gun
- Handkerchief
- Jackknife

- Pocket Comb
- Snacks (Danny's idea)
- Stamps - Penny Postcard
- Train Tickets

"Do you think we have everything, Mom?"

"I believe so, but if we forgot something, we can add it later."

"Do you think this will all fit in our suitcases, Mrs. A?"

"Yes, I do, Danny. They're very large and most of these items don't take up much space."

Danny smiled with relief.

"One last thing, boys. I think you should make a list of people you want to say goodbye to."

Our list included:
- Grandma and Grandpa Compton & Frisky
- Grandpa Tucker
- Lieutenant Tolna
- Mr. & Mrs. Reilly
- Mrs. Bradford (JB's Mom)

- Mrs. Mikas
- Otto Klump
- Queenie & Chub
- Sherm Tolna

It was difficult not to add others to this list, including Sheriff Connors. But we agreed that, because the next two days would be extremely busy, we had to prioritize.

"Jase, how much money should we take. We have a lot more than we need for the trip."

"I don't know, Danny. What do you think, Mom?"

"You shouldn't need more than a dollar a day -- on average. So $10 apiece should cover your needs. But you could add a little more -- just to cover emergencies."

Danny and I weighed this issue carefully and decided that we would each take $12."

"That's sensible, boys. If you need more, I can send it by telegram," Mom suggested.

I had wondered if that could be done but I didn't say so. Instead, I nodded my head, knowingly. Danny did the same. Then he wrinkled his nose at me and shrugged his shoulders again. Evidently Danny didn't know how that worked either.

After reviewing our lists, I began to feel very organized. It was a great comfort.

"What should we do first, Jase?"

"Let's start with our suitcases."

"Yours or mine?"

"Let's do mine this morning and yours this afternoon."

Danny nodded his agreement.

"I'll help if you like," Mom offered. "Something may need to be laundered."

"Oh -- that's right. We should add a *Dirty-Laundry Bag* to our suitcase list."

"Good idea, Danny. Good idea."

ON WEDNESDAY MORNING, DANNY and I were sitting on my bed, inventorying all we'd accomplished during the preceding 24 hours. Our suitcases were nearly packed. We had said goodbye to all but a handful of people on our list. More importantly we were feeling more relaxed and excited about the Nashville trip than at any time since we began earning money to pay for it. The prospects of a thrilling train trip to another faraway destination and of exploring Nashville with our friend JB were filling us with expectations of fun and adventures soon to come.

The sound of a slamming car door interrupted our reverie. When I heard the familiar sound of farm-lady shoes scurrying and scuffing up our front walk, I immediately identified our visitor.

The front door banged open, and she announced her arrival in typical fashion. "Yoo-hoo! Anybody home? Marie! Jase! Where are you?"

It was Grandma Compton.

"Here I am, Grandma!" I yelled. "In my bedroom with Danny. Mom's gone shopping."

"For goodness sakes," she exclaimed as she entered our room. "You look as if you're all packed and ready to go. When does your train leave?"

"Tomorrow night -- Thursday -- at 11:33 p.m."

"Wow! That's late. When do you arrive in Nashville?"

"Late Friday afternoon -- at 5:55 p.m."

"Laws! That's a very long trip. Me-oh, me-oh, my!"

"We've been waiting for you to come so we could say goodbye," Danny fibbed, smiling impishly.

From experience, he knew what effect his words would have on Grandma. She immediately forgot her concerns about our schedule and merely melted. She and Danny shared a mutual admiration society that not everyone could understand or appreciate.

"Well, here I am, Danny. And Grandpa too. He's out in the car, holding Frisky after her first car ride. She was a bit *surprised* by -- by the way I drive. Hee! Hee!"

Having only learned to drive at age 50, Grandma had surprised everyone in the family. Because of her high-speed reckless driving, none of my aunts, uncles, or cousins would set foot in her sporty 1934 Terraplane Coupe. But Danny and I savored it.

To us, the most appealing aspect of Grandma's driving style was that she only used two speeds, stop and full. And full speed for her Terraplane ranged upwards from 80 mph. People from miles away could track our course by the 50-foot-high rooster tail of yellow dust, shooting up behind us as we roared over Barrington Township's narrow dirt roads.

Danny and I embraced Grandma's driving style because we knew her secret. The minute she learned that Amelia Earhart, the renowned aviatrix, had been retained to sponsor and promote the Terraplane Coupe, Grandma simply *became* Amelia. With Amelia at the throttle, white scarf thrown over her shoulder, we imagined ourselves being transported around the country in our own personal P-51 *Mustang* fighter plane.

Frankly I was surprised that Grandpa had risked riding to town with Grandma. Normally he made every excuse imaginable to avoid being a part of what he called *Grandma's Barney Oldfield act.*

To understand the meaning of that remark, Danny and I had sought the assistance of the Riverton Library. We learned that Barney Oldfield was a famous race-car driver. In 1903, he was the first-ever to drive at the speed of a mile-a-minute (60 mph) on an oval track. And he set a record, 100-mph lap at the Indianapolis Speedway in 1914. He was also a valued test driver for the Ford Motor Company.

Admired for his extremely high-speed and dangerous auto-racing technique, Oldfield was a hero to American boys and young men during the early 20th century. His accomplishments led to the expression, "Who do you think you are? Barney Oldfield?"

"Let's go see Grandpa and Frisky," Danny urged.

Grandma led the way. We saw the pair sitting quietly, at last, in the passenger seat. When Frisky saw us coming, she began to bounce up and down in anticipation of a good ear-rub.

"Hello, boys. Your friend Frisky is excited to see you."

After an appropriate amount of affectionate petting, Frisky excused herself to curl up again in Grandpa's lap.

"The trip was a bit taxing for this little girl," Grandpa offered with a wink.

"Oh, Dad. There you go again, about my driving," Grandma scolded, quite insincerely.

Then she turned to us. "I know you boys are busy so we won't stay long. We just wanted to say goodbye and give you a little something for your trip. Here. Tuck these in your suitcases for emergencies."

She handed us each a tin container about the size of a large cigar box. Our names were marked on the lids, which were secured by a number of tautly-wrapped, large rubber bands.

Grandma gave us each a big hug. Grandpa shook our hands. And Frisky licked our fingertips.

As we said our last goodbyes, Grandma's face clouded over. Before she started to cry, she hopped in the Terraplane and tromped on the gas pedal. Within seconds, her *P-51* had roared out of sight.

"Whew! That made me tired," I admitted.

"I'm tired too. Let's open Grandma's cookies. Which do you want -- oatmeal or molasses?"

"Cookies? How did you know? I --." I stopped myself, because I knew Danny never answered that question. How he knew was part of his trademarked mystique, which he guarded closely.

When we returned to my room, Danny unwrapped the rubber bands from around his tin and removed its cover to reveal two large collections of cookies neatly wrapped in waxed paper. Just as he predicted they were his favorites, oatmeal without raisins and dark, thick molasses cookies.

While we nibbled Grandma's delicacies, I unwrapped my tin. Lifting the cover, I wondered aloud, "What's all this?"

"Let me guess," Danny suggested.

"Okay, smart guy. I dare you to give it a try."

"First, a jar of wheat -- to make wheat gum. Right?" Danny announced with authority

"Check," I admitted.

Danny continued the inventory as I checked off each item.
- Jar of Wheat, marked *For Wheat Gum*
- Spare Shoestrings (2 pair)
- Compass
- Spool of Tan Thread & Needle
- Little Screwdriver
- Package of Horehound Drops
- Package of Sen-Sen
- Bottle of Homemade Black Cough Syrup
- Stationery & Stamps
- Sharpened Pencils (2)
- Safety Pins (4)
- Bottle of Ass-Burns

When Danny finished his inventory, he asked smugly, "Did I miss anything?" Of course, he hadn't. Once again I was amazed by his ability to know things that he couldn't possibly have known. But for some reason, on this particular occasion, I refused to answer his question. After being completely whipped, I guess I didn't want to give him the satisfaction.

Apparently sensing my attitude, he offered a rare explanation. "Grandma Compton gave us the exact same things when we went to Camp Harmony. Remember?"

By golly, he was right. Unlike Danny and Grandma, I'd never thought of Nashville as camp.

10 ALL ABOARD

WE DROVE BOTH FAMILY CARS TO THE TRAIN station. This allowed Danny to ride with my family and tuck both our suitcases in the back of his family's station wagon. Because Queenie and Chub were eager to see us off, they also joined the party. I hadn't seen much of Queenie since the night we walked hand in hand to Pete's, both of us sharing our great concern for Danny's welfare during the kidnapping episode.

Our families had decided to treat us to a going-away supper at the Chop Suey Diner. After we were seated at the oversized circular booth at the far end of the diner, Mom and Mrs. Tucker presented us with identical, brown leather, Buxton wallets, large enough to accommodate our $12 travel money and train tickets as well. Carefully they'd printed our names and addresses on the identification card, displayed in the leather-framed, plastic window next to the wallet's fold. We placed our valuables in our wallets and slipped them into the buttoned back pockets of our *new* long pants.

For the trip, we had decided to wear long-sleeved shirts, our new belts, and dress shoes. Finally because we'd chosen not to splurge on a Pullman sleeper, we took our jackets in case the coach car became chilly during the night. We had stuffed the jackets into our YMCA gym bags, figuring that there would be plenty of room in the bags to bring back souvenirs or gifts we might acquire in Nashville.

In short, we had thought of everything.

Our meal at the diner was very memorable. We all selected the full turkey supper special, cooked to perfection and served with dressing, gravy, mashed potatoes, and peas. Danny showed us his stuff by consuming an entire turkey drumstick, along with ample servings of all the trimmings.

Because there were eight of us dining that evening, both Nikki and Mitsu Nakayama waited on us. As usual, the young Japanese women were their ever-alluring selves, gracefully bowing and gesturing with their petite ivory hands as they accommodated our every need with remarkable agility. That night, even their slightly pseudo-Japanese accents were pleasing to my ears. I'd heard them speak in plain, unaccented English on a few occasions. But this was a special occasion so on with the show.

With the Allies having defeated Germany and now completely focused on bringing Japan to its knees, I wondered whether the widespread acceptance of the Nakayamas by our community would endure. If there had been any lessening of community support, I'd not observed it. That pleased me greatly because I admired this hardworking Japanese-American family. I was proud that Rivertonians treated them with kindness and honest respect.

After supper, Mr. Nakayama bestowed an unexpected gift on Danny and me. A large, brown-paper sack filled with a dozen succulent turkey breast and Swiss cheese sandwiches on fresh kaiser rolls, garnished with lettuce and mayonnaise. My favorite! In his heavily accented English, he told us to enjoy them on the train and wished us an accented *bon vorage*. As we were leaving the diner, the entire Nakayama family bowed deeply to us. We waved thank you and goodbye as we headed for the station.

What a perfect send-off!

The platform of the Ann Arbor Railway station was aswirl with dozens of departing passengers, whose family and friends were there to bid them farewell. People also came to welcome the arrival of passengers on inbound trains. Mr. Tucker and Dad checked our suitcases at the baggage check-in area. On the way back, they determined that our train, the New York Central #78 arriving from Bay City, was right on schedule.

Because our train would arrive within 20 minutes, the boarding process would soon begin. We placed our baggage-claim checks safely in our wallets and re-buttoned our back pockets. Then we joined the others in upbeat small talk to kill time while we waited.

Danny, still clutching the bag of turkey sandwiches, smiled broadly as our train pulled into the station. I was relieved to know that his normal priorities were in good working order.

We walked toward our car and joined the line of departing passengers that gradually shortened as they stepped aboard, heading for their seats. At the same time, we all became eerily quiet, as if some great cataclysmic event was about to befall us.

Of all people, Queenie broke the silence. "I'd like to say that I'm very proud of -- and happy for -- Jase and Danny. They're off on a Nashville adventure to see their friend JB. And they earned every penny for this trip themselves. I say it's time to congratulate them."

At that, much to everyone's amazement, she gave Danny a big smacker, right on the cheek. Just as I was about to tease him, she planted a big one on my cheek too. I could feel my face burning. But apparently no one was affected except me. On the contrary, they were thanking Queenie for realizing it was appropriate to congratulate Danny and me. I regained my composure as best I could and relished the moment.

As I was about to step aboard, the porter standing there reached out to steady my elbow. However, before he could do so, I heard a voice behind us.

"Just a minute, Eddie."

The porter hesitated and turned toward the voice. "Yes, sir, Agent Connelly. What may I do for you?"

The agent who had sold us our tickets was heading our way.

"Eddie, these young lads are friends of mine. I want you to look after them. When they reach Jackson, please turn them over to the porter on New York Central #45 and ask him to do the same for them when they reach Chicago. They're connecting with the Pennsylvania Railroad #308, *South Wind*. Could you do that for me, Eddie?"

"Yes, sir, Agent Connelly. It'd be my pleasure. Consider it done." After glancing at our tickets, the porter declared, "Master Addison and Master Tucker, welcome aboard! If you need anything at all during our time together, don't hesitate to call for me. My name is Eddie. I'll check on you from time to time. And I'll see that you make your connection in Jackson."

Tipping his cap to our families, he continued. "Perhaps you'd like to say goodbye to these nice folks -- after that I'll take you to your seats."

We did exactly as Eddie suggested. Our goodbyes were short but friendly. Soon Eddie was leading us to our seats. While Danny preferred the window seat, I wanted the aisle.

"These are the best seats on this coach. Please note the luxurious shiny leather and soft upholstery. Gentlemen, just relax and enjoy yourselves. I'll be back when I'm through assisting my other passengers."

We thanked Eddie, and he gave us a quick salute and marched off to fulfill his other duties.

"Boy! He's pretty sharp. We're lucky to have him here to help us."

"You got that right, Jase."

Apparently members of our family agreed. While the train chugged out of the station, all of them were still on the platform, shaking hands with Agent Connelly and patting him on the shoulder.

All I could think of was Danny's incredible train-history lecture when we purchased our tickets. Danny had a way of bringing us very good luck.

Suddenly I was filled with a feeling of admiration for my dearest friend.

"Danny, can you believe we're finally on our way to Nashville?"

"Yes, Jase. We did it!"

DESPITE OUR JOURNEY'S SMOOTH start, Danny and I would learn later that not all train travelers during World War II were as fortunate. For the sake of historical accuracy, we would like to share what we learned from seasoned train travelers whom we met on our Nashville trip and from our reading of accounts of wartime travelers after the war ended.

During the war, train stations were jammed with the servicemen moving to training camps, posts, or ports of embarkation on the Atlantic and Pacific coasts. American railroads carried 97 percent of military freight, including supplies and equipment, and transported two million service personnel each month. Pullman cars were reserved for the troops, leaving citizens to sleep as best they could in coach seats. Each night during the war, 30,000 military passengers slept in Pullman cars.

On many railroad lines, a daily event was the passing of troop trains going from coast-to-coast. Troop trains carried entire military units, including their personnel, equipment, and supplies. Individual members of the armed forces, traveling under orders, purchased tickets on trains carrying both military and civilian passengers.

Frequently high-priority, troop trains forced civilian trains onto sidings, delaying civilian train schedules for hours.

Civilian train passengers often endured what many characterized as cattle-car conditions. Some passengers expressed gratitude for merely being provided a place to stand. People slept in the aisles. They ignored rules about not standing in the vestibules, the enclosed areas at either end of the passenger cars, while the train was moving.

Often top vestibule windows were opened to allow air to circulate through the crowded coaches. Cinders and smoke from the coal-burning engines regularly entered the vestibules and the cars themselves. A cinder in your eye was an unpleasant but not uncommon experience.

On the other hand, during the trip, Danny and I enjoyed watching the lights of towns as they whizzed by in the middle of the night. Waking up to see the sun come up was an exciting experience for most people including us. Although our coach seats weren't ideal beds, we found it was easy to sleep because the *clickety-clack* of the rails produced a sleep-inducing cadence.

We learned from experienced rail travelers that we could tell where we were during the day because telegraph poles adjacent to the tracks were evenly spaced. At each mile, a pole was marked with a number. Because train orders contained strict speed restrictions, places to slow down were identified by the mile-pole number. These numbers also provided an unsophisticated but effective way for passengers to keep track of where they were on the trip.

Some passenger trains had dining cars that could accommodate about 40 people. The lines were always long. But porters did pass through the train selling sandwiches and small bottles of milk, as well as Hershey and Baby Ruth candy bars. Eager to conserve our funds, Danny and I subsisted on the dozen turkey sandwiches given to us by Mr. Nakayama. Of course, we did dip into our trip money to purchase milk.

During the war, ticket fares for short distances of 15 to 25 miles were only about 25 cents. For longer trips, like ours, scalpers were known to sell black-market tickets for $10 to $50 extra. Travel agencies often charged a $20 service fee to purchase tickets for longer trips.

On balance, railroad travel was no more burdensome on American citizens than many other aspects of life on the home front. Rationing, shortages of goods commonly available before the war, and other such sacrifices were endured with a can-do spirit by most Americans back then. First and foremost, when we suffered such inconvenience, we tried to be mindful of the needs of our fighting men overseas.

As we sped through the night toward our first stop in Jackson, Michigan, Danny and I hadn't a care in the world. Unfortunately that was soon not to be the case.

I WAS PRECARIOUSLY PERCHED on top of the moving bean drill, setting markers for Grandpa Compton in the south field. The rhythmic *clickety-clack* of the drilling mechanism had nearly lulled me to sleep.

"Jase! Jase!"

I heard Danny calling to me, but I couldn't see him through the clouds of choking dust thrown up by the hooves of the workhorses and the wheels of the drill, the soil cutters, and the dragging chains.

"Jase! Wake up!"

Someone was shaking me.

"Eddie's here to take us to our next train. Wake up!"

I finally realized where I was. As I had done a dozen times since leaving the Chop Suey Diner, I patted my buttoned back pocket to insure my wallet was still safely in place.

"On, no!" I leaped to my feet and frantically searched all around me for my wallet. I thought I was losing my mind. It had to be there.

Danny and Eddie, having no explanation for my bizarre behavior, stared at me as though I were crazy.

"My wallet's gone!" I screamed. **"My wallet's gone! I've lost my train tickets! My baggage-claim check! And all my money!"**

"Are you absolutely sure?" Danny asked, patting his own buttoned pocket. "Mine's here."

"Danny, did you take it? Tell me! Is this a stupid joke?"

Eddie hadn't said a word. He simply observed my angst with great concern. Finally he laid his hand gently on my shoulder and assured me, "Master Addison, everything is going to be all right. Stay here. I'll go find the man who can help you."

Without further ado, Eddie turned and scurried up the aisle toward the dining car.

We were alone. After looking at each other in terror, we began another desperate search of the area around us. We looked everywhere. Under our jackets. On the shelf above us. All around the seats across the aisle, in front of us, and in back of us.

Nothing! My wallet was nowhere to be found.

By this time, every person in our car was wide awake. We could hear their loud whispers of concern.

"That boy's lost his wallet."

"Maybe he was robbed."

"Poor thing. I wonder where his parents are."

"Maybe they're orphans."

"Who'll help them?"

Eddie suddenly appeared at the front of our car. He was quickly making his way toward us. Following close behind him was a burly man with curly black eyebrows and a thick black moustache. The man was dressed in a professionally tailored, black gabardine suit, heavily-starched white dress shirt, and black silk tie. On his large head sat a somber homburg hat. But the man's most prominent feature was the large silver star pinned to his left breast pocket. As he came closer, I read the engraved words:

New York Central Railroad
Bureau of Detectives

"It's the law!" Danny announced loudly.

A startled gasp burst forth from our fellow passengers.

After shaking our hands, he informed us, "Boys, I'm Lieutenant Donovan with the Railroad Detectives."

We introduced ourselves and, as Lieutenant Donovan instructed, we told him how and when my wallet had apparently disappeared. While we spoke, the lieutenant carefully listened to our words and studied each of us. I assumed he was assessing character and credibility. He took notes in a little black notebook, which he slammed shut when we finished speaking.

"Jase and Danny, I believe you're telling the truth, but for the record, I have to ask this. Are you completely certain that you had your wallet when you boarded this train?"

"Yes, Lieutenant Donovan. I'm certain. Before we fell asleep, we both bought a bottle of milk to drink with the sandwiches we brought with us. Milk costs five cents. I paid for mine with a dollar bill from my wallet. I put the 95 cents change in my right pant pocket."

I reached in, extracted the change, and showed it to Lieutenant Donovan.

"I returned my wallet -- with the $11 -- to my back pocket and buttoned it. After our snack, I promptly fell asleep."

"As I said before I believe you --."

Before he could finish, an older man who sat two rows ahead of us, stood up and yelled. "Hey! My wallet's gone too. It was in the inside pocket of my suit coat. The coat's been right here on my arm rest since we left Riverton. There go my train tickets -- and my driver's license. Doggone it!"

"What about your money?" Lieutenant Donovan asked.

"It's safe. I keep it in a money clip in my pant pocket. I learned to do that the hard way. I been dipped before."

"Let me finish up with this young man. Then I'll be right with you, sir," Lieutenant Donovan told the man.

"Dipped? What does that mean, Lieutenant?" Danny asked with a puzzled look.

"Pickpocketed. It's the slang word that pickpockets use to describe themselves. Dippers."

Eddie's eyes were as big as saucers. "Lieutenant, could JD be back in business?"

"I hope you're wrong, Eddie. But when I'm through here, I'll contact Jackson State Prison to see if he's still their guest. Whether it's him or not, this certainly is his M.O."

"Who is JD?" Danny inquired.

"It's the nickname railroad people use to describe a pickpocket named Rupert Evans. It stands for the *Jackson Dipper*. He used to work trains and railway stations in the area around Jackson. In his early career, he focused strictly on wealthy passengers. He was very skilled in his chosen profession. He did very well by all accounts. The legend is he's got $100,000 stashed away someplace."

"Why didn't he just retire?" I asked.

"Hard to say. Most successful criminals have big egos. Maybe he thought he'd never be caught. But he was wrong. About ten years ago, he made a foolish mistake that cost him a short stretch in prison. After his release, he was a changed man. He'd turned downright vicious -- seemed out to hurt people, not to make a fortune stealing from them. He shifted to weaker victims -- women, old men, and children."

"How'd he find himself back in prison?" Danny asked.

"He was arrested and convicted of first degree manslaughter. His pickpocketing essentially caused the death of a poor old man with a serious heart condition. That was a couple of years back. Because he got a ten-year sentence for that one, he should still be behind bars in Jackson Prison. I'll check on it when I finish taking statements here."

"He's certainly had a long career with only two arrests. He must be very illusive," Danny suggested.

"That's an astute observation, Danny. He's got a very useful talent. As a former actor, he's a master of disguise. Why, he could be one of any of a dozen men right here in this car."

After hearing those words, I felt a chill run up my back.

The lieutenant's story of JD had temporarily distracted me from the dire situation in which Danny and I found ourselves. Reality came crashing down on me again. I felt nauseous and fear gripped my chest. I was dizzy. I had to sit down to regain my equilibrium.

After my anxiety attack passed, I told Danny, "We can't continue on this trip. We need to turn around and go home."

Lieutenant Donovan shook his head almost violently. "None of that talk now, son! We'll write you another set of tickets when we arrive in Jackson. Then we'll retrieve your baggage from this train and recheck it on NYC #45. You'll be whole before you reach Chicago. And you'll never miss a train doing so. You'll arrive in Nashville right on schedule."

"But I lost my baggage-claim check. How'll they find my suitcase?"

"It'll be easy and quick if it has a name tag on it. Most people don't bother. Hope you're not one of them. Does it have a name tag?"

Danny answered for me, "Both our bags have name tags. We got some very good advice on that subject from a man we know who works at the J.C. Penney in Riverton."

"Then you're in the chips."

"But what about Jase's travel money?" Danny demanded to know. "He had $11 in his wallet. We'll need that for our 10-day stay in Nashville."

"We'll have to --."

Danny interrupted him. "And what about the value of Jase's brand new wallet?"

Then he reached into his pocket and extracted his wallet. "This is exactly the same as the one that was stolen from Jase. We got them as going-away presents right before we boarded the train. They're brand new -- adult size -- brown leather -- Buxton wallets."

"I see that. Can you prove what they cost?"

"Sure. Look here. The price tag's still attached. $5.00."

"That's good. Jase will claim a total of $16. All right, Danny?"

"The amount's correct, but how soon will Jase have the money?"

"We'll have to submit an expedited claim to the railroad's insurance company. That'll take a few days. But wherever you are -- when it comes through -- we'll wire it to Jase. How's that sound?"

"How long will it take?"

"Shouldn't take more than four days. That's assuming today -- Friday -- is the first day."

Apparently my *agent* didn't care for the terms of the deal. So he offered an alternative, doing so in a way that only Danny could conceive and successfully execute.

"You say Jase will have his money within four days. You're pretty confident that you can make that happen. Right?"

"It's a sure bet."

"Does that mean you're a betting man, Lieutenant Donovan?"

"Well, I've been known to lay down an occasional wager."

"Good! Then I have one for you. Here it is. You pay Jase $15 out of your pocket right now. If the claim comes in within four days, you get to keep the entire $16. If the claim comes in after four days, you wire the $16, and Jase keeps your $15 as well."

"Well, I don't know?"

"You claimed it was a sure bet, sir."

Danny had him. The lieutenant reached into his wallet and withdrew $15 in crisp new bills. He held them out to me. But before I could take the money, he pulled it back. "I have one small condition."

"What's that, Lieutenant Donovan?"

"I just cashed my paycheck, and I would like you boys to write me a note to my wife, explaining where this $15 went to. I don't want her thinking I bet it on a horse. Could you do me that favor, boys?"

"You bet, Lieutenant Donovan. We could do that. Right, Jase?"

In case we needed them during the trip, I'd removed a pencil and a sheet of stationery from Grandma Compton's emergency supply box before packing it in my suitcase. I was confident this situation counted as an emergency. I handed them to Danny.

Danny smiled at Lieutenant Donovan and asked, "Now, what's your dear wife's name?"

BY THE TIME WE arrived at Jackson, thanks to Lieutenant Donovan and Danny, my disposition had changed from panic to tranquility. When the train stopped, the lieutenant proved to be a man of his word. He dispatched Eddie to retrieve my suitcase and to recheck it straight through to Nashville. Eddie promised to bring my new baggage-claim check to the stationmaster's office where Lieutenant Donovan would be making arrangements for my new ticket and checking on the status of Rupert Evans, a.k.a. JD.

"You fellas come with me. My business there will only take a few minutes. When I finish, we'll get you aboard the #45 for Chicago."

The stationmaster listened to the lieutenant's explanation of how I *lost* my ticket.

"I'll have our ticket agent issue a replacement -- right away." Looking at Danny, he asked, "May I borrow your ticket, son? It'll save a lot of time writing the replacement."

Danny dug out his ticket and handed it to the stationmaster.

"I'll be back shortly," he promised as he left his office.

Lieutenant Donovan picked up the telephone on the stationmaster's desk and instructed the operator to connect him with Jackson State Prison.

"Hello. Jackson State Prison? Good. This is Lieutenant Donovan from the New York Central, Bureau of Detectives. I'm calling to check on the current status of your inmate -- Rupert Evans. I --. "

A scowl immediately swept over the lieutenant's face. "When did you say this was? How on earth did he manage that?"

He looked at us and shook his head. "Did you put out an APB? Good! I assume you copied our office. I was the arresting officer so I have a vested interest in this fellow."

He nodded and concluded his call. "Thank you for telling me."

"Boys, just as I feared. JD escaped from a work gang about 48 hours ago. He went right straight back to what he knows best -- dipping."

"Wow! He's fast. Isn't he?" I speculated.

"You ought to change his nickname from JD to Rapid Rupert," Danny suggested.

For the first time since we'd known him, Lieutenant Donovan let out a very loud guffaw. It startled Danny and me.

"What's so funny?" the stationmaster asked as he entered his office with my new ticket. "Here it is. And here's yours too."

He handed tickets to both Danny and me. "I think my ticket agent broke a speed record. You boys better head for your train. Oh, I almost forgot. Eddie brought this new baggage-claim check for you, son. He had to get right back to his train which departs about now. But he wanted me to wish you well on the rest of your trip."

He handed me my new claim check. I was sorry that I hadn't had an opportunity to thank Eddie for all he'd done for me and to say goodbye.

"Come on, boys. Let's get to your train. I'm going with you. I've got a hunch about our old friend, JD. Or should I say *Rapid Rupert?*"

With that he let out another rip-roaring guffaw.

Danny looked at me and winked.

"We're on our way!" I exclaimed excitedly.

WITH THE HELP OF Lieutenant Donovan's badge, we boarded the train before the other passengers. When the porter returned from escorting a couple to their seats, he looked at us and smiled. I was startled. "Eddie! I thought you left the station -- on our last train."

"Oh! You two young gentlemen must be Master Addison and Master Tucker. I'm Freddie. Eddie's my twin brother. Hello, Lieutenant. I have three seats for you, but they're not very close together. In fact, they're separated by two coaches. Two in one. One in the other."

The resemblance was uncanny. I concluded that Eddie and Freddie must be identical twins.

"Freddie, any vacancies in the sleeper?"

"No, sir, Lieutenant. Booked solid."

"Okay, Freddie. I'll take the single. Thank you for accommodating me. I was half expecting to spend the rest of the night on my feet."

Turning to us, the lieutenant admonished, "Now you boys try to get some sleep. It's almost two in the morning. We'll arrive in Chicago in just over five hours. Remember to change your watches when we arrive. Chicago's on Central time -- like Nashville."

"Freddie, please escort these boys to their seats. I can find my own way. What's my seat number?"

On the way to our seats, Freddie explained, "I didn't have much time to talk to Eddie -- but I understand you had your pocket picked. Is that right, Master Addison?"

I gave Freddie a brief description of the crime.

"So sorry to hear about that. I'll check on you through the night. Make sure you're doing all right."

After we were seated, Freddie asked, "Would you like me to put your sack on the shelf above you, Master Tucker?"

"No, thank you."

Danny's answer didn't surprise me. He hadn't let go of that sack since we left the Chop Suey Diner. At times, he squeezed it so hard that I feared our ten remaining turkey-and-cheese sandwiches might become one molded mass of turkey paste.

"May I do anything for you before you fall asleep?"

"We're going to have a midnight snack," Danny replied, patting his sack. "Turkey sandwiches. Is there some way we can get some milk to go with them?"

"Yes, sir. Two bottles of milk. Coming right up."

After Freddie was out of earshot, Danny looked at me and asked, "You wanta use up some of your change?"

I nodded and reached into my pocket for a dime.

When Freddie returned, he handed us each our milk. I attempted to hand him a dime. But he refused to take it.

"Eddie made me promise to look out for you. Tonight your milk is on New York Central! Anything else you need?"

We thanked Freddie. I put my dime back in my pocket while Danny extracted two partially-squashed, lopsided sandwiches from his bag.

I hadn't realized how hungry I was. Then it struck me. Danny had lasted nearly four hours, fueled by only one relatively small sandwich. I wondered how he did it. So I broached the subject. "You must be pretty hungry, huh?"

"Not really. But I think we should eat one more sandwich before we fall asleep."

"Now that doesn't sound like the Danny Tucker I know. Why the change?"

"I'm pretending that we're in a lifeboat in the middle of the ocean."

"What?"

"A lifeboat. You know -- our ship was sunk by a Japanese submarine. All hands were lost except for the two of us. We're drifting in the middle of the Pacific. And we don't have oars. Or sails. Or anything. We could be out here for months. So we have to conserve our food. All we have is this bag of turkey sandwiches."

"Where did this come from?"

"I read the true story about sailors who survived in a lifeboat for 42 days. It was in my Dad's *Argosy* magazine."

"And all they had was a bag of turkey sandwiches?"

"No, silly. They had a very small supply of hardtack and chocolate bars."

"Milk?"

"No!"

I could tell Danny was losing patience. But at two in morning, after being robbed and having had under an hour's sleep, I was a bit thin myself.

"Danny, here's how I see it. In 15 hours -- not 42 days -- 15 hours, we'll pull into Nashville's Union Station. JB will be there. He'll take us to Stony River Academy where we'll eat a huge supper in the dining hall. We've got ten turkey sandwiches left. That means we could eat two sandwiches every three hours and still make it just fine."

Danny had turned so I couldn't really see his expression. But his silence told me he was weighing my words.

"Jase, do you want one or two sandwiches?"

"I'll have two, sailor."

CONSIDERING ALL THAT WE had experienced earlier that night, sleep came quickly. Although I wouldn't discover it until I awoke, I'd fallen asleep before finishing my second sandwich. The last of my milk remained unfinished as well.

This time my sleep was colored ink-black. Someone had pulled the plug and my internal screen was blank. Not a dream in sight.

"No! No! It can't be lost. For the love of Mike -- where has it gone?"

The anguished cry of an old man reverberated around the coach. No passenger could have slept through it.

Suddenly Freddie entered our coach, snapped on the overhead lights, and ran toward the man.

"Sir, what is it?" he pleaded. "Are you hurt?"

"I've been robbed -- all my savings. My wallet's gone. Help me -- please."

"Porter, I'm a nurse. Let me tend to this gentleman while you bring help," offered the young woman, seated across the aisle from the victim.

"Sir, this lady will stay with you while I find the person who can help you. He's just two coaches up. He'll be here shortly," Freddie assured the old man. "Don't worry! You'll be just fine."

Freddie dashed forward toward Lieutenant Donovan's coach. In less than a minute, both men returned. Just as he had in my case, the lieutenant took charge.

"My name is Lieutenant Donovan. I'm with the New York Central, Bureau of Detectives. Please tell me what's happened. Everything! Don't spare the details."

Lieutenant Donovan removed his little black notebook from his coat pocket and began taking notes.

"My name is Ray Howard. I live in Jackson. My wife died this past winter. I was invited to live with my daughter and her husband. They have a house in Chicago.

"Yesterday I closed my savings account -- everything that we'd saved over the course of our lives. I had the bank teller give me all of the money in hundred-dollar bills. So it'd all fit -- in a special wallet I bought. The wallet was in my inside jacket pocket. I thought it'd be safe there because the pocket had a zipper on it."

"How much money are we talking about, Mr. Howard?"

"There was $17,500."

"Was this special wallet in your jacket pocket when you came to the station?"

"Yes, I could feel it through my jacket. Naturally I was concerned about it. I suppose I must have checked it every ten minutes. It was there when I got on the train -- when I took my seat here -- and just before I fell asleep. But when I woke up, it -- it was gone."

"What about your train ticket, driver's license, and so on?"

"That's in my regular wallet in my back pocket."

He reached behind himself, pulled out his *regular* wallet, and opened it up.

"Everything seems to be here. Even the $20 bill I put there for use on this trip. Yep, it's all still there. Whoever did this just got my savings money."

"Well, sir. Whoever did this is still on this train and so is --."

Before Lieutenant Donovan could finish, an old, gray-haired woman in a blue dress, sitting in an aisle seat near the front of the coach stood up and screamed, "Hey! My billfold's gone too. It was inside my purse. My purse has been right next to me in this seat since we left Jackson. There go my train tickets -- and my driver's license. Doggone it!"

"What about your money?" Lieutenant Donovan asked.

"It's safe. When I travel I keep it in my -- well -- under my clothing." She patted her bodice. "It's still here. I learned to do that the hard way. I been dipped before."

"Let me finish with this gentleman. Then I'll come and get your report, madam."

While the lieutenant continued questioning the first victim, I whispered a thought in Danny's ear. He understood my message and nodded. We both rose from our seats and walked to the front of the carriage. We opened the porters' closet. I removed a broom with a long handle. We started back to our seats. Just as I passed the gray-haired victim, I stopped and turned around.

Danny stopped beside the lady and said in a kind voice, "I'm sorry you were dipped before madam. It's not a pleasant experience, especially if you're an old man or an eleven-year-old boy."

Danny's words were visibly upsetting to the woman. She stared at Danny and slowly shook her head. Then she reached for Danny's throat. Before she could touch him, I quickly slipped the broom handle under her hat and lifted it off her head. The hat wasn't all that was removed. The netting that extended downward in front of her face and her gray hair also came off, revealing a regulation, prison butch haircut.

I quickly pulled my broom back and jammed it through the arm rests of the two seats in her section, trapping her in her seat.

Danny smugly shook his finger at the woman. Then he yelled, "Lieutenant Donovan, it gives me great pleasure to introduce Rapid Rupert."

LIEUTENANT DONOVAN PROMPTLY ARRESTED, handcuffed, and locked away Rapid Rupert in a sturdy wire cage in the baggage car. Normally the cage was used for transporting dangerous animals. Therefore, it was most appropriate that the Jackson Dipper was occupying that space.

When the lieutenant entered our coach, he went directly to Mr. Howard and presented the stolen special wallet, containing his life savings. "We found this tucked out of sight in *Miss Rupert's* dress. I did a quick count and all $17,500 is there. But you should count it too."

Mr. Howard counted the money quickly and nodded at Lieutenant Donovan. "It's all here, Lieutenant."

"Good. Now I suggest you and I head for the mail car. We can turn it over to the postal clerk there for safekeeping until we arrive in Chicago. Then we'll retrieve it, and I'll escort you to a branch of the Northern Trust Bank in Union Station. They'll cut you a cashier's check made out to you. That way your savings will be safe until you deposit the check in a bank of your choice after you settle into your new home."

"Thank you, Lieutenant. I'm so grateful to you. I lost a good deal of money when there was a run on my bank -- in Jackson -- during the Depression. I've distrusted banks ever since. But it nearly ruined my life this time. Shall we go to the mail car now?"

After returning from the mail car, the lieutenant sought us out. "Boys, before you go back to sleep, let's go to the dining car and chat. I've got some questions and some information for you. I'll bet you've got the same for me."

After we'd sat down, Lieutenant Donovan told us that he was a bit embarrassed to have been Rupert Evans' last arresting officer and yet, that night, he'd failed to recognize Evans on two occasions.

Then he asked us the $64 question. "How did you know that gray-haired lady was, in fact, Rupert Evans?"

Because I'd been the first to draw that conclusion, Danny deferred to me.

"You told us a couple of things that stuck in my head. In the case earlier tonight on the other train, the old man who *claimed* he'd been robbed, stated he'd learned the hard way to hide his money in his pocket because he'd been *dipped* before."

"Those were his exact words. I wrote them down in my little black notebook. How did that help you?"

"When we asked you what he meant by *dipped,* you told us that *dipper* was a slang word that *pickpockets* use to describe *themselves.*"

"Good catch, Jase. So you concluded that the old man could have been a pickpocket himself."

"The thought entered my mind. But it didn't stick until I heard the gray-haired lady use almost the identical words herself. Then I began to wonder if we weren't dealing with two pickpockets -- an old man and an old lady."

"But you still weren't sure."

"Then I remembered that you called Evans a master of disguise. I concluded that we could be dealing with *one* very clever pickpocket. Even the disguises made sense because you also told us Evans was now choosing weaker targets -- old men, women, and children. But there was one thing the old man and old lady had in common that took me a while to figure out."

"What was that?"

"They both claimed to have lost their driver's licenses to the pickpocket."

"I don't understand."

"If they were accused of being pickpockets and required to identify themselves, they were covered. The *purported* pickpocket stole their driver's licenses, giving them a perfect defense."

"And a perfectly solved crime, my boy. Well done!"

My face turned red. Yet, somehow I managed a weak *thank you.*

"Now I have some news for you. One of the items *Miss* Evans was carrying in a secret pocket sewn into her dress, was a key ring filled with two types of keys. First, locker keys from nearly every train station within 300 miles of Jackson. Most likely these lockers are filled with disguises and loot. Before boarding NYC #45, I'll bet Evans stowed your wallet in his Jackson locker, Jase. That's also where he swapped costumes."

"What's the other kind of key?" Danny asked.

"Safety deposit boxes -- from at least two dozen banks in this same area. I imagine, when the judge orders these boxes opened, we'll find Evans' stash of ill-gotten treasure. And there's some good news for you boys in all this."

"Good news?"

"If this treasure is returned, you boys may be looking at some real, big-time reward money. And you'll have to learn how to deal with the press. This will make real news. What do you think of that?"

Danny assumed our side of the conversation.

"We've solved a number of crimes and vanquished any number of villains. We've been involved in more press conferences than I can remember. We give an exclusive to one reporter because he tells our stories with fairness and integrity. One of our recent cases resulted in our capturing an army deserter. That one brought us a $100 reward.

"But monetary rewards are not as important to us as recognition for doing good deeds for our neighborhood, our hometown, and our country. We've each received three United States Medals of Courage. J. Ebert Hoover presented the first one, when we were on the Don McNeil radio show. Our second one was presented by President Roosevelt in the White House. We even had a chance to chat with Winston Churchill on that occasion.

"I can't think what we did to receive the third medal. But it was probably something to do with national security. We're good at protecting our country from the bad guys. Right, Jase."

"Most of what Danny told you is true. But we still have one area to work on. Don't we, Danny?"

"What's that, Jase?"

"Exaggeration."

"Oh! Right. I knew that."

11 THE SOUTH WIND BLOWETH

WE ARRIVED IN CHICAGO RIGHT ON SCHEDULE, exactly 6:15 a.m., Central time. Freddie had agreed to lead us to the track where we would board our connecting train, the Pennsylvania Railroad #308 or the *South Wind* as it was called. The prospect of traveling on a train with a fascinating name like *South Wind* had captured my imagination. I could hardly wait to get aboard. Danny shared my excitement.

As we followed Freddie, we passed by the engine of our train which had stopped where our track met the platform. It was still huffing and hissing as we walked by.

"We arrived on Track #3 on the North Platform. These tracks have odd-numbers. The *South Wind* departs from Track #10 on the South Platform where the tracks are even-numbered. Here at Union Station, there are 24 tracks, divided equally between the two platforms," Freddie informed us.

When we stepped onto the platform, we looked both right and left to observe the dozen tracks coming into the North Platform. All but a few were occupied by trains busily loading or unloading scores of passengers.

"To get to the South Platform, we'll walk through the concourse -- that wide area between the two platforms. After we locate Track #10, I'll take you up and show you the mezzanine -- it's located between the platform and the street level. Lots of interesting restaurants and shops there. Then I'll take you up to the street level so you can see the hall."

The Great Hall was Union Station's ornate Beaux-Arts main waiting room, situated under an enormous vaulted skylight. The entire area was replete with statuary and dozens of elaborate, large-scale clocks that allowed passengers to keep close tabs on their time. From the Great Hall, splendid wide marble staircases led downward to the mezzanine or platform levels below.

Standing in the Great Hall, Danny and I couldn't help ourselves. Just like two country bumpkins, we stared upward at the immense skylight. We agreed that the glass ceiling was even higher than the peak of the tallest barn in Chippewa County.

Unfortunately Freddie's next porter's assignment was on a train departing more than an hour before we would board the *South Wind.* Because his duties commenced well before departure time, he had to leave us. We understood completely, thanked him for looking out for us, and bid him farewell.

"Don't forget the *South Wind* leaves from Track #10 -- from the South Platform at 8:00 a.m.," he reminded us one last time before heading to his train.

"Thank Eddie for us next time you see him, Freddie," Danny hollered before he was out of earshot. He gave us a thumbs-up and waved a last goodbye.

Freddie had suggested we check out the USO Canteen on the mezzanine level. "The soldiers, sailors, and the USO hostesses always make young fellows like you feel welcome," he assured us. "Especially since you're traveling alone."

We decided to take Freddie's advice and explore. We walked by a newsstand where bold headlines announced another milestone in the war in the Pacific:

U.S. NAVAL SHIPS BOMBARD
JAPANESE HOME ISLANDS

I realized that it had been three days since I had thought about the war. That was a record for me. Danny seemed to read my mind. "Jase, let's try to read the newspaper when we're in Nashville."

"Good idea, Danny."

When we arrived at the mezzanine level, we simply followed the sounds of boisterous voices and lively music that we assumed were emanating from the canteen. Even though it was early in the morning, the canteen was bursting at the seams with at least 200 soldiers and sailors seated or mingling inside the wide-open canteen entrance.

USO volunteer hostesses in neatly-pressed uniforms were bustling about, carrying tray after tray of donated goodies to the hungry and appreciative servicemen. Danny astutely inventoried the fare. "They've got doughnuts and coffee, pop and ice cream, and sandwiches -- club sandwiches mostly -- and iced tea. Hmmm. Pretty good, huh?"

The servicemen buzzed with excitement when their servers arrived. I wasn't sure what pleased them the most, the arrival of the scrumptious food or the pert young hostesses who delivered it.

"Hi, boys. Come on in. Have a sandwich and some pop," offered one of the friendly hostesses.

"Yeah! Sit here with us," a young sailor offered. "Where you guys from? And where ya headed?"

As we were relating the nature of our trip and what had happened along the way, our sandwiches and pop arrived. Danny, still clutching the turkey sandwiches, decided to relax his grip and placed the now-stained, paper bag under his chair.

We thanked the sailors and hostess over and over, admitting that we felt guilty taking food and drinks away from our men in uniform. But we were assured that there was plenty for everyone.

"Where are you from, sir?" Danny inquired of the sailor who had invited us in.

"Originally I'm from Iowa. But I enlisted right after Pearl Harbor. I've been serving on a destroyer out of Norfolk, Virginia. That's a big navy town. For the past three years, we've been hunting German U-boats -- submarines -- along the Atlantic coast. Had pretty good luck too. Sunk three U-boats, all told. But now that Germany's surrendered, I've been reassigned to a destroyer operating out of Pearl Harbor. That's where I'm heading now. I hope to sink a Jap sub or two before it's over."

"Sir, have you been home since you were in the navy?"

"First of all, I'm a non-commissioned officer. A first-class petty officer. You don't have to call me *sir*. And yes, I'm just coming off a seven-day leave. I got to see my family -- and my girl in Ames. That's where I'm from -- Ames, Iowa. Lots of Amish around Ames. They're mostly conscientious objectors."

I knew about the Amish. We had a few Amish farmers in the area around Riverton. But I didn't know the meaning of *conscientious objectors*. From the slight shrug Danny transmitted to me, he apparently didn't know either. But neither of us interrupted to ask.

"So you're heading for Nashville. You don't by chance go through Louisville, do you?"

"Yes, the *South Wind* goes through Indianapolis and then Louisville," I told him.

"I hear they got a swell canteen there. Check it out," he suggested.

We agreed. Based on our limited experience, canteens were fine places as far as we were concerned.

We chatted with the sailors at our table for nearly another hour. Without exception, they were extremely polite, gregarious, and welcoming, just as Freddie had predicted. And the hostesses doted on us as if we were full-scale members of the military.

When the large clock on the wall across from the canteen read 7:30 a.m., I suggested to Danny that it was almost time to meet Lieutenant Donovan at Track #10.

When we stood up to leave, our sailor friend made us a promise. "You boys don't have to worry about this war. We'll have this thing wrapped up and those Japs put to bed, long before you're in high school. Yes, sir. It'll be our pleasure to save you guys the trouble."

After exchanging farewells, Danny retrieved our sack of sandwiches and we headed for the South Platform.

"Did you notice that nobody offered his name? And nobody asked us for ours?" Danny observed.

"Curious. Why do you think that was, Danny?"

"They've been fighting the war for two or three years. Could be they've learned it's best not to get too close to anyone. After all, lots of soldiers and sailors have lost their lives. Maybe you'd prefer them not to be your close friends."

"Maybe so, Danny. Maybe so."

THE USO CANTEEN AT Union Station in Chicago sparked within me a profound and lasting interest in the remarkable phenomenon of track-side canteens during World War II. Like wildflowers, dozens of canteens spontaneously sprang up in cities, towns, and villages across the vast network of America's railways. Their emergence resulted from the need of everyday Americans to say *thank you* to those in our armed services who sacrificed so much to defend our country and to keep its citizens out of harm's way.

The larger canteens in major cities like Chicago were complex organizations, operated by hundreds of volunteers, often including Hollywood entertainers. Many were funded by thousands of dollars in contributions from a broad spectrum of donors. Located in major rail hubs, these were the *canteen supermarkets*, designed to serve a large volume of traveling servicemen and servicewomen.

Other canteens were far more modest. They were the *mom-and-pop grocers* of the track-side canteen world. They served their *customers* donated homemade cookies and pies, sandwiches and soup, and coffee and tea. These were the canteens that sprouted up along the tracks in smaller American towns and villages.

Which best served the needs of our traveling soldiers and sailors? They both did by providing American military men and women friendship, welcome, and home-cooked food.

Here is a glimpse of just a few track-side canteens that I have learned about since the end of the war.

On the morning of December 17, 1941, in North Platte, Nebraska, a small group of women arrived at the Union Pacific station. These mothers, wives, sisters, and fiancées were waiting for the troop train, transporting men of Nebraska's 134th Infantry from Camp Robinson to an unknown destination. They'd been told the train would arrive about 11:00 a.m. Shortly after noon, a train did arrive, but not that of the 134th. Disappointed, they were informed that the 134th would surely arrive later, about 3:00 p.m. As news spread by word-of-mouth, a larger crowd gathered.

When another train finally arrived about 4:30 p.m., over 500 friends and relatives had assembled, carrying baskets of fruit, cartons of cigarettes, Christmas gifts, and cookies for their men. The Nebraskans cheered at the sight of the smiling soldiers but soon learned that these men were from Kansas.

Overcome by their friendly spirits, the people showered the Kansans with the gifts they'd brought for their own relatives. While the train departed, the men's thumbs were sticking up, out of the open windows, and the women were crying openly and wishing them well. This was the first time that anyone had met the Kansans' train, and the men's morale was raised enormously by the friendliness and generosity of the people in North Platte.

After this heart-warming experience, the town was determined to give other servicemen the same send-off. Eight days later on Christmas Day, and only 18 days after Pearl Harbor, volunteers met every train from 5:00 a.m. until midnight. They greeted the men, served them a Christmas dinner, and wished them a *Merry Christmas.*

That Christmas Day marked the beginning of the *North Platte Servicemen's Canteen* located in the North Platte depot. From that day until the end of the war, they met every train. Housewives made sandwiches, cakes, and cookies while younger women met each train, serving coffee and providing conversation. On certain days, men's organizations prepared and served food, washed dishes, and swept floors. Young children collected magazines, raised cash, or worked in the kitchen.

Volunteers sometimes performed personal services by sending soldiers' telegrams, writing letters, mailing birthday and anniversary cards, administering first aid, or sewing on buttons and mending tears in clothing. Platform workers distributed candy bars and matches, answered questions, and served the wounded men on hospital trains. Women behind magazine racks distributed tons of entertaining magazines and decks of cards to ease the long hours of travel. Sometimes the women met as many as 32 trains a day, serving more than 8,000 servicemen during that period.

Nebraska and Colorado communities, some as far away as 200 miles, took turns providing food for the canteen on regularly scheduled days. By the end of the war, $137,884.72 had been contributed to the North Platte canteen. With the involvement of almost 55,000 volunteers, the canteen had served more than six million servicemen.

Following the establishment of the North Platte canteen, a spontaneous grassroots effort spread across the country. Towns located along railroad routes began establishing track-side, free canteens for soldiers. While trains stopped for only a ten-minute layover, volunteers served free sandwiches, coffee, cookies, and cakes. But most importantly they gave away smiles, hugs, words of encouragement, and a taste of home.

By the end of the war, 125 towns across the United States, from New England to California, operated track-side canteens.

In Lima, Ohio, a canteen fed the servicemen traveling on passenger trains of three railroads, passing through during World War II. Initially troop trains were not to be served, but the Lima women passed food through the coach windows anyway. This canteen continued through the Korean and into the Vietnam Wars. Over 10,000 women fed over four million soldiers and sailors during these three decades, making it the longest-running effort in the nation.

According to Scott Trostel's book, *Lima's Operation Kindness*, the Lima canteen offered, at no cost to those in the service, the following:

- **Sandwiches** (Roast Beef, Roast Pork, Baked Ham, Chicken, Turkey, Barbecue, Bologna/Ham Salad, Meat Loaf, Egg Salad, Cheese, Chicken Salad, Goose, and Rabbit)
- **Fried Chicken**
- **Desserts** (Cakes, Fruit Cake, Brownies, Doughnuts, and Gingerbread)
- **Cookies** (Peanut Butter, Oatmeal, Molasses, and Sugar)
- **Pies** (Lemon, Apple, Cherry, Peach, Raisin, Strawberry, Pumpkin, Raspberry, Blackberry, Rhubarb, and Pineapple)
- **Hard-Boiled Eggs**
- **Popcorn Balls**
- **Candy Bars**

- **Fudge**
- **Drinks** (Coffee, White Milk, Chocolate Milk, Orange Drink, Orange Juice, Tea, and Hot Chocolate)
- **Ice Cream**
- **Fruits** (Apples, Oranges, Bananas, Grapes, Pears, Peaches, and Cherries)
- **Miscellaneous Items and Services** (Cigarettes, Matches, Tobacco, Chewing Gum, Magazines, Newspapers, Postcards, Writing Paper, Pencils, Telephone Calls, Telegrams, Bus Fare, Train Fare, and Taxi Fare)

In Crestline, Ohio, the canteen served 1.2 million soldiers traveling on the Pennsylvania Railroad. The construction of the canteen building was paid for by the school children of Crestline who donated their pennies.

Over 1.3 million troops stopped at the canteen in Dennison, Ohio, on the Pennsylvania Railroad where they were welcomed with bologna and cheese sandwiches, fruit, candy bars, and drinks, provided by citizens of seven counties.

In Troy, Ohio, The West Street Ambassadors, a group of nearly 40 young women, operated the Junior Girls Canteen. Residents of Troy and communities in six counties supported their efforts. Each night, even in the rain, they offered snacks from a cart sheltered by a patio umbrella.

On Christmas Eve of 1944, a troop train from Texas rolled into Troy. The temperature was near zero and the men's spirits were low. Baskets of neatly wrapped gifts were brought on board, and shouts of *Merry Christmas* were heard in the still night. In early 1945, five men wrote notes of appreciation from the trenches during the Battle of the Bulge. This was the only canteen in the country operated by teenagers. They fed over 600,000 troops during the war.

Alongside the New York Central Railroad, citizens of Bellefontaine, Ohio, erected a little white hut. Here soldiers quickly filed through a buffet line, choosing from sandwiches, desserts, fruit, candy bars, cigarettes, and drinks. Then the men relaxed on the platform while the locomotives were changed. Sunday school classes, high school classes, grange members, farmers, and local merchants and manufacturers stepped forward to help. This canteen, one of twelve in Ohio, was run by wives of New York Central Railroad men. It served as a track-side model, and provided lunch for over 700,000 men during the 45 months of World War II.

This poem, written by Virginia Fortney in 1945, was included in *The Columbus Avenue Miracle*. It was printed on the back of cards, given to the troops that stopped at the Bellefontaine Canteen.

Is everything ready? The train is in!
Here come the boys; look at them grin!
Hello there, Sailor! Hi there, Marine!
You're welcome to the Bellefontaine Canteen.
Right this way, Private, Lieutenant too;
You girls Khaki, Green, and Blue!
Help yourselves to the sandwiches, cake, and pie.
Our coffee urn is never dry.
Or if you'd rather, there's milk or "coke."
It's all donated by generous folk -
Whose prayers are with you constantly -
And anything you want is free.
Where are you from? What's that medal for?
You look too young to be in this war.
Send us a card. Or even better,
If you have time, write us a letter.
Here comes the conductor. "All ready, men?"
Goodbye! Good luck! Come back again!

This poem sums up the atmosphere created by track-side canteens. These are only a few of the remarkable stories about women meeting strangers with love, a friendly greeting, and a taste of home as the servicemen and servicewomen headed off to the unknown in Europe or the Pacific.

BEFORE OUR ARRIVAL IN Chicago, Lieutenant Donovan had proposed a plan. We would ask Freddie to lead us to the track from which the *South Wind* was scheduled to depart. Because we had nearly a two-hour layover between trains, we could spend part of that time exploring Union Station. But we had to be back at the *South Wind* by 7:40 a.m. to board.

During our layover time in Chicago, the lieutenant would turn over Rupert Evans to the Chicago police. Then he'd telephone the stationmaster in Jackson and ask him to open the pickpocket's locker. If my new wallet was in the locker, the lieutenant would arrange for the stationmaster to send it to me in Nashville. Then the lieutenant would meet us at the *South Wind* to tell us whether the wallet was on the way or not.

True to his word, Lieutenant Donovan was waiting for us at Track #10. More importantly he was all smiles. "You're in luck, Jase. Your wallet and all your cash are on their way. Mailed -- Special Delivery -- to the Nashville address you gave me earlier. How's that sound?"

"That's really swell, Lieutenant. Really swell. How about that, Danny?"

Danny didn't respond. Instead, he wrinkled his brow and stared at Lieutenant Donovan.

"What's the trouble, Danny?" the lieutenant asked.

"What about the wager?"

"Huh! With everything that's happened today, I almost forgot about our bet. Now let's see. When Jase gets his wallet -- after he arrives in Nashville -- he'll be whole. That is, he'll have his $5 wallet and the $11 in travel money. But he'll also have my $15! So now he'll have to give that back to me," he declared, holding out his hand.

I reached for the lieutenant's money, but Danny stopped me. "Not so fast, Jase."

I paused while Danny reminded us of the terms of the wager. "Lieutenant, the key element of our wager was to see how long before Jase received that claim money. You had four days to get it to Jase. Today -- Friday -- is the first day. This wager isn't over until Jase receives that wallet and money. If he receives it in four days or under, he'll send your $15 back to you. But if it takes more than four days, Jase keeps your $15. That was our bet. Right?"

The lieutenant seemed taken aback by Danny's words. He rolled his eyes and put his hand under his chin. He was evidently searching for some flaw in Danny's logic. After racking his brain for nearly a minute, he shrugged his shoulders and admitted, "You're right, Danny. That was the gist of our original wager. The bet's still on."

"As I recall, you told us the wallet and money were being sent by Special Delivery. I assume you mean the Special Delivery mail service provided by the U.S. Post Office Department. Is that so?"

"Yes, sir. That's the one."

"So there will be no question about exactly when Jase receives that wallet and money. I mean he'll be required to sign a receipt, stating the time and date. Correct?"

"I agree completely. That receipt will determine the winner of the wager. On my word of honor," Lieutenant Donovan stated solemnly.

We all shook hands. But I noticed Danny was looking very smug. I suspected that neither the lieutenant nor I knew what Danny had up his sleeve. But I was certain it was something.

"Danny, I didn't hear you say, 'On my word of honor,' " I observed.

"Do you doubt me?" he replied slyly.

I decided that I wouldn't answer his question. I had my honor to consider as well.

After a round of goodbyes, we sincerely thanked Lieutenant Donovan for all he'd done. He promised to keep us abreast of the disposition of the Rupert Evans case. "And especially any possible reward money," he reminded us.

As we settled in our seats, I asked Danny, "All right, now let's have it. What are you not telling me about the Special Delivery service?"

At first, Danny ignored my question by delivering the following non sequitor, "Boy, isn't this a luxurious train. Just think! We're going to spend all day on the *South Wind*. We won't even have to change trains before arriving in Nashville. Just think!"

I gave him a dirty look.

As he reached for his crumpled sack, Danny changed the subject. "You want another turkey sandwich, Jase?"

"Talk! You dirty rat!" I snarled, using my very best Humphrey Bogart brogue.

Danny laughed and finally relented. "Jase, what day is this?"

I was so tired and confused that it took me a minute to come up with the answer. "It's Friday. What does that have to do with it?"

"If you mailed a regular letter to yourself in Riverton today, when would that letter be delivered?"

"Let's see. Because of the weekend -- probably not until Tuesday."

"What time on Tuesday?"

"Sometime in the middle of the afternoon."

"Do you know when that same letter would be delivered if you mailed it Special Delivery?"

I honestly had no idea. I shook my head.

"A *Special Delivery* letter would get there on Tuesday morning. And not before."

"Why is that, Danny?"

His answer was baffling. "Because the only thing *special* about *Special Delivery* is the special delivery time."

"Huh?"

"The letter will arrive in Riverton, probably sometime Monday night. If it's been sent by *Special Delivery*, someone will make a special trip out to your house and deliver it on Tuesday morning. That's what *Special Delivery* means!"

"Danny, what you're telling me is that -- *the only thing special about Special Delivery is the special delivery time.*"

"You got it, Jase. Now tell me when does the four-day time limit expire?"

I counted on my fingers. "Day One expires at midnight Friday. Day Two -- midnight Saturday. Day Three -- midnight Sunday. Day Four -- midnight Monday. It's Monday, Danny! Not Tuesday!"

Danny nodded his head smugly. Then he stuck out his hand.

"What?" I replied brusquely.

"Jase, you almost gave the $15 to Lieutenant Donovan."

"I guess I --. I wasn't thinking."

"I think it'd be best if we put your $15 in my wallet."

Reluctantly I agreed and handed him the money.

After stowing my money away in his wallet, Danny took a huge bite of his mashed turkey sandwich.

Suddenly I felt exhausted. I realized that we'd been awake nearly the entire night before. I closed my eyes and all went black.

"MASTER TUCKER, PLEASE WAKE up. We're coming into Louisville. Master Addison, please wake up now," the porter implored as he shook my shoulder gently.

"What time is it?" I yawned.

"It's half past one. We'll be in Louisville in 15 minutes."

"Louisville? What happened to Indianapolis?" Danny wondered.

"You gentlemen were sleeping so soundly -- I didn't have the heart to wake you. You didn't miss much. We only stopped briefly in Indianapolis -- just three minutes. But we'll be in Louisville for over an hour. I thought you might like to stretch your legs. Union Station is an interesting place to visit. You'll see lots of soldiers and sailors at the USO Canteen there."

"Thank you, porter. We didn't get much sleep last night."

"I heard all about that. You gentlemen are celebrities. But you both fell to sleep right after you boarded -- just after 8:00 a.m. You got over five hours of sleep."

"How'd you feel, Danny?"

"Hungry. Want another turkey sandwich?"

"No, thanks. Why don't we get something different in the Louisville station?"

"Good idea. These sandwiches are getting moldy. We'll be in Nashville for supper in three -- or maybe -- four hours. Porter, could you please dispose of this sack for us?"

"Be my pleasure, sir," the porter replied, picking up Danny's sack gingerly, using only two fingers. "Don't forget. We depart at exactly 2:56 p.m. You don't want to miss the train."

Upon entering Union Station, we were swept up and carried along by a throng of servicemen. Our *herd* was greeted by a young woman, wearing the familiar USO hostess uniform. She smiled and handed us each a small brochure entitled, *Welcome to Louisville's Union Station.*

Danny opened the brochure and began summarizing its contents for the benefit of everyone around him. "Union Station was built by the Louisville and Nashville railroad. Opened in 1891. The largest train station in the Southern United States. Serves over 50 trains a day. Cost over $300,000 to build. Wow! Exterior is *limestone ashlar* -- whatever that is. Roof -- slate. Walls -- marble from Georgia. Ceramic tile covers the floor. That's good."

After thumbing ahead, Danny stopped and told us, "There's an 84-paneled stained glass skylight! Just like Chicago, Jase. It's part of the barrel-vaulting tower -- never seen one of those. Oh, Jase -- here's the best part. There's a USO Canteen -- just off the atrium. I know where I'm having lunch. How about you?"

"Can't beat the price," I admitted. "But before we go, let's find a drinking fountain. I'm thirsty."

We stopped and looked around us, but the crowds of people blocked our view. We couldn't see anything beyond a few feet.

"Can I help you, lads?" We turned to see a large police officer with a friendly face. His badge told us his name was *Clancy.*

"We're looking for a drinking fountain, sir."

"They're over by the restrooms -- just over by the --. Just follow me, lads."

We fell in behind Officer Clancy, weaving our way to the far wall of the atrium. When we arrived at our destination, the policeman pointed at the fountains and announced, "There ye are, lads. Help yourselves."

Mounted on the wall were two white porcelain drinking fountains. A large sign above one read, *White Only.* Above the other, *Colored Only.*

I was confused. "Danny, do you think they call normal water, *white water?*"

"Maybe so, Jase. But what's *colored water?*"

"Got me! Maybe it's flavored with something. Why don't you try it? I'll try the white."

We walked up to the fountains and were about to sample the different types of water when Officer Clancy intervened. Laying his large hand on Danny's shoulder, he admonished, "I wouldn't do that if I was you, son."

"I just wanted to taste some of the *colored* water. We don't have that in Michigan," he explained.

"It's not *colored water*. It's water for *colored* people."

Danny stared at me with a confused look on his face. Then he turned to Officer Clancy and pleaded, "I'm not sure what you mean, sir."

"There are fountains for *white* folks -- like you and me. And there are separate fountains for *colored* folks -- like those folks over there. You know -- nigras," he explained, pointing at a black family sitting nearby. "The same is true for the restrooms. On that side, there's two *colored* restrooms -- a men's and a women's. And on this side -- two *white* restrooms."

Danny and I looked at each other knowingly. We finally got it. But it was hard to assimilate immediately.

Officer Clancy, sensing our difficulty, caringly advised, "Things down here in the South are done differently than up north. It's our custom. Don't worry. You'll soon get used to it."

We smiled and nodded compliantly.

"Now how else may I help you, lads?"

"Could you tell us where the USO Canteen is located?"

"Right behind you, lads. Right over yonder," he replied, pointing over our heads.

The canteen entrance was less than a hundred feet away. Swing music and raucous laughter poured from its door. We turned and walked briskly toward the deafening noise.

"Now wait just a minute, lads! You forgot your drink of water," the police officer reminded us.

"It's all right, Officer Clancy. Thanks just the same. They'll have pop for us in the canteen. All colors -- strawberry, orange, and lemon. But we don't mind."

Officer Clancy shook his head and waved goodbye with an exaggerated swipe of his arm. As he disappeared, I could tell by his body language that he was still talking to himself.

We enjoyed the same welcome at the Louisville canteen as we had in Chicago. We ate our fill of club sandwiches and drank two tall strawberry pops. As the hands of the clock approached the top of the hour, we sloshed our way back to the *South Wind*.

Once we were back in our seats, I asked, "Danny, do you think Nashville will be as *Southern* as Louisville?"

"Not a chance, Jase. Not a chance."

12 POWS IN AMERICA

Author's Note:

The Cottonwood *series is replete with stories involving German POWs in America during World War II. POWs were frequently transported to their camps and work assignments by train during this period. War Department policies governing their treatment as passengers were a constant source of frustration and resentment by servicemen, servicewomen, and civilians alike.*

Strictly following the rules spelled out by the Geneva Convention, POW passengers were granted priority berthing and dining while American military and civilian passengers traveled in coach or settled for standing-room-only reservations on trains.

The U.S. citizens including members of congress accused the War Department of coddling the POWs, but the Pentagon staunchly defended these practices. To allow you to make your own assessment of the issue, I've presented a full treatise on the subject below. I invite you to read the facts and judge for yourself.

DURING THE WAR, AMERICA EXPERIENCED A CRITICAL labor shortage. The 16 million Americans serving in the armed services made up more than ten percent of the country's population at the time. Therefore, the booming defense industry's demand for labor more than exceeded supply, even counting the millions of women who joined the work force. The need for semi-skilled workers in farming, food processing, and forestry was particularly acute.

Because the Geneva Convention authorized us to compel German enlisted and non-commissioned officers to work, businesses or individuals like farmers contracted directly with the Army for POW laborers and paid the prevailing wage rate which averaged 52 cents per hour.

The POWs worked an eight-hour day, six days per week. They were paid 80 cents a day plus a 10-cent daily allowance for personal items. 90 cents per day was about what a U.S. Army private was paid during the war. The rest of their earnings went to the U.S. government to pay for housing the prisoners and to finance the war effort. Half of their pay was deposited in savings accounts that they could take home after their repatriation

The other half was paid in the form of canteen coupons. Camp canteens, operated by POWs, sold cigarettes and pipe tobacco, soft drinks, ice cream, candy, and, in most cases, beer and wine. POWs could even order items from the Sears Roebuck catalog using canteen coupons.

UNLIKE THEIR AMERICAN COUNTERPARTS in Germany, German POWs held captive in the United States were hardly *roughing it*. They enjoyed an abundance of food, including delicacies they hadn't seen in years like coffee, eggs, and meat. Ironically, at the same time, American citizens were deprived of these same items because of rationing.

Some of the first German POWs to arrive in America were soldiers from General Erwin Rommel's Afrika Korps. These tough fighters were used to surviving on meager rations. Until they became accustomed to the large quantities of rich food, most became ill.

While POWs in America gained weight while in captivity, American POWs overseas lost weight. Camp menus were tailored to German taste, and meals were prepared by POW cooks so the prisoners would eat more and waste less. POWs told the German

Red Cross to discontinue sending food items to them. These just weren't needed in America.

Many camps allowed pictures of Adolph Hitler to hang in the Mess Hall. POWs were often transported to camps on railroad Pullman cars. While they were served three meals a day in the dining car, their military police guards were only authorized to order two meals a day.

In the camps, POWs had pets including cats, dogs, monkeys, and canaries. After Mussolini's defeat in 1943, Italian POWs got permission to go on sightseeing trips and attend dances and dinners in local Italian communities.

Because POWs had regular visiting hours for family members living in America, tracking down distant relatives became a major activity for many of them.

POWs were allowed to send postcards and letters home from the camps. This correspondence often resulted in the desire to tie the knot, and POWs were able to marry their sweethearts back home by proxy. Weddings, arranged through the Red Cross and conducted by local clergy, featured all the trimmings including cake, flowers, and best man.

But no bride!

IN THEIR LEISURE TIME, POWs took courses for college credit accepted by 19 universities in Germany and Austria. These courses were taught by local college professors. Credit hours were to be recorded in a logbook prepared by the German High Command just at the time when Germany was losing badly on the Russian front and the Allies were poised to invade Normandy.

In the camps, choirs and orchestras were established, using instruments donated from the communities in which the camps were located. Public concerts were held to thank the donors. POWs learned crafts and skills, including oil painting, sculpture, furniture making, carpentry, and *locksmithing*, of all things.

Sports teams were organized, using equipment furnished by local YMCAs. Volleyball, soccer, and Ping-Pong were very popular with the Germans. The public was invited to the camps to watch the matches.

Community groups donated books, stationery, games, hobby materials, phonograph records, magazines, and newspapers to the camps. Some camps allowed POWs to publish their own newspapers.

POWs watched English language movies which would be stopped from time to time to allow for translation. They seemed to enjoy propaganda movies like *Why We Fight* and anti-Nazi movies like *Watch on the Rhine*.

DURING THE WAR, 40 German generals and two admirals were interned in American POW camps. By design, they were treated with great deference because of their likely influence in Germany after the war. Retired American officers of the same rank were assigned as their liaison officers and guides. These Americans were all graduates of West Point and Annapolis which insured they were well-versed in the nuances of military tradition and courtesy.

These high-ranking German officers were taken on tours of shipyards and war plants to impress them with the size and vitality of the American war machine. All German officers regardless of rank were given radios to listen to whatever they wished. They were amazed at the openness of the news in America.

Officers had spacious private quarters with gardens, their own chefs, and full pay and benefits. These officers were granted paroles if they swore not to escape. They were provided with U.S. Army cars and drivers which they used to tour the countryside around their camps at will.

And not one paroled German officer ever attempted to escape!

Five hardened German submarine officers were allowed to travel *unescorted* together on a train to their new POW camp, Camp Blanding, Florida. They had no dress uniforms for the trip so they were allowed to wear the uniform of a U.S. naval officer with one exception. They wore small Nazi lapel pins so they couldn't be accused of being spies. During their trip, there were no problems from the five or from Americans along the way.

NATURALLY SOME AMERICANS ACCUSED the military of coddling the POWs but the War Department refuted the charge by citing these benefits. First, when word of our generous treatment of POWs reached the German army, it would encourage more of them to surrender and thus shorten the war.

Second, such treatment made for docile POWs who required fewer guards. This meant more American soldiers could be sent to the front lines.

And third, the POWs were more cooperative and worked harder at their jobs thus helping in the war effort.

Though it may be hard to believe, serious consideration was given to a top secret proposal to allow POWs to transfer to the U.S. Army as the *German Volunteer Corps* to fight against the Japanese in the Pacific.

Most German POWs cherished their time spent in America during the war. This was particularly true of those who worked on American farms. Although fraternization was supposedly not allowed, farmers generally ignored the rule, plying hardworking POWs with tobacco, beer, wine, and extra food. No one was there to object because small details of three to five POWs were assigned, without guards, to area farms.

POWs ate at the dinner table with farm families who became very fond of their POWs. When the war ended, both the POWs and the farm families were saddened when they parted.

After the war, farmers sent gifts of much-needed foodstuffs and warm clothing to the POWs and their families. They visited them in Europe decades later.

In appreciation for the sincere hospitality of their American hosts, some POWs donated their savings accounts to local Community Chest campaigns. And more than 5,000 former POWs immigrated back to America after the war. More attempted to do so, but with so many displaced persons knocking at the American door, immigration was extremely difficult.

POW ESCAPE ATTEMPTS WERE rare. Of the more than 426,000 POWs in America during the war, only 1,583 *escaped*. And of those, only 22 were never recaptured. To put this in perspective, the escape rate was far lower than that of the U.S. Federal Prison System at the time.

Most POWs escaped to break the monotony of camp or to seek the companionship of local young women they'd met at work. The majority of the escaped prisoners returned on their own within 24 hours because they didn't want to miss the creature comforts of camp, including good food and a comfortable bed. And where could they earn such good money? Or enjoy the extensive educational and recreational opportunities provided back at camp. Besides, if they did escape, where were they going to go? In short, they had it pretty good.

However, there were a few determined POWs who earnestly attempted to escape. And, in a sense, you can't blame them. Being prisoners of war, it was their duty. There was no provision in the Geneva Convention to prevent or condemn you for trying. The idea being, if you escaped or even attempted to escape, the enemy would be required to spend more resources tracking you down and guarding you.

Obviously some POWs took their duty very seriously, especially the Japanese. In all, 56 POWs were shot and killed while attempting to escape from camps on American soil.

FORTUNATELY MANY POW ESCAPE attempts not only failed but were downright laughable. The following examples fall into this category:

The Great Escape

In a cold drizzle on Christmas Eve of 1944, a group of 25 officers and enlisted German POWs escaped through a tunnel from Camp Papago Park, located in Phoenix, Arizona. The camp was the repository of 1,700 of the most ardent Nazi POWs in America.

The escape was led by Submarine Captain Jurgen Wattenburg who believed fervently that escaping was his solemn duty.

The digging of the tunnel had been facilitated by camp guards who willingly furnished digging tools to the POWs when they requested permission to build a volleyball court. Over the course of three months as the tunnel was dug, the POWs stuffed dirt from the tunnel into pant pockets with holes in the bottoms. To cover up their tunneling activities, they walked around camp to distribute the dirt. Incredibly the resultant tunnel was 178 feet long and three feet in diameter.

In the camp woodshop, they'd constructed canoes in three sections to make them easy to transport through the tunnel. They tested the canoes for water-tightness in the camp showers and pronounced them seaworthy. From maps they'd acquired, Wattenberg and his officers devised a plan calling for them to wade down the Cross Cut Canal pulling their canoes behind them until they'd reached the Salt River. Once there, they would launch their canoes and float down to the Gila River and on to the Colorado River which would take them into Mexico.

Under cover of a noisy Christmas party contrived by their fellow POWs, the officers and men made it through the tunnel with their canoes. When they arrived at their first destination, they were shocked to discover that the Salt River was nothing but a muddy bog created by the recent rains. They failed to take into consideration that, like many of Arizona's rivers, the Salt was bone dry most of the year.

Not to be discouraged, they carried their canoes another 20 miles to the Salt's confluence with the Gila River, only to discover that the Gila was nothing but a series of large puddles. The discouraged POWs sat on the riverbank with their heads in their hands and cried in utter frustration.

Cold, wet, and hungry, Herbert Fuchs, one of the enlisted POWs, decided to throw in the towel. Flagging down an unsuspecting motorist, he requested that he be taken to the sheriff's office where he surrendered. The sheriff called the camp and told them that he had one of their prisoners who wanted to *come home*. Until the sheriff's call, camp officials were blissfully unaware of the escape.

Within days, all 25 POWs were returned to Camp Papago Park. Most required hospital treatment for exposure to the elements and exhaustion. This was not a glorious homecoming.

The Long Arm of the Law

Although the details are sketchy, this example provides an important lesson, Never fool with the FBI.

A German POW whose name was Ernst Meer escaped from Camp Reynolds, Pennsylvania. He hopped a freight train that carried him to Kentucky where he secured employment on a horse farm. After several weeks, he was tracked down by a diligent FBI agent named Johnson who arrested him and returned him to Camp Reynolds.

Meer wasn't happy about his lost freedom so after a few weeks he decided to escape a second time. This time his plan was to get as far away from Pennsylvania as he could. So he hitchhiked to California where he planned to enjoy life without constantly having to look over his shoulder.

Months later, Agent Johnson was in California investigating an unrelated case. Walking back to his hotel, Johnson just happened to spot Meer walking toward him on the opposite side of the street. He crossed the street and rearrested the POW.

Naturally Meer was impressed with Johnson's ability to track him down. So he begged Johnson to tell him how he'd done it.

Johnson simply replied, "We have our ways."

Meer reformed on the spot and never attempted to escape again.

Mountain Law

Three German submariners who were POWs at Camp Crossville, Tennessee, were assigned to a crew cutting timber in a remote area of the Cumberland Mountains. Left alone for a period, the trio decided to escape by fleeing into the dense forest.

They wandered aimlessly for several days, lost in the rugged mountain country. When they came upon a cabin in the woods, they attempted to get a drink of water from a pump. An irascible Granny appeared at the cabin door, aimed her squirrel rifle, and told them to, "Git!"

Unschooled in ways of mountain folks, the Germans ignored her. So the Granny took aim and fired, killing one of the Germans. When the sheriff informed her that she'd killed a German POW, she broke into tears.

The sheriff implored, "Well, shucks, Granny. What did you think you wuz aiming at?"

She replied, "I thought they wuz Yankees."

13 STONY RIVER ACADEMY

WHEN WE PULLED INTO NASHVILLE'S UNION
Station, I was so excited that I couldn't speak without shouting.
Danny was grinning so broadly that his teeth seemed to have
disappeared behind his owl-like ears.

Despite the horde of soldiers, sailors, and just ordinary citizens
milling about the platform, the minute we stepped off the train,
we spotted JB. In anticipation of our arrival, he had climbed up
onto the front rack of a luggage cart to place himself well above
the crowd. He madly waved at us until we waved back to let him
know we'd spotted him.

"Nothing like a friendly welcome!" Danny giggled excitedly.

By pointing toward the baggage-claim area, JB let us know
where to meet him. We nodded our agreement and began pushing
our way through the crowd.

Soon we joined the long line of arriving passengers eager to
claim their luggage and get on with their Nashville plans. With
quiet efficiency, luggage was speedily distributed to its rightful
claimants. Even before JB reached us, we'd exchanged claim checks
for our two suitcases.

When he arrived, we put down our luggage and exchanged
hugs with our friend. Apparently JB had come directly from
basketball camp because he was still dressed in his rich, forest-
green sweat suit. Over his left breast pocket, the Stony River

Academy school crest, comprising interwoven bay-laurel wreaths and noble Greek athletes hurtling through space, was embroidered in brilliant gold thread. In addition to looking fit and healthy, JB seemed to have grown an inch or two since I'd seen him last. After thinking about this, I dismissed the idea. After all, he'd only been gone about six weeks.

"Boy! Am I glad to see you two fellows! How was the trip? Long one -- wasn't it? Did you get much sleep? Coach Lewis is waiting for us in the parking lot. He's looking forward to meeting you. Do you need a hand with your suitcases? Wait until you see the Stony River Academy campus. Boy! I can't believe you're here. I couldn't get to sleep last night. Thanks for sending the telegram. It was the first one I ever received. I still have it. Want to see it?"

Evidently Danny and I hadn't been the only ones excited by our arrival.

We walked up the steps to street level and onto the sidewalk that crossed the wide sets of tracks and led us to the parking lot beside an elegant, blinding-white building. The bronze plaque next to the main entrance told us this was Nashville's main post office.

When we entered the parking lot, I saw a tall, rugged man, who reminded me of Gary Cooper, standing next to a wooden-panel, four-door station wagon. The man was also wearing a green SRA sweat suit. He waved at us, opened the rear door, and hollered, "Welcome to Nashville, y'all. Put your luggage back here."

After we'd dropped our suitcases and gym bags in the back, the man grasped our hands and shook them vigorously. "I'm Coach James Lewis. Based on everything Johnson has told me, I'm very eager to meet y'all. I hope you'll enjoy yourselves during the next ten days. Johnson's got an agenda all planned for your visit. When you leave Nashville, I guarantee you'll know more about our fair city than many Nashvillians. Are you ready to head to SRA?"

"Before we go, I have one question," Danny declared. "Who's this *Johnson* person?"

Not knowing Danny's quirks, Coach Lewis was perplexed. JB and I secretly smiled at each other as we watched the coach trying to determine how to answer Danny. Finally he took a stab at it. "I was referring to Johnson -- here. You know -- Johnson Bradford," he offered hesitantly, patting JB on the arm.

"Oh, you mean JB? I'd forgotten he once went by *Johnson Bradford*. That was before he became a Rivertonian," Danny explained. "Isn't that right, JB?"

"That's right, DT," JB countered, winking at the coach and me. *Touché.*

WE EXITED THE PARKING lot and turned onto the street that passed in front of the post office and the train station. Until that moment, I hadn't really noticed the striking architecture and ornate finish of these two buildings. I wondered if we would have time to examine them further.

"This street is Broad," Coach Lewis told us. "If we'd turned right, it'd have taken us to the center of downtown Nashville. Tomorrow I believe JB plans to show y'all the many tourist attractions in that area."

"JB, does your agenda include spending a little time checking out the train station and post office? Those buildings were extremely interesting to me. I'd like to look around inside them."

"Yes, indeed. We'll do that first thing in the morning."

"Coach Lewis, what direction are we heading right now?" Danny inquired.

"We're basically heading southwest. Up ahead, we'll take the right fork in the road. That puts us on West End Avenue. We'll stay on West End past Vanderbilt University and Centennial Park. After a couple of miles, West End becomes Harding Pike and a few blocks later we'll be in Belle Meade, the suburb where SRA is located."

After a few blocks, JB pointed out, "That's the Vanderbilt campus on the left where Vanderbilt University Hospital is located. My mother was a nurse there. And that's where she met my father when he was a resident."

JB stopped abruptly, but I remembered that Mom had told us the rest of the story. JB's parents were married in the summer of 1932, long before the war. Wanting to serve his country, Dr.

Bradford joined the navy and was assigned to the medical staff aboard the *USS Arizona*.

He was on duty that Sunday morning when the Japanese attacked. Tragically the Arizona was sunk and he was killed. Mercifully his remains were recovered and sent home to his family, who made arrangements for him to be buried in Arlington National Cemetery, just outside Washington, DC.

"There's Centennial Park. It has a huge swimming pool. If we can work it in, I hope we can take a swim there before you leave," JB informed us.

"What's that building with all the columns?" I inquired.

Coach Lewis replied, "That's the Parthenon -- or at least Nashville's version of it. Of course, the original is in Athens, Greece. When Tennessee celebrated its centennial in the late 1800s, this park was the site of the Tennessee Centennial and International Exposition. A full-scale replica of the Parthenon was built in the park for that occasion.

"As a temporary structure, it soon began to deteriorate. In the early 1900s, it was leveled and construction of a permanent replacement was begun. After ten years, the Parthenon you see there was finished."

"If we go swimming at the pool, we can take a closer look at it," JB added.

During the drive, Danny and I shared the latest Riverton news with JB, and he filled us in on his duties at camp.

"Wow!" Danny exclaimed. "That was the Belle Meade Theater. Wasn't it? I recognized it from the postcard you sent me, JB. How high is that tower above the theater?"

"As I recall, it's about 130 feet tall. When it's lighted at night, you can see it for miles around. The Belle Meade Theater is thought to be the most elegant suburban theater in the South," Coach Lewis told us.

"Maybe we can go there some evening after camp," JB suggested.

Within minutes after we passed the theater, Coach Lewis announced, "We've just entered Belle Meade. There's city hall, coming up on the left."

"On the right -- directly across from city hall -- is a stand of tall trees that perhaps you fellas will recognize," JB told us.

We stared out the car window. Then we turned to each other and nodded. "They're cottonwood trees -- just like the big one in the middle of our sidewalk on Forrest Street. Cottonwoods! All the way down here in Nashville. Who would have thought?"

"In May -- when they release their cotton fluff -- driving along here is like driving through a Michigan snowstorm," Coach Lewis told us. "We thought we'd point them out so you fellas would feel right at home."

"Thanks, Coach Lewis," I responded. "We appreciate your thinking of us."

When we turned left onto Belle Meade Boulevard, I was stunned by the grandeur of the city. It nearly took my breath away. A median strip of grass and trees. Stunning homes set far back, away from the street. Lush landscaping, including wide swaths of carefully manicured flower gardens. Meticulously mown lawns. This was indeed a very special place.

Danny rendered his one-word assessment, "Wow!"

We turned onto Stony River Road and before us stood the elaborate wrought-iron entrance gate to the academy. A uniformed guard waved us through.

"Welcome to Stony River Academy!" Coach Lewis proclaimed. "First stop -- your dormitory. JB will check you in and show you to your rooms. You'll have a few minutes to freshen up but you'll probably want to unpack your luggage after dinner.

"Oh, I forgot to mention -- Dorothy -- Mrs. Lewis is joining us. I'll park the car at the dining hall and meet y'all there."

"Great! I was hoping Mrs. Lewis could join us," JB replied with a smile. "You fellas will like her."

"Great!" Danny replied with a matching smile.

I was simply not prepared for Stony River Academy. When JB told us he was assisting with a basketball camp that summer, I expected to see a campground with tents, cabins, or, at best, white wooden barracks.

As I glanced around the campus, I observed that each of the dozens of buildings was constructed of reddish-brown bricks, gray slate roofs, and perfect white-framed windows. The rich, green lawns were mown closely and each building was nestled in a billowing wreath of enormous boxwood shrubs. The campus was much larger than I expected. From my initial survey, I estimated that it would cover about a third of Grandpa Compton's 100-acre farm.

"How many students attend SRA?"

"When school's in full session between September and June, there are about 400 students on campus. About 75% are boarding students and the rest are day students from the area. Of course, there are also over a hundred faculty and staff here as well. During the summer session, these numbers are greatly reduced. This week we have about 120 students and campers on campus. Only one dormitory -- this one -- is open in the summer."

We followed JB into the dormitory and stopped behind him at the front desk where a middle-aged man, dressed in a black suit, white shirt, and red tie, greeted us. "Masters Tucker and Addison, I presume."

We nodded our heads.

"Welcome to Stony River Academy. I hope your stay with us will be a pleasant one. Please sign the guest register -- right there," he advised, shoving the black leather book in our direction. "Here's a pen."

"Is this a dormitory -- or a hotel?" Danny whispered as he signed his name.

"We like to think of Radnor Hall as both," the man informed us.

"Classy!" Danny affirmed, winking at the man.

"Quite," he replied.

"Master Tucker, you're in Room 203. Master Addison -- Room 204. Master Bradford is already in Room 205. You three have adjacent rooms. Here are your keys. The elevator is to your left. Thank you -- and again -- welcome to Stony River Academy."

"Follow me, fellas," JB instructed. When we arrived at our rooms, before disappearing into his room, JB advised, "Take a few minutes to freshen up. Then we'll walk over to the dining hall."

"Jase, I have a question."

"What is it, Danny?"

"Do you know how to *freshen up?*"

"No! How about you?"

Danny uttered a one-word reply, "Southerners!"

AFTER WE WERE RE-FRESHENED, Danny and I knocked on JB's door to let him know we were ready for *dinner.* We quickly learned that when Nashvillians said *dinner,* they were referring to what Rivertonians called *supper.* And the noon meal that Rivertonians call *dinner* is called *lunch* by Nashvillians. I decided it was just one more quirky Southern tradition that Danny and I would have to adjust to.

On our way to dinner, JB answered some of our questions. For one thing, we'd heard him refer to the place where we were going to dinner as both the *cafeteria* and the *dining hall.*

"That's because it's both. Breakfast and lunch are served cafeteria style, but dinner is formal. At dinner, a waiter takes your order and serves you. To get around the confusion, most people just call the place by its official name -- Robertson Hall."

That made sense.

"JB, we never thought to ask, but should Jase and I have brought our coats and ties to wear to dinner? We left our blue blazers and ties at home. Governor Dewey bought them for us so we could go to dinner with him at the City Club in Owosso. Mr. Bentley was there too. He's an ambassador -- somewhere in South America."

"Governor Dewey? Do you mean Thomas E. Dewey, the man who ran against President Roosevelt last fall?"

"Yes. We became friends of both candidates. We helped both of them with their political campaigns," Danny informed him nonchalantly.

"Danny, sometimes I don't know whether to believe you or not," JB sputtered.

"Oh, Danny's telling the truth, JB. We knew both men and we did help with their campaigns."

"But how -- Oh, never mind. You can tell me later. Now, the answer to your question is that you don't need coat and tie. I should have thought to tell you before you came. But it was a good question because most schools like ours require summer students and campers to wear coats, white shirts, and ties for dinner -- and even for classes.

"Since we're located in the South -- where the summer temperatures are usually pretty high -- and because many campers come to meals straight from the gym or the track, wearing SRA sweat suits, we did away with jackets and ties during the summer sessions some years ago."

"Is that unusual for a private school like this one?"

"Yes, it is, Jase. Very unusual But our summer standard is very popular with students, faculty, and administrators alike. We still have very high academic and athletic standards so we can afford to relax this rule -- at least during the summer -- and still be a highly sought-after school."

Robertson Hall was elegantly appointed. Dark wood paneling, highly polished mahogany dining tables and chairs, and honey-colored parquet floors created an atmosphere of formality softened by warmth. I tried to estimate the seating capacity of the facility.

"JB, what's the capacity of Robertson Hall?"

"It's a bit over 200. During the full session, we need two seatings. To serve dinner to all resident students and faculty, underclassmen eat at the early seating. Upperclassmen and faculty -- at the later seating."

Because of our relatively late arrival, the dining hall was almost empty. But at the row of tables at the far end of the room, we saw Coach Lewis and a very tall, attractive lady standing with a formally dressed gentleman that I assumed was the headwaiter. Evidently they were waiting for us to arrive before being seated. I was struck by the politeness of Nashvillians. They treated each other with a degree of civility that seemed slightly foreign to us two Michiganders.

When we arrived at the row of tables, I noticed that on each was a silver holder with a card that read, *Faculty*.

"Dorothy, I would like to present Danny Tucker and Jase Addison. Fellas, this is my wife, Mrs. Lewis."

"How do you do, boys?" she said with a cheerful smile. "Welcome to Nashville. And welcome to Stony River Academy.

We've looked forward to your visit for weeks now. Haven't we, Johnson?"

We shook hands with Mrs. Lewis and told her how pleased we were to meet her. Then Danny looked at JB and winked.

JB caught his meaning. "Mrs. Lewis, when I moved to Riverton, I learned from Danny and Jase that 'not a single person living in the State of Michigan has two last names.' So they call me *JB*."

"Why, that sounds charming -- simply charming, I'm sure. From now on, JB it is," Mrs. Lewis averred in her delightfully soft Southern accent.

No wonder JB promised that we would really like her.

"Shall we be seated?" Coach Lewis suggested.

The headwaiter helped Mrs. Lewis with her chair, opened a leather-bound menu, and handed it to her. Then he handed each of us one as well. "When you've had a minute to consider the menu, I'll return and tell you about our specials tonight."

After the waiter left, Danny asked, "Jase, doesn't this remind you of the City Club in Owosso?"

"Danny and Jase had dinner with Governor Thomas E. Dewey at the City Club in Oswassa -- did I pronounce that right, fellas?"

Before we could answer, Mrs. Lewis told us, "I believe the proper pronunciation is Owassa, JB. Last year, I had the pleasure of meeting Governor Dewey at a basketball tournament in New York. We chatted for a while. He told me about his Michigan hometown. He's done a fine job as New York's governor. A very impressive gentleman indeed. Don't y'all agree?"

Danny and I enthusiastically concurred. Neither of us bothered to correct her pronunciation of Owosso. I don't know about Danny, but I actually preferred her version because it sounded so pleasantly Southern.

JB urged us to order some genuine Southern cooking. Following his suggestion, we ordered the Southern fried chicken with cheese grits, collard greens, and freshly baked biscuits. Based on our first sampling, Danny and I stated that we definitely preferred Southern over Northern cooking any day. JB looked very smug.

While we were waiting for our desserts, I inquired, "Did Stony River Academy play in the New York basketball tournament?"

"No, it was the Nashville *Bomberettes* playing for their fifth AAU national championship," Coach Lewis told us.

"Who are the *Bomberettes?*" Danny asked.

"What's AAU stand for?" I wanted to know.

"Mrs. Lewis plays on a championship basketball team? Why, she's the star of the team!" JB told us proudly.

"Now, we mustn't exaggerate, JB," Mrs. Lewis admonished. "I'd be glad to answer your questions. AAU stands for Amateur Athletic Union. It was founded in the late 1880s to support men and women players and teams in almost every sport. Since very few colleges had basketball teams for women, most women's teams were sponsored by businesses.

"Here in Nashville, the Consolidated Vultee Aircraft Company sponsors a women's team called the *Bomberettes*. Like many companies that have become prosperous during the war, it sponsors several sports teams."

"Where did that name come from, Mrs. L?" Danny asked.

"Since Vultee manufactures dive bombers, the name *Bomberettes* was a natural one. Unlike other women working in defense factories, we *Bomberettes* team members work clerical jobs to minimize the opportunity of our being injured working on the assembly line."

"Tell the boys about this year's team, Dorothy."

"Well, this year, our '45 team has become the most dominant women's basketball team in the United States. With an average height of six feet, our team is one of the tallest teams in the country. In the AAU tournament, we simply overwhelmed the opposition and closed the season with 49 wins and no losses. And two of our team members were selected for the AAU's All-American team."

After the war, I learned that when the defense industry began to wind down, the *Bomberettes* were left without a sponsor. Southern Beer Company, a Nashville beer distributor, decided to support a men's basketball team to promote the *Budweiser* brand and a women's team to promote its lower-priced brand, *Cook's Goldblume*. The *Bomberettes* became the *Goldblumes*.

"Wow! This is certainly a basketball family. Isn't it?" I observed.

"Let's put it this way -- we never lack for something to talk about," Coach Lewis told us. "And it sure keeps us busy on the weekends. For example, tomorrow the *Bomberettes* play an exhibition game in Birmingham. So while you boys are touring Nashville, Mrs. Lewis will be driving to Alabama and back.

"I'll be here meeting with my staff to discuss plans for the camp in the upcoming weeks."

Mrs. Lewis wondered, "If y'all like and are available on Sunday, I know you'd love to hear the Fisk Jubilee Singers. They're performing downtown -- at the 10:00 a.m. service at the First Presbyterian Church. Because they're so popular worldwide, they seldom perform here in Nashville. How's that sound?"

"That sounds great, ma'am!" Danny declared for both of us.

Something about Danny's response struck me as strange, but I couldn't put my finger on it.

Coach Lewis had an idea as well. "After church, I thought we could take in a professional baseball game. The Nashville Volunteers play the Memphis Chickasaws at one o'clock at Sulphur Dell. Their ballpark's not far from downtown."

"Great!" I responded enthusiastically.

"But I have a question. What do those team names mean?" Danny asked.

"Tennessee is the *Volunteer State* so that explains Nashville's official team name, but everyone calls them the *Vols*. The Chickasaws are named for an Indian tribe that inhabits this region of the country, but everyone calls them the *Chicks*."

"That makes sense."

"Then we're all set." Mrs. Lewis spoke for all five of us.

"Boy, look at the time. You fellas haven't even unpacked yet. And you must be bushed from your long train ride. Why don't we call it a night?" the coach suggested.

Danny and I replied with simultaneous yawns.

JB told us that, on the weekends, breakfast was served from 6:00 to 8:00 a.m. He suggested we catch the 8:30 a.m. bus to downtown. We agreed to go to breakfast at 7:00 a.m.

We all said good night.

After closing the door to my room, it struck me. Danny had used the word, *ma'am*. That was the very word that caused Danny to suspect JB of being a sissy.

Instead of going directly to bed, Danny stuck his head into my room and announced, "Isn't Nashville a great town?"

"Yes, ***ma'am***. It certainly is."

Danny's face turned red. He'd been caught.

I let him off the hook. "Good night, Danny."

"Good night, Jase. Y'all sleep well."

Danny was acclimating very quickly!

WHEN WE ENTERED ROBERTSON Hall, I was surprised to see a long cafeteria line set up to our left. It hadn't been there the evening before when we had dinner with Coach and Mrs. Lewis.

"Where on earth did that come from, JB?"

"It was there last evening. But we couldn't see it because it was hidden behind the west wall. Before serving breakfast and lunch, sections of the wall are pushed to either side and folded together. Then -- voila! You have a cafeteria line. Pretty clever. Huh?"

"Boy, I'll say! Very ingenious."

During my brief exchange with JB, Danny had wasted no time. He had already taken a tray, selected his silverware, and entered the serving line. Suddenly my heart sank. I remembered Danny's first experience with a wide array of food at the MEM cafeteria.

My initial impulse was to ask Danny to change his behavior this time. But I quickly realized that would be pointless. Instead, I chose to examine the length of the serving line, hoping to see selections up ahead that would meet my breakfast needs and allow me to skip ahead of Danny.

I didn't want to be one of the ravenous students and campers stuck behind him. Those diners wouldn't stand a chance of eating breakfast any time soon.

"Do you think we can avoid another MEM cafeteria fiasco, Jase?"

"How did you know about that?"

"Danny wrote about it in one of his postcards. He promised it wouldn't happen here -- but I have my doubts. How about you?"

"Well, miracles do happen I suppose. At least there's no cashier. That eliminates one potential bottleneck."

After I'd selected my breakfast, I looked down the line behind me to check on Danny's status. JB did the same.

"Where'd he go? I don't see him anywhere. Oh, well. Let's go find a table, Jase. I guess we can catch a later bus."

Since most of the tables near the end of the serving line were occupied, we headed for an area of empty tables. Our attention was focused on the other side of the hall when we *heard* the miracle. "Hey, you guys. Where are you going? I saved two chairs for you -- right here by me. Hurry up! We gotta catcha bus!"

NASHVILLE VISITORS GUIDE

WE CAUGHT THE BUS AT THE CORNER OF BELLE
Meade Boulevard and Stony River Road. It was right on time.
The bus fare, a dime, was exactly twice what we paid at home. The
bus was configured differently as well. All the seats faced forward.
The only open seats were located three rows behind the driver. In
Riverton, Danny and I always sat in the seats running parallel to
the side of the bus, immediately across from the driver. We chose
this prime location because it enabled us to assist the driver with
his duties.

We performed our job diligently. Notifying him of each
upcoming stop. Warning of cars about to turn into the street
ahead. Greeting people as they stepped onto the bus. Shouting
goodbyes when passengers departed from the back door. Pulling
the stop-signal cable for those laden with packages. Collecting
fares and depositing them -- **Bam!** -- into the fare box. And finally
helping the driver make change by doing his arithmetic -- aloud!
We knew that Riverton bus drivers were extremely grateful for our
help by the way they thanked us, over and over, when we left the
bus.

Because the seating configuration was poorly designed,
Nashville bus drivers were deprived of the benefit of our services.
When I mentioned this to Danny, he reminded me that we were
on vacation and we shouldn't have to work. Good point.

"This bus will take us down Belle Meade Boulevard, past Cheekwood and then --."

"What's a Cheekwood?" Danny wanted to know.

JB turned away from us and pulled something out of his back pocket. With his back to us, he read the following:

Cheekwood is the 100-acre country-place estate that dates to the early 1930's when it was created for Leslie Cheek and his wife Mabel Wood. To name their property, the couple combined their last names - Cheek and Wood.

Leslie Cheek was a wholesale grocer who invested in his cousin's special blend of coffee that was served exclusively at the Maxwell House Hotel in downtown Nashville. In 1929, the blend was sold to Postum for 45 million dollars. With the proceeds from the sale, Mr. Cheek invested in IBM stock and purchased this land in West Nashville. The Cheeks hired landscape architect, Bryant Fleming, to design their mansion and to landscape the property. Together the Cheeks and Fleming toured Europe to buy furnishings for their home.

The European trip resulted in the decision to build a Georgian-style home of limestone that was quarried on the property. They also purchased antiques for the house and gardens, shipping these back to Nashville in four box cars. Leslie Cheek's interest in botany led to his travels through the South to purchase boxwoods for the property and to establish a trial boxwood garden at Cheekwood.

I'm not sure why but Danny and I looked at each other and smiled foolishly.

"The bus will also pass the entrance to Percy Warner Park. It's one of two adjacent parks. The other -- called Edwin Warner Park -- is a few miles south of here. They're connected by a hiking trail. The two parks encompass thousands of acres of rugged and hilly woodland. There're a number of trails for hikers, as well as equestrian trails -- for people to ride horses. On the other side of Percy Warner from here, there's a steeplechase course where the *Iroquois Steeplechase* is held every May."

"What's a steeplecourse chase?" Danny inquired, contorting his face.

"That's *steeplechase course*. In horse racing, there are two types of courses -- flat and steeplechase. Flat is an unobstructed, dirt course like they have at most racetracks. And steeplechase is a course having many barriers -- fences, hedges, and ditches -- that the horse and rider must jump over on their way to the finish line."

"Why's this steeplechase called *Iroquois*? Isn't that the name of a nation of Indian tribes -- up in New York or Canada?"

"Yes, it is, Jase. But it's also the name of a famous racehorse who won a dozen major races in America and in Europe in the late 1800s. After his racing career ended, Iroquois was purchased by the owner of the Belle Meade Plantation. At the time, Belle Meade was an internationally renowned thoroughbred breeding farm. Within a short period of time, Iroquois became the *Leading Sire* in America. He strengthened the Belle Meade bloodline and was responsible for producing a number of other famous racehorses. Sorry. I can't remember their names. As you might have guessed, I'm not a big fan of horse racing."

"We're not either. Right, Jase?"

"I know a lot about workhorses, though -- especially Grandpa Compton's two teams. But he doesn't race them. He works them."

As our bus wound its way through the streets of Belle Meade, I was again struck by the sheer number of estate homes, built on multi-acre, meticulously landscaped lots. These homes reminded me of those we saw on West Oliver Street the fall before when Governor Dewey gave us a tour of Owosso.

"Jase, what was the name of that street in Owosso?"

"West Oliver."

"Yes. That's it. Does Belle Meade remind you of West Oliver Street?"

"It does. But there were only a dozen or so especially fine homes on West Oliver. Belle Meade has hundreds."

"JB, how many people live in Belle Meade? And how many homes are there in the city."

"As I recall, in the 1940 census the population was just over 2,000 people. It's still growing. So today I'd say there probably around 2,200 people living in the city. Assuming there are about three people per home, there are around 700 homes in Belle Meade."

After we turned onto Harding Pike, JB observed, "In a few minutes, we'll pass the Belle Meade Plantation. It was built by General William Giles Harding. He was the son of John Harding who founded the plantation in the early 1800s. During the Civil War, Union and Confederate forces fought on the front lawn. Evidence of the skirmish is still visible in the form of bullet holes in the mansion's stone columns. At the end of the Civil War, 125 slaves who worked the plantation were emancipated."

"How large was the plantation?" I asked.

"At its height, it covered 5,400 acres, including a 600 acre deer park where visitors were able to hunt wild game imported from all over the world. President Grover Cleveland was among those who visited the plantation. To accommodate the President's enormous body, the owners had to construct an extra-large bathtub."

"You've got to be kidding!" Danny exclaimed.

"I'm very serious. Belle Meade was a destination for some of America's most important dignitaries, especially people interested in thoroughbred horses. But unfortunately, despite decades of success as the country's oldest and largest thoroughbred breeding farm, by the early 20th century, Belle Meade Plantation had fallen on bad times. Finally the Harding family heirs were forced to auction off the property.

"Today the only remaining evidence of Belle Meade Plantation is the 30-acre plot of land -- fronting on Harding Pike -- where you'll see the mansion, the horse barns, and a few other outbuildings, including original slave quarters and the smokehouse. There it is. Take a good look."

We stared in awe at the colonial-style mansion. After we passed it, Danny asked a very good question. "JB, how do you remember all these details?"

"Well, the plantation has always interested me. I've read almost everything ever written about it. But just before moving to Riverton, I wrote a term paper about the plantation for my U.S. History class at SRA. I guess I'm sort of an expert on the subject. Besides I got some extra help from Mrs. Lewis."

Coming clean, JB pulled a compact handbook from his back pocket. It was entitled *Nashville Visitors Guide.*

"She gave me this to study before you fellas arrived. I read up on the places we'll be seeing during your visit. But I didn't memorize it. If you don't mind, I may have to read some of the information."

"Boy! Can I see that, JB?" He handed me the *Guide.* I leafed through a few pages. "Wow! This is great information. Look at this, Danny," I said as I handed him the *Guide.*

"Where's the section on Belle Meade Plantation?" Danny asked as he flipped through the pages. "I want to know what happened to the rest of the 5,400 acres."

"I can answer that," JB told him. "It was developed into what's now the City of Belle Meade. To give you an idea, Deer Park is now a Belle Meade neighborhood."

"Oh, now I get it. Hmmm! Wonder what it's like living in a game park," I mused aloud.

AFTER HARDING PIKE BECAME West End Avenue, the number of people boarding our bus began to grow. We were stopping at nearly every intersection to pick up one, two, or more new passengers. The new riders were a diverse group.

There were older, nicely dressed ladies evidently on their way downtown to shop. There were soldiers, who usually boarded in pairs or threesomes and spoke with accents that told us they were from all over the country. A few soldiers were black but most were white. Regardless of color, like us, they were tourists, checking out Nashville. There were women wearing white dresses of domestic workers. Many, but not all, of these women were black. There were also businessmen in suits, white shirts, and ties. Then too there were students carrying textbooks and notebooks, perhaps headed to Vanderbilt University, Peabody College, or Fisk. Some of them were black as well.

After observing the growing numbers passing by my seat, I wondered how full the bus had become. I leaned out into the aisle to survey our load. Looking toward the back of the bus, I observed something I'd never seen before. I elbowed Danny and pointed toward the back. Because he was seated in the window seat, he had to stand. He looked and quickly sat down.

"The whole back of the bus is filled with black people. Everyone in the front is white," Danny whispered. "Why's that?"

I shrugged my shoulders and whispered, "Let's ask JB later."

At Union Station, we exited the bus with others who were mostly soldiers. The platform area was filled with hundreds of people. At a glance, I guessed that at least half of them were in uniform.

"Let's push through the crowd and go inside," JB suggested. "You'll really be amazed by what you'll see."

I looked at Danny who nodded and pointed his head toward the main entrance. Knowing Danny, I interpreted his response to mean, "Let's wait until we're inside and find a quiet place to talk."

It took us a full five minutes to elbow and twist our way through the bustling mass of humanity. How we managed to stay together was a miracle. Once we got closer, I paused to examine the building's façade. JB pulled out his *Guide* and read an historical overview:

Union Station in Nashville is a Romanesque masterpiece, known for its tall, ornate clock tower at the top of which stands a statue of the Roman god Mercury. Inside the soaring main hall you will see the 128-panel stained glass ceiling and finely detailed gilt plasterwork. A shoe-shine station is located just inside the front door.

Union Station opened in 1900 to serve the passenger operations of the eight railroads providing passenger service to Nashville at the time. The station reached its peak in recent years as a shipping-out point for tens of thousands of U.S. troops. To meet the needs of military personnel, it's also the site of a popular USO canteen

The station is also renowned for being haunted by the ghost of a man who was responsible for the maintenance and operation of the clock located in the top of the tower. For 12 years, he's said to have regularly climbed 11 flights of stairs to keep the clock in good working order. No one seems to know the circumstances of his death or why he'd choose to be a ghost, but many claim he haunts the clock tower.

After the war, I learned of a second ghost at Union Station. It was that of a woman who was waiting at the station for her fiancé to return from World War II. Instead, she was greeted by the news that her fiancé had been killed in action. In her despair, she allegedly climbed up the 11 flights of stairs to the top of the tower and threw herself down the stairwell. Again there is no explanation for her choice of afterlife occupation.

Even though it was the third Union Station we'd visited in recent days, we were most impressed with the Nashville version. JB was justifiably proud of the first stop on our tour.

After delivering far more than the required number of positive comments, we felt it was time to broach *the* subject. Drawing upon his deep reserve of sensitivity, Danny blurted out a question, "Why on earth do *certain people* have to sit in the back of the bus -- when the rest of us don't? What's that all about, JB?"

While JB was obviously caught off guard, his response managed to catch me off guard as well. "That's because they're colored people, Danny."

Danny pressed on. "You mean there's a *colored* and *white* section of the bus. There's a *colored* and *white* drinking fountain. And there's a *colored* and *white* bathroom. Right?"

"Exactly," JB answered as calmly as he could.

"Well, tell me, JB -- do *you* think that's right?"

JB took a while to answer. Then he said, "Personally I don't think it's right at all."

After turning to me with a look of profound relief on his face, Danny replied, "Happy to hear that, JB. We don't either."

"I'm glad we're in agreement, Danny. But let me caution you -- there are many good people in the South who would disagree with us. These people fiercely protect their right to choose their own customs. Regardless of the rightness or wrongness, they greatly resent anyone from the North coming down here to try to convince them to change their customs.

"There are also many good people down here who feel that these customs are very wrong. But they realize it's going to take a long time to change the way many people think and act in this area.

"I'd advise you to be sensitive to how people down here feel about their customs and traditions. You don't have to agree with them, but I hope you will respect them. I truly believe, if we can continue to treat each other with civility, the time will come when the color of a person's skin won't pass the *so-what* test."

"Thanks, JB. That's good advice. Don't worry about us. Right, Jase?"

We all shook on it.

"Let's go see the post office."

"Did I hear you fellas say you're going to the post office? I'm late for my train. Could you mail these letters for me -- please?"

"You bet we will," Danny promised, taking the soldier's letters. "Good luck, Sergeant."

The soldier smiled, saluted, and immediately took off running toward the platform.

"Now we *have* to go to the post office," Danny announced. "We're on official military business."

AS WE LEFT UNION Station, I noticed a large U.S. Army truck parked at the curb. Danny and I were accustomed to seeing this type of truck carrying POWs to and from the canning factory in our neighborhood back in Riverton. Adding to my assumption that it was a POW carrier, in the back of the truck, there were two armed MPs, waiting with ominous tommy guns cradled in their arms.

"Boy! That looks familiar. Doesn't it, Jase?" Danny declared. "Wonder where the POWs are?"

From behind us, came Danny's answer. "Please make way, boys."

We wheeled around. Marching in our direction was a squad of a dozen POWs, dressed in the familiar olive-drab work uniforms with the large letters, *PW*, stenciled in white dye on the front and back of each prisoner's trousers and work shirt.

The POWs were accompanied by two armed MPs, a private and a sergeant. Evidently the squad had just arrived by train. Each POW and MP was carrying a small duffel bag. Familiar baggage tags were tied to the bags' hand straps. While I had no way of knowing from where they'd come, my experience told me they were most likely heading for new work assignments.

I decided to test my theory. "Good morning, sergeant. My friends and I are familiar with German POWs. We assume they're being transported to a new work assignment. Are we right?"

The sergeant stopped and smiled at us. "Well, I'm very impressed. You're exactly right. Where'd you learn about the deployment of German POWs?"

"We're from Riverton, Michigan. There's a German POW camp -- just outside of town. Every day, we see trucks like this taking POWs back and forth to work -- right in our neighborhood."

"Hold it! Hold it! Don't tell me! They work at the Chippewa Canning Corporation. Right?" the sergeant exclaimed with a broad grin. "And I bet they work under the watchful eye of my old friend, MP Sergeant Rick Prella. And their POW crew leader is a former Luftwaffe officer named Otto Klump. Am I right about that too?"

Needless to say, you could have knocked us over with a feather.

"My name's Sergeant Max Mellon," he said, smiling warmly and extending his hand.

We shook his hand and introduced ourselves.

"What on earth are you boys doing in Nashville?"

We gave him a quick explanation, told him where we were staying and how long we'd be there.

When all the POWs were seated in the back of the truck, Sergeant Mellon helped the other MP up onto the truck. Before departing, he paused long enough to tell us, "We just brought this squad of POWs here by train -- from Camp Crossville, Tennessee. "They're skilled construction workers. Moving them to a new branch camp being established where a new VA hospital's being built."

"Where's that, Sergeant Mellon?" JB asked.

"I got it right here," he replied, removing a slip of paper from his pocket. "160 White Bridge Road."

I recognized the name of the street. It had crossed our bus route right where Harding Pike became West End Avenue.

"None of us knows Nashville. Not even the driver. He just brought the truck down from Fort Campbell. We're going to have to get directions. But wait. You don't happen to know where it is -- do you?"

"Sure, I can tell you. It's only a mile or so from Belle Meade -- where Stony River Academy is located. So I know the area well."

JB proceeded to give the sergeant a set of very clear directions.

"Gee, thanks, JB. That'll save us time. We got to run now. But if the camp is near your school, why don't you drop over sometime before Jase and Danny leave. I'd like an update on things in Riverton. I've been gone for almost a year now."

We promised Sergeant Mellon we would definitely come by before we left Nashville. JB suggested that we could go by ourselves while he was involved with the basketball camp. After all, he reminded us, he was relatively new to Riverton, and we had a lot more knowledge of the POWs. He had a good point. However, his offer was destined to be obviated owing to events that were soon to unfold in our lives.

The sergeant thanked us again, told us he hoped to see us soon, and hopped into the truck's cab. As they pulled away from the curb, the driver honked his horn and Sergeant Mellon waved. We waved back. Following suit, every MP and POW in the back of the truck waved back at us as well.

"Guys, everywhere we go, someone either knows you -- or knows someone who knows you. It's uncanny."

"JB, remember we're international heroes. As such, we have a widespread and impressive fan club," Danny advised him.

"Danny, what you have is a widespread and impressive *ego*. Come on! Let's go to the post office and mail those letters," I ordered.

"You two are something else," JB avowed with a laugh.

"Indeed we are," Danny agreed.

THE EXTERIOR OF THE Nashville Main Post Office was breathtaking. From JB's *Guide*, we learned that massive slabs of white marble covered its steel frame. But the moment we stepped inside, we were awestruck. In my mind, the Riverton Post Office, built during the 1930s as a part of FDR's New Deal, was the most majestic building in the world. But it paled in comparison with this streamlined building.

Looking down the broad expanse of its Art Deco lobby, I was struck by the unadorned yet classical look of the room. This seemed more like the Grand Palace of the Ruler of the Universe in a science fiction movie. The intricately tiled floors and black-marble wainscoting, as well as the cast-aluminum of the twelve icons in the grillwork, were highly polished.

Our eyes traveled from one end of the long lobby to the other, where two flights of black-marble stairs led to second-floor offices. We were mesmerized by one frieze of four icons in the grillwork above the counter. These sleek icons depicted an airplane, a ship, a locomotive, and an automobile, representing the modern modes of transportation used to deliver the mail.

"Have you ever seen anything like this, Danny?"

"Not even in my dreams. I bet there isn't another building in all of Nashville that comes close to matching this one. Right, JB?"

JB was all smiles. Clearly our reaction pleased him. Evidently he knew how awestruck we would be. Union Station was elegant. So far this was the highlight of the trip.

"We better get on with our official military duties, Danny," JB responded, deflecting Danny's question.

A postal clerk from a nearby window motioned to us, "Hey, boys. Come over here, please."

"Have we done something wrong?" Danny asked in earnest.

"Oh, no. Nothing like that. From your reaction when you entered our fine post office, I assume you're first-time visitors. We're about to begin our morning Behind-the-Scenes Tour. It includes a trip through the underground passageway to Union Station. I thought you fellas might enjoy it. No charge! How about it?"

Without conferring with JB or me, Danny yelped, "You bet we would! When do we start?"

"See that door over by the stairs. Please meet me there."

We walked across the lobby and waited for the clerk to open the door.

"I'll take you down to the supervisor who'll conduct the tour. He's waiting for folks on the lower level. That's where we deposit bags of mail into different carts before they're moved over to the train station. Follow me, please."

The clerk locked the door behind us. We followed him across the area behind the counters to another wide door that opened into a cavernous room where mail was being handled. On the other side of this area, we saw, through massive bay doors, over a dozen mail trucks backed up to a wide loading dock. Men were carrying bag after bag of mail from the trucks and emptying them onto three wide conveyor belts.

The clerk introduced us to his supervisor, who wasted no time in getting started. Apparently we were his only sightseers that morning.

"Good morning, gentlemen. Welcome to Nashville's Main Post Office. We're one of 41,792 post offices operated throughout America by the U.S. Post Office Department. Despite the fact that America is at war, your post office department is projected to deliver over 37 billion pieces of mail this year, including over 21 billion pieces of first-class mail. In the process, we'll generate revenues of over $1.3 billion with only $1.1 billion in costs. Yes, not only are we profitable, but we're one of the largest businesses in the world with over 278,000 employees.

"During your tour of this facility, you'll observe that the post office depends heavily on America's railroads to help us route and deliver mail to our postal customers. In fact, as we speak there are over 10,000 trains -- traveling all over the country -- hauling special mail cars where postal personnel are at work preparing mail for delivery in every city, town, and village along that train's route."

He turned and pointed at the trucks being unloaded at the dock. "Those trucks are bringing mail that was picked up from collection boxes all over the city. Collectors do this at least twice, and sometimes as many as four times, a day. That mail is placed into bags on their trucks.

"When they return here, the mail in those bags is dumped onto the first three conveyor belts. See the men and women there. We have 30 people cancelling newly-collected mail -- 24 hours a day, seven days a week. They do nothing but stamp every piece of mail, imprinting the name and location of this post office and the date. You've seen cancellation imprints on the letters you've received. Right?"

We all nodded.

"That's a very critical step. Often important legal matters -- like payment of obligations -- depend on having mail postmarked by a certain date.

"Once the mail is cancelled, it's placed on the second set of conveyor belts. Right here in front of us. See these folks here. They're our sorters."

He pointed to a set of conveyor belts, slowly moving stacks of mail past the line of sorters. "These folks are sorting the mail by destination -- and placing the mail in the appropriately marked mailbag."

We watched as two dozen sorters, positioned next to the slow-moving conveyor belt, plucked off individual pieces of mail and tossed them into canvas mailbags which were hung, open-mouthed, inside sturdy frames behind the sorters.

"When a bag is full, it's carried over and placed on one of those carts parked near the opening of the train station passageway. When a cart is full, sorters push it over to Union Station where it stored in wait for the next train heading to that destination -- or I should say to the mail distribution center closest to the destination."

We watched as a sorter removed one of the bags from the frame and carried it to a cart. Then he returned, picked up an empty bag, attached a destination tag to it, and hung it back onto the frame. Turning to a fellow sorter he said, "Give me a hand pushing the Detroit cart to the station."

"That's our cue, gentlemen. We'll go with them."

We followed the cart into the dimly lighted passageway that led to Union Station. When we emerged, we found ourselves inside a special caged-in area adjacent to the baggage-check area.

"Mail is kept under lock-and-key here in this cage until it's time to load it onto the proper train. When that train is scheduled to arrive, we send two men over here to load the bags into the mail car and bring the cart back to the post office. We guard the safety and security of the mail very closely. In fact, those postal personnel working in the mail cars on trains are armed. That's an example of how far we go to protect America's mail.

"Well, this ends our tour, gentlemen. Any questions before we part?"

Danny had one. "Why are mailboxes always painted that greenish-gray color?"

"Why are the collection boxes painted olive drab? That's a very good question. Until the end of World War I, the boxes were painted bright green. But when that war ended, the War Department gave the Post Office Department its vast surplus of olive-drab paint. This became the standardized color and, I'd guess, it'll remain so for at least the next ten years. Why do you ask?"

"I need to find one of those boxes. I promised a soldier I'd mail these three letters."

JB RECOMMENDED THAT WE tour Nashville's downtown on foot. Being seasoned walkers, we readily agreed and headed down Broad toward our next destination, the Ryman Auditorium.

"Okay, tour guide. Give us your spiel on the Ryman," Danny ordered.

Reading from his *Guide*, JB gave us an overview:

The Ryman Auditorium, located at 116 Fifth Avenue North, was built at the height of religious revivalism in Nashville. Between 1888 and 1901, Thomas Green Ryman, a recent convert to Christianity, had this tabernacle constructed as a place where Reverend Sam Jones could preach revival services. It was known as the Union Gospel Tabernacle until 1904 when it was renamed for Ryman. Since it was the largest auditorium in Nashville and had excellent acoustics, eventually it was used more for concerts and conventions than for religious events.

In the history of country music, the Ryman and WSM are forever linked. WSM are the call letters of Nashville's National Life and

Accident Insurance Company's radio station. The letters match the company's slogan We Shield Millions. *The station was founded in 1925 and, during its first year, WSM began to broadcast the Grand Ole Opry.*

In 1932, WSM constructed a unique diamond-shape broadcast antenna, providing 50,000 watts of power. WSM also secured clear channel *status, making it one of only 40 American radio stations to be granted exclusive use of its frequency, 650 AM. These factors combined to create WSM's vast area of radio coverage, especially at night.*

After WSM moved the Grand Ole Opry to the Ryman Auditorium in 1941, country music fans all over North America could hear the Opry broadcast live from the Ryman every Saturday evening. Today WSM is a national broadcasting powerhouse whose heartbeat emanates from the Ryman Auditorium.

When we turned off of Broad onto Fifth Avenue, the Ryman Auditorium stood before us in all its glory.

"Wow! It's huge. It takes up most of the square block. Can we go inside?" Danny wanted to know.

"The Ryman's not open now. But next Saturday night, Roy Acuff will be hosting the Grand Ole Opry show and radio broadcast. The ticket price is only 25 cents. Want to go?"

"Yesssss!" Danny hissed.

"Just think, Grandpa and Grandma Compton will be listening to the Opry on WSM, like they do every Saturday night -- way up in Riverton. And we'll be seeing the show -- in person -- way down here in Nashville. This is absolutely amazing! Absolutely amazing!" I exclaimed.

"Next I'd like us to see --."

"Let's see some food. How about lunch?" Danny suggested, interrupting JB.

"As I was about to say, next we'll have lunch at Harvey's, one of Nashville's largest department stores. It's not far from here -- at the corner of Church and Sixth Avenue."

Our tour guide briefed us along the way. "I remember when Harvey's opened in 1942. It's my favorite store because it's like going to a carnival. Here in downtown, there are two other department stores -- Castner-Knott and Cain-Sloan. They're elegant -- but a bit stuffy to me. Harvey's is definitely the fun place to shop. It even has a phonograph department with listening booths where you can preview records."

"Wow!" I exclaimed.

"Sometimes circus clowns in full costume stroll around the store and stop to chat with you. But the best clown of all is the owner himself, Mr. Fred Harvey, who makes his rounds, wearing fuzzy bedroom slippers."

"Amazing!" Danny replied.

We entered the store and headed for the luncheonette on the first floor. We sat at the counter on chrome stools. Soon we were devouring thick and tasty grilled-cheese sandwiches, followed by mammoth slices of Harvey's famous apple pie. As we exited, we noticed that you could buy your choice of a German chocolate, carrot, or coconut cake and have it packaged in Harvey's signature white box, tied with a colorful cord. Danny agreed that the desserts were definitely one of Harvey's most attractive features.

"I forgot to mention. The store's slogan is *Harvey's Has It*," JB added.

Author's Note:
Fred Harvey purchased carousel horses from the old Glendale Park Carnival off Franklin Road. After the war, when he installed the first escalator in Middle Tennessee in his store, he mounted the brightly painted horses next to the escalator handrails for the children to pet as they traveled from floor to floor. He also added a Monkey Bar restaurant where diners could watch monkeys, swinging from the top of their cage to the bottom and back again. In the toy department, he installed a full-scale carousel which was operated by Max Lowenstein, a Buchenwald death-camp survivor.

"My mother asked me to pick up a package for her at Cain-Sloan. You won't mind taking it home for her, will you? The store's right next door."

We exited the casual atmosphere of Harvey's and entered the elegant Cain-Sloan. I couldn't help notice that people were dressed in their finest. Men wore suits and ties with shiny leather shoes. Women wore fine dresses, high-heeled shoes, white gloves, and pert hats. Little girls were dressed as if they were flower girls in a wedding. Even young boys wore long pants and dress shirts. We were glad we were wearing our new long pants. Cain-Sloan shoppers certainly did it up right.

JB located his mother's item, but before leaving the store, we glanced around for a final look. Our eyes roamed from the cosmetic area to the jewelry counter to the glove department. There we saw a lady who appeared to be waving at us. She was seated on a stool with her elbow resting on a square velvet cushion. When we waved back, she gave us a funny look.

We watched her with curiosity, trying to determine why she waved at us. We finally deduced that she was being fitted for a pair of gloves. After having her hands powdered with talcum, she *waved* at us again, as the saleslady stretched the fingers of a pair of gloves and slipped them on her customer's raised hand.

We smiled at the lady and gave her a final wave. She smiled back but didn't wave this time.

OUR NEXT DESTINATION WAS the Arcade where JB promised we could buy postcards highlighting Nashville's popular tourist attractions. He told us the Arcade occupied a full city block encompassed by Fourth and Fifth Avenues North and Church and Union Streets. The two-level, glass-covered mall whose entrances were framed by identical Palladian facades was modeled after an arcade in Milan, Italy. Built in 1903, the Arcade became Nashville's first shopping center.

Walking through the Arcade, we passed tiny restaurants with outdoor seating, a shoe-repair shop, a small post office, a fruit stand, a hair salon, a bakery, and myriad small specialty stores. One of them was the Planter's Peanut Shop where an employee, dressed in a *Mr. Peanut* suit, was handing out free samples. He told us that the shop had been roasting peanuts since 1927.

JB pointed ahead to a quaint tobacco and candy shop. Once inside, our noses were treated to a pleasant mixture of rich tobaccos and the essence of lemon, orange, and coconut. Danny and I took all of 35 seconds for each of us to select a dozen brightly colored postcards.

"Let's write these now and mail them at the post office here," Danny suggested.

"I don't have my address book."

"I was thinking of just sending cards to people whose addresses I know by heart -- like my folks."

"Oh, all right. Good idea."

The store manager loaned us each a pen. We quickly scratched notes to our parents, our grandparents, and to JB's mother. That took all of five minutes. We returned the pens and thanked the manager.

"Let's go to the post office here. I'm sure they'll have one-cent stamps."

Danny was right. To cover all our cards, he purchased two dozen stamps, affixed some to the addressed cards, and tucked the rest into his wallet. When he placed the wallet back in his pocket, I remembered the $15 I'd gotten from Lieutenant Donovan that Danny had deftly separated from me for safekeeping. I looked forward to Monday evening when we would know if we'd won the wager.

"To the Capitol," JB announced as he marched us out the north door of the Arcade.

The walk from the Arcade to the Tennessee State Capitol Building was only a couple of blocks, but the change in elevation must have been a couple of hundred feet. By the time we reached the front steps of the imposing building, perched dramatically on a grassy, tree-studded hill, we were huffing and puffing. During my brief time in Nashville, I'd realized something about the area around Riverton. It's *very* flat.

We arrived just in time for the 2:00 p.m. tour. Our guide, an attractive young lady, proudly informed us she was a history major at Vanderbilt University. We were among a dozen tourists who followed her up the stairs and into the building. She informed us that the state capitol, completed in the mid-1800s, was modeled after a Greek temple in Athens. Its slender three-story tower was topped with a square cupola. It's one of only 11 state capitols that do not have a dome.

We were told that its architect, William Strickland, also designed the First Presbyterian Church, where we would hear the Fisk Jubilee Singers on Sunday morning.

Both the exterior and interior walls, as well as the columns were of Tennessee limestone, quarried about a mile from the site. Instead of wood, wrought iron was used for the roof trusses to reduce the threat of fire.

Because of the limestone walls, marble floors, and high ceilings, the interior was cool, just like the Riverton Water Works. What a relief it was on this very hot and muggy July day! Marble staircases led to the second floor where the legislative chambers, the library, and the governor's office were located.

As we climbed the stairs, we noticed a chunk missing from the bannister. Our guide pointed out that this was caused by bullets during a heated legislative battle in 1866 over ratification of the Fourteenth Amendment to the Constitution that granted citizenship, due process, and equal protection to all citizens, including former slaves. I recalled Belle Meade mansion's exterior walls and columns had been riddled with bullet holes during the Civil War.

On our tour, we were surrounded by historic touches, from busts of famous Tennesseans like Andrew Jackson to the 1930s friezes depicting the women's suffrage movement. A glimpse into the Governor's reception room featured murals from the 1920s when it was still acceptable to paint pictures of *happy slaves*.

From this floor, we were afforded a spectacular view of the city. We looked down on the barge-filled waters of the Cumberland River, snaking its way through Nashville. Along its banks we could see old Fort Nashborough, built by the original settlers to protect themselves from marauding bands of Indians who travelled by canoe up and down the river.

We thanked our guide, said goodbye to our fellow tourists, and headed for our next destination, the Hatch Print Shop, located on Broad, just east of Second Avenue.

"The Hatch is about four blocks from here, but it's an easy walk. All downhill," JB assured us.

"It's about time," Danny wheezed. "My legs are a bit tired. And I'm really thirsty."

"After the Hatch Print Shop, we'll take a local bus to the Elliston Place Soda Shop. Not far from Vanderbilt. Your kind of place, Danny. I've saved it for last!"

"What's it called again?" I asked.

"Elliston Place Soda Shop. But most locals just call it the *Soda Shop.* Everybody in town knows exactly which soda shop you're referring to, because it's the most popular -- and the best."

Danny gave JB a wistful look and thanked him. Sometimes Danny was very easy to please.

When we arrived at the corner of Fourth Avenue North and Church Street, JB announced, "Here's the Maxwell House Hotel." Pulling out his *Guide* as a reference, he continued:

The Maxwell House Hotel opened in 1869. With five stories and 240 rooms, it was the largest hotel in Nashville. Seven U.S. Presidents have stayed here. The hotel reached its height of popularity in the 1890s.

While staying at the nearby Hermitage Hotel, President Theodore Roosevelt declared the coffee he drank there was Good to the last drop. *The coffee was the blend from the Maxwell House Hotel. At that time, it was a regional brand, marketed by the Cheek family. For decades, Roosevelt's words have been used as a slogan to market Maxwell House Coffee.*

When we walked into the Hatch Print Shop, we were taken by surprise. Every surface was covered, from floor to ceiling, with posters announcing music performances and a wide variety of show-business events. The multi-colored works displayed a multitude of artistic styles. The range of featured performers extended from country to popular and from modern day to old timey.

JB told us that the Hatch was one of the oldest letterpress print shops in America and was famous for its block-printed posters. Looking around us, we could see why. A cursory check of prices told me we didn't have enough pocket money to purchase a Nashville souvenir at the Hatch Print Shop.

"Maybe someday, Jase," Danny assured me, once again seeming to read my mind.

"Are we going to walk to the Soda Shop, JB?" Danny asked, apparently eager to get there.

"We'll take a local bus to West End and Elliston Place and walk a short distance to the soda shop. After that, we'll use our transfers to take another local bus back here. Finally we'll transfer to the Belle Meade bus, which will take us to SRA."

"Oh, I understand," Danny mumbled, clearly indicating to me that he did not.

"How much will all this cost?"

"Just the initial dime fare, Jase. The transfers are free," JB replied.

"Oh, I understand," Danny announced enthusiastically. "Just like in Riverton."

This time he got it.

15 BACK IN ACTION

THE DOWNTOWN BUS EXCHANGE WAS AN ARRAY OF paved driveways located in the area laying between First Avenue and the Cumberland River. Arriving buses entered off First, pulling all the way forward and then stopping to discharge and then load passengers. When full, as soon as it was clear, they departed onto Broad.

We boarded the West End local bus well before its departure time. As a result, the two seats directly behind the driver were empty. As usual, Danny preferred the window, leaving the aisle seat for me. JB sat in the seat directly across from me.

Within minutes, the bus was nearly full. The passengers closely resembled those that we'd seen that morning. Young and old. White and black. Military and civilian. Well-dressed and work-dressed. In short, it was another diverse group.

Just as the driver reached for the lever to close the door, a large man wearing a set of wrinkled, white coveralls ran down the sidewalk toward us and pushed his way through the door and onto the bus. Immediately I thought there was something odd about him. Danny must have felt the same way because he nudged me slightly with his elbow.

"Excuse me, sir. Your fare," the driver reminded the man. "You forgot to deposit your fare. It's ten cents, please."

"Eh?"

"Ten cents!" the driver repeated a little more loudly. This time he rubbed his first two fingers with his thumb, the international sign for money.

"Maybe he's deaf," Danny speculated in a low voice.

The man reached inside his coveralls and extracted a handful of coins and offered them to the driver. The driver selected a dime and dropped it into the coin box.

"Thank you, sir. Please take a seat. We're about to depart."

While the man stood next to me, waiting for others ahead of him to be seated, I closely examined him once more, confirming my initial impression. He was indeed odd.

Danny nudged me again, lifting his foot and pointing at it. I grasped his meaning and glanced at the man's shoes. But wait, these weren't shoes at all. Nonetheless they looked familiar. Suddenly I remembered. Turning to Danny, I whispered, "German jackboots!"

He nodded his head in response. Silently his lips formed the letters, "P-O-W."

I slowly nodded my agreement.

I watched as the man moved to the back of the bus. Perhaps to be as far away from the driver as possible, he sat down next to an older man in the last row of seats. I turned to Danny and pointed with my thumb toward the back.

Danny rose and looked for himself. Then he sat back down and concluded somberly, "Apparently he's not familiar with Southern customs."

"Jase, what's going on?" JB whispered.

I quietly related our suspicions about the last passenger. JB looked for himself. Then he nodded his agreement. "What'll we do?" JB whispered.

I pointed at JB and then at the driver. He shook his head and pointed back at me. He was right. I knew what to say. So I patted my chest and nodded in agreement.

Leaning forward, I tapped the driver on the shoulder. When he turned slightly toward me, I whispered my suspicions in his ear. The driver leaned into the aisle, took one look, and immediately reached out his window to beckon a police sergeant, standing on the sidewalk. When the officer came to the window, the driver whispered in his ear. The police officer whispered his instructions to the driver who nodded his head.

The driver left his seat and stood in the aisle. "Folks, I'm afraid I have some bad news. We're having mechanical difficulties with this bus and will have to change to another bus. I would appreciate y'all taking the same seats in the new bus as you have now. We'll unload, starting with the back row first. Then the next row -- you follow the back row folks -- and so on. That's right. Thank you."

Among the first people off the bus were black passengers and our suspected POW. When the suspect stepped off the bus, he was immediately taken into custody by a contingent of Nashville's finest. They marched him off to a nearby squad car, pushed him into the caged-in backseat, and slammed the door.

Then the police sergeant returned and spoke to the passengers standing outside the bus, "Sorry for the inconvenience, folks. Y'all are free to reboard. There's nothing wrong. Thanks for your cooperation."

As the last of the puzzled passengers climbed aboard the bus, the police sergeant spoke to the driver, "Joe, I need you and those three boys to come down to the station. We'll make arrangements to get a substitute driver here as soon as possible."

We waited until the driver collected his jacket, lunch-pail, and morning paper. Then we followed him off the bus. When the police sergeant finished talking on his squad-car radio, he walked over to us and shook each of our hands. "Thank you, men. We've been on the lookout for this fellow for a number of days now. He escaped from Camp Forrest earlier this week. His name's Korff. Apparently he's a bad actor.

"We focused our search efforts on Union Station and here at the bus exchange. But it looks like you young gentlemen are better at spotting wayward POWs than we are. I've called ahead -- I need you to come to police headquarters and tell your story to the chief."

Addressing the driver, he said, "You too, Joe."

Naturally we accepted his invitation. After all, we heroes were used to acclaim.

BY THE TIME WE arrived at police headquarters, word of our role in capturing the escaped POW had spread among the press corps. As we walked up the front steps, we were quickly surrounded by a dozen reporters and photographers. We were peppered with shouted questions and flashbulb bursts.

JB resembled a deer in the headlights. His eyes were as big as saucers. "JB, we've been through this before. Don't look their way. Just stare at the sergeant's back and keep walking. Soon we'll be inside. It's just like cutting through the defense in basketball."

Apparently my advice to JB did the trick. He smiled and his demeanor changed to dead serious. I'd seen that look before, just before he burst through the opponents to sink the ball. He'd be fine.

When we arrived at the chief's office, we received a welcome we hadn't expected. The office was filled with high-ranking officers and one distinguished gentleman wearing a finely tailored suit and tie. There was also an army captain whose insignia I recognized as that of the U.S. Army Military Police.

"Gentlemen, I'm Chief Braddock. Congratulations on a job well-done. You've earned the unqualified respect and gratitude of the Nashville Police Department."

We each introduced ourselves as the chief shook our hands. Then he turned to the well-dressed gentleman, "Mayor Stout, may I present Masters Addison, Tucker, and Bradford. And Mr. Joseph Curry."

"I'm honored to meet y'all," the mayor boomed, vigorously shaking our hands. "As you saw on the way in, members of the press are eager to meet y'all formally. But before that, the chief and I would like to hear how you knew to alert the police. How did you recognize this escaped POW? Let's start with you, Mr. Curry."

The bus driver quickly deferred to us, informing the mayor all he did was listen to my whisper, deem it important enough to alert the sergeant, and pass the information to him.

"So, Master Addison, it was you who tipped off the driver. Is that right?"

"Yes, sir. But before I did so, I conferred with my friends, Danny and JB -- Masters Tucker and Bradford -- to make sure they concurred."

JB gave me a smile, silently thanking me for including him on our crime-stopper team. Aside from the acclaim he rightly earned on the basketball court, this was his first experience being a hero like Danny and me.

"Exactly why did you conclude this man was a German POW, Master Addison?"

"There were a number of reasons, Chief Braddock. First, he was wearing white coveralls that didn't fit him -- they were much too large. Also, he had his white coveralls on inside out. I figured he was trying to conceal something. And unlike the other men on the bus, he wasn't wearing a hat.

"When he got on the bus, he didn't know where to put his fare. And when the driver confronted him, he didn't seem to understand. I don't think he speaks English very well. Apparently he doesn't know the value of our money either because he let the driver choose the correct fare from his handful of coins. That reminds me -- his hands were very clean and soft-looking. They weren't the hands of the worker he pretended to be. And he wasn't carrying a lunch-pail or a toolbox like other workmen we'd seen this morning on the bus. "

"Master Addison, I'm impressed. Anything else?"

"Yes, Your Honor. He was unfamiliar with your custom of reserving the back of the bus for black passengers only. He sat down next to an elderly, black gentleman in the last row of seats."

"Very interesting."

"Most importantly his footwear convinced me that he was a German POW."

"Footwear? For goodness sake! What was he wearing that gave him away?"

"German jackboots! They're worn by POWs who are former members of the SS. These boots are the knee-length -- shiny, black leather -- hobnail boots. You've seen them in newsreels worn by storm troopers *goose-stepping* down the street in Nazi parades."

"Yes, I've seen them. You know a lot about this subject for such a young man."

Danny joined the conversation. "From our experience with former members of the SS, I'd guess that Korff refused to wear standard army-issue work shoes. The pride and arrogance of this group of POWs are well-known. After they're in our POW camps for a while, they put aside their pride, join the rest of their comrades, and enjoy the benefits of being a POW in an America-based prisoner of war camp."

"My goodness, Master Tucker. You certainly know a lot about this subject, as well."

Danny ignored the compliment and added, "If you check, I'll bet he was captured relatively recently -- probably in Sicily or Southern Italy."

Turning to the others in the room, the mayor announced, "Gentleman, I think we have just heard from experts on the subject of German POWs. Captain Isley, what's your opinion on what these young gentlemen have told us."

The MP captain replied, "I concur 100 percent with everything the boys said. They're right. Korff is a former member of the SS -- captured in Sicily. I suspect these boys are from a town that's home to a POW camp. Right, boys?"

We nodded our heads. "We're from Riverton, Michigan. Camp Riverton is a German POW camp just on the outskirts of town."

"You aren't, by chance, the boys responsible for capturing a number of escaped POWs from Camp Riverton? And wasn't one of you kidnapped by POWs on two different occasions?"

"That's us, Captain. I'm the one who was kidnapped -- twice. But I outwitted them -- both times," Danny announced, once again, inspecting his fingernails.

BEFORE THE PRESS CONFERENCE, we met with Mr. Jeffries, Chief Braddock's press secretary, who briefed us on the key members of the Nashville press corps. He focused on the top crime reporters from the *Banner* and *The Tennessean*, as well as the lead radio correspondents from WSM and WLAC. Most likely these reporters would pose a majority of the questions. He assured us that they were tough but fair. That being the case, Danny and I knew with our experience with the press we'd have no problem answering their questions. But JB felt very uncomfortable. This was his first experience with the press. Moreover, JB felt his role wasn't that significant. Reluctantly we concurred that JB's participation would not be required.

Mr. Jeffries gave us the format, which sounded to Danny and me like a repeat of the news conferences during the MEM robbery case. He estimated that the conference probably would not wind up until well after five o'clock. Furthermore, he requested we stay afterwards to assist him in drafting a press release. We agreed, but we told Mr. Jeffries we needed to let Coach Lewis know that we'd probably be late for the six o'clock seating. Since the coach was attending an all-day meeting at the school, Mr. Jeffries dispatched a police car to the school to contact him, explain the situation, and inform him that a car would return us to SRA as soon as we were finished.

To open the press conference, Chief Braddock made a statement, followed by a few remarks from Mayor Stout. After introducing the MP captain, the city attorney, the arresting officer, Danny, and me, the chief opened the floor for questions.

Because our experience relating to misconduct of German POWs was considerable, we credibly answered each and every question that members of the press posed. Aside from details unique to this case, there weren't many questions that we hadn't fielded before.

Danny and I thought members of the Tennessee press corps were considerably more polite and civil than reporters we'd experienced in the North. In fact, this observation applied to everyone we interacted with in Nashville.

Our only difficulty was understanding the words of the questioners who pronounced everything with a Tennessean accent. This wasn't a new problem. Since arriving in Nashville, we'd noticed that Tennesseans pronounced certain words differently than we Michiganders. For example, we would ask, "How do you *feel?*" When Nashvillians asked the same question, we heard, "How do you *fill?*" In contrast, if we asked, "Did you *fill* the tank?" Nashvillians seemed to say, "Did you *feel* the tank?" During the press conference, we listened intently to hear and understand every word.

One reporter hit upon a question I had wanted to ask myself. "Why did Korff wear those coveralls inside out?"

Chief Braddock stepped forward. "I believe I can handle this one, gentlemen. Captain Isley, please chime in here if I get off track. When Korff escaped from Camp Forrest, he was wearing the standard POW work uniform, adorned with prominent white *PWs* stenciled front and back. Somewhere near Tullahoma, he hopped a freight train heading to Nashville. When his train entered the Gulch, he evidently decided to hop off and hide."

The same reporter raised his hand. "Chief Braddock, if I might --."

"I -- ah, yes. What is it?"

"I'm from Memphis -- could you tell me what you meant by the *Gulch?*"

"Having come from an old Nashville railroad family, I could indeed. Back in the late 1800s, the Louisville and Nashville Railroad Company decided to build Nashville's Union Station. To serve this new station, the L&N developed a site now known as the Gulch. There they built an expanded railroad yard with more than three dozen tracks and a massive roundhouse. Trains arriving at Union Station passed through the Gulch and unloaded under a long shed of nearly 500 feet, constructed of steel, wood, and slate. That, sir, is what we here in Nashville call the *Gulch.*"

"Thank you, Chief Braddock. Please continue."

"Let's see. Where was I? Oh, yes. Here's what we believe happened. Korff hopped off his train, ran across the tracks, and hid in the garage of a nearby filling station. There he removed his POW work uniform and slipped into a set of white coveralls he found hanging in the garage. They were far too large for him, but at least he was free of those POW duds, which we later discovered wadded up and stuffed under a stack of old tires. Evidently he felt safe enough in those white coveralls to make his way to the bus exchange at the end of Broad. That's where these two young POW hunters nabbed him. Anything else?"

"Excuse me, Chief. I'd originally asked if you knew why he wore them inside out."

"So you did. So you did. The answer is because he chose to hide in an American Oil filling station. The company's logo -- the American flag -- was proudly displayed above the left breast pocket. Apparently he was uncomfortable operating under *our* flag."

The Tennessean reporter posed another question that was difficult for Danny and me to answer.

"Given that Germany has surrendered. And that these POWs will soon be repatriated. Why did Korff choose to escape now?"

Danny deferred to me and I gave it a try. "We've become acquainted with a number of POWs -- especially those who work at the canning factory in our neighborhood. Generally they fall into two categories. Those POWs who've fallen in love with America and would give anything to stay. And those who are so concerned about their families back in Germany that they would give anything to be home -- right now. But at this point in time, POWs in these two categories would never choose to escape. So I guess I really haven't answered your question. Sorry."

"Perhaps I can help, Jase," offered Captain Isley. "There are some Nazis in our POW camps who face prosecution for war crimes when they're repatriated. Whether they're tried by the Allies or later by good Germans, they face long prison sentences or worse."

"Thank you, Captain. That makes a lot of sense," the reporter agreed as he took his seat.

"Why didn't I think of that?" Danny wondered aloud.

"I thought you probably already had, Danny."

"You're right again, Jase."

CHIEF BRADDOCK AND MAYOR Stout made a special effort to see us before they left for other pressing business. They thanked us for our service to America, Tennessee, and Nashville. It was humbling, at least for me. We said goodbye and followed Mr. Jeffries back to the conference room where he'd prepped us.

"Could you hold up for just a second, boys?" Captain Isley called as he wove his way through the crowd.

"Go ahead, fellas. I'll get the typewriter set up in the conference room. See you there when you finish with the captain."

"Before I left, I wanted to shake your hand and thank you for your service to our country. I doubt that anyone knows that you have both been the recipients of United States Medals of Courage.

But I wanted you to know -- I think that's really something for fellas your age."

"How did you know about us? We try not to talk about our awards a lot -- especially in public." I looked at Danny who seemed unusually sheepish for a recent offender in this area. Not everyone in our partnership was totally comfortable wearing the cloak of public modesty. But I was hoping my words would induce a change for the better in you-know-who.

"I heard of your accomplishments when I was attending a conference on POW camp security in Washington earlier this year. But your names hadn't stuck with me. This morning I saw Sergeant Mellon who was escorting a contingent of POWs to a branch camp here in Nashville -- on White Bridge Road. He told me he'd run into you two at Union Station this morning. Because he'd been stationed at Camp Riverton, he was very familiar with your accomplishments. He went on and on. In short, he's quite a fan of yours."

"We thought he was a nice fellow. In fact, he invited us over to have lunch with him at the camp."

"I hope you can make it. The sergeant's really looking forward to it."

He shook our hands one more time. Then he stood tall and saluted both of us. Danny returned his salute. I simply smiled. He waved goodbye and left the police station.

As we wandered back to the conference room, Danny reinforced what the captain had said. "We've got to make it out to Sergeant Mellon's camp. He's counting on it."

I agreed and suggested we schedule our visit at a time when JB could join us.

When we entered the room Mr. Jeffries was seated behind a huge *Underwood* typewriter. Before he could say a word, Danny told him we would be pleased to help with the press release, but he had a couple of requests.

"What are they, Danny?"

"First, would you please send this press release to Chuck Nichols at the *Riverton Daily Press* in Riverton, Michigan? We want JB's mother to read this story in Monday's paper."

"Done! What's the second one?"

"We'd like you to include JB as one of us. And also it'd be very kind of you to mention that his father graduated from the Vanderbilt School of Medicine. Could you also say that his father was killed in action while he was serving aboard the *USS Arizona* when it was sunk by the Japanese at Pearl Harbor?"

"I'd be honored to include this information. Thank you for bringing it to my attention."

I was touched by Danny's thoughtfulness.

JB WAS WAITING FOR us in the reception area of Chief Braddock's office. When we entered, he asked excitedly, "How'd it go?"

Mr. Jeffries answered for all of us. "It went extremely well. However, upon reflection, I'm truly sorry that you weren't standing up there with Jase and Danny this afternoon. I apologize for being inconsiderate. You should have been there too."

I sensed that JB was caught off guard. "No, I should --. Thank you," he sputtered. That was all he could muster.

"Chief Braddock wants to say goodbye to these three young men," the secretary advised, breaking the mood. "I'll tell him you're here."

Once again, the chief was effusive in praising us for our assistance in recapturing Korff. "I hope to arrange for our fair city to express its gratitude to you three gentlemen in some meaningful way," he promised. He shook our hands with added vigor and bid us farewell.

Mr. Jeffries informed us, "We have a car waiting to take you to Stony River Academy. I hope you haven't missed your dinner."

We told Mr. Jeffries how much we enjoyed working with him. He thanked us again as we hopped into the backseat of the police car. Leaning in the window, Mr. Jeffries' last words were, "Officer, please deliver these three young men to Stony River Academy as soon as possible."

Evidently the officer took him quite literally. After exiting the garage, the officer hit his siren, stomped on the gas, and warned, "Hold onto yer hats, boys!"

Cars in front of us sought the protection of the curb, creating a clear path as we sped out Broad and down West End.

"Ever ridden in a police car with its siren on, boys?" our driver inquired while, of all things, looking at us through his rearview mirror.

JB shook his head nervously and deferred to us. Danny answered his question forthrightly, "We've been fortunate to do so on numerous occasions, officer. But I must say -- you're one of the most skillful high-speed police drivers we've ever encountered."

"Ya don't say?"

"Yes, sir. I *do* say," Danny assured him.

"Well, I swan! Giddyap, Napoleon!"

JB and I had to bite our knuckles to keep from bursting into laughter. But Danny shushed us out of our giggles. And we obeyed.

When we reached Belle Meade, our driver evidently thought it was safe to turn off his siren and flashing lights. By the time we reached the school's front gate, he was driving at a snail's pace. "Where shall I drop y'all?"

"Please turn at the next right and drop us in front of that first building, Officer," JB instructed.

After waving goodbye, I suddenly felt exhausted. It had been a long day. JB gave us our instructions. "I spoke to Coach Lewis before we left the police department. He's arranged for a late meal in the dining hall. We're due at 7:00 p.m. That allows us plenty of time to --."

"*Freshen up*. Right, JB?" Danny suggested mischievously.

"Why yes! That's it exactly, Master Tucker," JB shouted, throwing his arm around Danny's neck and treating his scalp to a good old-fashioned Dutch rub.

WHEN WE ENTERED ROBERTSON Hall, we saw Coach and Mrs. Lewis seated at the same table we'd had the evening before. There were no other people in the dining hall. The headwaiter stood at attention, awaiting our arrival. He was grinning from ear to ear. "Welcome, gentlemen. Welcome," he declared as he seated us. "Oh, my! I'm honored to serve you!"

Mrs. Lewis looked at him quizzically. Coach Lewis grinned knowingly. The headwaiter quickly regained his composure. "This evening we arranged a late dinner for you. I'll check in the kitchen and return with our suggestions."

After we had exchanged greetings, Mrs. Lewis demanded to know, "What on earth was that all about?"

As if we'd rehearsed it, we boys and the coach all shrugged our shoulders simultaneously and played dumb. This wasn't the response Mrs. Lewis expected. "Now wait just a minute here," she ordered. "Somebody 'fess up. What's going on?"

"Apparently our headwaiter heard the special newscast on the radio this evening. It was on just before you arrived home, Dorothy," the coach replied in a cajoling tone.

"Special newscast! Well, for goodness sake. What about the special newscast?"

"Well, according to the mayor and the chief of police, our three dinner guests are heroes. Reportedly they single-handedly captured a dangerous German prisoner of war who had escaped some days ago from Camp Forrest. For their feats of bravery, they were treated with an afternoon with Mayor Stout, Police Chief Braddock, and the Nashville press corps."

"I'm flabbergasted. Is this true, boys?" Mrs. Lewis wanted to know.

"No, ma'am. Not entirely," JB said humbly. "As I told the press secretary from the police department, Jase and Danny were entirely responsible for capturing the POW. I was just along for the ride. And that's the truth."

Danny had reached his limit! He stared coldly at JB and then turned to me. "I don't know about you, Jase. But I'm fed up with JB's broken record."

Turning back to JB, he asked, "JB, why are Jase and I in Nashville?"

"Ah -- because I invited you to visit me?"

"Why were we in downtown Nashville today?"

"Because I wanted to show you the sights."

"Why did we get onto that local -- West End -- bus?"

"Because I knew it'd take us to the Soda Shop."

"So who's responsible for Jase and me being in downtown Nashville, Tennessee -- sitting on the West End local bus -- when an escaped POW, wearing stupid German jackboots, just happened to stumble aboard?"

"I -- I guess I am."

"For the first time today -- you got that right. The three of us captured that POW. Get it?"

"Got it, Danny."

"Good. We missed our Soda Shop snack so I'm really famished. Let's eat!"

16 THE BALL BOUNCES

ON SUNDAY MORNING, WE WERE NEARLY LATE FOR breakfast, even though the cafeteria remained open until eight o'clock on weekends. Because we'd tumbled, exhausted, into bed an hour after dinner, I calculated that we had enjoyed a full ten hours of sleep. We really needed it.

By the time the Lewises picked us up at the dormitory, we were well-rested, well-fed, and ready for another full day. Our first stop would be the First Presbyterian Church in downtown Nashville.

"We don't normally leave this early for church, but it's necessary today because of the Fisk Jubilee Singers. They're so popular that people will travel for hours to hear them perform. Officially the service is scheduled to begin at ten o'clock, but by half past nine every seat in the church will be filled."

When we entered the church, I could hardly believe my eyes. It was by far the most unusual place of worship I'd ever seen. Luckily we found five seats together and not far from the pulpit at that. When we were seated, for our benefit, JB softly read a section from his *Guide:*

First Presbyterian Church, located at 154 Fifth Avenue North, was built in 1848. The Egyptian Revival style was popular during this era because archaeological finds in Egypt were being highly reported

*in American publications. The exterior of this historic landmark
includes Egyptian style lotus columns and a winged sun disk. Interior
elements include stained glass windows, woodwork, colorful columns,
and a perspective painting of Egyptian scenes on the sanctuary walls.
This is the best surviving ecclesiastical example of Egyptian Revival
architecture in the United States.*

"What this doesn't tell you is that everyone in Nashville refers
to this church as *First Prez,*" JB confided.

"Y'all probably don't know about this, but during the height
of the maneuvers near Nashville -- in the months leading up
to the Normandy invasion -- around 80,000 servicemen were
in Nashville on weekends. This church served as a refuge for
soldiers. Volunteers from the congregation operated what we
called the Servicemen's Lounge, located in the church basement
just beneath this sanctuary.

"On weekends, off-duty soldiers came here for a luxurious hot
shower, a place to sleep, companionship, and a hearty breakfast at
no charge," Coach Lewis informed us.

"When the 160 cots were filled, the church allowed up to 300
weary soldiers to make themselves comfortable anywhere they
could find space," Mrs. Lewis added. "It wasn't uncommon to
see two soldiers sleeping on the piano. This lounge was the first
of its kind in the United States. Dozens of representatives from
churches and charitable organizations in other cities have come
to see the operation firsthand."

"While we don't have those large numbers of soldiers today,
still every Saturday night dozens of soldiers stay in the lounge,"
Coach Lewis told us.

The crowded church was abuzz with anticipation. When
the minister arrived at the pulpit, he raised his hands. Soon
the church was quiet. We proceeded through the usual service,
excluding the singing of hymns. I assumed the minister was
saving the music for the Jubilee Singers. Having dutifully
delivered the prescribed quantity of Christian message, the
minister immediately transformed himself into a master of
ceremony. From the way he performed his new role, it was clear
to me that he'd garnered considerable experience in show business

somewhere along his career path, which I learned later ended at the Vanderbilt Divinity School.

"Good morning, folks. Many of you are visiting us for the first time this morning -- in order to enjoy the upcoming performance of one of the world's most renowned singing groups.

"On behalf of the congregation and myself, I bid you welcome. We cordially invite you to join us for some refreshments after the service -- refreshments prepared by the ladies of the church and served in our basement meeting hall.

"By now the soldiers who slept there last night have set off to explore Nashville. Or, judging from the number of military folks we have with us here in the sanctuary, perhaps some of them are still here.

"Whenever we're blessed by a visit from the Jubilee Singers, we're joined by many who are hearing this fine music for the first time. I'd like to share with those folks a little something about the long and brave history of the Jubilees.

"In 1866, immediately following the War Between the States -- in an abandoned Union hospital barracks in Nashville -- the American Missionary Association established the Fisk Free Colored School to educate former slaves.

"When donations by former abolitionists to support the institution declined, nine former slaves with extraordinary voices formed an *a capella* group. To save their school, they traveled to towns along the former Underground Railroad in the Northeast, introducing their audiences to Negro spirituals -- those songs sung by slaves before the War. In 1871 in Oberlin, Ohio, a public performance marked the first time their secret music was sung outside the plantation fields or the closed doors of their cabins and churches.

"The group was called *The Jubilee Singers*, a Biblical reference to the year of Jubilee in the Book of Leviticus, Chapter 25. The Jubilees expanded their tour to Europe to raise money for Fisk. Slowly their beautiful voices began to change attitudes among predominately white audiences as they broke racial barriers in the United States and in Europe -- where they sang in cathedrals and performed in palaces for the royal families in England, Holland, and Germany.

"In 1873, their European tour raised funds to build Fisk's first permanent building, Jubilee Hall. In this Victorian Gothic building -- one of the oldest structures on campus -- hangs a floor-to-ceiling portrait of the original nine Jubilee Singers. This work was commissioned by Queen Victoria during the 1873 tour as a gift from England to Fisk. The Jubilees continued their American and European tours, raising enough money to turn Fisk into the full-fledged university it is today.

"Please join me in welcoming the Fisk Jubilee Singers."

The minister turned toward the stage behind the pulpit and benevolently breached normal church protocol by leading the applause.

The Singers filed proudly onto the stage. Without hesitation their voices soared above us in gloriously pure tones and splendid harmony. They mesmerized us with soulful renditions of traditional Negro spirituals including:

- *Steal Away*
- *Swing Low, Sweet Chariot*
- *Down by the Riverside*
- *Nobody Knows the Trouble I See*
- *Soon - Ah Will Be Done*

When they finished, the audience stood and applauded for a full ten minutes. The Jubilees took three *curtain calls.*

It was one of the most inspiring performances I'd ever witnessed.

When the applause died down, the minister once again took up his position behind the pulpit. "Thank you. Thank you for your generous applause. Thank you. Ladies and gentlemen, I have yet another gift to share with you. Before the service this morning, I received a communiqué from Nashville mayor, The Honorable Harry L. Stout. I'd like to share his message with you."

Deliberately the minister reached into his pocket and removed an official-looking envelope from which he slowly extracted what looked like a piece of parchment. He placed a set of spectacles on the end of his nose and with great aplomb read the following:

July 22, 1945

My dear Reverend Jasper,

I have it on good authority that among those in your audience, today, which is assembled to enjoy Nashville's treasure, The Fisk Jubilee Singers, are three very special young gentlemen.

These individuals bravely and single-handedly acted yesterday in this city to subdue and to bring to justice a dangerous escaped Nazi prisoner of war. In doing so, they exhibited courage far beyond their years.

For their service to the United States of America, the State of Tennessee, and the City of Nashville, we're deeply grateful.

Please pass along my personal best wishes to Master Jase Addison, Master Daniel Tucker, and Master Johnson Bradford, who is the son of a fallen hero at Pearl Harbor, Doctor Jackson Bradford of this fair city.

If you would be ever so kind, please respectfully inform them they are to be honored at City Hall on Tuesday evening next at seven o'clock. At that time, each of these gentlemen will receive a much-deserved Key to the City.

Well done, young gentlemen!

Yours sincerely,
Harry L. Stout
Mayor
Nashville, Tennessee

We were completely flabbergasted.

When he finished reading the note, Reverend Jasper, whose name was now apparent to us, asked, "Would the honored young gentlemen please stand to receive an expression of our thanks here this morning?"

JB and Danny looked at me for guidance. I answered by standing up. They followed suit.

As we attempted to accept gracefully the outpouring of near-raucous acclaim from those around us, one important thought completely dominated my thinking. Unwittingly or not, Mayor Stout has just caused the three of us to upstage the Fisk Jubilee Singers.

I made a mental note to apologize to them if the situation ever presented itself. I guess some of that Southern civility had rubbed off on me too.

BY THE TIME WE made our way through dozens of well-wishers at the church, it was already past noon. Coach Lewis encouraged us to hurry to the car. "On Sunday afternoons, there are overflow crowds at Sulphur Dell. People arrive early to watch the teams take the infield -- or to get seats in the right field corner of the stands -- where players give autographs.

"On top of that, the army brings busloads of army airmen from Smyrna Army Air Field to the Sunday games. Technically the ballpark only seats 8,500. Of course, when the big league teams stop here to play, we somehow manage to jam in a few more thousand fans."

"Big league teams? Aren't the Vols a minor league team?"

"Yes. The Vols are a Class A1 minor league team in the Southern Association -- just like their opponents today, the Memphis Chicks. But traditionally big league teams, traveling home from spring training in Florida, stop off at minor league parks along the way and play exhibition games.

"The Vols are in the Chicago Cubs farm system. We've seen the Cubs here on numerous occasions over the years. Even Babe Ruth played here once. That was a standing-room-only occasion."

"Why's the ballpark called Sulphur Dell?"

"I can answer that," JB asserted, looking in his *Guide*. "Apparently the site of the ballpark was once called Sulphur Springs Bottom. It was a bottomland or a dell -- where an artesian sulphur spring was located. The original ballpark -- called Athletic Park -- was built in 1870, and it's been home to the Nashville Volunteers since 1901."

JB scanned his *Guide* for more. "In 1908, Grantland Rice, a Nashville sports-journalist at the *Nashville Tennessean,* referred to the ballpark as Sulphur Spring Dell -- later it was shortened to Sulphur Dell."

"Excuse me for saying -- but aren't sulphur springs awfully smelly?" I suggested.

The coach chuckled. "Well, now that you mention it, that's not the only odor we have to contend with at the ballpark. First, there are odors of livestock from the stockyards and fumes from the gas works nearby. When the wind is right, it can be overpowering. And there's the snuff factory -- just down the block. From there you get can smell sour, burnt tobacco, coming your way. Of course, it seems that every man in the stands smokes cigarettes or cigars. Mix all that with the aroma of grilled hot dogs and freshly popped popcorn -- and there you have it. The Dell Smell."

"Ye gads!" was Danny's contribution.

"If we're going to disclose everything, we have to mention the dump," Mrs. Lewis added.

"The dump! You mean there's a dump here too?" I asked incredulously.

"This is *the* last word on this smelly subject," Mrs. Lewis promised. "Y'all heard the terms *bottomland* and *dell,* but the land on which the ballpark was built was really one huge sinkhole. For decades, it was filled with Nashville's garbage and trash. To be honest, it still smells like a dump."

"That's not so bad," Danny assured her. "Jase and I spend hours every day searching for buried treasure at the Riverton City Dump."

"That's very commendable, Daniel," Mrs. Lewis responded politely, attempting to make the best of it.

"Well, in the interest of telling the *whole truth and nothing but the truth,* the mountains of garbage under the ballpark resulted in a rather *hilly* outfield," admitted Coach Lewis. "This is particularly true of right field which slopes steeply -- at about a 45-degree angle -- starting right behind first base, upward toward the fence. When you're almost to the fence, you reach a 10-foot-wide shelf. That's at about 224 feet from home plate. Some people call our right fielders *mountain goats* that *graze* on their terrace along the fence -- that is when they're not running downhill for short pop-ups and ground balls."

"When Babe Ruth was here, he said, 'They have a right field that goes straight up in the air,' " Mrs. Lewis added.

"Needless to say, if you can hit to right field, you have a good chance of hitting it out of the park. In addition to the hilly terrain, the fence is only 262 feet from the plate. That's why the right fielder stands up there on the shelf. Left field is more normal at 334 feet and center is a respectable 421 feet."

"I've never heard of a ballpark like this one," I admitted. "But I guess both sides are favored equally."

"Exactly, Jase," the coach declared. "Sulphur Dell may be an odd ballpark, but it's *our* ballpark and we love it."

"That's all that counts, Coach," Danny affirmed.

WE FOUND FIVE SEATS in the lower deck about 20 rows up from the Vols dugout. They were excellent seats. The minute we sat down, I checked with Danny, "Smell anything?"

He shook his head. "Maybe there're no smells on Sundays."

"Or maybe they moved the sulphur spring, the livestock yards, and the dump because they knew we were going to be here."

"Don't be silly, Jase. How would they know we were coming?"

We both laughed and settled into our seats. The seats around us filled very quickly. The last two empty seats in our section were immediately in front of Danny and me. Actually they weren't really seats per se. Throughout the ballpark, fans were seated on hard wooden, bleacher-like planks. There were no separating armrests or backs. But I estimated the space in front of us would accommodate two fans.

Before long, two older gentlemen took those seats. Judging from their Nashville Vols baseball caps and uniform shirts, they were avid fans. They were also gregarious and genuinely friendly, introducing themselves to their neighbors seated on either side and in front of them. Then they turned around to say hello to us.

After shaking our hands, one asked, "Are you young fellas ready to see the Vols take these Chicks to the woodshed?"

Danny answered, "What's the woodshed?

"Why, I suspect you're new to Sulphur Dell. And from your accents, you may be new to Nashville. Am I right?"

"Yes, sir. We're from Michigan -- down here visiting our friend, Johnson Bradford, who's here this summer helping with the basketball camp at Stony River Academy," Danny said, pointing to JB.

"Stony River -- well, for goodness sakes. Hello, Coach Lewis. Mrs. Lewis. I didn't see you at first. How are you?" Turning to his companion, he commented, "Jack, look who's here."

The Lewises and the two older gentlemen appeared to know each other. They smiled, shook hands, and exchanged warm greetings.

"How'd the Bomberettes do in Birmingham, Mrs. Lewis?"

"Luckily we won another one. Thank y'all for asking"

"Great! Then you're still undefeated. That's very good news indeed. Congratulations."

I looked at Danny. From the alarm in his face, I knew he'd read my mind. JB had that same look. Apparently we'd been so absorbed in the POW capture and press conference that we'd completely forgotten to ask Mrs. Lewis about the Birmingham game. I was filled with feelings of profound embarrassment. I promised myself I'd apologize as soon as we were in the car.

Our friendly neighbor's words redirected my attention. "Both of us had grandsons who played basketball for SRA under the careful tutelage of Coach Lewis. That's going back a few years now," he explained to us. "Johnson Bradford. You've played for Coach Lewis recently. Isn't that right? Sharpshooter extraordinaire as I recall."

"Yes, sir. That was before we moved to Michigan. Coach invited me to assist him with the camp this summer. That's why I'm back down here. My friends, Jase and Danny, came to visit me."

We were interrupted by the PA announcer's request that we stand for the playing of the national anthem. Everyone in the stands stood and placed their hands over their hearts or, in the case of those in uniform, saluted the flag. As the scratchy recording wafted out over the field, the voices of over 8,000 enthusiastic patriots nearly drowned out the antiquated PA system. When the anthem ended, the crowd cheered at the top of their lungs.

When the din subsided, the PA system played *Three Blind Mice* to announce the arrival of the umpires on the field. Minutes later, the Vols' pitcher delivered his first pitch, a perfect strike, and the game was under way. The pitcher was hot, quickly striking out the first two batters. The third batter mishit a fluke ground ball that bounced down the baseline right into the mitt of the first baseman who stepped on the bag to end the inning.

As the Vols ran off the field toward their dugout, I noticed something very unusual about the left fielder. Turning to Coach Lewis, I asked incredulously, "Does that fielder only have one arm?"

"That's right, Jase. With so many baseball players in the service, the Vols signed a one-armed outfielder. He bats one-handed fairly well and he's darned good in the outfield. He fields the ball on the run, tucks the glove and ball under his opposite armpit, plucks the ball out of the glove, and makes the play -- all in one smooth motion. His name is Brown -- can't remember his first name."

That was a new one on me. I thought to myself, *I'll have to tell Grandpa Compton and Dad about this extraordinary player.*

In the bottom of the first inning, the Vols' hitters were hot. They hit the cover off the ball. When the inning ended the score was 5 to 0. Having gone to the bull pen twice, it looked like a long day for the Memphis Chickasaws.

During the lull between innings, vendors filled the aisles, hawking various food and drink. The hot dog seller's song rose above those of his fellow vendors, "Red hots! Red hots! They're really, really ready, and really, really hot. With a pickle in the middle and an onion on the top. Red hots! Red hots!"

We all ordered a red hot and a Pepsol, a local carbonated red-pink beverage with a pepsin flavor not unlike cinnamon. The hot dog and Pepsol only cost 15 cents. I made a secret wager with myself that Danny would down at least four of these combinations before the game ended.

Our new acquaintances, took the occasion to entertain us with some Sulphur Dell lore. The first man told us, "When we were boys, the field was surrounded by wooden fences. Since the lumber used had lots of knotholes, we'd take our jackknives and pop them out to create peep holes to watch the games through.

"After a while, the Vols management decided to use knot-hole-popping as a basis to bring more families and kids to the games. They created the *Knothole Gang*. A Gang member bought a general admission season pass, and the card was punched each time a game was attended. After every four punches, the next game was free."

Jack continued, "We kids could see games from a number of locations outside the ballpark. Sometimes there'd be a boxcar parked on the railroad tracks on the other side of the fence over there. The top of the car would be covered with kids watching the game.

"To see the game, you could also climb up on top of Whetby's Produce building on Jackson Street or the Atlantic Ice Company building, where many home-run balls landed. But the real break came when management decided that on Saturdays, all kids would be admitted free."

Jack's friend added, "In the past, when trains passed along the tracks outside the ballpark over there, they'd spew cinders all over the third base side of the stadium and out in the parking area. As kids, we all wore short pants. If you happened to fall down, your knees were badly scraped by sharp cinders."

"Sounds like it was a lot of fun growing up around this ballpark," I said.

"It was the best childhood you can imagine."

"Yep, the very best," his friend assured us.

THE FINAL SCORE OF the game was 12 to 3. A pretty good showing for the Nashville Vols whose 1945 losing record was a great disappointment, especially after winning the league championship in 1943.

In my mind, they'd played a near-flawless game because Danny and I were in the stands. But that's the way we international heroes think on these occasions.

We said goodbye to the two gentlemen in front of us. Once again we all shook hands and they wished us a pleasant visit. We went our separate ways and before long we were pulling out of the parking lot in Coach Lewis' station wagon.

When we cleared the heavy traffic around the ballpark, I bit the bullet. "Mrs. Lewis, we owe you an apology. We failed to ask you about your game yesterday. I'm very sorry."

"Jase Addison, don't you spend another second thinking about it. Your day yesterday was filled to the brim with events requiring your full attention. By the time y'all arrived home, you were exhausted. I don't know how y'all stayed awake through dinner last evening. Please don't bother your head about it."

"I'm sorry too, Mrs. L.," Danny told her.

"Me too," JB added.

"Everything I said to Jase applies to you two as well. Not another thought about it. Please."

Up until this time, the coach hadn't uttered a word. As a matter of fact, he seemed preoccupied. His wife interrupted his reverie. "James, were you going to ask JB to meet with you before dinner?"

"Hmmm? Oh, yes. Johnson, when we arrive back at the school, would it be convenient for you to meet with me at my field house office? I want to tell you about my meeting yesterday, go over the master schedule with you, and ask your advice on some outcomes of that meeting."

"Yes, sir. I'd be happy to meet you there. Would it be all right if Danny and Jase came along? They could shoot some baskets while we meet."

"You bet. Why don't you freshen up, and then we'll go straight to dinner from the field house?"

"Sounds good, Coach."

After the Lewises, dropped us off at the dormitory, Danny asked, "Jase, do you have any freshen-up lotion I could borrow? I'm clean out."

The three of us got a chuckle at that one.

"Wear your basketball shoes, fellas. You're going to like what you see at the SRA field house. Just a wee bit different than the Riverton YMCA gym."

JB was right about that. The field house consisted of two full basketball courts. One was for practicing and the other for playing opponents. The bleachers associated with the playing court, I guessed, would hold at least 2,000 people. Beyond the two courts, an area nearly as large as two basketball courts was devoted to other indoor sports, including gymnastics, wrestling, volleyball, and weight lifting and conditioning. In the basement under the field house, there was an Olympic-sized pool with locker rooms for men and women.

I had never seen such a complete, shiny-new, and opulent indoor sports facility. I could only imagine that many colleges would be happy to have such a facility available to their athletic departments.

We looked across the court and saw Coach Lewis seated at the desk in his office. The large glass window allowed him to look out onto the practice court. He waved at us and we waved back.

"See those bins over by the bleachers? They're filled with basketballs. Grab what you want and have fun while I'm in talking to the coach."

So we weren't chasing balls after every shot, we extracted four basketballs from the bin.

We warmed-up with a few easy set shots after which we mixed in some jump shots. Finally we added a few layups. We were getting nicely warmed up when Danny suggested, "How about some one-on-one games?"

"Okay, half-court. You take the ball out first."

We scrimmaged with each other for about ten minutes, exercising both our offensive and defensive techniques. Since we hadn't played basketball since early spring, I was surprised by how sharp our playing was. We were blocking each other's shots, dribbling past each other for easy layups, and swishing long jump shots.

After about 15 minutes, we decided to take a break. I looked over at Coach Lewis' office. Both JB and he were staring out the window at us. Then they opened the door of the office and walked toward us.

Danny and I looked at each other. "That's curious, Jase. Wonder what's up."

"Boys, you were playing some fine basketball out here. Johnson had told me you were good, but he didn't do you justice. For your ages, you're both excellent players. You may be able to help us out of a fix we're in -- if you'd be willing."

"We'd do anything to help, Coach," I told him, meaning every word of it.

"Yeah, anything, Coach," Danny assured him.

"Well, without going into a lot of detail. We misjudged the number of campers that we have signed up for this coming week and for the weeks following that. We allowed two of our staff members to depart this past week -- to spend vacations with their families.

"We thought our camp enrollment would drop off significantly but just the opposite occurred. We can get help in here by the week after next, but we're behind the eight ball this coming week. I'd very much like you to join our camp staff in the same role that Johnson plays.

"What do you say?"

It didn't take us a microsecond to consider the request. We simultaneously yelped, "Yes!"

We all shook hands. The coach thanked us profusely and promised to meet with us an hour before camp started in the morning to outline our duties. He thanked us again and returned to his office.

Bursting with excitement and joy, JB, Danny, and I bounced up-and-down with glee. We were about to tear out of the field house when the coach flagged us down.

"Wait up, boys! I almost forgot something important," he hollered as he approached carrying two packages. He handed

Danny and me a package and announced, "You're going to need these in the morning."

"What's this, Coach?" I asked nervously as I opened my package. "Oh, wow! Is it really for me? Thank you, Coach Lewis. Oh, wow!"

Danny held his rich, forest-green SRA sweat suit up to his body. While doing so, he caringly caressed the school crest with his fingertips. "Looks like a perfect fit to me, Coach. Thank you so much. We'll be proud to wear these."

I don't remember walking to Robertson Hall that night. I suspect my feet never touched the ground.

17 KEY TO THE CITY

WHEN THE THREE OF US, DRESSED IN OUR OFFICIAL SRA coaching sweat suits, walked into Robertson Hall for breakfast, the noisy room suddenly became still. The campers stared at us as if we were men from Mars.

"It looks like the boys are wondering who the new coaches are," JB observed.

"So are we," Danny replied cryptically.

But I knew what he meant. Frankly I was extremely nervous about our new roles. While Danny and I had both experienced pregame jitters, the jitters I was having before my first coaching experience were quite different. Self-doubt was beginning to tarnish the glow of having been selected by Coach Lewis.

Danny seemed to read my mind. "Nervous, Jase?"

"You bet!" I answered honestly.

"Me too," he admitted. "Frankly I don't really feel like eating. How about you?"

I never dreamed I'd hear those words from Danny. But I had to agree. "I think I'll just skip breakfast today."

Instead of trying to convince us it was all in our heads, JB assured us that our anxiety was normal. "I couldn't eat a thing all the way here on the train. All I could think about was whether or not I could cut it."

"How'd it work out for you?" Danny inquired, tongue in cheek.

"On my first day, I actually did okay -- but I was extremely hungry afterwards."

We all chuckled, which relieved the tension a bit.

In deference to our temporary fast, JB hurried through his breakfast. Before we knew it, we were walking into the field house. Coach Lewis looked up from his desk and welcomed us with a smile and a wave.

Wasting no time, the coach sat us down in front of the blackboard and outlined his program. "Our campers fall into two groups, junior-high and elementary school -- that's grades four through six. JB and you two fellas will coach the elementary-school campers. My assistants and I will take the junior-high group.

"After rest and lunch breaks, we only end up with about five hours a day to teach these campers the fundamentals. Or, as JB will attest, to break their bad habits and reteach them the basics. Everyday -- for both groups -- we spend an hour on each of four fundamental basketball skills."

The coach wrote four words on the blackboard:

• Dribbling
• Passing
• Shooting
• Defense

"Then we end each day with an hour-long, shirts-and-skins scrimmage. That allows the camper to apply what he's learned -- under our watchful eye, of course. Any questions so far?"

"I assume you have specific drills for each of these areas."

"That's right, Jase. Judging from your skills, you're probably familiar with most of them. I'll quickly run through them so we can go out on the floor where JB and I can demonstrate any you're not familiar with."

The coach quickly inventoried the drills for each of the four areas. "For the SRA high-school team, I use two-ball dribbling drills including pound-it, two-ball kills, alternating piston, and one-high, one-low. But frankly many of our junior-high campers have difficulty with two balls. And we've seldom seen an elementary-school boy use two balls successfully. Unless you want to spend your day chasing down errant balls, you probably should stick to one-ball dribbling drills. To coach passing skills, we use shuttle passing, double-circle passing, and dodge-it drills. I assume you're familiar with these."

We both nodded our heads.

"Naturally we combine shooting with rebounding. As one player shoots, the others compete for the rebound. We teach shooters the layup, the hook, the set shot, and free throws. In defense, we teach both individual defense -- one-on-one -- and zone defense. How are you fellas on zone defense?"

"We use it on the YMCA team all the time. So we know it well," I told Coach Lewis. "Unless you use a different kind of zone defense," I added, looking at JB.

"It's virtually the same as we coach here, Jase," JB confirmed.

Before the campers arrived, JB and the coach demonstrated the two-ball dribbling drills in case we wanted to try them. Because we were familiar with the other fundamentals, by the time the first campers arrived, we felt relaxed and ready. We divided the elementary-school campers into two groups. Danny took one and I took the other. JB was the floater, moving from one group to the other to help campers who were having difficulty.

By lunchtime, our appetites had returned in full force. Danny selected his usual gigantic feast. I settled for a normal but robust meal. As he munched away with relish, Danny observed, "This camp counseling's a kick. I think I might apply for a job here next summer. How about you guys?"

While I chuckled, JB cautioned, "One day at a time, Danny."

DESPITE OUR EXHAUSTING FIRST day, we were still wound-up after dinner. Perhaps it had something to do with Coach Lewis' announcing to everyone within earshot that Danny and I were *natural-born coaches*. To say the least, his comment nearly knocked our socks off. Mrs. Lewis told us she was *pleased as punch*. Neither Danny nor I knew exactly what that meant, but we assumed she was quite happy for us.

"Are you fellas tired?" JB asked when we arrived back at the dormitory.

"You kidding? I'm so excited I could stay up all night! How about you, Jase?"

"I'm wide-awake too."

"Good. Let's pop into the game room. Maybe we can find something to occupy ourselves for a while before bedtime."

The game room contained four polished-oak tables and chairs. On the shelf near the door, there was an assortment of games. JB inventoried our choices, "Checkers. Chess. Playing cards. Backgammon. Snakes and Ladders. Parcheesi. Mr. Ree. Battleship. Game of the States. Monopoly."

"Monopoly? What's that like?" Danny asked.

"It's a good game for three people. Have you played, Jase?"

"Yes, I have. Let's play. You be the banker, JB."

JB opened the board, placed the Chance and Community Chest cards on the appropriate squares, organized his Monopoly money by denomination, and counted out our opening share of $1,500 apiece in Monopoly play money. "We're all set. Everybody choose a playing piece. I'll take the racecar."

"Battleship," I responded, lifting the small metal token from the board. It's your turn, Danny."

For a long time, Danny stared at the remaining pieces. Instead of choosing, he asked, "Tell me again. Why do I need one of those little things?"

"We'll all put our pieces on *Go*. When it's your turn, roll the dice. Whatever the dice add up to, move your piece that number of places."

"Oh, I see. Then it's important. Any more racecars?"

That did it!

"Danny, hurry up and pick a piece. It's getting late, for crumb's sake."

"All right, Jase. I think I'll choose the cannon -- so I can sink your battleship," he threatened, winking at JB.

I wasn't amused.

JB gave him an overview of the rules and the object of the game. Danny responded with his usual number of silly questions followed by his usual off-the-wall comments. JB patiently answered his concerns. "Yes, if the card says *Go to Jail*, you must go to jail. No, you can't move your piece backwards. I realize the houses look like *doghouses* but they still cost what it says on the Title. No, you can't put houses or hotels on railroads or utilities. You can't use two playing pieces."

You get the idea.

Two hours later Danny had evolved from a naïve amateur to Monopoly mogul. In record time, he had managed to bankrupt both JB and me. He counted his cash showily and announced his winnings, "I have $14,190. I also have all the hotels and all the properties. The bank only has $240 and you two guys have zero. So I guess I win. Right?"

Neither JB nor I gave Mr. Smug the satisfaction of an answer.

"Hmmm! I'll bet -- you're afraid to tell me I haven't won yet. Hand me the dice. I'll roll again."

"No! Danny, you've won. The game's over," JB declared with finality.

"Oh, I see. Good! Let's play another game. How about it, Jase?"

"This has been a long day. Let's go to bed," JB asserted.

"I think I'll stay here and practice rolling the dice," Danny announced.

"Are -- are you serious?" I sputtered.

"Gotcha!" Danny responded.

Author's Note:

In 2007, long after the war ended, according to the terms of the Official Secrets Act of 1939, the British government declassified information relating to how the lowly Monopoly game played an important role in winning World War II.

Beginning in 1941, a great number of British airmen found themselves imprisoned in POW camps behind German lines and in need of maps to assist them in escaping. Paper maps were noisy when crinkled, often wore out before they could be used, and turned to mush when wet. MI9, the British secret service, sought out John Waddington Ltd., a British company that had perfected the technology for printing on silk. Coincidentally this firm was also the British licensee for the Parker Brothers game of Monopoly.

A small, sworn-to-secrecy division of Waddington printed silk and rayon maps that depicted routes to and locations of safe houses and other places where escaped prisoners could find refuge. These maps covered the regions in which certain camps were located. Codes printed on the box covers assured that each set reached its designated camp.

Maps were folded and inserted in a Monopoly playing piece. Another small piece held a magnetic compass. Small metal tools were included, as well as high-denomination German, Italian, and French currency that was hidden in stacks of Monopoly play money. British crews were told that "special edition" Monopoly sets would be marked with a red dot, which looked like a printing error, in the Free Parking square.

Rather than include them in Red Cross packages, these top-secret Monopoly sets were sent to German prison camps by private, often fictitious, organizations. If they were discovered, the Germans would have no justification for stopping Red Cross packages from reaching POWs. Decks of cards, the board game Snakes and Ladders, and pencils were also used to conceal maps for prisoners. Many British airmen, flying over German-occupied Europe, inserted silk maps into the heels of their boots or sewed them into their uniforms in case they were shot down.

During the war, some 35,000 prisoners returned to the Allied lines before the war ended. It's credibly estimated that about one-third of them were aided by the top secret contents of a simple Monopoly game. I find it ironic that so many British POWs were able to take advantage of Monopoly's Get Out of Jail Free *card.*

OUR SECOND DAY WAS a great improvement over our first. Instead of being impatient with campers' athletic ineptitude, we accepted our campers as they were and simply did our best to help them improve. When they did so, we commended them and gave ourselves credit for a job well-done.

If, for some reason, they seemed not to improve, we didn't take it personally. Instead, we renewed our efforts to teach them, using creative new approaches that we devised as we went along. By midmorning, the campers were playing basketball at a much higher level than before and, more importantly, both the campers and we were much happier about it.

At our morning rest break, I noticed that Danny's shoestrings were untied. Normally I wouldn't have mentioned it to him, but I was aware that during our drills we counselor-coaches were often moving at a high rate of speed. Stepping on your own shoestrings could lead to serious injury. I pointed at the loose shoestrings. Danny bent over and pulled them both tight. Oddly enough, both strings snapped.

"Shoot!" he spat. "I don't want to restring these with knots in them. Where do they sell shoestrings here on campus?"

"Gee, Danny. We'd have to take a bus down to West End for them. Sorry," JB told him.

"Wait a minute! There were two pairs in Grandma Compton's emergency supplies tin. Where's that tin, Jase?"

"It's on my closet shelf, next to my dress shoes. Here -- take my room key. Go change your shoestrings. JB and I'll keep the boys busy until you return."

"Good idea!" Danny said as he grabbed my room key and sped out of the field house.

JB and I set up the two groups for circular-passing drills. JB oversaw one and I the other. When we'd been at it for some time, I realized that Danny had yet to return. A glance at the clock told me it was nearly time to break for lunch. And still no Danny.

"Jase, it's almost noon. We better head for Robertson Hall."

"Good idea, JB. But I wonder what's become of Danny?"

"Who knows? Danny marches to the beat of a distant drummer."

When we entered the dining hall, I looked across the room and saw Danny sitting alone at a large, round table. He waved at us and pointed at his table.

"I guess he wants us to join him."

"Look! He's already served himself lunch. Why on earth didn't he return to the field house? Or if he was bound and determined to come here, why didn't he wait to go through the line with us?"

"You got me, Jase."

"More distant drumming, I suppose."

By the time we joined Danny at his table, he'd finished his lunch. I decided not to mention his bizarre behavior, at least, not until I'd finished my lunch.

"Danny, I thought you were coming back to help JB and me. What happened to you?" I snapped.

"After I finished restringing my basketball shoes, I was on my way back -- when I was stopped."

"Stopped by who?" I asked bluntly.

"By official business. I'll tell you about it later." Danny nodded toward the head table where the summer school faculty and the camp staff members were seated.

What did they have to do with it? I wondered. I had no idea why, exactly, but I gave him a pass. I didn't have the energy or patience to pursue the subject any further.

After observing my capitulation, Danny changed the subject. "We should have brought our blue blazers to wear to tonight's Key-to-the-City ceremony at the mayor's office."

"It's too late for that now," I told him. "We'll just wear our long pants and clean shirts. That should be formal enough for summertime in Nashville."

"I have a better idea," JB suggested. "Let's all wear our SRA sweat suits."

I looked at Danny and he looked at me. We both nodded. "That's a top-notch idea, JB," Danny replied.

"Bully!" I agreed, imitating old Teddy R himself.

AFTER THE KEY CEREMONY, JB was ecstatic. Having been the recipients of a number of honors and awards, Danny and I were understandably rather blasé about the whole affair.

"This was the greatest thing that's ever happened to me!" JB professed effusively. "How about you guys?"

Danny responded with a noncommittal look of great forbearance. When I caught his attention, I shook my head ever so slightly to signal Danny to exercise restraint. He got my message and nodded back his reassurance. "JB, I can understand how you feel. How many other native Nashvillians like yourself have ever received the key to your own city?" Danny asked with sincerity.

I smiled approvingly.

We joined the mayor, other city dignitaries, and reporters in the city-council meeting room for punch and cookies. As Grandma

Compton would say, the mayor was full of himself. He slapped backs and shook hands with everyone, talking and laughing extremely loudly. As he gestured wildly, his punch splashed on those standing near him.

"Gentlemen, let me shake your hands one more time," he boomed, working his way through the crowded room toward us. "Have you ever received a greater honor?"

I sent Danny another precautionary signal. But this time, Danny refused to heed my warning. "Only once or twice, Your Honor," Danny said meekly, baiting the hook.

The mayor, who had evidently failed to do his homework, swallowed Danny's bait. "Oh, psshaw! Master Tucker, I do believe you're pulling my leg."

"I'd never do that, Your Honor." Danny loved to play his fish before reeling him in. To be honest, I felt a little sorry for the poor mayor.

"Come on, now! Tell me. When have you ever received such prodigious public acclaim?"

Danny felt *forced* to inventory our record of achievements for the mayor and the reporters who had circled around us to observe this exchange.

"Well, the first time was when J. Edgar Hoover awarded each of us a United States Medal of Courage on Don McNeil's *Breakfast Club* radio show in Chicago. Our appearance there was arranged by our good friend, Thomas E. Dewey. He took time off from his presidential campaign to set it up. Jase and I helped both Governor Dewey and President Roosevelt with their campaigns."

I was amazed. This time Danny even got Mr. Hoover's name right.

"The next was when President Roosevelt gave us our second Medals of Courage at the White House. On that occasion, the President took us to the British Embassy for a top secret meeting with the British Prime Minister, Winston Churchill. He told FDR that he wanted to meet us too.

"Then there was --."

The mayor's face had turned a deep shade of purple. Evidently he'd stopped breathing. Danny had noticed too. "Are you all right, Your Honor?" he asked compassionately.

Sputtering and gasping, the mayor looked at his wristwatch and announced, "Gentlemen, I must leave. I have an important telephone call coming in from Washington. President Truman is seeking my advice on how to avoid making a fool of yourself after award ceremonies. I mustn't be late."

With that the mayor shook our hands one more time and hastily exited the room.

The reporters who had heard Danny's recitation circled around us, demanding to know whether Danny was telling the truth. Mr. Jeffries, the police press secretary, fielded their questions. "Gentlemen, I can assure you that young Daniel Tucker spoke the truth. Here's an advanced copy of the press release I drafted this afternoon after a long conversation with Chuck Nichols, a reporter from the *Riverton Daily Press.*"

He handed each reporter a copy.

"Mr. Nichols confirmed every fact that Master Tucker told the mayor -- and then some. Gentlemen, these boys are truly American heroes."

That was our exit line. We pushed our way through the throng of reporters who followed us to the Lewises' station wagon. With some difficulty, we pried open the doors and found sanctuary inside the car.

"Y'all are certainly popular with the press," Mrs. Lewis chuckled. "Will y'all autograph my basketball?"

Her question provided the perfect comic relief. We all laughed heartily.

After we said good night to the Lewises, we headed for our rooms. It had been a long day. I unlocked my door and was about to step inside when Danny stopped me. "Just a minute, Jase. I have something for you."

He unlocked his door and went into his room while JB and I looked on. Within a second or two he emerged with my wallet in his hand. After he handed it to me, I opened it and found my $11 nestled safely inside.

"When did this arrive?"

"This morning -- when I was in your room changing my shoestrings. It came by Special Delivery -- I signed for it."

"I thought I'd have to sign."

"I signed your name. Because I was in your room, the mailman thought I was you."

"So we won the wager. That's great! We get to keep the $15. Right?" Danny didn't answer. He just smiled instead. "Danny, what about the $15?"

"I sent the $15 to Mary Donovan."

"Who's she?" I demanded. "And why did you send our money to her."

"She's Lieutenant Donovan's wife. Remember? I wrote her the letter to explain why the lieutenant's paycheck money was short by $15. I remembered her address."

"But we won the bet, Danny."

"I know, but the lieutenant helped us -- when he didn't have to. He gave us that money out of his pay. So I simply returned the favor. I knew you'd approve."

I shook my head and admitted, "Of course, I approve, Danny. Thank you."

BY WEDNESDAY, OUR CAMP routine went as smoothly as clockwork. Feeling confident and contented, we decided to take in an evening movie at the Belle Meade Theater. By eating dinner at the first seating, we could walk to the theater for the seven o'clock showing of *The Fighting Sullivans*. This film was making a second run in theaters, following its premier the year before.

When we mentioned our plans to Coach Lewis, he was all smiles. "That's a terrific movie. Mrs. Lewis and I saw it last year -- when it first came out. We can compare notes after you've seen it. Why don't we pick you up and go out for ice cream? You haven't been to the Soda Shop yet. We'll go there."

Naturally that suggestion was music to Danny's ears. "All right!" he yelled.

After a leisurely walk, we entered the Belle Meade Theater. I was amazed by its striking art deco design. The Chippewa Theater back in Riverton was downright plain compared to the Belle Meade. We walked by the *Wall of Fame*, where we saw a huge square of white marble on which were inscribed the autographs of dozens of movie stars, singers, and other celebrities who had visited the theater since its opening in 1940. Surrounding the marble square were scores of autographed photographs mounted on the wall, each depicting a recognizable celebrity shaking hands with Ed Jordan, the theater manager.

JB proudly watched as Danny and I swooned over the names and images. "That's Frank Sinatra -- and there's Bing Crosby. Isn't that Doris Day? I recognize this lady too. Oh! That's right. It's Helen Hayes. Hey, look! It's Smiley Burnette -- Gene Autry's sidekick. And there's Irene Dunne. Wow! Is there anyone who hasn't been here at this theater?"

The lights in the lobby dimmed, signaling us to take our seats. After the newsreel, previews of coming attractions, and the cartoon, the featured attraction flashed to life on the huge screen. Since that night in Belle Meade, I've seen this film over a dozen times. As a World War II history buff, I've also read extensively about the Sullivan brothers. Much of the material in the following paragraphs does not appear in the film itself.

The five Sullivan brothers, named George, Frank, Joe, Matt, and Al, were born and raised in Waterloo, Iowa. On January 3, 1942, when they enlisted in the U.S. Navy, their ages ranged from 20 to 27. Their enlistment was conditioned on their serving together so all five were ordered to join the crew of a light cruiser, the *USS Juneau*. While participating in the Guadalcanal Campaign in the Pacific, the *Juneau* was forced to withdraw after being struck by a Japanese torpedo on November 13, 1942.

While their ship was departing from the Solomon Islands area with other damaged U.S. Navy warships, it was struck by a second torpedo fired by another Japanese submarine. Evidently the second torpedo hit in close proximity to the *Juneau's* ammunition magazines because the ship exploded and sank very quickly.

Captain Gilbert C. Hoover, senior officer of the battle-damaged task force, decided not to delay the escape of the other ships by searching for *Juneau* survivors. He ordered the remaining ships to continue on a course which would return them to the Allied base at Espiritu Santo. He also signaled a U.S. B-17 bomber in the area to notify Allied headquarters to send aircraft and ships to search for the survivors.

About 100 of *Juneau's* crew had survived and were floating in shark-infested water. Refusing to break radio silence, the B-17 crew did not relay the search request until they'd returned to base, hours later. Compounding the problem, the request went unnoticed for several days.

Finally aircraft were sent to search the area. Eight days after the sinking, only ten survivors were pulled from the sea. These men reported that Frank, Joe, and Matt had died instantly. Al drowned the next day, and George survived for four or five days. Overcome with grief and in a weakened condition, George allowed himself to slide from his raft into the water.

The *Fighting Sullivans* became national heroes and were recognized in many ways. President Roosevelt wrote their parents a letter of condolence. Pope Pius XII sent a silver religious medal and rosary. And their parents were invited to speak at more than 200 war plants and shipyards on behalf of the war effort. They also toured the country selling war bonds.

In 1943 and again in 1995, the Navy commissioned destroyers both named *USS The Sullivans* with the appropriate motto of *We Stick Together.* The City of New York named a 1,400-foot pier on Staten Island in their honor. In 1944, the brothers' story was told in the film that I viewed for the first time at the Belle Meade Theater. Later their hometown of Waterloo named a convention center, a street, a public park, and a museum wing in their honor.

DURING THE WAR, 90 million Americans went to the movies at least once a week. When you consider that America's population was only 134 million, this is an incredible statistic. There were several reasons for the record-breaking attendance.

First, immediately following Pearl Harbor, movie executives, producers, directors, and actors alike signed on to do their part. In contrast to recent times, Hollywood produced movies that stood solidly behind our military and the rightness of our cause. In fact, wartime movies were shamelessly super-patriotic. Thus, Americans came to the movies to escape and to have their spirits lifted. They also came to stay abreast of the war's progress as depicted by the latest newsreels shown before each feature attraction.

Prior to and during the war, Academy Award nominations for the Best Picture and Best Story included these patriotic films:

- 1939. *Blockade, Test Pilot*
- 1940. *Foreign Correspondent, The Great Dictator*
- 1941. *Sergeant York, Night Train to Munich*
- 1942. *Mrs. Miniver, Wake Island, Yankee Doodle Dandy*
- 1943. *Casablanca, For Whom the Bell Tolls, The Human Comedy, In Which We Serve, Watch on the Rhine, Action in the North Atlantic, Destination Tokyo*
- 1944. *Since You Went Away, The Fighting Sullivans, A Guy Named Joe, Lifeboat, None Shall Escape*
- 1945. *Anchors Aweigh, Objective Burma!*
- 1946, *The Best Years of Our Lives, The Stranger*

In 1942, the Best Picture award was presented to *Mrs. Miniver*, a serious World War II drama. As the war progressed, films offered relief from the war and movies became more varied in theme. In 1943, *Casablanca* won the Best Picture award.

In 1945, *Anchors Aweigh*, a musical comedy, follows three sailors on shore leave in San Diego during the war. The film is well-known for the musical scene where Gene Kelly dances with the animated Jerry Mouse. The movie received the awards for Best Music and Scoring of a Musical Picture, as well as nominations for Best Picture and Best Actor (Gene Kelly).

THE CROWD SWEPT US out of the theater and onto the street. Quickly we spotted the Lewises' station wagon parked on West End Avenue about half-a-block away. We jogged up the street, opened the rear car door, and slid in.

"Anybody hungry?" Coach Lewis inquired as he pulled out into traffic. The three of us answered affirmatively. "Good! We're off to the right spot."

Luckily we found a parking space almost immediately in front of the restaurant. A large neon sign in the window spelled out *Elliston Place Soda Shop*, which I read aloud to help me remember the name.

A colorful neon sign attached to a pole at the entrance depicted a thick, creamy milk shake. On entering the shop, I noticed three different seating arrangements. Straight ahead was a lunch counter with revolving, black leather-covered stools. Behind the counter on the red and white checkerboard-tiled walls were placards, featuring malted milk, banana pudding, and banana splits, all specialties of the house. Placed on the floor, which was a similar pattern in larger green-and-white tiles, were stand-alone, Formica-topped tables with slender, wrought-iron chairs. Against the right wall were green vinyl booths, each sporting a table-top jukebox.

Without asking, Danny quickly slipped into a booth, slid all the way in, and placed himself right next to the jukebox. After perusing the record titles for a microsecond, he asked, "How long has this place been here?"

"It opened in 1939 -- just before the war in Europe began," Coach Lewis replied.

"My parents used to eat here when they worked at Vanderbilt University Hospital. That was before my father entered the navy. This is still my mother's favorite meat-and-three."

"What's a meet-and-free?" Danny wanted to know.

"It's *meat*-and-*three*. That's a Southern-style restaurant that charges a reasonable, fixed price for one serving of meat -- your choice of, say, sugar-cured ham, fried chicken, or pork chop -- with three servings of vegetables from the daily roster of a dozen or so choices. Most offer mashed potatoes, baked squash, turnip greens, fried bite-size rounds of okra, black-eyed peas, and congealed salad -- that's the Southern name for Jell-O. This all comes with corn bread or rolls. And sweet tea -- if you're a real Nashvillian. For dessert, you could choose a banana split, a piece of silky-smooth chess pie, a banana pudding, or a frosty piece of lemon icebox pie."

"Before we leave, we just have to come here for lunch or supper, Jase," Danny suggested. "But tonight is dessert night."

"Have you decided what you're ordering, Danny?" Coach Lewis asked.

"I'm thinking about a double chocolate malt."

"What do you mean by *double?*"

"I mean two of them. I'm pretty thirsty. I got really hot in the movie theater."

The coach sniggered and looked at Mrs. Lewis, who rolled her eyes, ever so subtly.

Our waitress took our orders and returned with five nickels to exchange for Danny's quarter. "Jukebox money," he explained. "We'll vote on which five songs to play. Says here these are all on the *Hit Parade* list. So we should know them all."

"Dorothy, do you remember when *Your Hit Parade* was first broadcast on the radio?"

"It was back in the mid-thirties. Was it 1935?"

"That's exactly right. Boy! That was ten long years ago."

"Okay! Everybody ready to vote? I'll read the entire list first. Then we can go back and vote on each song. Here goes."

He read the following list very quickly:

1. *Sentimental Journey* by Les Brown and Doris Day
2. *It's Been a Long, Long Time* by Bing Crosby with the Les Paul Trio
3. *Rum and Coca-Cola* with the Andrew Sisters
4. *Till the End of Time* by Perry Como
5. *My Dreams Are Getting Better All the Time* by Les Brown and Doris Day
6. *Bell Bottom Trousers* recorded by Louis Prima
7. *Don't Fence Me In* by Bing Crosby with the Andrews Sisters

"Remember, we each get five votes. I'll keep track of the voting. Whichever songs get the most votes, wins. Then I'll play the songs with my nickels. Agreed?"

On the first ballot, each of the seven songs on the list got three votes.

"All right. Some people didn't vote five times. Who was it?"

"I think that was me. I only like a couple of songs on the list."

"Let's try it again. Remember! Everybody vote for five songs."

By this time, the waitress was setting our desserts on the table.

"Danny, maybe I can help move this forward," Coach Lewis suggested. He requested the waitress to break a quarter into a dime and three nickels. "While we eat our ice cream, please play all seven songs. Okay, Danny?"

Danny smiled, slapped a nickel in the coin slot, and punched in his first selection. Before it had started to play, he opened his mouth and poured about half of his first chocolate malt down his throat. As he pinched the bridge of his nose together to relieve the severe pain caused by the freezing malt bomb, Doris began her *Sentimental Journey.*

At times like these, I wondered whether our Nashville trip would end up being a *senti-mental journey* or a *semi-mental* one.

BY THE TIME WE finished dinner on Thursday evening, we were exhausted and ready for bed. Our schedule had been so demanding, we were beginning to run out of steam. We were also concerned about running out of money. The $12 we'd each brought to Nashville had shrunk to about $5 apiece. We knew we had to conserve much of what remained for our train trip back to Riverton. We couldn't count on a sack of turkey-and-cheese sandwiches to sustain us during our upcoming travels. Of course, Danny's return of Mrs. Donovan's $15 certainly helped the Donovan household budget, but it did nothing to strengthen our financial health. Still I had no second thoughts about Danny's decision. It was indeed the right thing to do.

We changed into our pajamas and met in my room to finish writing postcards. We divided the list of our friends and neighbors, including the Matlocks, the Tolnas, the Zeyers, and Mrs. Mikas. However, regardless of who wrote the card, we both signed our names. In addition, I wanted to send cards to my cousins. Because this would take more cards than I'd purchased, Danny gave me some of his.

The one piece of news we included in every postcard was our plan to attend the Grand Ole Opry stage show and radio broadcast on Saturday evening at the Ryman Auditorium. We urged our family and friends to tune in and imagine us sitting in the audience right there in Nashville.

Our postcard project was nearly finished when we heard a knock on my door. "It's me guys -- JB! Open up. I want to share some nifty news from this afternoon's *Nashville Banner.*"

We opened the door and JB hurried into the room. By the way he nervously shook his newspaper at us, we could tell he was very excited. "The Shrine Circus is in town! It's at the ballpark -- at Sulphur Dell. Let me read what's in the paper."

Danny stared at me. "We better recount our money, Jase."

JB apparently didn't hear Danny. Instead, he began reading, very rapidly. "Says here -- again this year -- the Al Menah Shrine Temple in Nashville -- is sponsoring Tom Packs' Three-Ring Circus -- for six performances between July 25 -- that's yesterday -- and July 29th -- that's Sunday, the day you leave for home.

"The general admission ticket price is $1.20 for adults and only $.60 for children. There's an evening performance on Friday and Saturday. If we go to the Grand Ole Opry at the Ryman on Saturday, we could go to the circus tomorrow night.

"Mr. Jack Norman -- the General Chairman of this year's circus -- says the Shriners have already sold 47,500 tickets. With only 8,500 seats in the ballpark, there'll be a lot of standees. This means the Shriners will be making a huge donation to the Shriners Hospital for Children. Isn't that wonderful?

"Here are some of the acts -- The Great Jansley and his Hollywood Sky Ballet. A.E. Selden, the Stratosphere Man. The Flying Valentines. Will Hill's Elephants. Joe Greer's Horses and Ponies. And Spiller's Seals.

"And listen to the best part -- the clowns include Bozo Harrell, Jimmy Davison, Gabby DeKoe, Rube Curtis, and Red Carter. Isn't this great news?"

I couldn't recall ever seeing JB demonstrate so much fervor. Frankly I was inclined to ask him if he were all right.

"Jase and I were just counting what's left of our spending money. We're not sure we have enough to go to both the circus and the Ryman."

"Oh, shoot! I almost forgot. Coach Lewis wanted me to tell you that the Shrine Circus and the Grand Ole Opry are on him. His way of thanking you guys for your help this week. He'll thank you in person tomorrow at the awards ceremony. Each Friday at the end of a camp session, we present campers with Certificates of Completion. It's a nice way to acknowledge everyone's contribution to a successful camp experience."

"You know, JB. I've always wanted to go to the Shrine Circus," Danny admitted. "Tell me more about those seals."

THE WEEKLY AWARDS CEREMONY was a particularly memorable SRA tradition. Each camper received a formal certificate and was congratulated by his coach-counselors on his successful completion of the program. In turn, the campers were encouraged to express their gratitude to their coach-counselors for the excellent training they'd received.

Our campers were extremely generous in their comments about Danny and me. Their words were totally unexpected and a very special gift, which we humbly accepted. Coach Lewis reinforced their sentiments by thanking us profusely, citing how we performed admirably with little or no previous experience and after having been pressed into service at the last minute.

The coach reiterated these same sentiments on the way to Sulphur Dell where his gift, the Shrine Circus, far exceeded our expectations. To our surprise, Mayor Stout, wearing a red Shriner's fez, was called upon to thank the Potentate of the Nashville Shriners for his exceptional job of organizing the circus.

Evidently the mayor had spotted us as he took the stage because he asked Danny, JB, and me to stand and be recognized as the latest recipients of the Key to the City. Naturally he substantially exaggerated our role in the capture of POW Korff, who by that time was probably tired of hearing how he'd been brought to ground by us three boys. Even so it was a bit heady to receive a standing ovation from nearly 8,000 circus fans, 15 clowns, and a dozen barking seals.

Mayor Stout was obviously most proud of his Shrine membership because he told the crowd about the Shriner's admirable record of accomplishments in Nashville and throughout the world.

In 1920, the Shriners began the philanthropic work of raising money to build a Shriners Hospital for Children, specializing in the treatment of children with polio. Care is offered at no financial cost to the patient or the child's family. The only requirement is that children must be under the age of eighteen and treatable.

Since the beginning of World War II, Shriners have sponsored war bond drives, led Civil Defense work in local communities, served in the Armed Forces like Generals MacArthur, Wainwright, and Doolittle, or served as President of the United States like Roosevelt and Truman.

On the way home, Danny deemed Mayor Stout's performance to be *stouthearted*. We all agreed that Danny had nailed it.

18 THE LAST HURRAH

DANNY AND I AGREED THAT WE SHOULD TAKE FULL
advantage of our last full day in Nashville. There were four items
on our agenda:

- Swim at the Centennial Park public pool.
- Visit Sergeant Mellon for lunch at the POW branch
  camp.
- Purchase *GooGoo Clusters* for gifts and travel snacks.
- Attend the Grand Ole Opry.

After a good night's sleep followed by a bracing shower, we
dressed and headed for Robertson Hall. The night before, we'd
agreed on our *uniform of the day*. We donned our SRA sweat suits
and carried our SRA gym bags, in which we packed swimsuits and
bath towels, both inscribed with the SRA coat of arms. As you
might have surmised, we intended to make a statement.

According to our plan, we entered the dining hall just seconds
before the cafeteria line closed. After a hearty breakfast, we headed
for the bus stop to catch the nine o'clock bus. Twenty minutes
later we disembarked at the Vanderbilt campus, crossed West End
Avenue, and entered Centennial Park.

Instead of heading directly to the pool, JB suggested we alter
our course and take a close look at the Parthenon, which we'd
only seen from a distance. It was good advice. As we approached

the rectangular building, we counted 17 columns on the long sides. Atop the six columns on each end was a triangle whose apex formed the peak of the roof.

With help from his handy *Nashville Travelers Guide,* JB explained, "The triangle is called a pediment. There's a similar one on the east side as well. Carved into both pediments are figures representing Greek gods and goddesses. You see, the Parthenon is a temple dedicated to Athena, the goddess of wisdom. On this side, the two central figures are Athena and her uncle Poseidon, god of the seas. Notice the fine carving of the people and the detailing of the horses and chariot. Let's walk around to the east side where the two central figures are Athena and Zeus, the god of the sky and ruler of the gods."

The enormity of the building and its splendor were breathtaking. We walked slowly past the columns to the east side, mesmerized by this magnificent structure.

"Can you imagine a monument like this being designed and built by the ancient Greeks more than 2,000 years ago?" JB asked. "That was centuries before the steam shovel or modern design principles used by architects today."

"This is very impressive indeed. But someday I'm going to Athens to see the original," I vowed.

"Monuments always make me hot. Let's go for a swim," Danny suggested. JB and I looked at each other and smirked.

Danny led the way to the swimming pool, despite the fact he had no idea where the pool was located. After having spent nearly every day for more than a year with Danny, I'd dutifully followed our clueless leader on countless similar occasions. But Danny fooled even me that day. He efficiently guided us directly to our destination by simply following the throng of people, carrying sundry swimming and beach paraphernalia for a day at the pool.

When I first laid eyes on the Centennial Park pool, I immediately attempted to estimate how many times larger this gargantuan swimming facility was compared to our neighborhood pool located in Trumble Park. It was like comparing a rain barrel to the Pacific Ocean.

What struck me most was the huge number of people who were actually in the pool. There must have been well over a hundred swimmers splashing, paddling, floating, and stroking their way here and there over the pool's surface. Even at this early hour, hundreds more men, women, and children were stretched out on beach chairs, towels, or blankets that covered the extremely broad deck and wide lawn that encircled the vast pool.

"Look at those diving boards, Jase," Danny exclaimed. "They must be ten or twelve feet above the water. At home, ours are no more than three feet."

"You're right. But what's even more unbelievable are the kids who are up there diving in headfirst. Some of them can't be more than five or six."

"Let's go to the locker room, rent a basket, and change into our bathing suits," JB urged. "I need to cool off."

"Too many monuments, I bet," Danny asserted confidently, claiming the moral high ground.

AS THE MORNING WORE on, the number of swimmers, divers, sunbathers, and general roisterers at the pool grew exponentially. Despite the best efforts of conscientious parents, lifeguards, and security personnel, out-of-control young boys were racing around the pool, threatening bodily harm to older Nashvillians who had come, seeking peace, tranquility, and an occasional cool breeze, unavailable in their stifling homes.

We three SRA elites were fast tiring of the noise and turmoil emanating from the can of human sardines into which we'd unwittingly allowed ourselves to be packed. From experience, I knew that Danny did not suffer situations like this lightly. Yes. He was the first to crack. "Ye gads!" he shouted. "Let's get out of this rattrap."

JB and I rose, gathered our towels, and followed Danny into the locker room. Within a few minutes, we were boarding the outgoing West End Avenue bus that would take us to White Bridge Road. JB glanced at his watch and announced, "We should be there well before 11 o'clock. So we're in good shape."

"That's excellent news. I'm getting hungry," Danny informed us as if it were necessary in his case.

"Hey, fellas, I just remembered something," JB told us.
"Remember the day we met Sergeant Mellon. I thought I'd be
coach-counseling at the SRA basketball camp -- and you two
would be visiting the POW camp without me. Funny how it
turned out. All three of us end up working at SRA. And I come
along when you visit the POW camp."

"I'm glad things worked out this way, JB," I said.

"Me too," Danny agreed.

We got off the bus and walked down White Bridge Road
toward the POW camp. "It's only about five blocks -- on the right
hand side," JB announced as we marched along.

When we arrived at the building site, we observed at least
a hundred men in constant motion. Yelling and waving at each
other, they transported tools and building materials by truck,
by wheelbarrow, and by hand to the center of their attention, a
sparkling Veteran's Administration hospital, rising inexorably out
of the dirt and dust at its base.

Our observant eyes discerned the many trades whose skills
had merged to produce this structure -- bricklayers, carpenters,
electricians, metal workers, concrete masons, and sundry unskilled
laborers. Some appeared to be civilians. Others were Army
Engineers. Still others were German POWs. Undoubtedly the
POWs escorted by Sergeant Mellon at Union Station were among
the skilled workers on this project.

We stood silently, observing this anthill of activity while
looking for the familiar face of Sergeant Mellon. But he wasn't
where we expected to find him. "Hello, boys. Welcome to Camp
White Bridge," boomed a voice from behind us.

We wheeled around to see Sergeant Mellon, standing next
to three POWs and a young man who appeared to be American.
"We just returned from the diner down the road. Until we get our
cooking facilities set up, we've been using army chits to purchase
our box lunches from the diner. Pretty good fare. Today we ordered
extra. So I hope you fellas are good and hungry."

Danny smiled involuntarily.

"Let me introduce you to these men. This is John Seigenthaler,
whose father's company is one of the main contractors in this

hospital project. In addition to working like a beaver for his father, John is also a qualified truck driver. He picks up our meals for us. John, I'd like you to know Jase Addison, Danny Tucker, and Johnson Bradford -- or JB -- for short."

We all shook hands, greeted each other, and smiled warmly. I was impressed by John, who was a handsome, mild-mannered young man whom I guessed to be about 18 years-old.

Finally the sergeant introduced us to the three POWs who were most friendly and welcoming, not unlike those men who worked for Otto Klump at the canning factory back home.

We followed them to a large tent with open sidewalls. Above the entrance, a hand-painted sign read, *Mess Tent*. Inside were about 20 picnic tables. In the rear, a wide serving table was covered with an assortment of box lunches whose contents were marked in black crayon. Five shiny 50-gallon garbage cans, filled with ice and soft drinks, stood next to the serving table.

"We feed the Army Engineers, MPs, and POWs here. A few contractors like John and his father's crew eat with us as well. They come straggling in between noon and one o'clock, depending on what their work allows. The other workers bring their lunches from home or drive to a nearby eating place on their own."

After serving ourselves, we sat down at the picnic table nearest the entrance. According to Sergeant Mellon, assuming there was a westerly breeze, this was one of the coolest tables in the tent. The three POWs took the table behind us. As soon as they were seated, they began to babble in German, interrupted by frequent outbursts of raucous laughter. This demeanor was very familiar to Danny and me. We had seen this same behavior on those occasions when we joined the POWs in the canning-factory dining room.

"I realize you three fellas were tied up with the basketball camp yesterday. It's too bad you couldn't have been here for lunch. We had a surprise birthday party -- even a cake and candles -- thanks to the owner of the diner."

"Whose birthday was it, Sergeant Mellon?"

"The 27th of July -- John Seigenthaler's birthday! That's whose it was. He turned eighteen. How about that?"

John's face reddened with embarrassment.

Upon hearing John's last name, the three POWs behind us began to chant very loudly, "SEE - GEN - THAL - ER. Nein! Nein! SAY- GAN - TALL - ER. Ja! Ja!"

After repeating this chant three times, the POWs broke into another chorus of raucous laughter.

Everyone at our table joined them, including John, whom I guessed had experienced this ceremony before. When he regained his composure, he confessed, "According to my POW pals, my family has mispronounced our name for about a hundred years. I checked up on this. And found out that -- by golly -- they're absolutely right." Then he started laughing again. Everyone joined him.

Afterward John turned to JB. "Johnson, I've had the privilege of seeing you play basketball -- on the junior-high level. You're one heck of a ball player. My brothers and I attended Father Ryan High School. SRA and Father Ryan have had some extremely competitive games. And I know your skills were responsible for a good share of SRA's success in recent years. It's a pleasure to know you."

"Thank you, sir," JB replied, out of habit. "Jase, Danny, and I play together up in Riverton, Michigan. We took a YMCA state title this past spring. The three of us have been working as coach-counselors at Coach Lewis' basketball camp this past week. Unfortunately they're heading back to Riverton tomorrow."

"Speaking of Riverton, you boys owe me an update on the news since I left there almost a year ago," Sergeant Mellon reminded us. "Come on! Let's have it!"

Danny and I decided to start with the story of how, earlier in the summer, Danny and Otto Klump were forced to fly to Milwaukee by way of Selfridge Field. With his characteristic degree of modesty, or lack thereof, Danny told the sergeant how he had personally saved the day by creatively using the phonetic alphabet. Normally it would have taken me about 15 minutes to tell this entire story. With Danny involved, it was closer to an hour and 15 minutes.

Even though I was reluctant to raise the subject, Danny insisted on relating the story of how the three of us had been given Keys to the City by Mayor Stout for capturing POW Korff.

As I suspected, Sergeant Mellon was very familiar with that story because Korff had escaped from Camp Forrest. But Danny insisted on telling the entire saga again.

When Danny finished, I ever so gently reminded him that Sergeant Mellon was interested in POW-related events in Riverton, not Nashville. He agreed and asked if Sergeant Mellon had heard about Hitler's top espionage agent who had come to Camp Riverton and helped his brother to escape. And how the Nazi agent robbed a Riverton bank. And finally how Danny had singled-handedly subdued the two fugitives at the lumber company out by the Riverton stockyards. By the time Sergeant Mellon could answer his question, Danny had finished the whole story. So it really didn't matter.

It was close to three o'clock when Danny finally ran out of material. We thanked Sergeant Mellon for lunch and left the POW camp. Long before Danny had stopped talking, John Seigenthaler excused himself and returned to his work.

Coincidentally, however, as we were walking along White Bridge Road on our way back to West End Avenue, John pulled up behind us in his truck. "You boys need a lift?"

We told him we were heading back to SRA.

"That's not far out of my way. I'll take you there."

"Oh, I forgot," I added. "We have to purchase some *GooGoo Clusters* to take home as gifts."

"Piece ah cake. There's a Hills Grocery just up ahead. You can buy them there. Hop in the back."

We accepted John's offer. Within a few minutes, we had purchased our *GooGoos*, and John had driven us back to the SRA dormitory. We thanked him, shook hands, and wished him good luck. He told us he hoped to see us sometime in the future.

Author's Note:
As it turns out, John Seigenthaler and I did see each other again, some sixty years later after my wife Joanne and I moved to Nashville. In some future Cottonwood *edition, I'll tell you how that really happened before Danny has a chance to rewrite the story for me.*

INSTEAD OF RETURNING DIRECTLY to his dormitory room, JB told us he'd go to the field house to insure Coach Lewis had arranged for dinner at the first seating. "That way, we can arrive at the Ryman Auditorium early and get some choice seats," he assured us. "You'll still have plenty of time to pack before dinner."

Neither Danny nor I had the heart to tell JB that we'd finished our packing earlier that morning. Frankly it didn't take us long. We only had one suitcase each.

When we entered the dormitory, I noticed that Danny had suddenly become quiet. I sensed something was on his mind. He confirmed my suspicion as we arrived at our rooms. "Jase, can we talk for a few minutes while JB's gone? A couple of things are bothering me."

I immediately agreed. It was uncharacteristic of Danny to reveal that something bothered him. Usually he merely confronted the subject and resolved it without ceremony.

"Let's talk in your room, Jase."

Danny sat in my easy chair and I sat on the edge of my bed. "What's on your mind?"

"Two things. *GooGoos* and the Centennial Park swimming pool."

I had no idea how these two subjects were connected. "What about them?"

"Let's talk about *GooGoos* first. How much did they cost?"

"Well, we bought seven boxes -- each one contains six *GooGoo Clusters*. Five boxes are for people at home. One box's for the Lewises -- a thank you gift. And one box's for us to eat on the train. They cost 25 cents a box. So that's -- ah -- $1.75."

"Do you think we'll spend more money tonight?"

"I guess we might -- on popcorn or something."

"Yesterday we each had $5. When we leave tomorrow, we'll be down to about $4 each. Right?"

I nodded my head.

"We won't have a sack of sandwiches going home. We'll have to buy all our food and drinks on the train or at a train station. And the trip is much longer. Do you think $4 will be enough?"

Suddenly a sense of panic gripped my temples. Danny was right to be concerned. Several questions rushed through my head. Why hadn't we brought more of the money we'd earned? Why couldn't Danny have waited until we got home to return the Donovans' $15? Most important, at this late date, what could we possibly do about this situation?

"Danny, I don't know whether $4 is enough? What do you think?"

"I'm not sure either, Jase. That's why I needed to talk to you about it."

This was a strange situation for me. Generally I was never very concerned about running out of money. When I was at home and running short, I merely investigated possible ways of making some money, made my choice, and produced the desired result. But I didn't see how we could do that before we left for Riverton. My head was spinning. Frankly I felt a bit foolish. I admitted this honestly to Danny. "How on earth did we get ourselves in this fix?"

Danny's response was eerily similar to what I'd just been thinking. "I feel a bit foolish for not bringing more of the money we earned -- and for returning that $15 before we got home. Unfortunately I think it's a bit late to remedy this situation."

"I feel the same way. I guess there's only one solution," I suggested. "Let's eat a *whole lot* of dinner tonight and breakfast in the morning. That way we won't starve before we arrive home."

Danny smiled. "I really like that idea!"

"For some reason, I thought you might."

We both laughed, very hard and very loud. I felt the tension in my temples ease. Danny smiled at me and I smiled back.

I thought I knew the answer to my next question, but I posed it anyway. "All right, Danny. Tell me -- what bothers you about the Centennial Park swimming pool?"

"I think you know, Jase. It's the same thing that bothers me about having two sets of water fountains, restrooms, bus seats, and train-station waiting areas. There wasn't a single black person at that pool today."

"Have you thought about why we think this is so odd?"

"Yes, I have. Back home in Riverton, there are no black people. We don't need customs and traditions that keep black people separated from us white people."

"Do you think, if we had black people, we'd have rules that told them where they could go and what they could do -- just because of the color of their skin?"

"I don't know, Jase. But I hope not."

"Then think about this, Danny. Why is it all the Mexican migrants who work at the sugar-beet factory and in the sugar-beet fields only go to the Grafton Theater and only sit in the balcony? Have you ever once seen a Mexican at the Chippewa Theater or riding a Chippewa Trails bus in Riverton?"

"Wow! Jase, are you saying we do the same thing as they do here in the South?"

"What do you think, Danny?"

"I think I could use a *GooGoo*," he gasped.

TO CELEBRATE OUR LAST evening in Nashville, we decided to don our best long pants and dress shirts and to polish our good shoes before going to dinner and the Opry. We were just folding our SRA sweat suits into our suitcases when we heard JB knocking at our door. "Hey, guys. Open up. There's a man here with a telegram for you."

Danny gave me a puzzled look. "A telegram? Wonder who it's from?"

We opened the door quickly. The telegram delivery *man* turned out to be a boy, not any older than us. Evidently he delivered his telegrams by bicycle because his right pant leg was rolled tightly and stuffed deeply into his right high-top stocking. I admired his frugal method of preventing his pant leg from becoming entangled in the uncovered bicycle chain. No money squandered on a pant-leg clip for our young delivery man.

"Western Union telegram for Jason Addison or Daniel Tucker," he announced in a sing-song, pre-adolescent voice.

"That's us!" Danny shouted, holding out his hand for the missive.

"Sign here, sir."

"You bet! Jase, give this young man a nickel, please."

Without thinking, I reached into my pocket and retrieved five pennies. When I handed them to the boy, he gave me a funny look. I suppose I'd just weighted him down some, making his pedaling job an iota more difficult.

But his practiced response belied my perception. "Oh, thank you, sirs. Thank you very much indeed."

"Quick! Open it, Danny," JB ordered, more excited than either of us recipients.

Before sharing its content, Danny took what seemed like an inordinately long time reading the telegram. Then he guffawed and slapped us both on the backs. He tossed the telegram on my bed. I quickly snatched it up and read its content, slowly and carefully as Danny had. I allowed JB to read over my shoulder.

Printed on familiar, Western Union yellow paper in bold, black ink, here's how it read:

WESTERN UNION
TELEGRAM
Michigan Central Railroad Depot
Jackson, Michigan

Time: *8:05 AM Eastern War Time*
Date: *July 28, 1945*
From: *Lieutenant Raymond Donovan*
         New York Central Railroad Bureau of Detectives
To: *Jason Addison & Daniel Tucker*
         Basketball Camp
         Stony River Academy
         Belle Meade, Tennessee
Subj: *Rupert Evans (JD) Reward (First Installment)*

Greetings Jase & Danny,
     First installment JD reward ($25) approved by Jackson St Prison for recapture. Second installment ($75) pending prosecution for additional crimes committed while JD free. More to follow.

> *At insistence of wife Mary, I have wired $25 to WU office, Union Station, Nashville. Claim immediately by showing return train tickets.*
>
> *Congratulations! Thanks again for $15 and for assistance in nabbing JD.*
>
> *Your friend,*
> *Lt. R. Donovan*

We took the Lewises' box of *GooGoo Clusters* and the telegram to dinner with us. We could hardly wait to present the gift and share news of our good fortune. After we ordered, we did so. They thanked us profusely for the gift. Upon reading the telegram, they asked us dozens of questions about how we'd gone about recapturing Rupert Evans. They were fascinated with our long story.

"Well, I can imagine that you'd like to collect that reward as soon as possible. I suggest we stop at Union Station. It's right on our way to the Ryman."

"That'd be great, Coach. It certainly would give us some peace of mind."

"We don't have to rush through our dinner, but we should try to leave here by the top of the hour. How's that sound?"

"Initially Jase and I had wanted to make this a long dinner. But that won't be necessary now. Right, Jase?" Danny quipped with a wink.

"Good! Then we're all set," Coach Lewis declared as he focused his attention on the large serving of barbequed ribs before him. "Hmmm! I just love ribs."

"I didn't compliment y'all on how handsome y'all look this evening. When folks go to the Grand Ole Opry, dressing up is certainly not a requirement. But I appreciate your extra effort to look your best. Thank you."

"Mrs. Lewis, you always say just the right thing to make people feel great," Danny told her with an unusually large dose of charm.

"Why, ah do declare. Master Daniel has acquired the mahners of a Southern Gentleman," she responded, slathering Danny with her Southern syrup.

We all laughed. JB had been right. We couldn't have had better hosts for our Nashville visit. The Lewises were super people.

Picking up her *GooGoo Clusters* box, she asked, "Do y'all know the connection between *GooGoos* and the Grand Ole Opry?"

Danny and I shook our heads. JB just smiled. I assumed he knew the answer to her question.

"Now, Dorothy. Before you start -- in fairness to Jase and Danny -- you should inform them that you're a GooGoo *ringer*."

"Oh, laws. Do I have to?"

Coach Lewis shot her a single robust nod.

"Oh, all right. One summer when I was in college, I worked in the marketing department at the Standard Candy Company, which is located here in Nashville. Back in 1912, Standard Candy began production of the world's first *combination* candy bar. To put it simply, this was the first time that multiple ingredients were combined in a mass-produced, retail candy product. Also, unlike other candy products, the *GooGoo Cluster* was not rectangular or square. It was a round mound, consisting of marshmallow nougat, fresh roasted peanuts, and real milk chocolate.

"When I worked at the company, most of the creators of the original *GooGoo Cluster* were already long gone. But some of the people there claimed that the candy was named *GooGoo* after a baby's first words. They also say that a *GooGoo* is so good that babies ask for it from the day they're born.

"Since the Standard Candy Company is a sponsor of the Grand Ole Opry radio show, *GooGoo Clusters* are the official -- and best-selling -- candy at the Ryman Auditorium. Because of this close connection with the Opry, many people have thought that *GOO* stands for *Grand Ole Opry*."

"So what you're saying is that Jase and I selected the perfect gift for you because it's our first time at the Grand Ole Opry. Is that it, Mrs. Lewis?"

"You heard me clear as a *bell*, Danny."

"Good! Now I know what *ringer* means."

BECAUSE CROWDS OF PEOPLE normally surrounded Union Station, Coach Lewis suggested that he drop Danny and me off on West End Avenue not far from the door leading to the Western Union counter. Then he'd find parking and, as he'd done the day we arrived in Nashville, he'd send JB to find us. We agreed and headed for the entrance.

Our timing was perfect. The young woman behind the counter seemed most happy to see us. "You're my only customers in the past 15 minutes. Usually we're extremely busy," she explained. "How may I help you?"

We showed her our telegram and our return train tickets as identification. After we signed a receipt, she inquired how we wanted our $25 *denominated*. This word was evidently Western Union insider jargon, but Danny comprehended it immediately, providing her with simple instructions. "Half and half."

When she looked confused, Danny helped her out, "$12.50 to each of us, please."

Our total time at Western Union was under five minutes. After tucking our cash away in our wallets, we looked for JB through the wide, floor-to-ceiling windows. I was surprised to see him staring at us through the glass.

"How'd he get here so quickly?" Danny asked.

His answer came when JB pointed toward West End Avenue and began to weave his way through the crowd in that general direction. We left the station and followed him to the street. Luckily Coach Lewis had found a parking spot in front of the Main Post Office.

"Gee, that was fast. Everything go all right?" the coach asked as we hopped into the station wagon.

"Perfect!" Danny assured him. "Let's *Goo!*"

I was the only one who understood Danny's pun. The Old Southern accent had done it again. It makes you wonder how we Americans managed to defeat Germany when all along we couldn't understand one another.

We parked about a block from the Ryman. Because the doors opened an hour before showtime, we entered the magnificent old church after only a few minutes wait. This allowed us time to purchase our tickets, find good seats, and then explore the venerated venue. I became aware that the number of people on stage was gradually increasing. Technicians tested microphones, amplifiers, and radio equipment. Stagehands arranged tables, chairs, and miscellaneous equipment. No one seemed hurried. The atmosphere was unusually calm.

What happened to the legendary stage fright? I wondered.

A few people dressed in cowboy attire walked out on stage, apparently to size up the place. Not being an avid country fan, I didn't recognize them. But I assumed they would be performing later on.

Meanwhile we wandered around the perimeter of the auditorium, studying the hundreds of photos of Grand Ole Opry performers over the years. There were established country, bluegrass, western swing, and cowboy stars. There were framed photographs of Roy Acuff, Eddy Arnold, Minnie Pearl (replete with hat and price tag), Pee Wee King, Bob Wills, Spade Cooley, Gene Autry, Red Foley, Ernest Tubb, and dozens of others.

"How do we know which of these people will perform here tonight?" I asked naively.

"Technically all -- or none of them -- could perform. During the week, most of these stars are on the road, performing wherever they can book their acts. On weekends, if the permanent Opry members are in town -- and if they care to -- they can perform at the Opry. When they're not enough permanent members to fill a show, the producers invite guest performers. Of course, those guests are hoping to impress the Opry producers who -- each year -- invite a few guest performers to audition for the honor of being selected as permanent Opry members," Coach Lewis explained.

"Since the war started, many of the performers -- both permanent and guest -- are overseas with USO shows. Or with the *Grand Ole Opry Camel Caravan* that was formed to entertain troops at military bases here in the states and the Panama Canal Zone," Mrs. Lewis added.

"Coach, there's one star who'll be here tonight," JB reminded him.

"You're right, Johnson. Roy Acuff is the host of the *Prince Albert Show* segment. Every Saturday night, that segment is broadcast to over 140 NBC-affiliated radio stations. So he'll definitely be here."

Our seats were just a few rows from the stage in the center of the main floor. We sat on hard oaken church pews, not the plush seats I was expecting. I noticed that many people were wise enough to bring their own cushions.

I watched as a dozen or more people still wandered about on stage presumably preparing for the show and the broadcast. I glanced at my watch and saw that we were just a few minutes from the start of the show. I was totally surprised. I'd expected a wide curtain to drop, covering all this housekeeping activity. But my expectation did not match reality at the Grand Ole Opry.

I soon learned that a cherished attribute of the Opry was its presentation of a *grand show* totally devoid of pretense, including artificial scenery or other unnecessary frills. What we were watching just before the show was what we would see throughout the evening. Even the commercials that were spliced between acts were read from sheets of paper by the master of ceremony. The sponsors were *Martha White Flour, GooGoo Clusters, Pepsol* soft drink, and other everyday products. The commercials were delivered convincingly using informal, honest, down-home, softly-spoken words. Very much unlike the shrill puffery I was used to hearing on the radio at home.

From the back of the stage, a dignified gentleman, wearing a conservative western-cut suit, white shirt, string tie, and cowboy boots, casually sauntered to a single microphone placed near the front of the stage on our left. As he did so, some half-dozen men, wearing street clothes and carrying instruments, took their places behind music stands to our right. I assumed they were members of the stage band. Several of the people who had been wandering around on stage took seats on two long sofas at the back of the stage. Presumably this is where they would sit until called upon to perform.

"Good evening, ladies and gentlemen. Welcome to the Grand Ole Opry!"

With those words, the stage band broke into lively country music. I was struck by the perfect acoustics of the old church. The notes and words of the performers could be heard perfectly in every corner of this massive auditorium.

We were off!

This was the beginning of one of the most entertaining evenings of my life. And to think, I hardly ever listened to the radio program. But there I was, witnessing the show, in person, at the Ryman Auditorium in downtown Nashville, Tennessee, while my family was listening to it on the radio in Riverton, Michigan!

I glanced at Danny whose eyes were sparkling as he tapped his toes to the rockabilly beat. Not surprisingly, he sensed that I was watching him. He turned to me and flashed two quick thumbs-up. I smiled and leaned back to lose myself in the total delight of that memorable occasion.

What a way to end our Nashville visit!

19 HOMEWARD BOUND

BEFORE WE LEFT HOME, TEN DAYS IN NASHVILLE
seemed like an extremely long time to spend visiting someone. In
our minds, this was especially true when that *someone* had a full-
time job during the week. Danny and I seriously considered the
possibility of our becoming bored. If this happened, we had agreed
to cut our visit short and come home early.

Of course, we never came close to being bored. The most
difficult part of our visit was finding time in our hectic schedule to
take advantage of everything Nashville had to offer. This was made
even more difficult by our having ended up with full-time jobs.

When our visit came to an end, we were both extremely sad.
During breakfast on Sunday, we tried to concentrate on the positive
aspects of our time in Nashville. Perhaps we overcompensated a bit
because I noticed that the Lewises and even JB appeared ready to
break into tears. While Danny and I inventoried the enjoyable
events we'd experienced together, the three of them were having
trouble controlling their emotions.

It was uncanny. The sadder they grew, the more manic Danny
and I became. As I think back on that moment, it was rather
bizarre.

To give us more time to spend with each other that last Sunday
morning, the Lewises suggested we not attend church. After we
finished breakfast, we lingered at our table. When it finally became

clear that the servers were waiting for us to leave, we rose from the
table and headed for the door.

Before leaving the dining hall, we paused to look back
on the place where we'd shared so many excellent meals and
pleasant conversations. For several minutes, no one said a word.
Demonstrating a side of himself that I'd seldom witnessed, Danny
suddenly emitted a deep sob. That broke the emotional logjam.
We all began to weep, closing our arms around each other to give
comfort and solace.

While we stood there for several more minutes, still no one
spoke. Finally Danny broke the silence. "If I don't use my hankie
soon, JB's shirtsleeve's gonna be soaked."

That brought down the house. We all laughed, cried, and blew
our noses together. It was a gratifying experience to share with
people for whom you felt such great affection. At last, we had cried
enough. We left Robertson Hall and headed to the dormitory to
collect our luggage.

Danny and I had each packed three boxes of *GooGoos* in our
SRA gym bags. The boxes were carefully nestled in our jackets to
soften the blow should we drop the bags or bang them against a
seat as we entered the train.

We had packed Mrs. Bradford's Cain-Sloan package inside
Danny's old YMCA gym bag, which we carefully stuffed into my
old YMCA bag. Without confirming it with JB, we agreed the
package most likely contained a piece of fancy lingerie, not readily
available in Riverton.

We placed the bags with our suitcases in the back of the station
wagon. Then, out of habit, both Danny and I removed our wallets
to insure we had our train tickets and our recently replenished
supply of travel money. We returned the wallets and securely
buttoned our pockets.

"All ready to go, fellas?" Coach Lewis asked.

"Yes, sir," Danny responded.

"Yes, sir," I echoed.

Pleased by our use of the Southern expression, JB smiled at us
and shook his head in disbelief.

OUR DRIVE TO UNION Station was largely a silent one. After all, we'd all had our say. Now it was time for us to thank everyone one last time, say goodbye, and leave for home.

Coach Lewis dropped us off at the station. "We'll park the car and be back soon. You fellas can check your bags. We'll meet you on the loading platform."

Danny and I carried our suitcases to the baggage-check area while JB carried our SRA gym bags.

While we stood in line, I noticed a neat pile of tagged mailbags in the nearby caged area. I smiled to myself as I remembered our tour of the Main Post Office. What an experience that had been!

After we had our baggage-claim checks in hand, Danny made an announcement. "I need to send a telegram. Let's go inside the station."

Without further explanation, Danny made a beeline for the Western Union counter. JB and I trotted behind him, carrying the gym bags.

When we arrived, the same young woman was at the counter. "Hello, there. I'm glad to see you again," she said with a smile. "How may I help you this time?"

"I need to send a telegram -- it's a reply to this one." He handed Lieutenant Donovan's telegram to the woman.

"I understand. Please draft your telegram on this form. I'll be right back."

Danny hunched over the counter and carefully composed his message. When he finished, he handed it to the woman. She counted the words. "That will be 40 cents, please."

Danny handed her the correct change which she placed in her cash drawer. Then she took Danny's draft to the teletype machine where she quickly typed his message and formatted the telegram. When she was satisfied, she pushed the *Send* button that shot the telegram over the wire and provided a typed and formatted copy for Danny.

She returned to the counter and handed the copy to Danny. "Thank you, sir. I hope to see you again soon."

Danny smiled and replied, "Me too." He folded his copy and placed it in his pants pocket. Looking our way, he suggested, "Why don't we meet the Lewises on the platform?"

Once again, Danny led the way. JB and I followed him, carrying the gym bags like a couple of red caps.

The Lewises arrived shortly after us. Before long, our conductor leaned out of the train and loudly announced, **"All 'Board."**

We exchanged a final flurry of thanks and goodbyes. Then we all hugged one last time.

Before we knew it, Danny and I were settled in our seats, feeling the vibrating quivers of the Louisville & Nashville #95, *The Pan American*, as the behemoth engine pulled us out of the station and chugged toward our first stop, Louisville, Kentucky.

Once we were under way, Danny reached in his pocket and removed the telegram. "You'll want to read this, Jase," he advised, handing it to me.

"Thanks, Danny. I believe I already know what it says."

I was right. When Danny is doing the right thing, he can be very predictable. See what I mean?

WESTERN UNION
TELEGRAM
Union Station
Nashville, Tennessee

Time: *11:55 AM, Central War Time*
Date: *July 29, 1945*
From: *Jason Addison & Daniel Tucker*
          Union Station
          Nashville, Tennessee
To: *Lieutenant Raymond Donovan*
          New York Central Railroad
          Bureau of Detectives
          Michigan Central Railroad Depot
          Jackson, Michigan
Subj: *Rupert Evans (JD) Reward (First Installment)*

Greetings Lieutenant and Mrs. Donovan,

     Thank you for first installment JD reward ($25). We collected same from WU immediately. We needed funds. Your telegram saved day.

> *We appreciate efforts in obtaining reward for us, but you played large role in nabbing JD.*
> *We want to split second installment on 50-50 basis.*
>
> *Your friends,*
> *Jase & Danny*

"Last time, you sent $15 to Mrs. Donovan. This time you sent her $37.50. What'll it be next?"

"Until I know the amount of our next reward, I can't be sure. But we'll work something out."

"Okay, Danny. Okay."

HAVING TRAVELED BY TRAIN to and from Chicago and to Nashville, we counted our return to Riverton as our fourth train trip. As seasoned train travelers, even before leaving Nashville, we'd studied our northbound schedule with certain objectives in mind. First, we didn't want to miss any meals. That was Danny's idea. Second, because we hadn't read a newspaper for nearly two weeks, we wanted to catch up on the latest war news. That was my idea. And, because this trip was going to take over 22 hours, we didn't want to be tired when we arrived home. On this we both agreed.

On the schedule, we recorded the events that would enable us to meet these objectives:

NORTHBOUND

<u>Louisville & Nashville RR #98</u> (*Pan American*)

Trip Events

Nashville	Leave:	12:20 p.m. (CT)	
		(Late lunch in dining car)	
Louisville	Arrive:	4:45 p.m. (CT)	
	(Nap - sleep thru Louisville 15 min. stop)		
Louisville	Leave:	5:00 p.m. (CT)	
Cincinnati	Arrive:	9:15 p.m. (ET)	

(Late supper in Cincinnati station)
(Buy magazines & newspapers)

Baltimore & Ohio RR #58
Cincinnati   Leave: 11:45 p.m. (ET)
                      (Nap - sleep until Toledo arrival)
Toledo   Arrive: 5:30 a.m. (ET)
                      (Early breakfast in Toledo station)
                      (Replenish magazines & newspapers)

Ann Arbor RR #51
Toledo   Leave: 7:55 a.m. (ET)
                      (Nap - sleep until Riverton arrival)
Riverton   Arrive: 11:47 a.m. (ET)
                      (Late lunch in Riverton - after arrival)

Danny retrieved the schedule from his gym bag and studied it. "Jase, when shall we go to the dining car for our *late lunch?*"

"It isn't even one o'clock yet. Don't you think we should try to wait a little longer? We won't be eating supper until almost ten o'clock tonight."

Apparently accepting my reasoning, he continued to study the schedule. "Maybe we should have two lunches today. One before our nap -- and the other after it."

"If that's what you want to do, Danny, let's go to the dining car."

He nodded his head enthusiastically. "Thanks, Jase."

I rationalized agreeing to the schedule change because having a full stomach would help us fall asleep more quickly. After all, being well-rested was also an important objective. Besides I have to admit I was famished.

WE RETURNED FROM LUNCH around two o'clock. The rhythm of the *clicking* train tracks was hypnotic. I didn't try to keep my eyes open. Instead, I surrendered to Hypnos and fell into a deep, dreamless sleep.

"Jase, wake up. We're coming into the station. Wake up!"

I was still half asleep and more than a little irritated from being awakened so abruptly.

On the other hand, I felt extremely refreshed. When I opened my eyes, Danny was looking at me with a smug look on his face, as if he was about to spring a surprise on me.

"Danny, we were supposed to sleep through the Louisville stop. Why did you wake me?"

"We did sleep through Louisville. We're coming into Cincinnati. We missed our second lunch. And now it's supper time. We're back on schedule. You hungry?"

I honestly thought Danny was pulling my leg until I looked out the window. Outside it was pitch black. No wonder I wasn't tired. I'd just had a seven-hour nap.

"Danny, did you sleep the entire time?"

"When the porter announced our arrival in Cincinnati, I woke up. We have over two hours here. Let's eat supper and buy some papers and magazines. We'll still have plenty of time to catch our train to Toledo."

That's exactly what we did.

While we carried our gym bags and reading material onto the B&O #58, I suddenly realized how luxurious the *Pan American* had been. I momentarily regretted having slept through most of that leg of the trip. Then it dawned on me that our plan was to sleep through most of our time on this train as well.

Something else occurred to me. I'd never been in Ohio before.

We'd bought copies of both *Life* and *Time* magazines and of the *Cincinnati Inquirer* and the *New York Times*. Surely these publications would allow us to catch up on the news we'd missed. I looked forward to reading them until I fell asleep again.

UNFORTUNATELY THE ARTICLE I read first made it extremely difficult for me to sleep later. As it turned out, Danny had the same problem. I'd chosen a *Life* magazine story with accompanying graphic photos depicting the horrors of a number of Nazi extermination, labor, and concentration camps in Eastern Europe and Germany.

Here are the words that kept me awake:

The Holocaust

Only one word adequately describes Nazi Germany's methodical persecution, imprisonment, and murder of millions of so-called enemies of the state since 1933. That word is Holocaust from the early Greek meaning sacrifice by fire.

How could such evil behavior occur among the nominally cultured, civil, and intelligent German people? The answer is simple. Adolph Hitler, cunning and tyrannical leader of the Nazi party, espoused the idea that Germans were a superior race.

Therefore, any race, religion, or political philosophy, not genetically a part of or in agreement with the viewpoint of the superior race, was deemed an enemy of the German state. The hatred of such internal and external enemies fed Germany's lust for blood and conquest.

Inferior groups included millions of Jews, tens of thousands of Roma or Gypsies, and 200,000 mentally or physically handicapped people. More than three million Soviet prisoners of war, supposedly protected by the Geneva Convention, were murdered or died of starvation, disease, or maltreatment. The Nazis killed tens of thousands of non-Jewish Polish intellectual and religious leaders. Other "inferiors" persecuted by the Nazis included Communists, Socialists, Jehovah's Witnesses, and homosexuals.

The Nazis deported millions of people from Poland and Western Russia for use as forced labor in German war plants where they worked without adequate food, clothing, shelter, or medical care, until they were dead.

Of all the groups Nazis considered enemies of the state, they despised Jews the most. Hitler and his Nazi followers blamed the Jews for Germany's humiliation after World War I and for the resultant economic chaos that wreaked havoc on that country during the 1920s and early 1930s. In 1933, when Hitler proclaimed himself to be Germany's head of state, his first priority was to target German Jews for persecution.

About half of Germany's half-million Jews fled Nazi persecution between 1933 and 1939, as did two-thirds of Austria's 180,000 Jews. But there was little chance of escape for the nine million Jews of Central and Eastern Europe. When their nations were overrun by Hitler's armies in 1939, they became the victims of Hitler's murderous *plot to annihilate Europe's Jewish population completely. In the end, an estimated six million Jews died in the Holocaust.*

The Holocaust lasted until the Nazis were defeated by the Allied powers. In recent months, hard evidence of this brutal regime's evil campaign against Jews and others has been discovered and documented by Allied forces that have retaken Europe's Nazi-occupied countries and Germany itself.

Martha Gellhorn, United Press foreign correspondent and third wife of novelist, Ernest Hemingway, accompanied American troops and witnessed grisly scenes when our forces liberated Buchenwald in Germany. "There can never be peace if there is cruelty like this in the world," she wrote. "And if ever again we tolerate such cruelty, we have no right to peace."

Below are photographs that typify the horrors awaiting American and Russian soldiers.

I flipped the page to find dozens of gruesome photos of scenes from liberated concentration camps. The names of the camps and their locations were posted above each photo, including the following:

- Alderney -- Channel Islands
- Auschwitz -- Poland
- Bergen-Belsen -- Saxony
- Buchenwald -- Germany
- Dachau -- Germany
- Drancy -- France
- Falstad -- Norway
- Fort de Romainville -- France
- Fossoli - Italy
- Grini -- Norway
- Herzogenbusch -- Netherlands
- Janowska -- Ukraine
- Kaiserwald -- Latvia
- Klooga -- Estonia
- Mauthausen -- Austria
- Mechelen -- Belgium
- Natzweiller-Struthof -- Alsace

- Sobibor -- Poland
- Sojmiste -- Serbia
- Theresienstadt - Czechoslovakia
- Treblinka -- Poland

I was certainly shocked by what I saw. But I wasn't sure what was most upsetting, the hundreds of carelessly discarded bodies or the stark ranks of the living-dead staring blankly at me through the camera's lens.

Danny casually looked over to see what I was reading. When he saw the photos, his reaction echoed mine. "Good grief, Jase, what horrible pictures! Are those dead bodies? And who are those emaciated people in striped pajamas? They look like they haven't eaten in months. Their bones are sticking out. Look at their sunken eyes. How can they be skeletons and still be alive? Are we sure we want to look at these pictures? Ugh!"

"They are pretty ghastly, Danny. But read the article before you make your decision whether to look at them." I handed him *The Holocaust* article.

When he finished reading, he affirmed solemnly, "I think it's our duty to study and remember these pictures, Jase. We don't want this to happen again."

IT WAS WELL PAST midnight when we finally fell asleep. Our seven-hour nap would have to carry us through the news-shortened night. We awoke just before our train arrived in Toledo at 5:30 a.m.

We carried our gym bags into the deserted train station and looked around. Next to a newsstand on the opposite side of the station, we spotted a lunch counter that was open for business. The newsstand was closed.

"Let's have breakfast. Maybe the newsstand will be open by the time we finish," Danny suggested.

He was right. About the time our breakfast was served, a stocky man wearing a *Cleveland Indians* baseball cap and a white apron opened a door behind the newsstand and lugged in two bulky bundles. He cut the rope that bound the bundles and arranged the latest newspapers and magazines on the shelves of his stand.

When we finished breakfast, we stepped up to the stand to replenish our stock of reading material.

"Morning, boys. What can I do for you?" the friendly man asked as he lit his cigar. "We got the morning edition of the *Toledo Blade* and the latest *Life* magazine. Shocking article about those horrible Nazi death camps."

"We read *The Holocaust* article. It was an eye-opener for sure. But we'll take a copy of the *Blade*," Danny told the man. "Any suggestions on another publication that covers the latest war news?"

"Yep. Yesterday's *Detroit Free Press* had a complete update on the war in the Pacific. I still got a couple ah copies."

We carried our bags and newspapers to the Ann Arbor Railroad ticket window. "Good morning, gentlemen. How may I help you?" asked the ticket agent.

"We already have our tickets for #51 to Riverton. When'll we be able to board?" I inquired.

The agent instantly produced an official railroad watch from his vest pocket, flipped open the lid, and quickly snapped it shut again. "The #51's due to arrive at 6:45 a.m. -- exactly 20 minutes from now. She'll be ready to board 15 minutes after that -- at 7:00 a.m. She'll depart at exactly 7:55 a.m.," he told us with great precision.

We thanked the agent and sat down in the waiting area to read our newspapers. Danny agreed to start with the Detroit paper. I took the *Blade*.

"Wow! Danny, look at this. A U.S. Army Air Corps B-25 bomber crashed into the Empire State Building. Fourteen people were killed, including everyone aboard the bomber."

"That's terrible. But look at this. Did you know that French Marshall Philippe Pétain is being tried for treason?"

"Remind me who he is."

"He headed the Vichy government that ruled the supposedly *Free Zone* covering southern France while the Nazis occupied and ruled northern France. Actually Pétain was just a puppet whose strings were pulled by Hitler."

"I remember now. *Vichy* brings to mind the movie *Casablanca*."

"Oh, my goodness! Did you know that Winston Churchill resigned as Prime Minister?"

"Why would he do that?"

"Because his Conservative Party was soundly defeated by the Labour Party in the recent general election. A man named Clement Atlee is the new Prime Minister."

"Maybe we should send Mr. Churchill a telegram too."

"Do you think he'd remember us, Jase?"

"He's the one who told FDR he wanted to meet us. Remember? Danny, did you know that Japan rejected the Potsdam Declaration?"

"What's that?"

"A document signed on July 26th by President Truman, Prime Minister Churchill, and the head of China's Nationalist Government, Chiang Kai-Shek. It demanded Japan's immediate unconditional surrender. Then on July 28th, Japan rejected the ultimatum."

"Now, what'll happen?"

"The Declaration stated that if Japan didn't surrender, it would face *prompt and utter destruction*. Whatever that means."

"That really sounds ominous."

Author's Note:
A short number of days later, the whole world would know just how ominous it would be for the stubborn Japanese government. The message would be delivered in the form of, Little Boy, *the first atomic bomb dropped on Hiroshima by a B-29 flown by Colonel Paul Tibbets.*

Exactly at 7:00 a.m. we headed for our train. Just as the ticket agent had predicted, the train was available for boarding. We stepped aboard and found two comfortable seats.

"Can you believe it, Jase? In less than four hours, we'll be home."

"I can't wait."

"Me, neither. We're scheduled to have lunch when we arrive."

BY THE TIME WE heard the porter announce our impending arrival in Riverton, Danny and I were completely updated on the latest news from the war front. On the other hand, although we'd been away from Riverton for less than two weeks, I felt completely out of touch with the news from home. I was eager to get home and learn what had happened during our absence.

In preparation, we removed our gym bags from the shelf above our seats and retrieved our baggage-claim checks from our wallets.

"I wonder who'll meet us at the station," I mused aloud.

"There'll probably be a band to welcome us home," Danny joked.

We both laughed. Then we heard it.

"Danny, it is a band -- playing the Riverton High fight song. Could that possibly be for us?"

"You gotta be kidding, Jase. Why would it be?"

As our train quivered, hissed, and screeched to a halt, Danny and I made our way to the front of the car.

When we stepped off the train, suddenly we were engulfed in a huge crowd of people led by Chuck Nichols and our parents. I glanced up at the depot and saw a huge banner strung across the front of the building. It read:

WELCOME HOME! JASE AND DANNY!

Chuck Nichols slapped us on the back and handed us copies of the *Riverton Daily Press*. I was astonished. The front-page headline read:

RIVERTON HEROES CAPTURE ESCAPED NAZI; AWARDED NASHVILLE'S KEY TO CITY

Welcome Home Ceremony Planned for Monday

Our parents rushed toward us and gave of us each huge hugs. "Welcome home, boys!" Mom exclaimed.

"We've missed you," Mrs. Tucker added.

"We're all mighty proud of you fellas," Chuck Nichols asserted. "Folks, I hope you can spare your sons for a few minutes. There's someone waiting for them at the podium."

Under the banner, on a makeshift platform, was the podium from the city-council meeting room at City Hall. Standing beside the microphone, Riverton Mayor Smith smiled as we approached.

He shook our hands and turned to the crowd. "Ladies and gentlemen, I am honored to present Riverton's own, Masters Jason Addison and Daniel Tucker."

The huge crowd roared their approval and applauded wildly. The mayor held up his hands to call for quiet. "Thank you, folks. Thank you."

Once the crowd was silent, he continued, "I'm privileged to extend my best wishes to these young gentlemen, their proud parents, and to you citizens -- who've come here this morning to honor them."

The crowd broke into applause once again.

"As you all know from Chuck Nichols' fine article, Danny and Jase were recently honored by the City of Nashville, Tennessee, for their courageous deeds -- deeds which resulted in the apprehension of a dangerous Nazi fugitive in that city. As an aside, these boys just never seem to be off duty. Even on vacation, they're on the lookout for villains -- whom they have an uncanny knack of subduing."

The crowd again applauded. While they did, Mayor Smith reached under the podium.

"Not to be outdone by the City of Nashville, the City of Riverton is proud to acknowledge our local heroes and to present them each with a Key to the City."

He handed us each a large wooden key which had been painted gold and inscribed with the word **RIVERTON** in bold, black letters. Each key was decorated with a bright red bow.

As the crowd cheered and clapped, Mayor Smith shook our hands. Flashbulbs exploded around us.

"Boys, would you like to say a few words?"

I nodded and moved behind the microphone. "Thank you, Mayor Smith. We're truly honored to receive the Key to the City.

Nashville is a very fine city -- and we had a great time there. But we're very happy to be home. Thank you, Riverton."

More cheers erupted.

Danny stepped to the microphone and expressed his feelings with four short words, "Let's all have lunch!"

In response to Danny's suggestion, the crowd roared its approval.

Danny turned to me and smiled.

Then he declared, "All's swell that ends swell!"

EPILOGUE

DURING THE SUMMER OF 1945, THERE WERE TWO events whose details were not fully disclosed until long after the war ended. One has been well-documented. In fact, the manifestations of this event play an important role in life today and promise to do so into the future.

I refer to the dropping of the atomic bombs on Hiroshima and Nagasaki. Since 1945, the development and deployment of ensuing generations of nuclear weapons have dramatically shaped the history of the world.

The other event, the sinking of the *USS Indianapolis*, has been all but lost in the haze of time and by the passing of those most affected by this tragedy. I refer to the 316 officers and men who were rescued after floating in the shark-infested sea for nearly five days. The number of those rescued must be considered in the context of an essential fact. A total of 1,196 crewmen were aboard when the ship was struck by two torpedoes, launched from a Japanese submarine.

Oddly enough, these two events are closely connected.

The Atomic Bomb

THE STORY OF THE development of the atomic bomb is a case study in American ingenuity, intellectual prowess, and just plain hard work. In 1938, when news broke that a German scientist had split the uranium atom, many Europeans and Americans feared that Hitler would build an atomic bomb. In his desire to create a superior race, Hitler had escalated his persecution of Jews, including many scientists. Among those fleeing to the United States were Albert Einstein, Enrico Fermi, Richard Feynman, and Harold Urey.

Earlier, Leo Szilard, a Hungarian scientist had immigrated to the United States. He has been credited with being the first scientist to conceive how an atomic bomb might work. On October 11, 1939, a letter, written by Szilard and Albert Einstein, was delivered to President Roosevelt, warning that Germany might be developing nuclear weapons.

Their words were so convincing that the United States began a secret research program to build an atomic bomb under the code name, *Manhattan Project*. Canada and the United Kingdom also became project participants. In 1942, as work began to intensify, Major General Leslie R. Groves, Jr. of the U.S. Army Corps of Engineers was appointed project leader.

Research and production were carried out at different facilities, including universities across the United States, Canada, and the United Kingdom. However, the project had three major sites:

- Production of plutonium at Hanford, Washington
- Enrichment of uranium at Oak Ridge, Tennessee
- Weapons research and design at Los Alamos, New Mexico

In August 1944, Groves estimated that atomic bombs would be ready for use by the spring of 1945. The Army Air Corps immediately began modifying 17 B-29s for combat delivery of atomic bombs.

The *Manhattan Project* was carried out in absolute secrecy. On April 12, 1944, following the death of Franklin Roosevelt, Vice-President Harry Truman was sworn in as President of the United States. The next day, Truman learned *for the first time* about the existence of the atomic bomb from Secretary of War Henry Stimson.

By 1945, the *Manhattan Project* had grown to include 40 laboratories and factories employing nearly 200,000 people. Among those working on the project were the world's greatest scientists. Through their combined efforts, an implosion test bomb known as *Fat Boy* was created. On July 16, 1945, under the code name *Trinity,* the first nuclear test was held in the New Mexico desert. This successful test led to the creation of two more atomic bombs that would be used against the Japanese to bring an end to World War II.

On August 6, 1945, an American B-29 bomber, *Enola Gay,* dropped a 9,000 pound bomb named *Little Boy* on the city of Hiroshima. The blast resulted in the instant deaths of 66,000 Japanese. The area of total vaporization from the blast measured one half mile in diameter. Total destruction measured one mile in diameter, and deadly fires extended for three miles from ground zero.

Three days later, a second and more complex plutonium-core bomb, *Fat Man,* was dropped on the city of Nagasaki. It weighed 10,000 pounds and annihilated about half of the city. The population dropped from 422,000 to 383,000 in a single second.

While both explosions were devastating, the destruction did not end there. Rain that followed the explosions was contaminated with radioactive particles. Many people, who survived the blast, died from radiation poisoning. Others suffered severe burns, fatigue, hair loss, nausea, and other serious symptoms.

Of course, there were positive outcomes stemming from the development of the atomic bomb, including the harnessing of nuclear energy for use in power generation, propulsion systems, and the development of sophisticated medical equipment.

The *USS Indianapolis* (CA-35)

UNDER THE COMMAND OF Captain Charles Butler McVay III, the *USS Indianapolis* was assigned to Vice Admiral Marc Mitscher's fast carrier task force. In March 1945, the task force provided pre-invasion bombardment of Okinawa. On March 31st, after having shot down six Japanese fighter planes, a seventh fighter managed to evade the *USS Indianapolis's* anti-aircraft fire and drop its bomb on the stern of the ship. The bomb crashed through the ship and exploded under the keel, tearing two large holes in the ship's bottom and killing nine crewmen.

The damage was so extensive that the *USS Indianapolis* was ordered to steam, on her limited power, across the Pacific for repairs and overhaul at the Mare Island Naval Shipyard in San Francisco. After repairs were completed, the ship was ordered to Tinian Island in the Marianas. She was carrying components and enriched uranium for the atomic bomb, *Little Boy*.

She departed Mare Island on July 16, 1945, and steamed at full speed to Tinian, from which both atomic bomb attacks on Japan were to be launched. The ship arrived there on July 28th, unloaded her cargo, and was immediately dispatched by way of Guam to Leyte where her crew was to receive training before proceeding back to Okinawa. After night fall, exercising his prerogative to do so, the captain ordered the ship to stop zigzagging, a submarine evasion technique, and steam straight and fast to Leyte.

Shortly after midnight on July 30th, she was struck by two torpedoes fired from the Japanese submarine, *I-58*. The ship suffered massive damage. Within 12 minutes, the ship capsized and plunged, bow-first to bottom of the Western Pacific Ocean. About 300 men from the crew of 1,196 went down with the ship. The rest, about 886 men, were thrown into the sea with only a few lifeboats. Many of the men were not wearing life jackets. Regrettably 580 of those in the sea died before their rescuers arrived.

Making matters worse, the missing ship's failure to arrive at Leyte was never noticed. Three days later an American aircraft on routine patrol spotted the survivors in the water and radioed for help.

This wasn't the only snafu. Before sinking, the *USS Indianapolis* had transmitted a distress call which was received by three communications stations, none of which acted on the call. Investigators discovered that one commander was drunk, another had ordered his man not to disturb him, and the third thought it was a Japanese prank.

In November 1945, Captain McVay was court-martialed and convicted of "hazarding his ship by failing to zigzag." This verdict seemed to contradict the fact that zigzagging was to be used, or not, "at the discretion of the commanding officer." Furthermore, the commanding officer of the Japanese submarine,

Mochitsura Hashimoto, testified that zigzagging would have made no difference.

Fleet Admiral Chester Nimitz *remitted* Captain McVay's sentence and restored him to active duty. By doing so, Nimitz let the conviction stand unchallenged. In 1949, Captain McVay retired and was given a *tombstone* promotion to Rear Admiral. The promotion was a customary practice designed to increase the retirement pay of retiring naval officers.

Captain McVay had the rare distinction of being the only commanding officer in naval history to have been court-martialed for losing his ship in combat. Over the 24 years following the court-martial, Captain McVay was accused of being a killer by families of those who were lost. Unable to resolve the guilt and shame associated with the tragedy, in 1968, he shot himself with a navy-issue, .38 caliber revolver.

However, many *USS Indianapolis* survivors, as well as the captain's sons, did not give up hope of clearing his name. Finally in 2000, after declassified military records raised the specter of a navy cover-up, the U.S. Congress passed a resolution expressing the belief that Captain McVay was innocent. Navy Secretary Gordon R. England ordered that Captain McVay's service record be officially amended to exonerate him from any wrongdoing in the loss of the *USS Indianapolis.*

Rear Admiral Charles Butler McVay III now joins his father and grandfather in the annals of naval history as three generations of honorably-serving U.S. naval admirals.

Author's Note:
I first became familiar with Captain McVay's case in 1982, when I hired his son, Charles Butler McVay IV, to work for Gary Slaughter Corporation in Bethesda, Maryland. Charlie McVay was an extremely competent employee who had a keen sense of humor. He was also a courageous man. You see, Charlie was the only legally blind person in our company. He relied on his sense of touch, his considerable wit, and the telephone to perform his job admirably. Unfortunately he died long before his time. Most who knew him attributed his early death to the stress of his father's case.

WORLD WAR II & THE *COTTONWOOD* STORY

For readers, who have travelled with us on this *Cottonwood* journey, we offer the following inventory of the major milestones of World War II addressed in the five *Cottonwood* novels:

Prior to *Cottonwood Summer*

1939
September 1 -   Germany invades Poland to start World War II.
September 3 -   Britain, France, Australia, and New Zealand declare war on Germany.

1940
June 14 -   Germany launches Blitz against England.
September 27 - Axis pact signed by Germany, Japan, and Italy.

1941
December 7 -   Japan bombs Pearl Harbor.
December 8 -   America declares war on Japan and enters World War II.
December 11 - Germany declares war on America.

1942
April 1 -   Japanese-Americans sent to relocation centers in U.S.
April 18 -   Doolittle conducts surprise B-25 raid on Tokyo.
May 8 -   American carrier forces defeat Japanese carrier forces in Battle of Coral Sea.
June 5 -   American carrier forces defeat Japanese in Battle of Midway.
August 7 -   Americans make first amphibious landing on Guadalcanal in the Solomons.
November 8 - Americans invade North Africa.

1943
May 13 -   German and Italian troops surrender in North Africa.
July 9 -   Allies land in Sicily.

1944
January 22 -   Allies land at Anzio in Italy.
May 19 -   Allies capture Monte Cassino in Italy.

During *Cottonwood Summer*

<u>1944</u>

June 6 -   D-Day: Allies land at Normandy in Northern France.

June 13 -   First German V-1 attack on Britain.

June 19 -   Americans shoot down 220 Japanese planes during the *Marianas Turkey Shoot.*

July 20 -   Assassination attempt on Hitler fails.

August 25 -   Allies liberate Paris.

During *Cottonwood Fall*

<u>1944</u>

September 13 - U.S. troops reach Siegfried Line.

October 20 -   U.S. Sixth Army invades Leyte in the Philippines.

October 25 -   First Kamikaze attack on U.S. ships in Leyte Gulf in the Philippines. (2,257 planes)

November 7 -   Roosevelt defeats Dewey in the Presidential election.

During *Cottonwood Winter*

<u>1944</u>

December 16 - Germans launch Ardennes counteroffensive (Battle of the Bulge).

December 26 - Patton relieves Bastogne in Belgium.

<u>1945</u>

January 17 -   German withdrawal from Ardennes complete.

January 26 -   Soviets liberate Auschwitz.

February 4 -   Roosevelt, Churchill, and Stalin meet at Yalta.

February 19 -   U.S. marines invade Iwo Jima, an island 650 miles south of Tokyo.

During *Cottonwood Spring*

<u>1945</u>

March 3 -	U.S. and Filipino troops take Manila.
March 9 -	Tokyo firebombed by 279 B-29s.
April 1 -	Allies discover stolen Nazi art and wealth in salt mines.
April 1 -	Final amphibious landing of war, U.S. Tenth Army invades Okinawa, a Japanese prefecture (state).
April 7 -	B-29s fly their first fighter-escorted mission against Japan with P-51 Mustangs based on Iwo Jima.
April 7 -	U.S. carrier-based fighters sink the super battleship *Yamato* and several escort vessels which planned to attack U.S. Forces at Okinawa.
April 12 -	President Roosevelt dies, succeeded by Harry S. Truman.
April 12 -	Allies liberate Buchenwald and Bergen-Belsen concentration camps.
April 28 -	Italian partisans capture and hang Mussolini.
April 30 -	Adolph Hitler commits suicide.
May 7 -	German forces surrender unconditionally to Allies.
May 8 -	Victory in Europe Day (V.E. Day).
May 25 -	Joint Chiefs approve Operation Olympic, the invasion of Japan.

During *Cottonwood Summer '45*

<u>1945</u>

June 9 -	Japanese Premier Suzuki announces Japan will fight to the very end rather than accept unconditional surrender.
June 22 -	Japanese resistance ends on Okinawa as the U.S. Tenth Army completes its capture.
July 5 -	Liberation of Philippines declared.
July 10 -	One thousand bomber raids against Japan begin.
July 14 -	The first U.S. Naval bombardment of Japanese home islands.
July 21 -	President Truman approves the order for atomic bombs to be used against Japan.
July 26 -	Winston Churchill resigns as U.K. Prime Minister after Conservative party defeated by Labour Party in general election. Clement Atlee becomes new Prime Minister.
July 26 -	Components of atomic bomb, *Little Boy*, are unloaded at Tinian Island in the South Pacific.
July 26 -	The Potsdam Declaration demands Japan's unconditional surrender.
July 28 -	Japan rejects Potsdam Declaration.
July 29 -	Japanese submarine sinks the cruiser *USS Indianapolis* resulting in the loss of 880 crewmen.
August 6 -	First atomic bomb, *Little Boy*, dropped on Hiroshima from a B-29 flown by Colonel Paul Tibbets.
August 8 -	U.S.S.R. declares war on Japan.
August 9 -	Second atomic bomb, *Fat Man*, dropped on Nagasaki from a B-29 flown by Major Charles Sweeney.
August 9 -	Emperor Hirohito and Japanese Premier Suzuki finally decide to seek an immediate peace with the Allies.
August 14 -	Japanese agree to unconditional surrender.
August 14 -	General MacArthur is appointed to head the occupation forces in Japan.
August 29 -	U.S. troops land near Tokyo to begin occupation of Japan.

After *Cottonwood Summer '45*

September 2 -   Japanese sign unconditional surrender on board
                USS Missouri in Tokyo Bay as 1,000 carrier-based
                planes fly overhead; President Truman declares
                Victory over Japan (V.J. Day).

September 8 -   General MacArthur enters Tokyo to assume head
                of occupation forces.

October 24 -   United Nations charter ratified by England,
                France, China, Soviet Union, and United States.

ACKNOWLEDGEMENTS

In 1999 when I began to write fiction, I never dreamed that a dozen years later I'd have completed five successful *Cottonwood* novels. Dozens of people have played indispensable roles in this long and rewarding effort. Here in *Cottonwood Summer '45*, the last book of the series, I'd like to take this opportunity to acknowledge them.

The inspiration for *Danny* was Billy Curtis, my very best friend when growing up on Frazier Street in Owosso, Michigan. Our boyhood adventures formed the basis for many of the *Cottonwood* stories. Sadly Billy passed away in June 2011. I was honored to speak at his memorial service held in Ovid, Michigan. Billy was loved by all who met him and we will miss him dearly.

My young and enthusiastic seventh-grade teacher, Mrs. Pat Vaughn, rescued me from academic oblivion by cleverly daring me to live up to my potential. Owing to her care and concern, my lust for learning was launched at precisely the right moment in my life. I will be forever in her debt.

Many *Cottonwood* story lines involved characters based on friends from families who lived in my old Frazier Street neighborhood, like the Curtises, Worthingtons, Hildebrants, and Mrvas. No author could find a following of more loyal and dedicated fans than these. I greatly appreciate their continuing friendship and support.

The *Addison, Harrison,* and the *Compton* characters were based on members of my own family. My parents, Charles and Mildred Slaughter, were accurately portrayed as *John* and *Marie Addison.* My uncle, James Waters, served bravely in World War II and provided a credible basis for the *Cottonwood* character *Van Harrison.* His wife and my childhood roommate, Aunt Dee, was *Aunt Maude.* My cousin, Jimmy Waters, was *Little Johnnie.* My maternal grandparents, Grover and Lavina Mitchell, lived the life of *Grandpa and Grandma Compton,* Terraplane and all.

Over the course of the *Cottonwood* series, my older cousin, Leonard Mitchell, generously provided fact after fact about the early years on the Mitchell family farm.

And during the writing of the *Cottonwood* series, I relied heavily on refresher training in the subjects of fishing, catching bait, and mushrooming from my old school friends, Bill Walter and Jim Bishop.

In this current novel, I relied on my college roommate and former Navy and American Airlines pilot, Chuck Nuechterlein, for his expertise in civilian aircraft circa 1945.

In Owosso, we're indebted to Piper Brewer, Director of the Shiawassee Arts Center, and her enthusiastic staff for their total commitment to the *Cottonwood* cause.

Here in Nashville, we are indeed fortunate to receive the continuing support and encouragement from our friends at Ingram Books, Humanities Tennessee, and the Nashville chapter of the Women's National Book Association.

The most challenging aspect of this book was to write six entertaining and informative chapters on Jase and Danny's visit to Nashville during the summer of 1945. As she has done for all five *Cottonwood* books, through diligent and careful research, my wife Joanne produced a series of comprehensive *backgrounders* that enabled me to depict credibly this fascinating city during the war.

We owe a special thanks to our friends, Jerry and Helen Hooper, Tom and Betty Ward, and Dick Frank, who were kind enough to read and authenticate the Nashville chapters. Their having lived in Nashville during the war gave them a perspective that we lacked. I appreciate their willingness to assist me by ensuring my depiction was an accurate one.

We also drew on the special knowledge and expertise of other Nashville friends. Lyle Key on information relating to trains, schedules, and fares circa 1945. Michael Zanolli, M.D. on shotguns and skeet shooting. Jerry Klein, D.D.S. on *The Holocaust* and its lasting lessons for us all. Larry Woods on Nashville basketball during the 1940s, not to mention his friendship and support on everything having to do with books in this rapidly changing business of ours. John Covington for his firsthand knowledge of Nashville's main post office long before it became the Frist Center for the Arts.

John Seigenthaler, renowned journalist and television host, has supported our efforts from the beginning and allowed us to include a vignette from his youth in this volume for which we are truly grateful.

I'd be remiss if I failed to mention the critical support of thousands of thoughtful and generous *Cottonwood* fans from all over the world who kept us going when the weight of yet another 400-page volume seemed at times overwhelming.

This series of books could have never come to be without the unqualified dedication, encouragement and support, and just plain hard work of Joanne. For these last dozen years, she has played multiple roles ranging from editor, researcher, critic, and book production liaison to in-house publicist. As an author and husband, I'm blessed to have Joanne as my partner.

Thank you all.

Gary Slaughter
Nashville
April 2012

READING GROUP QUESTIONS AND
TOPICS FOR DISCUSSION

1.   Reviewers have claimed that the book's setting (Riverton, Michigan) is a thinly disguised Owosso, Michigan, where the author grew up. Discuss the advantages of his using a fictional, as opposed to an actual, setting.

2.   How does the author make use of surprise in the story lines contained in the book?

3.   The author of the *Cottonwood* novels relies heavily on humorous characters, crisp dialog, and unusual circumstances to convey his writing style. Does this detract or add to the book's depiction of this perilous period of our country's history?

4.   Most of the stories in the *Cottonwood* series are told by the now-adult narrator, Jase Addison. What storytelling difficulties must the author overcome when writing in the first person voice? Why did the author tell the story as a "now-adult" narrator?

5.   The *Cottonwood* series takes place during the last 15 months of World War II. *Cottonwood Summer* begins on D-Day (June 1944) and *Cottonwood Summer '45* with the surrender of Japan (September 1945). Why did the author choose this period of the war?

6.   The *Cottonwood* series is G-rated. Not a likely bestseller in the opinion of many so-called experts in the book business today. Why did the author choose to violate this contemporary rule? What do you think it cost him?

7.   The first four *Cottonwood* novels have received a total of six book awards in the areas of general fiction, adult fiction, and young adult fiction. How do you explain this wide range of reader and critical acceptance?

8.   With all the controversy surrounding the alleged mistreatment of enemy combatants interned in American camps such as Abu Grab and Guantanamo Bay, why were German POWs treated so well here in America during World War II?

9.   What did you know about the period between VE Day and VJ Day before you read this book? Did this book teach you about or change your impression of this period in history?

10. Compare and contrast life on the World War II home front in Riverton with that in Nashville.

11. Discuss segregation in the North and in the South during the 1940s. How was segregation dealt with in the Armed Services during that period?

12. The *Cottonwood* series has been approved for use as American History textbooks for high-school students in the states of Michigan and Tennessee. Why would these books be effective tools for teaching history to young students?

13. What was the purpose of the WPA during the 1930s? Identify some of its most important projects. Were there any in your community?

14. Compare the role of the National Red Cross during World War II with its role today.

15. Who were important artists, cartoonists, and writers during World War II? Discuss the role they played during the war?

16. Who do you know who lived during World War II? What are their memories of this period in history?

17. A major theme of the *Cottonwood* novels is patriotism. Discuss how and why American patriotism has changed during the years since World War II.